13 Consequence Street

13 Consequence Street

Miriam Pina Vanek

Copyright © 2014 by Miriam Pina Vanek.
Cover Illustration By: Shannen Paradero

Library of Congress Control Number:		2014917280
ISBN:	Hardcover	978-1-4990-7736-0
	Softcover	978-1-4990-7737-7
	eBook	978-1-4990-7735-3

All rights reserved. No part of this book may be reproduced or transmitted in any form or by any means, electronic or mechanical, including photocopying, recording, or by any information storage and retrieval system, without permission in writing from the copyright owner.

This is a work of fiction. Names, characters, places and incidents either are the product of the author's imagination or are used fictitiously, and any resemblance to any actual persons, living or dead, events, or locales is entirely coincidental.

Any people depicted in stock imagery provided by Thinkstock are models, and such images are being used for illustrative purposes only. Certain stock imagery © Thinkstock.

This book was printed in the United States of America.

Rev. date: 11/26/2014

To order additional copies of this book, contact:
Xlibris
1-888-795-4274
www.Xlibris.com
Orders@Xlibris.com

Acknowledgments

I extend my sincerest gratitude to everyone who encouraged me in the field of journalism. To my late husband, Ed, my life partner, who motivated me, supported my educational empowerment and creativity, and who helped read my papers and poems. To my late mother, Olga Bobea, who loved life and lived independently and fiercely—te extraño mucho, Mamá. To my children, Dr. Edward A. Vanek Jr.; Deborah Vanek Tomeo, CEO; Arlene Vanek Szabo, RN, ONC, CCM; Cheryl D. M. Vanek, vice president; my granddaughter Gabrielle Tomeo; and all of my grandchildren for their motivation, help, patience, and understanding during these past two years while writing and crafting this story. To my cousin Maria Luisa Bucarelli, I would like to thank her for dedicating so many long hours helping to type and edit my original handwritten manuscript and for her moral support. To my publishing company Xlibris, thanks very much for patiently waiting for me to complete the manuscript and for all of your support. To my editor Xena, who has a special place in my heart for helping me to accomplish this dream. To my alma mater, Hofstra University (oh my Lord, those English professors at Hofstra are tough!), who helped me tremendously to improve my English. To the Spanish Department at Hofstra University and to the University of Salamanca, who awarded me with the highest honors. To the Kornfeld Studio, whose director and photographer made me feel at ease during my photo shoot with jokes and laughter. To the Hewlett Woodmere Public Library, whose endless inventory of books from the Orient and Africa to the Library of Congress helped me invaluably with my research. Thanks to Sherry "Charito" D'Antonio for a lifetime of friendship, laughter, and support. To the Intellectual Group, which meets at Bagel Boss, Cheryl

Bronstein, Michelle Felix, Paula Marks, June Minsley, Rivka Moses, Annette Szusteiman, Phyllis Weinberger, Congratulations to Phyllis for articles published in the News Day. Thank you so much for your constant support, exchange of ideas, friendship, and laughter.

I'd like to thank my sister-in-law, Aida Vanek for encouraging me to finish *13 Consequence Street*. She constantly told me, "Miriam, I can't wait to read your book." Aida and Steve managed to raise three beautiful and highly accomplished girls. Congratulations.

I realize that it takes the efforts and good intentions of many people to produce a manuscript. I thank every one of you who, in one way or another, helped me in my quest to publish *13 Consequence Street*.

Chapter 1

That morning, as I looked through the small window of my crowded and dirty room, I could see beyond the trees the fog that covered the meadow. The shadows that wrapped those trees seemed as if they wanted to squeeze with darkness the last ray of light from their old and dilapidated trunks. I could hardly see "Liberty Road" (as I call it); only the puff, cloud of smoke, and dust let me know that life keeps running along. It keeps on pushing forward to a world full of mysteries and adventures.

My name is Mary. I was sixteen years old then, tall and beautiful. A person knows when one is pretty. You could see it plainly in your mirror, or you could notice it by the look men and boys give you when you pass by them, swinging your hips, showing your open lips (just enough to show the tip of your tongue), and brushing with your hands your long and silky hair. It used to get my heart to run at a pace with all the stares, as if the universe kept on speeding to carry me to a new high full of desires and adventures.

We lived in a one-bedroom shack in the middle of nowhere. The house was so old and dilapidated, with broken-down front steps and porch. The street number, 31 hung from one of its hinges, turning the number around to look as number 13. To everyone, my address was 13 Consequence Street. We even received mail with that address printed on it! Luckily for me, the fireplace was located in the living room where I slept on an old dirty couch. It kept me warm from the ice, snow blizzards, and cold winds that were constantly hitting us with its howling sounds and freezing winds that penetrated through the cracks and holes of our small shack. The state is Ohio, situated right on the horseshoe bay where the Ohio River becomes part of the Mississippi River in the Ohio Valley. Every spring, when the snow melts on the highlands and cascades down into the Mississippi River, it fills with its force the Ohio River carrying along trees, rocks, and animals as if the river wants to wake up the town from its laziness and ignorance. Water from the Ohio River feeds the lowlands, saturating them with rich minerals excellent for the cultivation of grains. I suppose my father could have planted grains on our two acres of land instead of potatoes that are easy to plant and collect.

Every winter after looking through our small window at the vast icy covered plot, my father would swear that during the spring, he would start planting grains instead of potatoes. It was a never-ending dream, a product of his state of intoxication. We lived in the vicinity of Bloomington Town, not far from Louisville, which is the heart of Kentucky territory. We feel more like Southerners than the people from Bloomington. We speak with a Southern accent, like the music, and feel proud of being called a "hick" except me! I did not date those cowboy-boot boys with their beer cans and dirty jeans.

I was running away that summer. Our social worker at the school begged me not to quit school and to endure two more years until graduation. "It is best for you if you can present a diploma at the site of employment," she stated, but who needs a diploma anyway! It was just a piece of paper that my parents would not even look at. I could just see graduation time! My mother with her front teeth missing and both of them smelling like whiskey; it would be a nightmare. My parents were the perfect example of the Aegean pre-Hellenic race from Ireland. They were beautiful. Tall with pink complexion and deep blue eyes. I used to keep the only picture of them well hidden in my backpack. It was the only picture of their wedding; they looked so beautiful. I had a deceptive idea that my parents had died and I was raised by a couple of drunken relatives. I sold weed to three customers from Bloomington. I was very careful not to show any display of wealth. The last calamity I needed was to be arrested and to have to spend more time in this depressed town. The dealer called himself "Oleander," which is a poisonous shrub with fragrant flowers. No one knew where he came from. One day, he arrived into town driving a brand-new red Ford and settled for the business of distributing weed. The townspeople kept their mouths closed. For the first time, there was cash in the hands of some of these "hicks." Customers came from Bloomington and from Louisville.

I was a secondhand miniscule distributor, but that's the way I liked it. Not much money, just enough to get out of this town and survive for one year in New York City. I became paranoid as cash accumulated in my old backpack. I slept with it cuddled up against my body. During the summer months, I did all of my shoplifting in a variety store called the Jig. The owner is a fat but discreet old man with all eyes on my intimate parts. I would wear tight short pants that show very well my belly button and a cutoff short blouse that revealed my well-developed bosom. I approached him and touched his face with my soft manicured hands, my pink lips in the form of a bow, but never kissing him; and as I turned around, I brushed my silky and perfumed blond hair back to delicately brush his face. He stood there like he was hypnotized, with glazed eyes and a red face. I could have taken the store away, but I had to walk five miles into town. Sometimes I felt sorry for my parents. The look of pain in their faces disturbed me; where did that come from? As if alcohol had sucked up all of their illusions and had left them in a world of indolence.

Winter was like always—cold and miserable. Its dreadful frozen winds crawled into town and made it look deserted. Small farmers had gathered their crop and were now feeding their herd with the last scrap of hay they had gathered. A mist veil touched slightly the deserted brown fields. Hunger tinted brown the facade of each of their homes. It was time to collect unemployment checks. A time for beer, and homemade alcohol, and domestic violence. Cabin fever they call it. It was the same every year. After a long winter, spring came. Trees that not long ago exhibited their dead trunks, and branches, would be alive as if resuscitated from a deep and long lethargic state. Little flowers would burst up above the patches of snow that still covered the meadow. Birds of all sorts of colors would nest high above the trees, filling the air with their melodies.

I had one friend, a local girl with dark green eyes and black hair. Betty used to visit me, walking through ice-covered fields, wearing an old coat and no gloves. She looked so hungry that I often gave her one of my chocolate bars that I had pinched from the variety store. We talked about our dreams, looked through magazines and tried to make ourselves look like those beautiful models, with almond-shaped eyes and full mouths.

Soon, melons weighing up to sixty pounds could be seen, as well as apples, pears, and mushrooms. Walnut trees displayed their fruits and discarded their outer skin to show the nuts that are much appreciated. Better species grow on the highlands: Mete, Plummet, thorn apple, Datura-Metel, Strychnos Nux Vomica. Some of these nuts are poisonous like the Strychnos. Betty and I used to gather them during the summer months. We used to go to the highlands (keeping an eye out for bears) and gather them. She would know which of the nuts were poisonous; however, she did not know their names. I took these species of nuts in school and did a nice science project, winning a recognition. With all their colors and perfume, flowers would cover the dirt and stink of our old town. It was time for me to leave. I could not say that I was running away, as my parents knew about it and didn't care. They were probably just as anxious for me to go as I was anxious to leave. They could drink all they wanted without having to face me and see a disappointed look in my eyes. I endured late fall for the last time when the Ohio River veered its water into the lowlands and left its brown mud everywhere. They predict floods. The hard winter that scourged the town with ice and snow hit with force the highlands. The Ohio River clashed with its force the town, causing floods and numerous damages. There was fear that some of the homes would have to be evacuated. Townspeople were rushing by, buying supplies in speculation of what was going to happen! The local church that looked desolated before was now full of activities and packed with devoted parishioners. There were lots of activities and a sense of unity in town. People were talking to one another, others giving information. It was a great early spring! My last in Bloomington Village. I never admitted to anyone that I lived in Bloomington Village. I didn't want anyone to know that I was a hick. Besides, I did not look like the rest of the people that lived in this town.

What I mean is that I did not dress, speak, or act as some of the people around Bloomington. Girls were jealous of me. They hung around boys wearing their cheap-looking makeup and worn-out jeans and sweaters. They spit when I passed by them while their boyfriends whistled and carried on. I didn't care. One day I was going to come back to this godforsaken town rich and beautiful while all these girls will be married with cigar-smoking and beer-drinking hicks while a bunch of brats tagged around them.

Betty and I dreamed for hours. We liked wrapping around our bodies old pieces of cloth and trying to walk with one foot in front of the other like models do. Our faces looking as though we were mad at the world, we walked the plank, imagining the audience looking at us, their faces full of admiration. But asking ourselves "Who walks like that anyhow?" we laughed until tears ran free from our eyes into a pool of happiness and dreams. During the summer, I was going to New York to become a model then send for Betty. She was fourteen years old, so I will have plenty of time to make money and send for her.

I was heading for great adventures, just like a walnut shedding the rough outer skin to show a polished and well-refined me. Free like those courageous little birds that spread their wings, not looking down the valley below, their eyes fixed into the blue sky, feeling the wind, enjoying its beauty.

My mother approached me while I was in the kitchen pouring myself a cup of coffee. "Mary," she said, "I heard you talking to Betty yesterday, about you quitting school and going to New York. You are pretty and smart . . ." She stopped the tears running from her eyes and into a pool of remorse and continued. "You have good grades, you could go to college, be somebody."

"But, Mom," I said, "you both graduated from high school, you have a diploma. It is just a piece of paper. It doesn't guarantee anything. Besides," I said, "who will pay for college?"

The surprised look in her eyes told me that she was unable to compute in her mind any problem and bring it into a realistic conclusion. Alcohol may have burned some neurons in her brain and left her unable to think in a rational manner. All the hate I harbored inside of me despaired, as if I had just met her and a new beautiful relationship had taken place. Was I too tough and indifferent? Did they perceive in my eyes a look of complacency and detected my inner emotions? Was all this a result of my vanity? Did I show them that I loved them? We embraced for the first time in years, my heart beating wildly against a more slow and tired heart.

I spent my last days in Bloomington Village. Everything looked different to me. I observed that the town was full of flowers, fruits, and grains. The trees that two months ago were showing pale small leaves were now in full bloom with a display of flowers or fruits swinging delicately at the end of their branches. It was the power of nature. Just like us mortals, always changing, as if the centrifugal force that keeps the planet speeding will carry us along to happiness or pain and suffering.

I wished that I didn't make up with Dad and Mom! I wanted to walk out of the house and slam the door without saying goodbye. Instead, we were all crying when we said goodbye, embraced one another. There was a longing that was deep and painful in my heart. Betty was there too, crying with us. I had to push her away as the bus was going to leave. I looked back, their sad figures set against the old walls of the bus station.

I was sitting in a large and comfortable bus. Dark clouds were crowding my mind as the bus rolled along the highlands, the nut trees where Betty and I used to gather them. We passed through dirty roads with old-looking houses and beautiful lands with flowers framed against the dark green meadows.

Why was I so frightened? I read about the actresses and models that left home to become successes. Today, they were all famous and rich like I wanted to be. Of course, I didn't know how many of those girls got to be famous or if they just disappeared into vast cities, victims of coke dealers, prostitution, and even murder! My blood turned cold, and I could hardly breathe! I wanted to go back, to stop, but was afraid to do so. Those roads looked so isolated, and I was so lonely! Sweat dripped from my hands and into my lap.

The bus driver announced that we were fifty miles away from Pittsburgh. We were to going to change buses and wait two hours for another bus to take us into Jersey City, next to New York. We would have to change buses again to cross to New York through the George Washington Bridge.

The bus stop was beautiful. Flowers decorated the entrance, it was well kept, and trimmed bushes curved the thick walk that led to the entrance. The food was delicious! I ate like I never ate before. The bathrooms were clean and in perfect order. I was disturbed when I washed my hands and couldn't find the faucet knobs. I looked around in desperation, soap dripping on my pants and leather jacket. For the first time in my life, I felt stupid! A young girl with a long skirt and short hair approached me and, in a very polite way, told me to hold my hands close to the faucet. I felt my blood tingling my face that was turning red with shame. *Well*, I said to myself, *do I look like a hick?* Wearing my high-heeled leather boots, fancy jeans, and leather jacket? I said, "Thank you," and left the bathroom without looking back.

The next bus was going through Route 80 on the New Jersey Turnpike. I was anxious to get to New York; the state of New Jersey looked as though it had no end! It was a beautiful state! I wondered what it would be like living in one of those well-kept and beautiful homes. You could see them through the high trees, extensive land, with trees and beautiful flowers. My mind was taking long trips. How different my life would have been if we were living in one of those houses. My parents looking handsome! And proper just like in the old movies. Mother, standing at the doorway, her Aegean pre-Hellenic race showing through those beautiful deep blue eyes and tall stature. Her long blond and silky hair covering her shoulders while she kissed my father goodbye. A brand-new car parked in the driveway.

I was afraid to jump into my past and feel the warmth of those happy days. There were flowers and an orchard that my grandmother kept. The delicious smell of food in the kitchen! The shack that today stood next to our house full of debris and garbage had been Grandpa and Grandma's private rooms, a one-bedroom with a living room and a fireplace. It had polished floors, handmade curtains, and a bedspread. I slept in the cozy and warm living room on a pullout bed that disappeared during the day into a small sofa. I was so happy! The old beaten and dilapidated ghost of a car full of garbage used to be well kept. We used to take long rides in it through winding roads and sparkling lakes to picnic under a giant tree, sitting on green shining meadows. I remember thinking that I wanted to be just as beautiful as my mother was then.

We passed Sunbury Town and Lancaster. There were extensive plantations of corn, wheat, and vegetables. Some of the fruits had been collected, and the land showed its nakedness in contrast to other fields that were bursting with fruits. But where were the people? We passed by beautiful large and small houses, duplexes, condominiums, but there was no one in the streets, as though someone had carried away their bodies and left their souls trapped in their houses.

The bus driver announced, "Next stop, Patterson." I thought to myself, *Will this state ever end?* I was surprised because there were people on the streets! People of all sorts and ages. There was a rainbow of colors, all of them going about in a frenzy as if they wanted to catch up time that was slipping away by the seconds. I had time to think thoughts that were hidden away protected inside a shell. You knew they were there, but to get to them, you would have to jump into that scary and deep dark past.

We were traveling for two days through what was Indian territory. I remembered history, the raids against Kentucky and Pennsylvania; the kangaroo court led by Captain David Williamson in vengeance for the raids on Kentucky and Pennsylvania territories, led by other tribes sentenced to death; the innocent Wyandot tribe located on the northeastern Ohio Valley. John Heckewelder and David Zeisberger led the raid against those innocent Indians. The Wyandot tribe that was located by the Tuscarawas River was exterminated; only members of the tribe that were out hunting survived. Their blood fertilized the soil of this region. Some of the new

Wyandot that are alive today gather by the Tuscarawas River to honor those victims.

I like history. No one could put you down when you know history. Last year, there was an exchange of students. Some of those students were from Boston. Because of my grades, I was chosen to greet them, to show them around town, tell the history of our state and region. Naturally, I told them about the Wyandot massacre. One tall and slim blond boy stood up and said that he didn't know that the people of Ohio were murderers. "Well," I said, "you Yankees bought Manhattan for a couple of dollars. That was plain robbery, but I am not calling you a thief!" That kept his mouth shut for the rest of the stay.

Chapter 2

People were shopping, dragging heavy bags. Mothers were strolling along with their babies. Men were rushing about, holding black cases. Others were tending their shops. I remembered John Traves's Jig's Variety shop back home, where I used to pinch everything that I wanted. I was hungry then; hunger was no stranger to me. I was nine years old, wearing dirty shoes and a worn-out coat, a look of hunger written on my innocent eyes. Mr. John Traves, the owner of the variety shop, used to give me chocolate bars, pencils, everything I wanted. A look of lust written on his ugly brown face, he used to take me through the back door and into a room packed with boxes. A rancid smell that still scented everything I remembered. I was never hungry again. I used to pinch everything I wanted. I was not ready to face my past then. I wanted to forget and concentrate on my future. I kept repeating to myself, *Modeling, modeling, modeling*, until my brain became frozen and left me trembling and unable to think of my past. Then I saw it! So majestic, like a hanging gray fortress, with interminable lanes, the George Washington Bridge was set against the blue sky. My heart was beating against my chest like a butterfly, free and beautiful, to wither away to foreign lands.

The bus stop in Upper Manhattan was located at the end of the George Washington Bridge on the corner of Eighty-First Street. I strolled around Broadway. I was amazed by the vitality and the happy atmosphere that surrounded the neighborhood. One could feel happy and free. No one pointed a finger at you. No one cared. I felt that I belonged to that neighborhood, trailing with me a rush of Ireland in my blood, listening to the mother tongue with a trail of various accents. Immigrants from around the world displayed their trinkets, silk, watches, and jewelry set on tables, their fat owners sitting comfortably, smoking their long Havana cigars. The smell emanating from various restaurants numbed my senses. I was hungry. A *"Carne Asada"* sign displayed in front of one of the restaurants caught my attention. I stopped to look at the window. A man was flipping long steaks, hamburgers, chicken, and barbecued vegetables. That was my type of food. I felt like an immigrant in my own land. I was scared, feeling the emptiness one feels when away from home, the land I grew up in. I tried to forget the penury and to remember the times when my grandparents lived and I was a happy girl. I felt free, the freedom that lets you stroll along with a chain and an iron ball attached to one of your legs. I walked toward the park. I could see the George Washington Bridge far in the horizon. I saw large buildings with the giant trees that lined the long and winding sidewalks.

I walked toward a large building. The heavy door resisted my push. It was locked. Just then, I saw a Room for Rent sign and to press 44-31-8. I pressed the number on the digital box, and to my surprise, a lady opened a window and with a heavy accent asked me what I wanted.

"It is about the room," I said.

"Oh yes, the room! Come, come." A buzzer sounded, and the heavy door opened, its hinges screeching. There was a heavy thud behind me as I went through. The smell of food reached my senses, a smell so thick that it clung to the walls. It felt as though it could be scraped from the walls with a knife. I knocked on apartment 4D. A dark eye looked through the peephole. The heavy brown door opened. A petite woman with piercing dark eyes stood on the threshold. Her eyes looked as though she wanted to extract from my inner self my most guarded secrets.

"My name is Mary," I said, trying my best to be gracious.

"Oh yes, Maria, come in." The apartment was big and clear. The sunlight shone through the large brown old window in the living room.

We had five bedrooms. She was showing me the apartment. Five bedrooms? I practically shouted. In my days, apartments were big. This apartment was one of the few large apartments left in this building. As soon as an elderly person dies, the owner of the building makes two and sometimes three out of these apartments. The apartment looked so big and empty!

"Oh, don't worry about solitude," Doña Anna said. "Wait until the school is over! You will learn how to cherish these silent moments." My rented room was small and neat. It had a small window. I looked down to a decline of rocks so steep that cars below looked as though they were toys. Besieged by winds, I saw the Hudson River crawling past Riverside Avenue and under the George Washington Bridge. The Hudson waters rippled, shining like diamonds on that bright sunny day. I was tired and wanted to take a bath.

Doña Anna said to me, "You better hurry, *niña*, before the clan comes in rushing through the front door!"

I strolled on the busy streets of downtown New York, its herd of people rushing about like robots. Red light, stop. Green light, go. We all followed the rules, or else some of us would be trampled on under the hooves of well-dressed men and women. What strange city is this New York! A person could walk in one direction and see well-kept buildings with flower boxes, small trees adorning the boulevard, and small cafes with outside awnings and tables. Toward Fifth Avenue, there were tall decorated buildings with very expensive shops—Calvin, Tommy, Bulgari, Chanel, and Salons. Ten blocks away from the luxury of furs and expensive shops lay the ghettos. Dirty streets and empty souls paraded on the practically desolated streets. There were small bodegas and businesses with armed men across or inside their businesses. The impact of bullets ricocheted against the gray and dirty buildings. I used to walk to Central Park, the lonely fountain. The water oaks, maples, lotus, and elm trees were in full bloom that fall, their colored leaves drifting away in the cold wind. The sun was bright, shining against the blue sky and fluffy white clouds. I sat on the benches that lined the walk and bent toward the lake. I closed my eyes and remembered the happy days when Betty and I used to run like wild Indians, chasing squirrels and picking up nuts, our boots caked with the soft mud that remained from the hard winter and heavy rain. *Why?* I asked myself. *Why doesn't one realize when he or she is happy and only when misery is closing around him or her?* And feeling the lightning pain, that's when you do realize you were happy. I remembered how the boys stared at me when I passed by and the feeling of importance deep inside me. Betty, my dear innocent friend, with her skinny unnourished body and delicate frame. Our laughs, our joys, and our dreams.

I went to every fashion designer in New York City. The models were so young! Thirteen- and fourteen-years old, were parading with so much makeup and false eyelashes. Their abdomens stuck to their ribs. They had plumped lips, face and eye operations, and breast implants. They looked to me as if programmed on a computer and paraded to the public as a new model. My soft curves and full firm breasts and large blue eyes caught a lot of attention, and my long and well-shaped legs were not skinny. I did not look like the specters they wished me to be. Their bulimic bodies were dried out like a cast-off piece of hide.

Then I met Carmela, a beautiful Italian girl with healthy pink complexion and shining black hair. I had seen her many times in one of those long and dreadful interviews where they send you galloping from one model house to another until you despaired, become bulimic, and somehow accumulated the $200,000 for surgery to look like the spectral funny-walking doll they wanted you to be. I refused, I refused to endanger my life. For how long anyway? Competition is fierce, and you are considered old when you reach the age of twenty-eight. There had to be another way to of making lots of money. I was sitting on a bench in Central Park when Carmela stood in front of me. The sunlight hitting my face, I felt backed into a corner, sadness invading my clouded senses.

"Did you get an interview, Carmela?" I asked.

Carmela said, "No, I looked too healthy. What can I tell you? I like to eat spaghetti." Inside the modeling office, we were rivals; we could have torn each other's eyes out. We did not talk to each other at the modeling office, no. We looked at each other with suspicion after each interview.

But now, sitting next to Carmela, I felt relaxed. No mere interviews, no more diets, I didn't have to stare at a secretary that looks at you with aversion, stripping you out of your clothes the little fat left on your body that was bulging out like in an uncommon fat person. For the first time in many years, tears filled my eyes and cascaded like torrents on my hollowed cheeks. I poured out all of my fears, my life, my parents, and finally my dreams and my promises to Carmela. I couldn't see Carmela. Anyone could have been standing next to me! I didn't care. As if a premonition wave took hold of me and smashed me against the hard rock of my emotions, I heard Carmela like in a dream. She was shaking me, bringing me back to my senses.

"It is all right, Mary! Come, let us walk." We stopped at a cafe. The sunlight of a late October day bathed our souls with new hope and different dreams. We ate like starving hogs, stopping just to breathe, our eyes shining, a pink color restoring our yellow and sunken cheeks. I listened to Carmela with a faraway hypnotism, as if her words were a sedative that carried me to a different plane. Did I say we could make thousands of dollars? Moving together, finding a flat? It was just like Carmela. Whether I was in agreement with her or not, she took control; all those plans did not mean anything to me. Later on, it brought a flush of excitement to my tired and dilapidated brain. She handed me a list of tasks I should do.

"Buy the *New York Times*. Make a list of apartments for rent! Call the agency, not individuals. Two bedrooms, two bathrooms, close to Fifth Avenue or Central Park." I started to work like a marionette. Carmela was pulling the strings. I called for hours, but when I finished my second sentence, the phone was dead. There was a dreadful empty sound ringing in my ears. What was I doing? And I tried again, only to experience the same response. It left my soul with a scar so deep and painful that I was not able to erase it. I felt worthless, thinking that something terrible was wrong with me. The thought that I harbored long ago thinking that I could conquer the world was gone. I despised the hicks from my own town, who paraded on the streets, plunking my beauty as though I was the queen of Bloomington. What's happening to me? Tears ran down my flushed cheeks while I sat on a subway bench waiting for the A Train. I felt so lonely. No one stopped to ask me if I needed help. They pretended that I was not there. Pushing, running, fighting against time. Down the stairs, fighting the red light, the train is going to close its door! Run, run! I walked through the streets like a living zombie. I passed the park and the building that I was living in without realizing it.

I woke up to the street not far from the George Washington Bridge; I was confused and didn't know which way to go. "Atras, atras," I heard them saying. They knew me! I was the only blue-eyed and blond-haired girl living in the neighborhood. "Oh, gracias, gracias," I replied. I dragged myself up the four set of stairs. I could hear the laughing and the music in the girls' rooms. I passed by Rocky, the old dog. He looked at me with indifference; he was just waiting for Joe (whom they called Junior) to take him for a walk. Junior was the only person Rocky paid any attention to.

I collapsed into the arms of Doña Anna. "Niña, what happened to you?" I could not talk; it felt like an eternity since I left. I composed myself and told my story. Doña Anna said, "But, niña, where do you come from? Don't you know that a different accent sends the Yankees raving mad?"

I felt like a fool. And this is America! This country is composed of different states, with their own customs, ways, and accents. At this, Doña Anna interrupted me. "We are all Americans, niña. Some of us are from

South America, from Central America and others from North America—*Americanos todos!*" she said.

After a relaxing tea and a hot bath, I felt a little better. Why was I treated like a foreigner? I belonged here! Some of my relatives fought for this country. Our state pays high taxes to our government. To me, the Yankees are the ones that speak with an accent. My phone was ringing constantly; it was Carmela.

I didn't feel like answering it. It was not until the next day when I ventured to answer my phone. To my surprise, when I told Carmela, she burst out laughing. "Listen, come meet me at the same restaurant where we had lunch yesterday. I will explain to you it was my mistake, I should have realized it. You will laugh too when you hear me."

I kept on thinking, *What can it be?* Besides my accent, I mean. I dressed quickly and was sitting at the restaurant by 11:30 a.m. I had coffee, diet soda, water, bread; and Carmela was still not there. I started to feel scared; she did not answer her cellular. Finally, there she was! Confident and looking beautiful, a half smile was displayed on her half-open sexy red lips.

"How can you smile knowing what happened to me?" I said.

"Listen," she told me. "It has nothing to do with you personally." Oh, I couldn't wait what she had to say! "Listen, they thought you were black. They don't rent to blacks or Spanish unless they are famous or superrich. To tell you the truth, they wouldn't even rent to us unless we could pass for models and show them our portfolios. Luckily, I have modeled for Bulgari just showing my feet for a pair of sandals they were advertising."

Somehow, I did not feel right about it. "Listen," I said to Carmela. "I am going to stay where I am, I am certainly not going to live in a place where I am not welcomed."

A frightened look came to her deep green eyes. "You see . . .," she said, "it is our address that is going to land us a good-paying job. Without it, we have to look for work at the nearby cafeteria."

It was a thrill to sit across the extremely well-dressed real estate agent and lawyer. I stuck my nose up and looked at them with disdain printed on my arched eyebrows. My piercing blue eyes with a rebuttal look was clearly set on them. "Previous address?" they asked.

Carmela had thought of everything; she had dated occasionally a male model that was doing well. She had spoken to him, and he had agreed on giving to her his references. They asked, "Telephone number?" There it was! Carmela handed them his personal reference *I* (business) card. They looked impressed, for he was on the cover of some of the sexy magazines. They were not finished with us yet.

The real estate lady gave us a hard look and asked, "And you, could I ask you about your background?"

"No, you may not ask," I said, trying my best to force an English accent. She was confused; she did not expect a negative reaction from me or from anyone. Her superiority could not decipher at the beginning the meaning of my rebuttal. Taking advantage of the confusion, Carmela turned to the lawyer and said, "Well, where is the contract to sign?" The rent was $7,000 a month. I nearly passed out. Plus $2,000 real estate fees and $1,000 per hour to the lawyer. Two years' lease. I was thinking, *I have $40,000 left that will cover the two years' lease and living expenses if we did not have anything to eat.* We left the real estate building feeling important. Our luck was about to change! A feeling of delirium grasped our young and vulnerable souls.

It was hard for me to say goodbye to Doña Ana. "I am afraid for you, niña. You are too pretty, and New York is a very dangerous place for a girl like you. You are sensitive." That word kept harpooning me to this day! Was I too sensitive about my beauty, my downfall, my relationship with others? Was I too sensitive about Carmela? About Betty, my parents, and above all, Bloomington? Yes, Doña Ana was right after all. The word *sensitive* means to be "impressionable." I do get mesmerized by beauty, wealth. Even to this day where I am trapped inside these beautiful rooms, I admire the beauty of this mansion, the majestic grandeur of its gardens, the polished floors and ornaments, the high walls and checkout booth, the rigid and inflexible order of my abductors. I even look up to my jailer. I sense his presence, admire his toughness, his riding outfits and whip. I know it is an evil attraction. My body has the ugly, dark marks of his wraths. I am like a bird in a gold cage, singing of the beauty surrounding, eager to fly the clouds and yet afraid of its wilderness and majestic spaces. Captor of my soul, singing to delight my oppressor, caught in a delirium that shriveled my mind with the toxic poison of conformity. Only my dream kept me from becoming insane. I could not rest. It was when everyone was sleeping and the shadows clouded my senses with the frightening idea of freedom hit me.

I remembered the good days after we rented the luxury apartment on Fifth Street and Park Avenue, pretending we were rich, flaunting our beauty to the more elegant and aristocratic wealthy tenants. We were careful not to call too much attention; we never brought anyone to the apartment that did not look distinguished and proper. For the first two years, we looked for work at various modeling houses, only to end up disappointed by their false promises. Sometimes, however, we would find a clown that took our pictures and made us spend lots of money. He would say, "Honey, we need you lying on top of a white and fluffy fur." I would go out and buy a mink stole. Or he would say, with one of his knees bent and the right palm of his hand down, "No, no, no, that outfit will not do! You need to wear a gold outfit to bring out your sexuality!" I had my pictures displayed on a third-rate magazine with no pay. The only payment I had was a promise that someone will see my picture and offer me a contract. Carmela had a very promising job as a real estate agent. She changed her name; Suzy was her real estate name. She was doing so well that we were able to rent the apartment for another two years. Everything was perfect, until she landed a thirty-million apartment on Fifth Avenue. She came home so happy! We jumped on top of the couch screaming; what did we care about the neighbors? We could have bought the building!

What Carmela did not realize then was that she stepped on the holy ground of the queen of real estate, Mrs. Rockwell, named by her competitors as Mrs. Rock Hard. The lady had an office on Fifth Avenue with a tiger's head showing its large and pointed teeth—a perfect image of her. She went after Carmela with a vengeance, showing her naked pictures to Carmela's clients and calling her a prostitute. She called banks and other real estate in the area; we were practically thrown out of the apartment! Except that we had signed a lease for two more years and now we found ourselves with no job and two years' payments for the apartment. We couldn't buy anything. We lived practically on cold cereal. The rent! Before we could turn around, it was time to pay the rent again! We had to do something. We spent hours sending pictures, making telephone calls, and nothing. We were so hungry that we started to look like those bulimic models that hung around the modeling houses.

Depression clouded my senses. I sat for hours in a dark living room, staring at the TV screen with an empty look on my hollowed face. I couldn't think anymore; it looked as if destiny had swept away my emotions and left me there trembling. Nowhere to go, no more dreams. I didn't know it then, but that was the beginning of all my nightmares. The phone kept on ringing, but I couldn't hear it; I didn't know it was working. It was Carmela. "Where were you?" she shouted over the phone; the sound of her voice hurt my ears.

"What do you mean?" I couldn't place her for a minute.

"This is me! Remember?" Carmela sounded excited. That was like Carmela! In the middle of a crisis, she would get happy and contented at the whisper of any positive news. "Get ready, my friend! And don't worry about the rent, I will explain to you later." Just like that, she fixed everything with a phone call! I had gone through this road before with her. She would burst into our apartment with the most positive smile printed on her face, telling me about the various positions we were going to have. Be a company lady for a rich and aged person. The trouble was, when the lady's lawyers investigated our past and saw our practically naked bodies in the third-rate magazines, they thought we were prostitutes. Our address didn't help much; how could we afford a high rent with no jobs? That left us with a perpetual list of positions unavailable to us—traveling companion, nannies, etc. We tried various positions, but the plain-looking front desk secretary wouldn't even let us sit down, and the pretty ones didn't want any competition. Besides, how much can a secretary make? It wouldn't even pay a month's rent with both of us working. We were trapped!

And there we stood, Carmela with her self-assured way, laughing, radiant with happiness. Her face flushed with excitement! I could hardly look at her. How many times had she rushed about, yelling and carrying on with new expectations? I couldn't be bothered! I sat there like a mummy closing my ears to this new false adventure of hers, her words rushing through her red lips like spilled water into a fountain. She was raving about the apartment contract.

"Mary, Mary, I know how to get us out of this contract!"

Well, that caught my attention! "How, how?" I said. "No, Carmela, we are done with. We will be slaves for the next two years!" It was like the medieval times for us, where hard work, starvation, and deception await us. Every month carried a late fee. How many months did we owe? It was like a yoke was fixed on our necks, no different from the slaves we all read and see in pictures.

"Listen," she said, with a fixed stare in her dark green eyes. "These are modern times, and we are a lot more sophisticated than the slaves in medieval times. If you are smart enough, you could find a way out of difficult situations." She started to read some part of the house contract under the penalty of being evicted.

> No pets
> No noisy party after 12:00 a.m.
> No prostitution
> No religious ornaments placed on doors or hallways
> Only gentlemen and ladies allowed on the premises
> Failure of payment, etc.

"Carmela," I said, "I know that. Why are you bringing this problem right now?" I couldn't see it; my clouded mind was not able to assess the situation and bring it to a solution.

"Well, dear friend, we will do everything that is considered a penalty. We will make such a racket that will shock the distinguished and proper ladies on this building." She took a hat and handbag and started to walk her head up high, her eyebrows arched, imitating some of the ladies in the building.

I had to laugh. I joined in the mockery and said, "After you, my lady," taking an old hat to curtsied.

Carmela's model friend Ralph, who loved to be called Ralphie, took charge of all the different characters that night at our apartment. We had fun! Some of Ralph's friends came to the apartment properly dressed; however, others were gay and refused to dress any different from what they were used to, their hair high up, as if a bolt of lightning had hit them and left them frozen and scared. We spent most of the money we had to pay the rent on booze and grass. The phone rang constantly, the neighbors, the real estate agent, the lawyer. We answered the phone with a laugh of malicious intents set on our intoxicated lips. The police was at the door! We took the marijuana left and flushed it down the toilet. They were not stupid! The smell clung to the walls, the rugs, our clothing. They couldn't find any evidence. However, we were only eighteen years old! The law said we have to be twenty years old to be drinking alcohol. There were empty bottles everywhere, enough evidence to pack us up and take us to jail. However, some of the boys were in their twenties. They said, "No, the girls were not drinking, we were." They could have given us an alcohol test. But they looked at us with a sad look written on their hard faces and left.

I wanted a cute little dog that I had seen at the window in a pet shop located right around our apartment. I used to stare at this cute white-and-gray Pomeranian. I wanted to buy it, but when I inquired, I was taken aback by the price! Two thousand dollars! That was more than half of our rent money. I supposed I could have gone to a less expensive pet shop, but that was my Tinkle. I stared for hours, through the frozen cold and raining days, listening to his sharp and piercing high-pitched bark. He knew me! I was afraid that someone would snatch him and I wouldn't be able to see him again. My heart beat fast against my chest at the thought of losing him. With a job at a local bar, I had collected from tips one thousand seventeen dollars. Carmela let me take two thousand dollars that we had accumulated previously for the rent. I had two thousand seven hundred dollars, hoping that the pet shop owner would not mind the three hundred dollars missing. After lots of bargaining, I obtained a leash, a cute winter outfit, and some pet food. I brought Tinkle home, placing him under my winter coat, hoping that he wouldn't let out one of his piercing barks. He was too cold to be bothered! We walked about six long New York blocks, and he was freezing. The porter and the front desk fellow looked at me with a suspicious stare on their hard faces. I knew there were cameras in the elevator, so I did not take Tinkle out of my coat until we were inside the apartment. We made it!

I was so elated I even forgot all of our concerns and tribulations. We were to be at court in three weeks. A police officer had come to our door. "Is your name Mary Fletcher, ma'am?"

"Yes," I said.

"This is a citation for you and your partner Carmela Bellini to present yourselves in court on January 28." Just like that! We were a couple of weeks away from disaster. We could have landed in jail, and Carmela sat there looking confident with the same placid look reflected on her peaceful face. Tinkle was my comfort on the weeks that lay ahead. We took long walks through the park, even when the days were frozen and the snow clung to the tree branches. I remembered other winters, other times, not long ago and other dreams. Dreams that used to be so assertive, free of the negative conditions that clouded my mind then. *Oh dear Lord!* I prayed. *Don't let me go to jail!* I was devastated, and each day brought in more bad news. We couldn't afford a lawyer. I couldn't sleep at night. What would happen to the apartment, my clothes? Even the bed where I was lying down did not belong to me. It was all borrowed.

Not even my life belonged to me. The judge could sentence me to prison and leave me old and dry with years. Tinkle, my Lord! What would happen to him! I had to talk to Ralph. I tossed in my bed, unable to sleep. I was not able to sleep for days; I looked terrible. I had dark marks under my eyes, and my hair that used to be shining and healthy was dry. My heavy winter coat that clung to my body then was hanging loose, showing my skinny figure and long legs.

We went to court on January 28 and waited for hours in the uncomfortable benches that lined up the corridor. We saw our lawyer for about a half an hour. He was like a machine. He hardly looked at us. He was just checking information. He asked, "Where do you prostitute yourselves?" What? I was surprised. Imagine, prostitutes practically dying from hunger?

"Oh, Carmela, we are done for," I said.

He came back three hours later to tell us that the judge had postponed the trial. We didn't have to move. There was a law in New York City that prohibited landlords from dispossessing tenants who were unable to pay the rent. Hoorah for New York City! We would be able to eat, pay the gas, electricity. We stopped at a near restaurant but changed our minds because it looked like the restaurant was packed with well-dressed men and women. We figured they were judges and lawyers. How would that look for our case! We couldn't pay the rent, but we could eat in that fancy restaurant. We fled from that restaurant as if someone was chasing us.

Luckily, about two blocks away, we found a nice cafeteria. Imagine, Carmela said with her everlasting confidence. We didn't have to pinch the little food they served on bars anymore! We felt at home. Tinkle jumped on my lap. I was so glad to see him. Even his piercing bark did not disturb me! "You are safe, my precious pet!" I bought him food and a little toy that squeaked when he bit it with his sharp little teeth. I slept for ten hours. Luckily for me, I had a loud alarm clock. I had to pull myself out of bed, I was still tired, but I had to go to work. I missed two days off work, and I didn't know if I still had a job. My boss, Mr. Wilson, called me to his office and told me that he had hired someone for the afternoon shift. But he still had an opening for the evening. I knew about that shift. Usually, heavy drinkers come after six o'clock. Right after work! They come bossy and fresh. Sometimes a six-foot-three Irish fellow would knock the daylights out of another customer, and it would take two bouncers to kick him out. It was also dangerous to walk at night. Sometimes customers were waiting outside to see if you could date them. We knew what dating meant. They warned us about it. We used to go out together and take a taxi. Our pocketbooks were filled with generous tips. In three months, for the first time we had some sort of peaceful life. There was plenty of food.

There was money to pay the gas, electricity, insurance, transportation, telephone, cell phone, tips, etc. Carmela was not making that much money working in the afternoon shift, so I had to pay most of the bills and still save money for what lay ahead of us. The lawyer that the court assigned us never called when we wanted to talk to him; we had to go to court and make an appointment. He didn't even give us his card or telephone number. We sat in the courtroom from 9:00 a.m. to 3:00 p.m. We had one hour for lunch. We had our lunch far away from the fancy small restaurants that surrounded the court. All day long, I witnessed a display of cold horror. The police would bring a crowd of well-built young men dressed in orange. Their hands were tied, shackles on their legs, their rattling noise perturbing the dead silence of the court. They called them one by one. Their impassive faces lacked remorse or any rebellious trait while the judge looked in the computer their records and took the advice of some of their lawyers' attendant. Finally the lawyer was called (who probably was sleeping in some dark corner of the court).

"Your client was caught with five ounces of coke in his car while speeding on the Belt Parkway heading east."

"Yes, Your Honor, but this is his first offense. I throw this case on the mercy of this court!" All this was said on a hushed whispering voice to the lawyer $5,000 parole.

"How do you plead?"

"Guilty."

"Trial will be on . . ."

I heard my name bouncing through every wall "Carmela Bellini . . . Mary Fletcher . . ." as though I was in the depths of the Alps and its echo was bouncing against every rock and precipice on those mountains. My knees gave way to my skinny body. The lawyer helped me up.

"How do you plead?"

"Guilty on dispossession charges, not guilty on prostitution!"

To my surprise, there were cameras waiting for us outside. Flash! Flash! I couldn't believe it! "How can you afford to live in such a luxury apartment?" they asked. I couldn't believe what happened. How my dreams and my hard work turned around to bite me on my face? I felt carried away to another dimension; oblivion covered me. I saw lips moving as they were speaking, but I couldn't hear, could not understand what they were saying. I felt myself going down, falling. Good, I thought for a brief moment. I wished that I would die and close forever the pain, the agony in my life. Why didn't I go through a life of success, the wonderful experiences of joy, and at the end to faint rejected, spiritless, with an emptiness in my heart that was difficult to comprehend? I woke up on a hospital bed, the TV on the wall flashing! At the beginning, I couldn't comprehend it. Then I saw Ralph.

"Yes, I know them!" Ralph said to the press. "They have been trying to get into the modeling industry for a long time. Instead they have been working in restaurants and as bar attendants. I ask you, have you ever seen a prostitute that has no money to pay the rent?"

"It was nothing to worry about," the doctor said. My blood pressure was low. I had to eat more to gain at least fifteen pounds. The press was there. A group of people were applauding. I asked myself if I should laugh or cry. I ran through the steps of the courthouse and into Ralph's car where I was safe. I clung to Ralph and cried. Those were tears stored in my heart. They ran down my cheeks and purified my soul. I wanted to sleep for one hundred years. Maybe then there would be no corruption or young girls wouldn't have to sell their bodies to make a decent living. I did not have the strength to get undressed; I wanted to sleep for a hundred years. Instead, I slept for two days.

Chapter 3

Run out of the hospital. Carmela's words the night before did not make any sense; it kept on rushing about my brain. Contracts, television. Tommy, Bulgari, Chanel.

I must dress quickly. To call! Oh yes, Carmela, where is the phone? Oh, here, it's not working! Help! I have to get out of here!

Just then, a nurse came rushing in. "What are you doing? You are not dismissed yet! Get back to bed!" she said. I sensed the fury on her dark eyes and saw through the delicate material of her uniform the strong muscles on her chest and arms. She had a thick neck holding up a large head, with abundant black hair.

Pointing to the bed, she said, "You could have died! You are lucky. Anyone could see that you are anorexic." Later on, as I was undressing, I saw myself in the mirror. I couldn't believe what I was seeing! My skin was so tight to my neck that one could see clearly my collarbone. My arms and legs were so skinny. My stomach that before was tight and well shaped was a hole where my hip bones protruded. I was ruined! Who would want to photograph a skeleton? I thought my dress was dancing on my body. Somehow after I was dressed, had brushed my hair and put eyeliner on my eyes, and glossed my cheeks and lips, I looked okay. My heart pumped with excitement.

For the first time since I arrived in New York, I felt the sensation of well-being. I was going put on my silk stockings and heels and flew Chanel12.

"No, no," I said, "I don't know about any contracts." Far away, I saw Carmela and Ralph waiting for me. I ran down the steep courthouse stairs like a scared rabbit ready to hide. I was glad to see them. Those were beautiful years for us. Famous designers and modeling firms called on us. Carmela had her picture displayed in practically every top-model magazines.

I didn't get along with the photographers. They kept on telling me that my legs were too skinny, my hip bone protruded, and my knees . . . After what *seemed* to be a torture chamber (highlights that make one sweat, fans that blow away your eyelashes, uncomfortable benches to hold difficult positions), your bones become calcified and you feel like you need a crutch to get away from the studio.

"Look," I said, "go to hell!" I walked out and swore I will never come back. I never did. I concentrated on modeling. They loved me! My tall and skinny body was perfect for the rich gowns and crazy styles they exhibited. That year, Oscar De La Renta introduced beautiful black girls with a line of cream-and-gold gowns that were a sensation. Walking on the catwalk, with one foot in front of the other, I always remembered Betty and the laughter and happiness of those days. A smile would come to my lips and a sense of accomplishment. I made it! I did it! Carmela and I bought an apartment right on Fifth Avenue. Five million dollars, two levels, skylights, three bedrooms, and four baths. I took care of my parents. I purchased an annuity that will give them an interest of $1,000 a month and a new house. Betty was eighteen years old now. It has been four years since I last saw her. I sent for her, my heart full of expectations. She was the same Betty that I always remembered. Shy, thin, and poorly dressed. She looked as though she needed a bath. I didn't care. I hugged her until my arms were tired. Tears wet Betty's hair.

The next day, we went shopping. Her petite frame made her look like a child. She looked so beautiful that it broke my heart just to think about Betty. We were happy! We laughed and giggled, ran, ate, and visited every store and shop in downtown New York. I remember that we stopped at a jewelry shop. We were pointing at different rings and diamonds. Oh, we like this one, look at that enormous engagement ring!

"Someday," I said, "someone will be giving us a ring just like it." While we were kidding around, I noticed that Betty was repeatedly looking at a delicate white gold pendant. A half moon sprinkled with small diamonds. It was March, and Betty's birthday was in April. I decided to get the pendant as a surprise for Betty's birthday. That day, I hid the pendant under her napkin and prepared breakfast for the three of us. I saw the look of surprise and love reflected on her beautiful face! Since that day, she wore the pendant under her dress as a good luck charm.

I was so busy in the next two years that I hardly had time to look at myself. I traveled to France, Germany, Spain, Italy. At the beginning, it was very exciting; but after a while, it was nothing more than a routine. Carmela and I did not see each other for weeks. We used to leave notes on the refrigerator to let each other know the latest news. Our correspondence and bills were another big problem. Mail was constantly piling up. I was so exhausted that I hardly had the time to take my clothes off and get to bed. Betty usually helped me pack and unpack my traveling cases. We had to do something! We had missed some very lucrative contracts, and they lay there at the bottom of a plastic bag! Some of our checks were lost in the avalanche of papers. We hired a secretary and a financial advisor. Finally, we were able to relax and take short vacations.

Resting on the beach in the Bahamas, I could see the blue sky blend with the blue sea. The bright sun looked as though it was resting upon the ocean, giving reflections like diamonds to the gigantic waves. I was mesmerized by its beauty. It was the first time that I was able to relax in such a paradise! Oh, how I wished I could stay there forever! It must be something like this when you go to heaven! I told myself.

I felt tired most of the time. I just wanted to lie on the beach and fall asleep. Carmela was having fun. She danced until the late hours of the night. She made lots of friends and fell in love with a handsome fellow that looked as though he was a millionaire. I had my suspicions about him, but she looked so happy that I couldn't take that wonderful feeling away from her. Besides, I was worried about myself. I kept losing weight; I felt tired and old all the time. My sponsors kept on looking at me with suspicious eyes. I didn't look as good as I looked before. I decided it was time I should see a doctor. Everything in my life came with a force. It would scale up to the highest pinnacle of good fortune and then descend to the pits of hell.

I had the feeling something was wrong when the doctor summoned me to his office. "Well," he said, "your white cell count is too low. Of course, we will be needing more tests. You have to take care of yourself! Eat well, plenty of sun, and vitamins."

"But, Doctor, my job!"

"I can only advise you. After that, you will make your own decisions."

I had an exhibition in London in two days. I couldn't call at the last minute and cancel it. I had to do this show and then (maybe) take it easy for a while. No drinks! the doctor had warned me. Well, I stopped at a bar. I said to myself, "I wouldn't take the medications today. I will start tomorrow." What could I do to make a decent living? Showing my body was the only career I knew. I was sitting at the bar feeling sorry for myself when this man sat next to me.

He took a look at me and knew I was in trouble. He never thought about health problems; he probably thought it was about love. Well, I wasn't going to change his mind. I knew it was a terrific subject to start a relationship. So I faked a lover, as I didn't know he had someone else. My eyes were full of tears, tears to erase wounds, to penetrate in my soul positive dreams.

Joe came into my life when I needed a friend to put together my dreams, when I thought I was at the end of my existence. I said goodbye to modeling and opened a Discothèque with Joe in West Forty-Eighth Street. The Discothèque kept me busy without having the competition of traveling and the pressures those modeling houses put you through. God forbid when a photographer takes your picture when you are relaxing or going to the supermarket without makeup. Here at the Discothèque, no one cared if you look attractive or not. Everyone just wanted to have a good time. I kept on taking my medication and eating well. I did not have a hole in my stomach, and my hip bones did not protrude anymore. My cheek had that rosy complexion and my eyes that intense shining look that I had lost.

Betty was a problem. Carmela and I tried to get her a job. She was not photogenic. The photographers criticized her so much that most of the time she ran out of the studio crying. She was too short for modeling. We did not want to have her staying at the apartment alone for long periods of time. I decided she could help at the Disco. She was terrific. She got along well with the other girls and men.

As time was passing by, I noticed some change in Betty. She had that flush of love reflected on her face, that radiant beauty that saturated the young, when in love and we have to attract the opposite sex. Betty wore the majority of her dresses, blouses, and skirts that I had given her. But the high-heeled shoes, she wouldn't wear them. Too uncomfortable to be working on them, she said. She wore flat shoes. I was glad. Her petite figure and innocent face kept those rough individuals away from her. I noticed immediately a change in Betty. I said to myself that she was young. All the excuses we make to ourselves when we refuse to accept the truth.

One day, she was in front of me and I could hardly recognize her. She had high heels, lots of makeup, and her dark hair was now tinted blond. This was not like Betty! I panicked. There I was pretending to be her guardian; I brought her to the disco to work. I didn't even warn her about sex! I took her to a discreet room reserved for married people, politicians, and high government officials.

"Betty," I said, "you know about sex?"

"Yes," she said. "I spied on my brothers at the barn, on the grass, on the meadow. I know what a man does to a woman when he is in love."

"That is the problem, Betty! Most of the time they are not in love! You are old enough to have sex, but I want you to realize that there are consequences that could change your life completely. There is always the risk of getting pregnant or being infested with a terrible disease. I want you to ask yourself this question, 'Does he really love me?' Not because he is telling you so, but because you have observed him and know for sure that you are right for one another." I hugged her as if I wanted to protect Betty from all the misfortune she would face later on.

My heart stopped whenever I think of her. So young, so innocent! So much in love. She was like a little sparrow singing away in the middle of the jungle. A snowflake drifting away through the night. Oh, Betty, Betty. What evil bequeathed you? What monster trampled upon your beauty and disturbed your innocence? Did he rejoice to see the stamp of fear reflected on your beautiful eyes? Did you think of me! Oh, Betty, Betty. I sank on my knees and cried. Life was running away from me. Hate and pain was invading my soul. I wanted to scream, but no sound came. I was drowning on a sea of remorse and pain. My fragile soul thrashed about by the turbulent fury of affliction. There was nothing I could have done to save her. I would have liked to think that for the first time, she was in love.

A radiant smile reflected on her beautiful face, she said, "I am moving in with Ralph. He is wonderful and loves me. We are in love."

Joe knew Ralph some years back. He had warned me. He would bring young girls from Mexico and set them in the prostitution business, young girls who were kidnapped in Mexico and sent to the United States as slaves. A lot of money was paid for them, and their pimps always made sure that they got their money back, with high interest, once they were distributed to various bordellos. They were slaves. If they talked, they disappeared.

The rest were afraid to talk. Naturally with all the cash they had acquired, those pimps could open legitimate businesses. About seven months later, Betty came to the Discothèque and asked me if she could talk to me in private. I agreed.

"Ralph is opening a boutique no far from here," she said. "He wants to know if you could talk to some of the big modeling houses. He wants to be able to display some of their attires in his shop."

"Oh?" I said. "In his shop? Listen, Betty, why should I do that for him? Tell him if the shop was in both of your names, I will consider it."

"Oh, Mary!" she said. "I am afraid that he is going to be mad at me. When Ralph gets mad, there is no way to stop him."

"Really?" I said. "Tell Ralph if he lays one finger on you, he will see me in court!"

I used to go to their shop and buy clothing. Betty would set aside some clothing that she knew were my style. Sometimes we went out for lunch. Those were the good times for both of us. We had money, were young and full of life. "We made it, Betty," I said and we both laughed.

As I suspected, Betty did not have any say in their business. When I asked her, she said, "I do not have brains for business."

"Did you believe him?" I asked. Betty laughed. I could see that she was too much in love to care. When a woman falls in love, she loses her senses. She becomes a part of him, that other being that has captured her soul. She becomes his slave. She is prepared to go to hell for him. To tend to him and love him. A man perceives love in a different way. Love and sex are connected in a man's mind. When sex is declined, love (as he perceives it) disappears. A man will not leave his position, his ambitions, his opportunities to become a hero, to achieve and pursue his dreams for a woman.

Love is beautiful, but a dangerous road to travel. As if this feeling is bred in us, it brings us to the highest pinnacle of glory and then takes us down into the pits of hell. I understood Betty then. She was mesmerized as I will later be. We did not have the same strength of Martha Mitchel or Queen Isabel.

Martha who had the strength to fight an entire nation, and her husband, Secretary of State John Mitchell, on the belief that Water Gate should have never happened. The will of Queen Isabel I, who witnessed the brutal execution of her lover, to prove her strength to a Nation that was divided by different faiths.

We were affected by the same disease of Juana La Loca, the crazy queen of Spain, who made believe that she was crazy. So her husband Prince Phillip I, did not take her title of Queen away from her. We are like Nicole Simpson, the wife of O. J. Simpson, an ex-football idol and murderer. She knew he was going to kill her! And yet she moved close to his house on the false belief of love. He killed Nicole, but was found not guilty, contrary to the majority of the public opinion. In the future, I would be contented with my lover, happy to have the privilege of admiring a man and live my life through his life, being a part of him and loving him. Adoring and loving him, sensing his presence. Willing to give up my life for him. Swallowing my tears. Why this blindness? Is it fear? Or some sort of disease that makes us succumb to death or leave us paralyzed with fear? No one knows. It is a mystery.

William was a perfect gentleman, suave and courteous, spoke little. His words were calculated, a few just to convey his thoughts or to manipulate you. To make you believe (contrary to your own senses) that everything was perfect when you felt trapped and sad and hell is knocking at your door.

Chapter 4

I went to the fashion shop, the Petite Shop, to look for Betty. The day was beautiful. The sun was bright and hot, but the weather was cool enough to wear a two-piece suit. I was feeling happy at the thought of going out with Betty, strolling around Fifth Avenue, having an ice cream cone, and just laughing, remembering our good times at Bloomington when we were spiritually free but weighed down by emotional shadows. As if our spirits wanted to fly away but were trapped, unable to fly. I was walking along in New York. Free, young, and pretty. I felt like those days in Bloomington when I used to swing my hips and brush back my hair. In New York, no one looks at you with piercing with desire eyes. The hicks in Bloomington make you feel like a woman, throwing their hats on your path for you to step on or letting you know with words their feelings. We walk like zombies in New York. Our eyes have no focus, looking through the crowds, beyond the trees. I felt the sensation of happiness in the atmosphere, and yet, I was unable to capture it. It was an illusion. No one was going to make me feel sad today, I thought. I passed hordes of people on their way home. Pushing, running. The people thinking: *The meter! If I couldn't get to the meter on time, the ticket will cost me one half of today's salary. What did I care if someone drops dead in front of me! I have to keep on going. The babysitter! Oh my God, she will be charging me more! I have to get to that train! Get out of my way, you scum. Don't you see that time is money?*

I felt sorry for them. I knew what it was to have my happiness ruled by money. The competition, the madness. Red light, stop walking; green light, go. Sometimes you could not get to the other side of the sidewalk. You stop in the middle of the street terrified. Cars passed by you left and right, drivers hurling insults at you. *Who do you think you are? A light post?*

They yell, *Get off!* You are lucky if you make it to the opposite side of the sidewalk. A policeman is waiting for you, his shining police vehicle flashing red lights, obstructing the traffic. *What have I done! Jaywalking, madam, it is against the law. You are putting your life in danger. It is my life! Who cares!*

I was thinking so much that I passed the Petite Shop. "Turn back! My goodness! God forbid you are on the wrong side of the sidewalk. South you walk on the right, north on the left. Where do you come from?" they yell at me. After pushing and struggling, I get to the right side. Two blocks later, I walked into the fashion shop, "the Petite Shop." There was Betty! With the same shining eyes and love written on her face! For the first time, I felt jealous of Betty. *Why can't I fall in love? When can I experience the elated feeling of love? Why was I so dried out inside? What's wrong with me?*

There was Betty, looking so pretty, so young, so full of life, and so much in love. I felt ugly, and old. A dried-out piece of wood discarded in the middle of nowhere, rotting away, wasting my life. We waited for the rush hour to pass and for calm to settle again. We were hungry so we went to a nice restaurant to eat. I could see that she had hidden something away from me, so I asked her.

She laughed. "Oh, I could never hide anything from you! Ralph has business in Detroit and Portland. He wants me to help. He wants me in Detroit."

"In Detroit!!" I yelled so loud that some of the customers looked at us.

My ears were ringing at that moment. I was unable to listen to the customers' hushed conversations or the tinkle of silverware, as if the world had crumbled around us and only me and her existed.

Anguish was reflected in my shaking voice. "Oh, Betty, Betty, you innocent kitten." I knew she was not going to believe me. I knew then that she was lost and nothing anyone could say would make any difference. I tried to control myself and asked her. As a matter of fact, I asked her departure day. "Saturday? That is only three days away," I said. "Why didn't you tell us?"

"Oh," she said, "Ralph wanted it to be a surprise."

I guess she saw the incertitude reflected on my pale face, so she said, "It is okay, Mary. I am going to be making lots of money! Be happy for me, please, Mary."

Holding both of her hands, I said, "Betty, promise me that you are going to call me if anything goes wrong. Promise me!" Who will she call?

She promised, but I knew then that she didn't believe me; she was in love! Nothing I could say would make any difference. She loved Ralph and thought that Ralph loved her.

A woman would abandon her ambitions, her dreams of achievements for love. Those dreams never existed; they were an illusion. The only dream that existed in a woman's heart is love.

However, some women throughout history had achieved fame and glory. They had set outside the business of love and had stood up to a demanding strong will, intimidating spouse or lover. Queen Elizabeth from Spain was in every one of King Ferdinand's campaigns against the Moors in Spain. She stopped to give birth in a hut or road house, and two days later, she was on a horse ready for battle. She won the confidence of the troops and the respect of King Ferdinand. However, her daughter Juana fell in love with a handsome Germanic prince and almost lost her crown. He took every power away from her and disregarded her authority. Luckily for Spain, he died young. Juana is known throughout history as Juana La Loca, or Juana "the Mad One." She died in the most deplorable of conditions, locked up in an old castle. Her fault: falling in love.

Queen Elizabeth I of England, the virgin queen, had sat impassively and watched the horrible death of her lover. Catherine II of Russia had plotted with her lover and killed her husband. Those were strong women who stepped outside the business of love, concentrated on their well-being, and became famous. The young are rebelling today; they wanted to break old traditions by not submitting to rules, to follow the ancient rules of order; they refused to submit to the ancient order of laws. The hypocritical ones instead, leave the security of their homes to roam the streets and become prey to unscrupulous drug dealers, prostitution, pedophiles, and murderers.

Rebellion is a wonderful act if it has a purpose, if it has a goal. The pages of history are full of names of heroes, who had witnessed something wrong and have rebelled.

José Marmol, the Argentine writer, had written the novel *Amalia* against the Argentine dictator Rosas. Recently, Roxana Saberi wrote *Between Two Worlds*; she was imprisoned and charged with espionage in Iran.

Winzola McLendon wrote *The Life of Martha Mitchell*, a heroine who spoke clearly about Watergate and the corruptions under President Nixon's administration. She died penniless and lonely, betrayed by her husband.

Today, a boulevard displays her name. "Martha was right" was written on her tomb.

Today, the royalty of the world is trying to break the link that has separated people. Prince William of Wales and Prince Felipe of Spain are among the young royalty that have married beautiful, well-educated, and down-to-earth spouses. Recently, the duchess of Cambridge, the charming Kate, and Prince William have mesmerized the world with their simplicity. Prince Felipe and Prince William fought in the war in Afghanistan. They both took the same risks they demanded from their citizens, their life.

I could see that Betty was a rebel. Rebellious people have to go through their own experiences. They would not listen! And Betty was a rebel in love. A dynamite combination!

For the first year away from New York, Betty called frequently. We were able to get in touch with her through her cellular phone. She sounded happy, too happy for comfort. Then she called once a week. Sometimes she would interrupt our conversation with some suspicious excuses. "I got to go." And hang up.

She was not the happy-in-love Betty that was waiting with us at Kennedy Airport to board the plane to Detroit. She sounded afraid, as if yearning to say something, but afraid to talk to us. She would say, "Oh, it is nothing, just a lovers' quarrel, I am fine." Betty, I knew then! And I did not do anything to save you! It was that feeling in my heart. The inability, the incapability on my part to react to your message of misfortune. She was telling me, and I didn't listen. I shut my eyes to your misfortune, indifferent and cold. Forgive me, Betty!

Guilt wrapped my soul, strapping me to its shadows, dragging me along to the pits of agony. I went to Detroit. I looked for Betty in her former address. "No," the superintendent told me. "They moved about eight months ago. She was in the hospital about six months before they moved."

"Why was she in the hospital?" I asked.

The superintendent looked at me with an empty expression on his dark and sweaty face and said, "Look, lady, I just take care of this building, I do not mess around with the tenants!" Just like that! He left me there pale and shaking, indifferent to my suffering. "I will find you, Betty!" I swore right then and there. "Ralph, you wait and see."

I strolled the streets, I went to police stations, visited every bordello in Detroit. I showed her picture to everyone, a beautiful, innocent-looking girl, with a sensual mouth with a beautiful set of teeth. Oh, Betty, who dared strike you! I swore that I would find Ralph. He will pay for this! I dressed myself like a low-class prostitute: a very short dress, long high heels, false eyelashes, lots of makeup, a red wig, and a short leather jacket trimmed with fake fur. Looking like a prostitute, I was able to obtain lots of information. They looked a lot at Betty's picture. Some of them would say, "Well, someone that looked like her worked here six, four months ago. She sure is photogenic! She doesn't look like that now!" Others would simply say, "How long ago did she take that picture?" I was beginning to feel afraid. But I would reassure myself by thinking that she was alive. I found her in a middle-class bar prostitution place. We were standing next to each other, and she did not recognize me. She was dressed like a low-class prostitute, and I did not recognize that sad, ragged skinny-looking prostitute with hollowed cheeks and black dry hair. I knew then that Ralph Monda managed to take away her mind and body. Betty looked like a fake copy of her old self—a devastated soul, a dried out wound that love left within. He did what I fear the most—he made Betty a prostitute. She sold her soul for money.

"Betty!" I cried, pressing my arms around her fragile-looking figure! She pushed me away. She did not recognize me. "It is me, Betty, Mary." We embraced for what seemed to be hours, crying. Rocking our bodies, back and forth, I felt her pain through her delicate and fragile body. Touching her anguish, God, I prayed, give me strength, let me save this innocent creature! I knew then that I should have listened to her first. That I have to.

In my distress, I rushed to close a side window that was opened. A rank smell engorged the room. The smell of lust, of treason, of bestial play, of robbed innocence. We sat in a small sofa. A yellow light shone from above the back wall, giving Betty shadows and light, to her devastated and mutilated figure. We held hands. Betty told me that she was working as a prostitute. It was not Ralph's fault. She started to take drugs and lost her job as an administrator at one of Ralph's restaurants. "Well," she corrected herself, "one his *bars*. He warned me, Mary, I just would not listen! He turned on me. He kept warning me to no avail. What am I going to do, Mary? I love him, I can't live without him! I tried to kill myself, Mary. That's how much I love him!" Tears rushed down her hollow cheeks.

"Come with me, Betty. Remember? We were so happy together! You could start a new life! Find someone else that you love. Be pretty again!"

"I tried so many times to get off the drugs, but I couldn't, Mary. It is like a curse. The more you try, the more you sink into this dark and hollow self that no one should be allowed to be. So now you know! You probably despise me."

I said goodbye at the airport. I have no words to describe it. I just wanted to picture her picking up nuts on the highlands of Bloomington, gathering flowers, running through puddles, up and down the declines, hills, resting beneath the trees, our faces flushed with excitement. The cold mountain's wind blowing through our long matted hair. Oh Lord, what have I done to this innocent girl!

In between sobs, she said to me, "Well, I will be seeing you, Mary. Ralph said that if I behaved, he will send me back to the shop on New York. It will be like the old days."

I did not have the heart to tell her that Ralph had sold the Petite Shop. I said, "That would be nice, Betty, like the old days." Without looking back, I entered the departure line that led to the American Airlines plane. I sat with my knees touching painfully the back of the passenger seat in front of me. There was no place to move or to accommodate your tired arms. No room to breathe. I could imagine an elderly person or an overweight passenger. It must be a torture chamber for them. It was for me! I felt as though I couldn't breathe. I was trapped with sweat running down my face. I couldn't reach my bag that was some distance away.

I felt like six years ago. Lonely and tired. Cuddled up with my dog Tinkle to ward off all the misery I was experiencing then. I kept on asking myself why. As if destiny didn't have a beginning that guides a person to an end. My soul was scarred by the clawing of pity, trapped in a dark room, feeling the weight invading my devastated being.

I don't recall how many days was I plunged into oblivion. A bright light recovered all of my senses, when Carmela walked in and found me there, tucked away on the sofa, empty cans of soda scattered around me, and poop from Tinkle around our very expensive persian rug.

"The cleaning woman called me!" said Carmela. "You would not answer the bell." Carmela opened the windows, cleaned the rug, and brought me a hot chicken broth.

She opened the curtains and helped me to a hot bath. Was everything normal again? No. Back to the therapist. "I have a sense of everything coming down to pieces. I couldn't help but feel guilty about Betty. I took an innocent girl away from the protection of her brothers and delivered her to a sadistic monster." I envy Carmela. She did not feel guilty. She kept that positive attitude that was ingrained in her.

"It was not your fault," she kept on telling me again and again.

I didn't believe her! How can she go out and fall in love, keep her job, and act as if nothing had happened! A sweet smile was reflected on her beautiful face. She was in love! She had met someone in California. His name was Anthony. "He's of Italian descent just like me," she used to say. "He likes everything I do. The same experiences. The same customs."

I felt myself sinking. Where could I find a man with the same experiences that I had? The thought used to make me laugh. The same alcoholic parents? Living in a godforsaken dirty hut? Teasing, rubbing, manipulating? No, I couldn't have anyone share my own experiences or have the same background. Carmela had invited me many times before to join her friends. I had refused. I felt that I was not a good company, that I would sit somewhere bored with nothing to say. But on that particular day, I just came from a long walk in the park, carrying Tinkle against my chest, my face glowing from the long walk.

I knew that Carmela was moving into a different circle of life, with sophisticated people that tried to speak with an English accent. The circle of madams, discreet manners, soft blond hair tied up with pearls and diamonds, and sensual loose gowns, their mansions overlooking picturesque lawns or spectacular sea views. Once in a while, they would slip us into their circle as long as we were popular! We were an attraction, scandals and divorce tinting with shame our tumultuous lives. A good conversation topic. *Did you know? I read that you are well known and popular.* To demonstrate our diversity, we dressed differently, like models. False eyelashes, spectacular hairdos, low-cut expensive gowns, and very high heels that warded off most of the males attending the party.

I met William, a very tall, large-framed man, a magnificent specimen of his gender. One could detect the strong character, a suave but determined will showing in his intense blue eyes. William was a perfect gentleman. Suave and courteous. Speaks little. His words are calculated. A few, just to convey his thoughts or to manipulate you. To make you believe (contrary to your own senses) that everything was perfect, when you felt trapped and sad, and hell is knocking at your door. Your heart will tell you. I was ready to go to the utmost sacrifices by simply meeting that stranger for the first time. Oh God, I thought, I had the contagious disease of Juana La Loca, the crazy queen from Spain, that gave her crown away, the kingdom of Spain, and glory to a German prince. I was in a bliss of excitement without any recollection of the first ten minutes after the introduction of this man. I remembered the terrace. There was a bright moon casting shadows and light to the garden, the aroma of flowers burning my senses. The bliss of being kissed, by the ancient god Neptune and me being the goddess of love. I was in love! Like Tess of the D'Urbervilles, a novel by Thomas Hardy. She went to the gallows for the love of a man. Like Anna Karenina, the heroine in the novel of Tolstoy; she lost her husband, her son, her station in society for love. She committed suicide after the indifference of her lover. I was contaminated by that ancient disease called love that strike mostly women and have taken many of us into the road that leads to misery, evil treatment, and murder.

I couldn't help it! That same night, I lost my virginity. I traveled through the mysterious road that maidens dream about. I woke up in a sunlit room, with large windows overlooking a garden, flowers of different colors adorning the brick-edged paths that led to a gigantic fountain. Other paths led to different statues. I had a lot to do. Where was William? It was 7:00 a.m., and he was not in the bedroom. There was what I thought was another room. I opened the door, and to my surprise, the room was what appeared to be William's dressing room. The aroma of ebony filled my senses. Everything was organized by colors, seasons, style, sports. There were shoes of all colors, drawers and drawers of them. Everything was in wood—floors, walls, drawers, ceiling. At the end of a three-sided mirror and a bench, I opened another door. It was a sitting room. Books, enormous vases with oriental painting were on top of the mantle. I retreated and opened another door. It was a bathroom with two showers and a Jacuzzi. I opened another door, and it was a regular bathroom with two of everything. It also had a strange running water.

There was another door. *Oh Lord*, I thought. *Please let it be a door that leads me out of these rooms.* I was beginning to feel paranoid, the sweat running down my face. To my surprise, the door led to a corridor and down a spiral stairway. A sheet was wrapped around my body, my bare feet touching the cold floors. I turned around. I felt that I had to take a shower. I opened the bathroom door, and steam and hot water touched my tired body.

I remembered everything now. The lovely look in his eyes when I told him that I was a virgin, a sign of his love covering my body. I couldn't wait to see him! I had to wear the same gown. I didn't find my panties and stockings. Where was my bag? I wore my evening gown and brushed my hair. *Where am I?* I kept on asking myself. *Whose mansion is it? Where is William?* All these questions kept pounding my brain, leaving me full of anxieties. I felt fearful as if all those high walls, granite stairway, and luxury red persian rugs could lock me up and leave me there where I stood alone and trembling. A deep voice startled me.

"Allow me to help you, madam, please follow me." We walked through a large dining groom. William's lips gave me a cold and senseless kiss. I felt hurt, but he was a gentleman, in his house surrounded by his servants. I was entering a different world. *That was an excuse which, I later always managed to give William for his erratic behavior.*

We ate in silence, saying the polite words that one is obliged to say but no one is interested to listen. When breakfast finished, he stood up and offered his arm to me. We walked through a large glass door and into a garden. It was the end of April. The smell of the flowers filled my senses. I learned the names of all the statues I had seen previously through the bedroom window.

We walked through the wet bricks and toward the various statues that led to the fountain. We stopped at each statue, and William lectured me about their ancient history. "This is Apollo, the symbol for law, order, and morality. He is also the god of crops, herds, and music." I looked at William. He spoke of these gods as if he believed in them, as if these statues were also the gods themselves. The stern look of Apollo's face showed his zest for law and order. Across from Apollo was the statue of Zeus, Apollo's father, the punisher of guilt.

Next to Zeus was the statue of his wife Hera. Across from her was the statue of Artemis, Apollo's twin sister, the virgin huntress. She was also called Diana. The whole family was there! Only the statue of William was missing. He looked at me then, and a chill ran through my body. In this family, the same manly frame, intense look, delivery of law and order, the punisher of guilt. Oh, dear William. How come I did not detect the message you were sending? I could say it was our first acquaintance. I learned that his name was William Bruckner. He was born in England. His self-made rich father married a society lady. We stopped and faced each other. He held my hands in his large and smooth hands. When we left the mansion, William went off the road and parked the car behind some bushes. We made passionate love on top of my fur coat, his body covering mine completely. It was ecstasy. How did I live for so many years without the love of this man! Without his kisses, without his hugs? I lay on the humid earth naked, his jacket covering part of me, his body engendering life into my dried soul. I dressed. On the horizon, miles of marshes covered the ground. Their pale green leaves danced toward the direction of the wind, howling and deserted. Shadows and light covered the immense territory. One could hear the rhythm of waves and the smell of saltpeter in the air.

"We're close to a beach," I said. He just told me to hurry walking in front of him, not like before when we walked hand in hand toward our love nest, kissing, touching, anxious to consummate our desire. He walked without looking at me, serious, mad. A different William. Like Zeus, the punisher of guilt, or Apollo the god of law and order. Was he feeling guilty about our love? What did I do to upset him so? Later on, I got used to his sudden changes of moods. He could be a perfectly loving gentleman one moment and a mad out-of-control person the next, or he would be silent, calculating, the part of his character that I feared the most.

William would lie and say to me that we were having guests and to order flowers for the occasion. I was to be composed when the guests arrived. A cold look on the butler's face told me that something was wrong. I walked into the dining room. The table was set for two. Flowers that I had ordered were displayed on top of the polished furniture. He was not attired in his usual evening suit and red band covering his waist, but with a regular suit that he wore daily. His stern face showed no regret or knowledge. A cold disregard was displayed on his aristocratic self. No explanation. A chilling silence saturated with pity my aching and devastated soul. Dead silence met each of my questions. I was trapped in a web. He sat there like a spider waiting for his victims to stop moving, trying to get free. I was caught up in a web of intrigue, saturated by doubts, confused by guilt, thinking it was my fault. Tears ran down my expensive gown.

How dare he! I'll show him next time! I watched him, I said to myself. *Next time, I wouldn't believe him! He is not going to be able to make me feel like a fool again.* The servants looked at me as though I was crazy, a contemptuous look on their bewildered faces. I forgave William. I said to myself he was covering up, he was protecting me from an embarrassment. I guess William wanted to say "I am sorry," but his stern character forbade him to do so. He would go to all kinds of expenditures to cover up his lack of sensitivity. A heart pendant with matching earrings said the words that it was impossible for him to say "I am sorry." I should have run for my life after the party incident. Instead, I found myself admiring him, forgiving him.

I guess I knew then that it was going to be the beginning of a living hell. I just didn't want to admit it.

It was Christmastime. Workers were everywhere, downstairs, outside. Christmas decorations everywhere. "Who? Who ordered all these decorations?"

"Madam, we have a budget for every holiday and reception that is to take place during the year." the butler told me.

"Mr. Leeward, I was looking forward to go Christmas shopping." I remembered Carmela and how much fun we used to have buying the Christmas decorations. Decorating the tree. All of it!

I locked myself in my room and sat on the small balcony overlooking part of the garden. I could barely see on my right the statues of Apollo's family. William's rooms were on my right, in which balcony I stood three years ago and wondered about the statues. It seemed like an eternity had passed by. I felt old and ugly. William's mental torture upon me had left me with a sense of worthlessness. I was not the same Mary that was going to conquer the world when I left Bloomington, the Mary that looked down on the town's men and women. Mary, the beauty, the pretty, graceful, soft, effeminate. I think the good Lord had punished me for being selfish; I lived with guilt in my soul. A cicatrix, a mental scar that had left me dried and helpless. I was not excited anymore about Christmas or seeing Carmela. What could I tell her? I didn't even know if she would believe me. Who could? William the polite, well mannered, the elegant, rich, social. William with a stern, but suave personality. The envy of every society lady, and I, the simple Mary. The target of all gossip, the usurper of fortunes, the lucky stranger with a southern accent.

William was in control of everything, I heard him telling Carmela how sorry he was that I could not speak to her. "She is not well, she is imagining stories". He told Carmela about the party that never took place. He described every detail with precise evil instinct, insinuating frail mental capability on my part! I was devastated. My dear friend! The only person that I could talk to. It has been three years since I moved away from my apartment. I was so happy then! I kept on telling Carmela how much I loved him, how lucky I was that someone like William wanted me! I was captivated, madly in love, charmed. That was when Carmela asked me,

13 Consequence Street

"And William?" It was just like Carmela. She would say one or two words and leave you there in suspense. Hanging by the meaning of those two words.

He never told me that he loved me. I was almost happy for the first time in months. William was at his best. We took long rides, had lunch in out-of-the-way sophisticated small restaurants, tucked away by earthen vases packed with aromatic roses and large blue rhododendrons. We traveled to the Bahamas, walked hand in hand through white sparkling sand and small roads. We made love on the beach, bathed by the bright moon rays. I forgot about all of his moods. I thought so much about pleasing William that I forgot my own needs. I became an obliging companion, a serviceable slave. I erased from my mind any contradicting thought and repudiated any negative thinking about William. He was my god, my Apollo, and I his Diana, the virgin goddess. Was Zeus (her grandfather) jealous of Diana? And did He chase away from her every young male? I often wondered about the mythology and Diana while strolling through the garden and looking at Zeus's stern face and his intense eyes. That Christmas, I was as happy as I remembered. We were a regular couple. His change of moods was not as drastic as they used to be. He looked peaceful, contented, pleased.

Suddenly, I liked the Christmas decorations that I didn't before. Now, I liked every bulb, wreath, and decorations that adorned the halls, stairs, entrance, patio, windows, and front lawn. Even if it looked like a display of farce, a naughty attitude toward our friends of different beliefs. I asked myself, Who am I anyway? Those were his friends, friends that adored his English manners, his haughty personality, his suave self. *What do I care? Be happy, Mary, love yourself.* I didn't love myself at all. I kept on forgetting the abuse, ill treatment, and desolation that I was being subjected to by William. I kept on giving myself excuses about his behavior. Forgiving him every time he came back to me with tears in his eyes, pleading, promising that he was not going to do it again. He blamed everything and everybody for his erratic behavior; therefore he was free of any guilt and impudence to commit the same behavior again. I didn't know why I did not run for my life. All I had to do was open the door, run past the gate. Be free. Freedom was just a few miles away, and yet I couldn't take those first steps. I couldn't call the police.

He needed to keep abreast of the Wall Street market news. My computer was in his office; I could only use it when he was in his office. I had sent disarrayed messages to Carmela, but they were working hours and Carmela did not answer them. However, I had the feeling that William went into my e-mail and cancelled those messages. William kept the office locked.

I had my little dog, Tinkle. He was my companion, my little angel. I kept him always close to me. I didn't trust anyone. I opened the can of dog food and watched him eat it. I didn't care if that was strange behavior on my part. The staff thought that I was crazy anyway. All I cared about was Tinkle, my only companion, my only friend, my baby, and I was wondering if I was sterile. I knew that William had a child, a girl from his first marriage, Catherine. She *never* came to visit him, but I knew that she called him from his private cellular phone. William used to travel to London to see her. I visited a gynecologist to see if I was pregnant or if I was sterile. William accompanied me.

"You are still young. We have lots of time. We will get married as soon as you are expecting!" We sat at the doctor's office eyeing each other; I was feeling uncomfortable.

"When is he going to call us to his office?" I felt that I could not take the suspense any longer. William sat across from me, untouched, calm, serene. My heart skipped a beat when the phone in the secretary's desk rang.

"This way please," the secretary directed us toward the doctor's office. William insisted in coming with me to see the doctor. "After all," he said, "I am going to be the father."

"Oh, William, I am so happy! I hope that I don't disappoint you." We waited what felt to me hours when it was just a ten minutes' wait. I couldn't breathe; I felt that I was going to faint. *Hold on, Mary,* I said to myself. *This is what you were waiting for.* I didn't hear all the explanation the doctor was giving us. All I heard was, "I am sorry to tell you, you are not pregnant." Tears filled my eyes and ran down through my ash-colored face. William was there to reassure me. My period was missing because of lack of iron! Iron, iron—I was branded with a red-hot iron. I was put in irons; I was left behind the iron bars that was to become my cell. Another iron lock to imprison me forever. What is the mystery of this substance? When it comes from the ground, it is used to manufacture arms that had killed billions of people.

Gone were the days without money. I had danced in cheap and dark cabarets in downtown Manhattan wearing sexy outfits that revealed most of my breasts and revealing underwear covering up slightly my well-rounded back. Men would feel up my outfit with hundreds of dollar bills, even occasionally a thousand-dollar bill. These were usually attached with a telephone number. I ran for my life after the show into a waiting taxicab. Juan used to wait for me every night, looking out for any car that would follow us. Sometimes a customer would leave the show and wait outside for me to come out. I had to be careful not to let anyone know where I lived. It was a dangerous, but exciting life. I was so wise. I never touched drugs or went to bed with the customers. I was always looking out for danger, knowing what to do in any situation. I didn't let men fool me. I was an independent, self-sufficient woman. I knew about life. I traveled around the world, associated with high-society European ladies. I was recognized in the fashion world, and yet here I was enclosed in a golden cage, madly in love with a cruel man. I was unable to spread my wings, fly away into clear horizons, feel the wind on my face, unlock my soul, and let it go into the blue sky. I knew I couldn't do it. Our souls were bound; he needed me as much as I needed him. I sensed his moods when he was disturbed, happy, angry, devious, mad adverse, guilty, an impostor, a deceiver, and yet I didn't know about the rest of humanity; all I knew at that time was that, iron was the substance responsible for all my misery. The doctor explained that iron (in its ferrous state) together with globin and porphyrin form part of the red blood cells. I was anemic. I had to eat foods that contained iron, like beans, red meat, etc., as well as take vitamins.

Well, back to the drawing board, I said to myself.

It was Christmastime, and the house looked like a gigantic electric bulb. Mr. Leeward, attentive and formal, stood by the doorway. He read small cards that our guests gave him, and he in turn announced their names to us. I stood with a fake smile printed on my face, next to me a cold, well-mannered gentleman whom everyone adored.

My gown was a gold color, a small white velvet band covered with pearls under and around my breasts and back. My hair was in curls to my shoulders. Fake pearls adorned my ringlets at different angles. I couldn't wait to talk to Carmela. I approached her, but I was taken aback when I noticed a nice-looking fellow holding hands with her. No one has to tell me when someone is in love. I could see it plainly in their eyes. It is a light that glows from within your soul and reflect its rays in the person's eyes.

"Carmela, you are in love!"

"We are in love," Carmela corrected me.

There she goes again. She was right. I could sense Carmela's partner's sensible love. She was his queen, his love. He did not try to impress anyone at the party. He let her be the center of attraction. Unlike William, who tried to impress everyone with his suave manners and extreme courtesy. I was merely a toy, a conjugal piece of meat that his friends were forced to swallow. I hugged Carmela.

She showed me her huge diamond ring. "We are going to marry and move away to California next month."

What can I say to Carmela now? Could I spoil her happiness then? A chill ran down my spine that made me tremble. She must have noticed my state of mind because she asked me, "What's wrong, Mary? Tell me."

Oh, I knew then that it was the last hope I had to run away, to confide to Carmela everything. To be free, but then I looked up to her eyes. They were so clear. There was so much love on those bright green eyes that I didn't have the heart to confide, to tell her of the misery that I was subjected to. Would she believe me? There I was dressed like a queen, a handsome and refined man for a partner, living in a mansion full of guests. What could prevent me from running away? No, I couldn't say anything. I was alone, discarded, inutile. Everywhere I turned for help, a door was slammed on my face. Carmela was shaking me, her eyes deep into mine, serious, concerned, slashing into my soul to rob me.

"Tell me, Mary, talk to me!"

"It is just that I feel lonely, and now you are leaving me!"

"Come with us, Mary."

She didn't understand I was not going to listen to her any more than Betty listened to me when I was pleading with her to leave her lover. Carmela and I were in the bathroom, and we had locked the door. We couldn't go upstairs and into my bedroom. William was watching me. I could sense the power of his being. No, that was the last time I saw Carmela. My heart told me that it was going to be the last time. Carmela and I looked into each other's eyes and knew. We were twin souls, bosom friends just like Betty and I were a hundred years ago. I knew I was going to be punished. What I didn't know was why. Maybe it was that I talked too much with Carmela or that I had locked the bathroom door. William sensed our spiritual sensitivity and became jealous. He was condemned by a religious zeal of self-grandeur. If I have him, I should not want anything or anyone else, or he will strike without pity. He was Zeus, the natural ruler of man, the holder of the thunderbolt, capable of finishing the world. The eagle on his extended left hand will finish the carcasses of humanity. I felt afraid. We were walking as we had many times before. Talking or holding hands, or simply admiring the garden, walking toward the meadow.

I had not paid attention to William. I was admiring nature until he turned his face toward me, insulting me, talking between his teeth, squinting his eyes to an imaginary point on my face, acting as though he was pissed off. I was taken aback by his sudden change in his personality. Never before had he used those words. I ran, ran for my life, deep into the meadow, past the wall. I rested under an old tree for about two hours, wondering, thinking of leaving William like I did many times before. Why did I not keep on walking? Freedom was some miles away. I came back to the house and entered through the side door, far away from the Zeus family, up a small set of stairs. I hesitated. I was only in that corridor once before. I stopped to recollect my memory. To the left was the staff quarters (as William always corrected me when I said "servants"), another landing, and I came on back of the main stairway, up to my room. I was dirty, boots caked with mud, and sand all over me. I took a long bath. Steaming water soothed my tired mind.

For the first time in my life, I felt like having a drink. *I will take two as soon as I finish my bath*, I said to myself. That was the biggest mistake that I made. I opened William's sitting room. There was a bar full with all kinds of liquor. I didn't know what to choose. Scotch. Everybody drinks scotch. I took a small glass and filled it. I needed that! I thought. It made me feel happy I had no troubles. What am I complaining about? So William was mad for some reason. What couple does not get mad? He has his reasons. The market went down, he lost lots of money, who knows? I went down the stairs feeling happy. I forgot William. I felt like kissing him, dancing. I entered the enclosed patio where we usually had two glasses of wine with my lunch. I didn't dare stand up and walk to my room. I knew that if I stood up and tried to walk, I would be wobbling throughout the corridors under the stern look of Mr. Leeward's face. I started to laugh, very low at first, but then I burst into loud hysterical laugh. I couldn't help it. It was the liquor.

Living with a staff of people that tend to you from the inconveniences of life is magnificent, but you feel like you are constantly being watched. There is no privacy; there are a hundred eyes judging you, forming their own opinion about your character. They know all of your secrets, your intimacy as if a rolling camera is chasing you around and making them aware of every move you make. One has to be born into this luxury to feel comfortable about it. I fell asleep in a retractable armchair, the midday sun caressing my body.

It was five in the afternoon when I woke up. I felt relaxed and poised. I had a wrinkled dress and matted hair, but I didn't care. I went for a walk. The sky burst with color. The air felt clean. The sun was down toward the West. Bright colors of pink, yellow and green covered the sky.

William started to take long and short trips. At the beginning of these trips, I thought that he was having an affair. Why would a man disappear for one, two, or three days? There was not a trace of a woman's perfume, telephone calls, or suspicious exits, or guilty attitude on his part. He always came back composed, relaxed. No a trace of the impatient, disturbed self that he displayed the last time I saw him. Well, I learned how to relax too. I developed a taste for vodka that made me cope with the vicissitudes of life. I could see that he was surprised there were no more questions about his business trips, no more insinuations on my part. Did my attitude change William? Was it possibly a change in his character? I asked myself. Just then, when I was full of hope for an open door into salvation, wanting to believe, eager to experience true love, a love without suspicions, without fears, a peaceful existence with no regrets, no doubts, I was struck down again. This time with serious consequences.

Chapter 5

It was as if the only shred of dignity left on me was yanked, stripped away from me. William, in one of his deranged and treacherous moods, had given me a black whip. It was thick at the metal handle and dreadfully slim toward the end. I saw the look in his eyes as if he wanted to caress me, a wanton disgusting look burning throughout every inch of my body. I was shivering, as if I was in the cold stage of a fever, my body pinned against the wall.

"William!" I yelled. "What is this?"

He came closer to me. His deep blue eyes turning almost black, burning with fury. "Don't you forget, madam," he said, "I know of your past and your life as a harlot. I am warning you, madam, if you as much as try to step out of this house, if I see you looking or wanting another man, I will tear your skin out of your body inch by inch." While he was talking, he was caressing me with that terrifying whip. My face, neck, my breasts, my legs. I felt the cold metal handle on my body. I sensed a chill run through me, his hot alcohol breath on my face. He pushed me against the wall, giving me a bump on the back of my head. He threw me on my bed and proceeded to take my clothes off. He raped me and left me there, sick and dirty, trembling with hate, more vulnerable than ever. I heard the shower going and then silence. I lay on the bed for what seemed to be an eternity. Afraid to move, afraid to see his huge athletic figure against the door. I couldn't think. All I wanted to do was scrub my body, take off all the tracks he left on me.

William disappeared for one week. Mr. Leeward informed me, "He will be away for a week, madam." I didn't look at him; his suave manners didn't impress me anymore. I felt the disdain reflected toward me in his impeccable and educated speech. I didn't look at him. I simply said, "I will have breakfast on the terrace." After breakfast, I rested, a bottle of vodka next to me on the floor. The early sun bathed the meadow, caressing the trees. A smell of earth reached my senses, the song of birds. I was falling sleep. The effect of the alcohol took possession of me. I felt relaxed, contented.

Happiness with William was like traveling in a steam vessel during a turbulent storm, the high waves and howling wind racking the vessel while passing under the ship's stern. Its rocking force made you sick, leaving you trembling and scared. It is my life. I chose it. Living in a gold cage like a frightened little sparrow singing when it should have been crying, eager to spread my wings, but afraid to do so. Feeling uncomfortable in a free open space. Choosing to stay in my golden cage. Chirping myself to experiment happiness, looking myself in the mirror, willing to find my other self, my twin sister, that other person that was happy, free, and confident. That other self that sprouted from the earth to become a delicate flower. Who wielded my delicate stem? And let me there willing without sunlight? It was William. William the handsome, the brave, the smart. The love that stops my heart whenever I look upon his figure, the generous torturer, the sarcastic and devious person. The man that I love.

My life changed for the worst from that dreadful night that William raped me. No more pretenses on his part. He could sense my apathy. I knew his biggest secret. The English society did not accept his father or him. His mother looked upon him as though he was an outcast. They were ridiculed. Only his father's money kept his mother and later on his wife as a trophy for their acceptance. He was running away. Taking back everything that belonged to him. Getting even. He destroyed the world with his own hands. He could not be close to Catherine, his pure and only love, his child. With Catherine, he was like Zeus—open, completely naked, only an olive crown covering his head. His manly parts exposed, no sandals on his feet, no deceptions, manipulations. Not the sarcastic and devious person that he is, but the loving father. He was allowed to speak to his daughter on the phone and visit her from time to time. He was mad at the world, especially to women. It was his mother and wife that ridiculed him, scraped from him the last trace of dignity, robbed his most valuable jewelry—the beautiful, refined, and delicate Catherine.

He did not inherit the rough character of his father, the obtuse attitude which the father imposed to some members of the high society. After all, he had seen them begging at his office for a loan or a business deal. He had no regards for their misfortune. He knew their feigned, dissembled, and hypocritical characters. He knew them! They detected his cold and disregard attitude. William was left to fend himself, to experience the cold rejection of his mother and wife. He did not belong. He felt rejected, unloved.

He rejected others as well. Dancers, young girls that exhibited their well-endowed bodies, prostitutes (that he calls harlots), they should all be in prison. For them, he was the god Apollo, the averter of evil, presiding over religious laws and expiation: the accuser, the condemner, the executioner.

I rode with him in the turbulent storm of his howling and macabre moods like two sailors fighting the wind, its high waves damaging our souls, threatening our existence. William was in a good mood for over three months then. We dined on small tucked-away restaurants close to the sea, a full moon caressing our faces with its gentle light. Sometimes, the moon hid beneath the clouds and cast a lugubrious, somber shadow on William's face.

I could swear that I saw his burning eyes shining like those of a cat, or lion when they go hunting at night, or did I imagine it? I had too many glasses of wine. Liquor brings traces of my old self, that other person of long ago that used to laugh, that other person that strived to succeed, that believed herself beautiful. I notice that the sound of the waves or being close to the sea made William feel uncomfortable, and yet he always chose to dine in those tucked-away restaurants set by the sea.

I did not complain. I will be lying to you if I tell you that I didn't enjoy the luxury, the pompousness of being taken care of, the restaurants, the plays, and of everything that came attached to living with William. Was it worth it?

Very few men would subject themselves for love to abuse and security. They will kill, if they must, to regain their freedom. I envy them! No one could stop them. If they had to move to another town or country to improve their financial situation, they will not hesitate to fulfill their dreams. If the wife or girl they love do not approve, a man will not hesitate to leave that person. After all, attached to every lucrative move hides his manhood, the ability to choose among a howling group of females that are willing to sacrifice themselves for love or money. It gives men a sense of being in command, in charge of his manhood. The eternal warrior. The Attila, king of the savage hordes of northern Europe, maintained on his horse, villain scorching the earth, stamping his horse's hooves into enemy territory, winning the respect of other great men and the eternal love of women. We love the macho man, their security, their manhood, their ability to sweep you off your feet to experience the sense of his dominant self to feel that he loves you. A woman forgets that along with his desire hides his ego, the somber self that makes him a warrior, a conqueror, a hero.

I first met Zoraida after I moved in with William. I felt that I didn't need anyone to tend to me, to do for me the chores that I was used to do for myself. I felt uncomfortable having someone treat me as though I was a child. William insisted and I consented. She would tell me strange stories from that faraway and exotic land, Morocco. A very special girl, docile, attentive, and honest, she was almost just a child when she started to work for me. She reminded me of Betty—the same large and sad eyes, the same skinny figure, and innocent self. I trusted her with all of my possessions.

The first week I moved in with William, he presented me with a very expensive set of rubies—earrings, a ring, and necklace surrounded with diamonds, valued at $75,000 dollars. We were invited to the Richardsons' eighty-million-dollar penthouse on Park Avenue. I was not really invited—the invitation read "Sir William Bruckner and guest"—I knew I couldn't refuse. The Richardsons were one of the first investors in William's main business. The invitation arrived three weeks before the event was to take place. A very distinguished card, with gold letters and impressive envelope with their gold initials printed on it. I was going to wear a black gown with a red fine line of silk across my chest and around my waist. I knew that the ruby set was perfect with what I was going to wear. Zoraida opened the case where the set of rubies were always in and saw with horror that it was missing. We started to look everywhere for it. Definitely, it had to be in the house; none of the other jewels were missing. Our fickle hearts full of fears, we looked for about fourteen days everywhere. Removed mattresses and looked under furniture, rugs, shelves. We were so afraid, as if we had stolen the set ourselves and were waiting judgment.

Mrs. Blake, a stern-looking fearful matron (typical of the Hitchcock movies of the fifties), walked in. She was already looking at us with suspicion. "The cleaning up," we said to her, "it was taking place." I had asked Zoraida not to say anything to the rest of the staff. I was certain that we were going to find the set. Why would anyone steal such a high-priced piece of jewelry and leave the case laying in everybody's view? I asked myself lots of questions on those two weeks. I had to think of something before Mrs. Blake told William. I was devastated. I knew that he was going to blame me. I knew his reactions. As if a mirage was taking place in front of me, I could see William. The same unmoving aristocratic face, the same cold eyes. Not a word, just reaching for a half-empty bottle of vodka, and looking at the white crystal liquid, a somber look reflected in his dark blue eyes. He would walk out of the room without a glance, not a word of compassion, as if I were to stand on a corner, taunted and ridiculed, torn apart by his lack of understanding. I acted like a mad person, laughing hysterically, reaching for the crystal liquid, trashing furniture, breaking dishes, vases. How could I thwart his somber being? I knew I was lost. He tended a trap, and I was caught in it as though I were a quail deceived by the hunters, listening to other sounds trapped by the mirage of another self. And finally struck down by a cold hunter. I was the mad Mary, as guilty as Juana La Loca of long ago. I sat on a chair, a blanket covering my dilapidated soul. Without saying a word, not listening.

The police was there. Their shining brass and polished shoes. Asking questions that William answered for me. "No, no other jewelry was taken. We looked everywhere. Yes, the jewelry were insured. All the other jewelry are insured as well."

A pitiful glance cast from the police officers. "What's wrong with her?"

"Too much vodka, Officer."

They were two long weeks. Questioning, fingerprints, the insurance company acting more like police officers than the entire precinct. Their look of mistrust reflected on their somber faces. "Do you have someone?" they asked, their devious eyes staring at my bosom.

"How dare you!" I send them out of the house. Their pitiful small frames doubled up to resemble those of a mouse. Finally, it was over, a calm once again pervading our household. I enjoyed the peace that reigned during those periods in the house. Rides, lunches, but most of all, peace. Oh god, how I needed those periods of peace! They were like an elixir to my crumbled soul. I gave in to William. It was time to rejoice, to change to normal living. It never took more than six months, a year, or two. Suddenly, as if a tornado and a mass of howling wind had struck our household, our peaceful lives were shattered.

It was a beautiful afternoon, and William wanted to go for a ride, camp in the tall grass, have something to eat, and make love. He came into my room, pointing at his watch. "Eleven thirty," he said. "It is windy, I am taking the convertible."

William was giving last-minute orders to the staff that were gathered outside in the hall. I reached for a light tan summer hat that was placed on the top shelf of my closet. Its case was facing down, flapping its silk wings up, ready for me to grab them and swing it quickly over my head. God almighty! Out came cascading down over my head, down my face, and shoulders my set of rubies that we had looked all over the house. Once again, I was the laughingstock of the household. I could hear their comments and laughs while they were walking away, piercing like an arrow to my heart. The necklace hanging from my head and down the side of my face. A really comedy show! Even Zoraida had a smirking look on her face! I laughed, a howling laugh that sounded like a scream. A fearful howling, like the piercing scream of the wolf. I knew it was William. Two days before that fearful day, I had worn that hat and placed it on the shelf two days ago. Why? Why did William want to mortify me? What lies under his taunting methods? It gave me a chill thinking of what else could he be planning to hurt me. I played the fool, not letting him know that he hurt me, concentrating on the miracle of getting back my beautiful set of rubies. Of course, I wore it at the ball, sending waves of rumors. I made believe I didn't care, showing my well-developed figure to the overweighed matrons. I kept on looking to see if Carmela were among the guests. No luck, I had not heard from her for a long time. I wondered if my mail was interfered with. In fact, I was almost certain. I knew Carmela, and I was certain that she will investigate if she suspected that I was in some sort of danger. I asked myself, *Did she come to visit me?*

What did they tell her? How about a telephone call? What happened to Betty? I tried; I went to my old apartment. A young couple with two children was living in our old apartment. Beautiful thoughts came to my memory. Central Park! I strolled through its paved walks. My mind absorbing its beauty, forgetting my dreadful life, feeling more lonely than ever. I went back home, wondering how my escapade will obstruct my liberty from this moment on. I didn't care. Mr. Leeward opened the door and informed me that William was expecting me, waiting for me at the library. He sat behind his huge mahogany desk. A rigid look was reflected on his fickle face.

"May I ask, madam, where have you been?"

"Well, sir, I didn't know I have to keep schedule about my goings."

"You certainly don't. It is a big difference," he said, getting up from his seat, displaying his huge well-developed body. "I am not fond of vodka as you are, and I do not go about displaying a meek mental attitude. I am afraid, dear. You need some looking after."

That was the first time William obstructed my path, with an ignoble accusation he was telling me that I was mad. "Well, dear William," I said, "for the first time you show your ignoble self and let me know what was in your mind. Today you became a human being."

My escapade to my old apartment and downtown New York had its consequences. Taking the LI Railroad on my own brought upon my already isolated life the final clamp, the last bolt on my ebbing and turbulent life. Mrs. Blake was in charge of my confinement. An evil and lugubrious matron, her little beady eyes watched me as a raven looks upon his prey, ready to strike, her somber shadow obstructing my liberty. For my protection, William installed a very complicated alarm in the house. You couldn't open a window, a side door, or accidentally throw a metal on the floor. A loud thump would send the alarm screaming as if abominable monsters were tearing down the sky, sending panic throughout the household. I felt so vulnerable. The bars of my golden cage closed on me. I spent the next few months in a restless stage, staring at the statues, looking out the windows, the bright light swaddling the earth with beautiful colors. I hung around with provocative negligees, a bottle of vodka close by.

Finally, I made a decision. I put on a turtleneck sweater, a great suit, and comfortable shoes. In my bag, I carried three thousand dollars and my credit card. I was ready to walk out of the house. I set off the alarm, and I didn't care. I felt the wind on my face. Spreading my wings beyond the horizon, I walked out. I didn't look back, running until I couldn't hear that horrible siren any longer, my heart thumping against my chest. The strength of my body leaving me, obstructing my breath, I had to stop the rush of oxygen going into my lungs. I stopped to absorb some carbon dioxide and continued. I heard the police sirens blaring away, sounding like trained hounds on my path, their terrifying barking following the scent of my sweating body. I lay exhausted, cooling myself under the umbrella of a hazelnut tree, gasping for air. I had no more hope, no more strength left in my dilapidated body. I was dragged back into my golden cage, looking more mad than ever. Why should I have to explain?

No one would believe me. There stood William, the handsome actor, standing on the threshold, hovering over his reasoning to the police with a callous, insensible way. Who was going to believe me? I sat there, trembling, listening. Each of his words gnawed away at my soul, forever imprisoning me, wasting away my life, taking away my freedom. I remember my grandmother's words whenever she saw me sad: in every misfortune, there is always a shining star. As a young girl, I looked at the sky for that small shining star; however, I realized during my affliction what grandmother meant. It could be worse for me. Tears fell from my eyes as I thought of Betty. I could have fallen in love with someone like Ralph! I had everything I wanted. Except freedom. Was freedom so important? That shining star inside of you makes you look at the positive side. It prevents you from becoming musty, and a flush of excitement invaded my soul. I told myself that I had to be positive. Who wants to live with a drunk? A deranged woman who would like to escape on every opportunity? I thought about William. He could throw me out any time he wishes to, and yet he kept me here! Why? Is it love? Or an obsession? He made love to me, especially after every one of my humiliations. He seems to be aroused by his callousness, by the morbidity of each one of his perfidies. *Where is that shining star?* I searched my mind, and I couldn't find it. Only the comforts of living in luxury. Well, that is a shining star! I could be under a bridge or locked up in a mental institution. The thought of it chilled my mind and made me tremble.

I decided to conform, to follow the star, until it was my time to act. I was at the ebb of my life, inconstant, voluble. As if I were an old discarded, dilapidated object thrown out on the sidewalk of life.

First, I had to reduce my intake of vodka. That would take an enormous effort on my part. I decided to try and I did. Only four drinks of vodka a day. One after each one of my meals, an extra vodka before going to bed. I hardly ate thinking of my drink of vodka. I had to be careful not to reach for a glass of juice. My hands were trembling, and I did not want treacherous Mrs. Blake to notice it. The house was peaceful again. I gave in to every one of William's whims without complaining. The dresses he wanted me to wear, wearing lots of makeup, and provocative dresses or gowns. Never taking vodka in front of him, but drinking a variety of wine that he was fond of. Never drinking more than a lady should. I turned into a living doll, picked up or discarded as he wished it, torn apart by his lugubrious moods. He did not take me to the Richardsons' ball anymore. I was grateful! I imagined going to a ball for ten years and never making a friend!

William was taking a trip to England to see Catherine. It was going to be her graduation, her presentation into society: Count and Countess Ronald and Helen Portberg to Sir William Bruckner, etc., etc. I just glanced at it. Its gold edges and gold printed lettering. I was glad that William was going to England. I could do as I wanted, dress as I like to. I was looking forward to drinking myself to oblivion to forget my fragile existence. I asked William if I could go outside to feel the sun on my face, walk under the trees, feel the crisp grass under my feet, smell the aroma of the flowers.

"William, please," I pleaded. "I will be good. I promise not to run away." He felt so happy with the thought of seeing Catherine that he gave in, with a schedule, of course. I was to go out at 10:00 a.m. and be back at 1:00 p.m. for lunch. Mrs. Blake was in charge of my schedule, ready to obstruct me at the least delay on my part. I had to be careful. I knew she would do anything to make my life miserable. I asked William if it was okay to take with me Zoraida. I had to take advantage of the happiness William was experimenting then.

He agreed with a warning toward Zoraida, lifting my chin with his hand and looking deep into my eyes, saying, "Zoraida, I leave you the responsibility of bringing back this beautiful doll every day at the set schedule."

I have to admit that looking into his eyes and at his handsome virile face, it took me back to the days when I was so much in love. The magic of the moment, his manly figure, and then his urgent kiss upon my lips had sent chills over my eager body. I knew then that I couldn't get rid of the knot that attached me to this man. I realized then that I loved William. I also knew that he was extremely happy to see Catherine. He was walking on a fringe, a liberated soul. Being invited to the ball and being the escort to Catherine, walking into the immense ballroom decorated in gold, with twelve huge hanging chandeliers, sent pride to his wounded soul. It was not me that he was kissing.

I didn't care. Sensing his hot lips upon mine sent waves of desires that were buried inside of me for the longest time. I had to be careful; I knew that Mrs. Blake was to keep an eye on me, and she could lie to William. Every day in front of Mr. Leeward, I used to set my watch especially when I came back at exactly 1:00 p.m. I stood in front of the clock that decorated part of the hall and proceeded to tell the time that we had arrived, Mrs. Blake observing me with her beady dark eyes. I knew that she must have placed my set of rubies on my summer hat. It was

William's brazen character and tactics that I very well knew—he was the mastermind—that had probably told Mrs. Blake that he had found the set of rubies and ordered her to place the set without my knowledge back into my room. He was not going to take the blame for this act and come out as the lugubrious figure that he was.

So I had to be careful. William had managed to have a partner, an old devious person. Feeling like an old wrecked ship in the middle of a turbulent sea, Mrs. Blake's retirement years were not far away. No pension and no money, her savings had been squandered away by her only child, a son that she had trusted to invest her possessions. She lost everything. The constable came to her house with an order of possessions. She sat in her comfortable old chair while they took everything. She managed to save some of her clothing and coats by taking them to her sister's house. At the end of this nightmare, they asked her to stand up and take the last of her possession away from her, the chair where she was sitting on, she, feeling the penury inside her weary old heart. I knew how she must have felt. It reminded me of my first years in Manhattan. Broke, alone, in a difficult city. Wanted to be destitute by a group of wealthy and eccentric tenants. Taken to prison, accused of being a prostitute. My picture flashed in and out in the television news. My pride shattered.

What were they saying in my old town? The echo of their laughter rang in my ears. But I was young, merely a child. I had my life in front of me! I chose prison to be with the man I loved, the eccentric man, the psychotic being that had encircled my life in penury. Then came the time of peace, that wonderful time in my life that I cherished. I felt free opening the front door; it sounded to me like the clang of rusted old castle doors, the sentry on guard behind me, life and freedom ahead of me. We walked through the woods, the humid pasture under our eager feet.

We ran like two frightened hearts, feeling the wind, the sun warming up our drenched and paled bodies. I could have kept on running. What was that strange feeling of culpability that encircled my life and kept me voluble? Fear of the unknown, William obstructed my life. I was trapped in a web, suffocated by his fickle and evil character, living me fragile.

I was free! For two months we ran and talked without restrictions, my heart discarding lots of pains, hardships, and doubts. I finally found a friend. Someone that I could trust, a confidant to whom I could discharge all the agony that I suffered—my suspicions, my frustrations, my ambitions, and my fears.

Chapter 6

Nothing kept me from seducing William. We hurried through the garden. We could hardly keep our hands away from each other. Our lips clasped in a constant kiss. I liked the smell of his body, everything. I was trapped in his crazy love, brazened by the impurity of this perception without dignity. A semisavage love that asked no questions, expect no gratification.

Two days later, my period came. I was devastated. Why? My dear Lord. I had the courage to dispel my fears to William. He was not surprised nor mad at me. On the contrary, he hugged me and said, "Next time, my dear. I am certainly enjoying the fussing you are granting me. Not to mention the lovemaking!" I laughed through my tears. I did not expect his kindness. Like a slave girl grateful at the slight attention from her master. The next day, I went to see the gynecologist. I wanted to see the results of the tests. I waited for what seemed to me a long time. Looking at the other patients through the top of magazines, most of the women were exhibiting their bulged inflated stomachs. There was an envy look in my eyes. I thought then that children were being born every second to mothers that abandoned them, give them away, throwing them in the garbage from balconies, killing them. I cried every time I read about it in the newspapers.

What sort of monsters is this society creating? I asked myself. There I was, full of expectations, eager to have a child. A child to love and care. A child for William!

I sat there wondering, my heart full of hope, eager to listen, but afraid of the consequences. Finally I was called in. I couldn't tell by the doctor's expression if there were good or bad news for me. A middle-age distinguished-looking man with a sprinkle of white hair and dark green eyes sat rigid while reviewing some papers in front of him. A flush of excitement filled with hope my weary heart.

"Nothing is wrong with you. You are perfectly capable of conceiving." He stopped. I detected a look of pity reflected on his face when he said that to me. "It could be your husband."

He hesitated and continued, "It could be a number of reasons. I had to examine your husband in order for me to give you a correct diagnosis."

"It could be a number of conditions? Oh, not William," I said, ready to defend him. It was always me to blame for everything. I was certain I was responsible. Years of obstructing my path with lies had left me vulnerable with low self-esteem. "He has a daughter! It is me! I am the one that is barren, it is all my fault!"

"Madam, madam!" the doctor tried to shout over my hysterical sobs. "It is not you, you could have a baby. Relax."

But I could not hear him! I was certain it was all my fault. "You don't understand," I said. "I know that William is not sterile, I am."

I ran past the ladies, blind with rage, blaming myself for all the grievance I had inflicted upon William and upon myself. Not to be able to have a baby! The thought gnawed at my vulnerable and troubled self. I spent weeks that I hardly ate, locked in a sea of somber shadows. I lost my beauty. Deep lines were set around my mouth and around my eyes. I lost so much weight that it looked as though a shadow of my old self was looking at me from the mirror with terrifying eyes. I collapsed. Zoraida rushed in, her eyes wide, her face showing the stress that I had inflicted upon her delicate soul.

"Señora," she said. "You are going to harm yourself."

I looked with indifference. Why should I care? The doctor's test report was lying on top of the night table unopened. I knew what was the result. Why should I open them?

It was the first time when William first started to cheat on me. I looked with indifference when he was late and when he was absent from long periods of days. I didn't blame him. I couldn't conceive. What if he managed to have a child with someone else? I asked myself. Terror gripped every cell of my body. No, I could not let that happen! He will chase me out, discard me, leaving me fickle, troubled, sterile. I looked at myself in the mirror, my robe sliding slowly from my body. A ray of reflected light showed my devastated body. Brittle as a desiccated leaf. That's what I had accomplished in just one year? One year of penury. One year of self-immolation, of devastating pain and trepidation.

Fears that clogged my senses made me ugly, odd, shriveled like an old prune. I had chased William away and into the arms of another woman. I had practically punished myself. I had accomplished all these calloused, insensible acts of torture for being unable to conceive. I thought that I was selfish. I was torturing William for something he didn't have any fault at all. I decided right there and then to change, to be the wife that he would like me to be. Submissive, and be the victim of William's fickle character again. Food tasted terrible after so many months of starvation. The smell of food made me gag and then run to the bathroom.

Zoraida was great during that time. She prepared teas and broths to enhance my appetite. She read stories from that exotic land of hers. She bathed me, brushed my hair, and kept me company. She was the pivot of my recovery, the dart or javelin pounding away without rest to bring forth my old self. Would she be able to take away the lines that I had around my mouth? Bring the gold ringlets about my shoulders, take away the wrinkles on my neck? My breasts, Dear Lord, they looked saggy and wrinkly. They used to be so firm. William loved them so! Will he care for me again? It was a hard time for me and Zoraida. It took me six months to be able to walk without holding on to the furniture or whatever available support I encountered on my way. During those three years, I hardly saw anyone. We did not make noise. We spoke quietly, as if we wanted to hide my recovery from the world. I wanted it to be a secret. Let William do everything he wanted outside these walls, these walls that kept me in prison, with no visitors and no consolation from William. He acted as though I was dying. The TV in his room was kept low. He probably took the ring off his phone. I couldn't hear anything. No noise.

Sometimes, Zoraida told me, he would ask her about my condition. She would tell him the same words: "Fine, fine." He would walk away without a trace of pity. The same brazen William that I knew so well. Well, at least I thought. He didn't bring any woman into his bedroom. I agonized thinking that I would hear the moans and noises that one makes when making love. He was too much of a gentleman to let the staff know how he really was. I thought about Bloomington and the girls and boys that used to hang around with their dirty jeans. They probably had a home, children. They were probably happy with their family around them. Getting together for Christmas, weddings, everything that I didn't have.

I wondered if they had seen me in that condition I was in. Would they have laughed at me? They would probably not recognize me. Yes, this is me, Mary Fletcher, the person that laughed at you. The rich, beautiful, corruptive girl that mocked and teased you. The vain and treacherous person who thought I could grab away everything I wanted. Look at me now, no friends, no children. A prisoner of my soul, a decaying bag of flesh. Stacked away, discarded. The medical report was on top of my small desk. Would I ever have the courage to open it? It has been three years since my last visit to the doctor. Every day I used to look at it, pick it up, and release the envelope as if it was set on fire. It didn't matter then. I had to recover, to be able to look at myself in the mirror without remorse. Without this canker inside of me that dispels the odor of hate. Hate toward the conqueror, the subjugating knight that took me toward the wings of heaven and then dropped me into the pits of hell.

I thought about my parents and their strange lives. They looked like one, always together, enclosed in that small room. No ambitions, without desires, as if the world had encaged them and left in them no will. Were they happy? They loved each other. Always acting as one. Never complaining, never asking for love. Their love for each other was enough to cover the somber existence that they lived in. Who was I to criticize them? There I was, trying to destroy myself for a crazy love that paralyzed my existence. Without the fortitude of a man that truly loved me. I had that disease called love, that attacks females and leaves them desolate while facing a brazen strong specimen of a man. It is the animal world. The strong gorilla that passes on his genes to the submissive female clan. I had to admit I loved William! I missed him dearly. The only reason I had not tried to see him was because I dreaded to be rejected by him. I did not want to see a pitiful look in those deep blue beautiful eyes. I had to get well. Be Mary Fletcher again, not the phantom of what I used to be, the shadow of my old self.

During the time of my self-confinement, I received news that the police commissioner wanted to see me. I was not in any mood to receive or to speak to anyone, especially with the police commissioner. I didn't know if it was one of William's hidden scams. One thing I was sure of, and it was, that he probably wanted to see me was to tie the knot already squeezing my fragile neck. But why? He did not miss me on the Christmas balls that William continued celebrating every year. The answer for my absence William gave to the guests was "that I was in a delicate state."

With an impassive perverted face, he would add, "She sends her regards." Rumors of my forced confinement were rampant, of course. The police commissioner probably felt obligated to make sure that everything was normal. That I really was in a "delicate state." It was probably my love who made the suggestion. I had already gained ten pounds. Some pink color was showing on my sunken cheeks. My large dark blue eyes were bulging out of my face like two highlights.

Richard Kormer walked into my quarters with Dr. Alan Parker. They both used to see people in a worse state than I was in. They were not surprised to see me. They asked questions. "Are you being taken care of?"

"Very well, sir, I have a maid, everything I want is provided to me."

"Are you sick?" the commissioner asked.

"Take a look at me, Commissioner, have you ever seen somebody that is healthy looking like me?" I said.

Dr. Parker did the routine checkup they do when they want to get rid of you fast, like "Look at my finger, open your mouth, touch your neck," etc. They left, leaving a dreadful silence behind. Why didn't I say to them, "Save me, I am sequestered. Yank apart the yoke that ties me to servitude. Let my soul fly away into the blue"? Instead, I sat there trying to save William. Did I have everything material that I wanted? Yes. They failed to ask me how I was treated mentally. I would have lied anyway. I was not able to get away from the control William imposed over me. I felt that even after his death, I would still lie about his control and his manipulation. I could hear the music playing down, the reflection of the Christmas lights slipping through my curtains. I felt sad, remembering other Christmases when I was so young and beautiful, full of love, and in William's arms. The ecstasy, the mystery, his kisses, his love. I longed to see him. Not like this when my body is wrecked from hunger and my mind wondering, Could it be beautiful again? The bones that were protruding from my body, would they be covered again with smooth soft skin like before? I don't know, only time will tell. I felt like an intruder. Living in someone else's house where I did not belong. Did the distinguished guests ask him why was I still living in the mansion? Did he love any of them?

"Oh, Zoraida," I cried, "make it go away!" I didn't want to think. I didn't want to listen to the music, the laughter, the fun, the glamour. I pictured William in his immaculate white shirt, with pearls instead of buttons, and his red cummerbund around his waist, glittering, brilliant, eminent, shining. I had to take sleeping pills to keep me from going crazy.

"Make it go away," I begged, "make it go away!" It was a painful and a long recuperation. I sat on the balcony trying not to look to my right toward William's side of the garden. A rhododendron bush that used to be trimmed had grown tall and thick, so I could hardly see that side of the garden from my balcony. For a while I was glad. I didn't have to look at those terrifying statues any longer, nor was I able to see William on his daily walks. He probably walked through a different path, the path around the mansion, far away from my view. It was April in Long Island, a beautiful county full of trees and well-kept houses with manicured lawns and magnificent gardens. The smell of flowers was in the air. All sorts of creatures hopped around, building their nests, filling the air with their chanting calls. I felt alive for the first time in months. I sat on the balcony, the warm sun giving life to my body, filling my soul with hope. I felt lucky for some crazy reason. A leisurely life without financial stress doing what I wanted, within my confinement. Why was William keeping me here? How come the sheriff has not presented himself and handed me an order of eviction?

I started to question for the first time his actions, a dark cloud filling my senses. Did a macabre plot exist that I was not aware of? Was William's impeccable reputation full of callous and devious actions toward me? At the moment, I felt that I didn't have anything to lose. I went to my desk and opened the doctor's report. I remembered that my mind computed the words that I wanted to see. The content was not important.

There was nothing wrong with me but further tests should be made.

I felt like a lightning bolt hit my mind. What if William was sterile? Did he find out that Catherine was not his child? Was that the hate and the control he felt he had to exercise upon the opposite sex? Did he have the operation and made me think that it was all my fault? Oh, I knew his devious ways, the fact that he was so liberal about not using condoms. How he hated prostitutes. How the best thing in our relationship was when I told him I was a twenty-four-year-old virgin. He did not have to use contraceptives, he did not want to contract a venereal disease. He preferred women that were young and virgin! That's why he wanted me!

Someone in the house that was beautiful, inexperienced, and willing. He was like a female spider, attracting the male with the victims that she had carefully wrapped in her web, having sex with the male, then proceeding to devour him. His remains are a good source of vitamins for her eggs that are hatching in her stomach. William was always there; he knew every one of his qualities—handsome, rich, tall. A debonair person, a magnificent candidate for the opposite sex, he had it all. A harborer of victims, a devoted foe and hater of women. Who would be his next victim? It had to be a fragile, young, and lonely girl. A delicate being that will fall in love and become trapped like I was in a sea of sorrows, confined in a cell without bars, trapped in the laboring of hidden thoughts. Loving this man with all your might, knowing that you are trapped in the penumbra of your own soul, but unable to free yourself from the claws of the wild beast, from the bird of prey.

Chapter 7

Months passed by, lazy days of mental tranquility. Everything flew away, like leaves in September, scattered about by the force of the wind, going nowhere just like me. I was peaceful, tranquil. Not thinking, as if I did not want to bring back old memories, let my soul rest of the sorrows hidden inside my encaged brain. When will I see William again? Will I feel the same as before toward him? Will my knees become weak when I see him? Will I be able to stop this love that has confined me to misery? I didn't know. I will wait when my bones recovered the flesh I had lost and bring in life to my body. I imagined that William had another love. The thought of it made me tremble with jealousy. I didn't know who, I didn't want to know, but I looked at Zoraida one day and I knew she knew something.

I called her and asked her if William had another love, if he had brought her to the mansion. At the beginning, she kept quiet. She didn't want to look at me; she went down on her knees and started to sob, to murmur, to clamor against this terrible secret that she had encased within her heart and she continued, "Please don't tell Mr. Bruckner. He said it was for your own good, madam, but I knew better. He was looking at me all the time. He said that we will be on the streets, with no one to ever give us a job. Who is going to take care of you if he found out I told you? He was speaking to Mrs. Blake. I guess he wants to keep an eye on me—she has. Everyone in the household is watching me. It is terrible!" And she kept on warbling each word with a fearsome tone. I had to wait until she calmed down, trying to obtain by deduction of reason what Zoraida was trying to tell me.

My heart twisted to a knot. I had to know. I waited until Zoraida calmed down. I helped her off her knees and sat her on a chair. "I will not tell anyone about the secret that I was not supposed to know. I wouldn't hurt you!" She told me what I had been dreading to hear.

"He has a new girl! Mr. Bruckner, I mean, he brings her on weekends. They stay on the left wing, on the guest's wing. They take different rooms sometimes. But at night you could hear lots of noises."

"Tell me, Zoraida, how does she look like?"

"Oh, she is pretty, I mean, not as pretty as you. She is short, shy, very delicate. Dark brown hair and yellow eyes. Like the cats. They locked themselves in the room, only Mr. Leeward is allowed into their quarters. Sometimes they take walks in the opposite side of the mansion. She is very young, with a sexy mouth and perfect teeth. Sometimes they go for a ride in the red convertible and come back late. They come through the side door, next to the guests' parking garages."

I had to cover my mouth with a handkerchief to drown out my sobs when I heard about the rides in the convertible. I knew where he took her! To what I thought was our secret place. How dare him! I couldn't complain; I had imposed my own prison, did not see him for almost three years. I was punishing him for something he was not at fault. I deserved everything! There I was again, trying to defend William. I did not see the indifference he bestowed on me. He did not try to convince me to send for a doctor to visit me, to encourage me to eat and to get out of the room. To be gentle, to show love, to be a human being. I was nothing but a sexual doll. Now he has another victim, a young girl that is being captivated into slavery. Crazy in love with a devourer of souls, a sinister companion, a devoted torturer of women. A defiler of young girls. I felt like a piece of discarded, wasted shadow of a human being.

Now what! I asked myself. *Why I am still living here? Why not just walk away? Be free.* I read that when one is imprisoned for long periods of time, the person adapts herself or himself to the environment. If set free, they could not adapt themselves to the freedom of the outside world. They long for their previous lives. Some commit suicide and others try to get back into the confinement they had previously experimented, where they felt secure. Was this happening to me? How could I have felt secured with a man that lied to me, that beat me, that kept me imprisoned? Responsible for enabling me to have children, lying to me about having the operation. To let my hopes die of having a baby. Encouraging me to continue trying for the purpose of his own pleasures and now, bringing someone younger and attractive to our home, to our love nest. The home that we had shared throughout sunshine and tempests. The home I was imprisoned with the chains of love, dragging them throughout this house with the heavy clang of fear.

I thought about Betty. She was also a victim. I knew then why she still loved him and why she was defending him and blaming herself for all the ill that she was suffering. I didn't have to find out about her life. I knew then what her life was like. She was probably a walking prostitute. Discarded, infected, selling her body to the first devourer of souls. I cried thinking that it could have been me. What if I had found myself in the same situation back then with William? I cried for the millions of women that like me find themselves tied by the bonds of love, without escape, without dignity, warbling to a brazened male the words "I love you."

It was the beginning of fall, when the leaves changed to different colors. Little birds were anxious to fly jump from branch to branch to give strength to their little wings and then fly away, without looking back, to other places, to other worlds. It was a beautiful afternoon, the sun warming up the chill of the day. Saint Patrick's Day was the only time my mother and father went to Mass. They would wash up and dress with the only decent clothes that they had. After church, they celebrated. A large bottle of whiskey was opened. They talked and laughed, their pink complexion getting reddish as the time passed by. They looked contented, happy on their own, like a rare specimen adapted to a different world. There I was also, adapted to a different world, bounded, confined, and banished from everyone, not a child to hold gently in my arms, to caress, to kiss. I was barren like the dried leaves that covered the garden.

"Is she here, Zoraida?"

"No, no. They went for a ride."

Yes, a beautiful day for a ride. I must hurry and put some meat over these weary bones. I must look beautiful again! I didn't know it then, but I was ready to conquer William again. I went out for the first time. The staff looked so surprised that the proper Mrs. Blake dropped a very valuable vase that she was polishing. She looked at me with hate in her piercing black eyes. Only Mr. Leeward welcomed me in his usual refined manner.

He said, "Welcome back, madam."

"Oh no, Mr. Leeward. I was just going for a walk. Everything will be the same. I will keep away in my quarters. I thank you." I went out into the September breeze. I was afraid of the open field; the brick path felt rough on my feet. I hesitated, holding on to Zoraida's arm. I wanted to turn back to the security of those two large rooms that had kept me safe and comfortable.

"Let's go back, Zoraida," I said. This time, I stopped and resisted the push Zoraida was giving me. We sat in one of the benches that were set on the garden.

Some of the late-blooming flowers were exhibiting their beautiful yellow, red, and blue colors. After we had sat on the bench for a while, I ventured for us to continue, but stopped at the side of the open field that paralleled the extensive garden. These were William's woods until it reached a small lake. Lots of land, about five miles. You could see birds that are rare in these parts of Long Island. Sometimes, William goes hunting with his friends. I never went hunting. I didn't know how to ride a horse; besides, I didn't want to kill those poor creatures. There are woodchucks, owls, and all sorts of little animals that I used to admire.

I stopped again, I couldn't go on. I felt afraid of the open space; it felt strange to me. I didn't remember being so sensitive, so frightened as if I was alone in the world and the universe could swallow me up. I panicked and started to run toward the mansion. Zoraida tried to get hold of me. I couldn't hear her; I just ran until my heart felt as if it was going to burst. Finally, I was back in the garden, in my peaceful and sublime garden, surrounded by flowers and birds. I hurried to my rooms, to my confinement, to the hidden quarters of my existence. To a jail without walls, without bars. They were real. They were there! Deep inside of my mind, the chains and bars were as thick as two inches.

I had fallen prey to my own destiny, tied to the claws of my own existence. I felt as if a ghost was chasing me, trying to devour me, reaching at me with his fangs. I sat in the divan and asked Zoraida to close the drapes. I wanted to feel secure in my rooms, the doors locked, the room dark. It was my only escape, my dreams, that part of me he was unable to control. That part of your brain that enables you to travel to unknown worlds where you could see, touch, feel, and then transport yourself to unknown dimensions. In the dark of my room, I felt my mind wander to faraway places: To Dublin in Ireland, along the banks of the River Liffey. I climbed the Dartry Mountains, saw the vast green and peaceful plains below. I flew through the narrow streets of Florence, turning into the Ponte Vecchio and throughout the mountains between Italy and Austria. The Appalachian plateaus in Kentucky, the National Park with its volcanoes, mountains, rivers, and vast woods, where animals roam free and undisturbed by hunters. My mind raved about the highlands of the Ohio territory, where I came from. Playing and running with Betty with our muddy boots and our matted hair flying with the wind, our faces red with the cold of the mountain. Laughing, feeling free and happy. Collecting nuts, and dreams. Dreams harbored by beautiful illusions of our friendly love. To 31 Consequence Street, its number turned around to read 13 Consequence Street. My heart full with trepid sensibility.

I looked through the small window. The old dirty sofa bed in the same place. Betty and I trying dresses, walking the plank, laughing. I was able to take illusionary trips. Each time, they seemed to become more real. The psychologist told me that it was dangerous, that I was living in a world that did not exist, a world debouched by the imprisonment of my soul.

"What's wrong with dreaming?" I said. "Doesn't the prisoner dream of liberty? The caged bird to fly away? Doesn't the woman that births children to a cruel man dreams of liberty?"

I will keep on dreaming, I said to myself. *I will shout it to the world and say, "Dream until your vocal screams become a muttering sound and your weary body becomes wilted!"*

I woke up. Zoraida was shaking me with tears in her eyes. "Oh dear Lord," she said, "I thought that you were dead! I was trying to wake you up for the last two minutes. I was ready to call for help!"

A tray with food was set on top of a small rolling table and brought to me. I was not hungry at all but forced myself to eat. I had to get well. I will face that impostor in my own terms. I had dealt with beautiful young girls before. Back then when I was a model and fought to keep my job. This time, I will fight for my man. For the one I loved. The handsome, elegant, and wily man, the haughty and cruel man that I adored. Zoraida took care of me with such a love that can only be bestowed to a mother. Little by little, color came back to my dried and yellow skin and energy invaded my body. I wanted to go out. I had the desire to run through the woods just like before! My legs got stronger by the day. At the beginning, I did not venture too far. I was afraid of an attack of anxiety, which I used to experience when away from my quarters. I had a terrible feeling of hyperventilation until I felt as though someone was grasping my neck and chocking me. My feeble body shook, my large eyes turning upward. I couldn't afford another dreadful chapter in my life and expose once more my mental and delicate condition to everyone. I was going to win. I couldn't let that little impostor get William away from me! I longed for his kisses, to feel his manly figure next to me, his perfume, his eager and sexy mouth. I loved all of him. I didn't care about my confinement, my sorrows, my grievances, my hidden fears. I loved him as he was, cruel, a devourer of souls, clamoring to the world with bold and calloused instinct his tinted innocence, devastating my fragile being.

I saw her! I went around the garden to peek at them, to observe with incredulous eyes his new virgin. She was so petite and fragile that she looked as though she could have been his child. Light brown eyes and long shining dark black hair, as black as a raven's. She looked contented and in love. They walk hand in hand, William leading as always, taking control, having his way, she, following like a delicate young chick. She looked more than a victim to me, ready to yield, to sacrifice herself for that crazy disease that seems to attack only women—a frenzy madness that captures your soul and leaves you enchanted, vulnerable, encaged forever. For a brief moment, our eyes met. Those large brown eyes and thick eyelashes met mine. Dark blue inquisitive eyes that I knew so well told her for a brief moment of danger. She didn't listen. I stood there until their shadows blended with the leaves of the trees.

I remembered our walks. They were different! We looked like a couple, a couple in love. She was a child! She was just following. Innocent, vulnerable, as though afraid. *Oh dear Lord, this is incest. How could William fall so low!* He had met her at a fair where William was a sponsor for a charity. The police commissioner that was with William introduced them. She was selling pizza at one of the fair's stands. Her mother was there too, helping with the cooking. Richard Kormer and William stopped for a pizza in the very crowded booth, full of screaming children and impatient clients. She was wearing a very long skirt tied to her well-shaped figure. The slit in one side of her skirt facilitated her movements. At the same time, one could see her beautiful legs. Her black hair, large light-brown eyes, and petite delicate figure was the portrait of an exotic girl found only in the description of a damsel in the novel *One Thousand and One Nights the story of Nur-Ed and Enis-El-Jelis*. William probably thought her as a gypsy from a faraway and exotic land. He did not have to be debonair to capture her attention! Elegant and handsome with profound blue eyes, displaying his courteous manners and haughty personality, she couldn't help herself; she fell in love. She didn't know it then, but she was trapped. She would be lost into a world of lies and lascivious tempests. The victim's name was Elizabeth Pattini.

I came from a low white American class, the white-trash hicks, rednecks society. Elizabeth came from a low middle class, the ones that have been stamped with the title of belonging to "the American Dream" social status. To Elizabeth's parents, the relationship with a social rich person meant to be able to get into the middle or upper social class, a great jump into their social level. Within months, they moved from their modest home in Queens, New York, to a home in Manorville, in Suffolk, New York, not far from the Hamptons and William's mansion.

One can imagine the happiness that the Fletcher family was feeling. They were now the owners of a large beautiful house, a three-car garage, two-acreage property surrounded by a manicured garden. Magnolia trees and fruit trees were set past an Olympic-size swimming pool and Jacuzzi. Imported tiles with gold and pink designs were set around the pool. Two outhouses with tiled roofs were at the end of the property. One of them had a bathroom and the other was for changing clothes, with male and female signs in the designed house. Beautiful trimmed bushes surrounded these two outhouses. Only the red tiled roofs could be seen from the swimming pool area. A paradise that none of them ever thought that existed. What if their daughter was underage? Two years away from graduation. It did not matter to her parents. She could have never made all the money that was constantly flowing from William's pockets and into their meager existence. It was heaven. The relatives of Elizabeth's mother used to visit them; they thought that William was a prince, a holy god. The good Lord had blessed them with an angel, an angel out of the novels of Dean Koontz. It was a magnificent portrait of every immigrant's dream. The enchanting, elated, and sublime state of mind as if they all had been chewing the magic mushrooms in Carlos Castañeda's books *The Journey to Ixtlan* and *The Teachings of Don Juan*. The magic mushrooms work upon your mind. A person feels as though he could fly and visit places he or she has never visited before. It is also called "the devil's weed," a very proper name when referring to William's lascivious personality.

I didn't care, not yet. I had to concentrate myself with getting better, to look as though nothing had ever happened. To be myself again. To look beautiful for William, to conquer him again. To suffer all of his malicious mind games with me. Everything was better if I had William again. If I was in his arms again. *Oh*, I thought, *in six months' time, he will be mortifying Elizabeth. Displaying his abominable character.* Elizabeth would have realized by then what sort of man she was in love with. I had to admit that she was in a better position than I was in. I was much older, alone, with no family, nor friends that I could confide in. Elizabeth had a house, friends and family she could rely on. He brought her back on Monday mornings. She had all those days without William, surrounded by her family, forgetting the unpleasant moments, willing and anxious to see him again. She could relax on those days wearing jeans and sneakers, swimming, having fun with relatives and friends. On the contrary, I had to be prompt and ready, looking my best all the time, dealing with the staff that were not in my favor, vulnerable to his macabre mind games. *I will overcome, face the worst problems.* I was ready to become a martyr again. I was trapped in that crazy love that the majority of women suffers from. Do psychologists have a name for this type of behavior? Have they researched why some many women display this type of attitude in front of a wily devourer and debaucher of souls, knowing for sure that one day this calloused man will kill her? I remember the case of Nicole Brown. I was fourteen years old when O. J. Simpson was accused of murdering her. She knew he was going to kill her, Nicole stated, as in the book by Faye Resnick, *The Private Diary of a Life Interrupted*, page 164: "I feel sad and slightly scared. I look at his arms and think, God are these going to be the arms that will kill me someday?" He beat her up all the time and yet she insisted on reconciling with OJ. She used to say, "Maybe he's changed." Why did a beautiful and smart woman keep on seeing that abusive, impudent, and dreary man? I didn't know at the time the dangers I was exposed to. I had what I call "kitten love." They keep on boozing and playing with the murderer that takes them to the nearby pond to drown them. The abusive man will make us submissive passive. He is a tamer, subduer, housebreaker. He satiates his callous instinct with his victims. He is a devourer of souls. Fly away from him, don't look back! Save yourself. But what did I know then? All I thought was how to conquer William back. Yellowsy set a veil upon my eyes.

    I couldn't see the real William. He was a prince in my own mind, I chanted, sitting by the balcony. Did anyone listen to me? What did I care? Why did you leave me? Like the aurora flies each day, hidden its rays above the clouds and into the cosmic light of my dark existence. After your deception, I kept loving you with ascetic devotion. A devotion that kept me bound maid to your wielded experience. I was a slave of your wisdom, of your haughty and concerted being. You were my love. I miss your kisses, your love, our secrets, our walks. The days kept passing by, leaving pain within my heart. I knew you had another love. An innocent girl that like I was, believed and probably adored you. Where are the days, the months, and years that I dedicated to you? Are not my eyes just as bright as when I first met you? Where has the years gone? Did the lines around my eyes scare you? Did you want to run away from the ravages of age, that hidden phantom that is engraved within us and makes us shriek with fear? I will love you throughout the ages, when your body looked dried out and feeble, and the strengths in your legs keeps you wobbling. When agraphia will invade your brain and it will prevent you from writing letters to Catherine, I will still love you.

Zoraida wore bright colors always. I used to admire the light green with gold or deep blue with yellow printed in her silk scarf with lace trimmings. She wrapped herself in those beautiful colors to show her petite and well-formed body. However, lately she was wearing black or gray and avoiding my eyes. It was as if I could read on them the pain that was afflicting her. She was always so brave. I used to admire her laughs, her positive attitude; but yesterday, I saw the look on those dark and big eyes. I panicked. I was always afraid that William would take away the only person that I could confide on, the last human being that understood and protected me. The gentle soul that took care of me, that has been with me on the darkest hours of my life.

"Zoraida, what's wrong with you?" I asked through my teeth, afraid that she will listen to me and tell me something that I didn't want to hear.

"Oh, Ms. Mary, I don't want to upset you! This is my problem, and I have to resolve it myself."

"Tell me, Zoraida," I said, somehow relieved that her problem has nothing to do with her position in the mansion.

"Mama and Papa," she continued, "want to marry me to a rich old man that has two other wives. You have no idea how I will suffer! Locked up in a harem, with two other wives to mortify me and plot to make me miserable."

"Zoraida," I said, "harems are forbidden in this country."

"Oh, Ms. Mary, it is not in this country. It is in Marruecos, where my parents come from! It is our ways. Parents marry their daughters, give them away for money," she said, crying as though she were a baby.

"Don't worry, Zoraida," I said. "I will give your parents the money. They don't have to sell you! I wouldn't know what to do without you,

Zoraida! Come," I said. "Sit here and tell me everything what I have to do to save you from that old monster." We laughed. She sat across from me while drying the drops of tears running down her face.

"Well, his name is Mahmud. He is a very rich, old, and powerful man in Morocco. My father and my brother went to Morocco for a vacation. While sitting in an outdoor cafe, in the town of Moulay, a man approached them, surrounded by lots of men as it is accustomed by men of wealth and power in our culture. He introduced himself to Papa Hosein and my brother. Mahmud was a good friend of Papa Hosein when Papa lived in Morocco. Mahmud then was a poor fellow trying to make a living out of silk that he used to dye in beautiful colors. He couldn't afford to have a wife, a girl that he loved. Her parents were asking for lots of money in gold as the damsel was famous for her beauty. He worked day and night until he was rich and married her and could give her parents money.

"Mahmud invited them to his mansion. They were to visit him on the third. My father and brother were delighted with the riches of this man. The arched entrance was adorned by tiles of blue, gold, and yellow beautiful designs. The entrance led them to a large tiled patio with a large fountain, with sparkling clean water. The aroma of flowers surrounded the patio where the house was paved with marble and embroidered carpets of different colors. A perfume from the flowers that were hanging from the balcony was exhilarating. Finally, they were led by the servants to a larger room, on which was a table with all kinds of fruits, peaches, oranges, grapes of various colors, melons, mangos, pineapples, and other Oriental fruits that my brother could not identify were placed. In a second table were the wines and Buzah, a barley beer, cheeses, and cold cuts of rich spices, smells, and delicious taste. The third table was of main dishes, game, partridges, pigeons, lamb, beef. One-fourth of the table were various breads, flats, round, large. And soviets of all types. Two ladies that they assumed were his wives attended to the guests. But they were not allowed to sit on the table with their guests. Their heads were covered, and rich silks were wrapped around their fat bodies.

"They looked sad, with big large eyes that reflected their misery. One of them, the one called Helene had green eyes. You could very well see that she must have been a pretty woman before, but now she was looking sad and haggard, with a large stomach and fat fingers, adorned with lots of pearls and diamonds. My father felt bad about his economical condition. Didn't tell Mahmud that he was renting the land that surrounded their well-kept, but small house in the middle of a place called Suffolk, Long Island. He was proud of his children. He showed Mahmud a picture of me wearing my sarong and showing my belly and large chestnut hair. He told my father that he was looking for a third wife. He will give ten pounds of gold and two pounds of diamonds for me. My father and brother Omar were in the city called Moulay Idris, in the Mekenes Province, in Morocco, where the tomb of Idris is located. She founded the first Arab dynasty, and thousands of pilgrims are attracted to the city of Moulay Idris each year. Papa Hosein wanted to go and visit the city of Moulay and take my brother with him. That's how they met Mahmud."

She stopped talking as though she wanted to reflect about her present condition but couldn't continue. After clearing her throat and drying her eyes, Zoraida continued. "Well, in my culture, the father is the master. He is responsible for the welfare of his children and wives. Daughters do not marry for love. The dowry is for their own protection in living a solitary life away from their family. The woman, when she marries, belongs to her husband's family, this is why my father was contented with Mahmud's offer. He thought I was going to be happy being one of the wives of such a rich and powerful man. I was born here! This is my country, I don't know anything about Morocco. I cannot, I will not marry that old goat."

We laughed through our tears. I promised her that I would protect her, I would pay her dowry. She didn't have to marry and leave for Morocco. "You don't understand," she said. I could perceive the doubt covering her senses. Why believe me? Someone like me that had suffered all these cruelties. She has been a witness of all of my miseries. Would I be able to help her? Did I really make an effort to rescue Betty? Did I help my parents, or did I give them enough money to drown themselves in alcohol? "This time will be different, Zoraida, I promise you."

"My father could put a curse on me and never let me see my family again. Imagine, Ms. Mary, in Morocco, a Muslim woman wears traditional veil. They are completely covered in black, only part of their eyes are visible. They look like parading ghosts, giving away their dignity. A specter of their selves. A dreary punishment bestowed on their meager existence. What have they done to deserve such a cruel punishment? They could do the same thing to me!" I hugged her. I promised that I would help her, and I did.

Mahmud took Papa Hosein on his black Mercedes-Benz to visit some of the provinces and urban prefectures: Casablanca, Fes, Marrakech. In

Casablanca, modern cooperative apartments were everywhere, surrounded by palm trees and flowers. The courthouse in Rabat, with its tiled interior patio, fountains, hanging flowers of rare aroma inundated the atmosphere. One could also see among the crowds a Berber woman from the Dades Valley showing her facial markings and colorful sarongs. Mahmud took him to the Kasbah, this ancient city with tall walls and street vendors, their rich merchandise displayed for everyone to touch and see. They visited the town of Maghreb in northern Africa and the nine-mile-wide strait of Gibraltar that separates the continent of Africa from the European continent. He also took Papa Hosein to the phosphates mines in Casablanca, where workers work on the mines as though they were slaves from another era. The vacation was extended to two months. Zoraida's brother lost the opportunity to register in the Hofstra University for the following semester. Her father thought it was okay. He made the best deal of his life! Imagine, his daughter married to such a wealthy man!

He couldn't be happier. His daughter would have a secure future. Her children would be following the proper religion, not those fanatic Catholics or the hip-swinging chorus-chanting Baptist, and Protestant nuts he has watched on television. Above all, she would living in a Muslim country, where the laws of the land and the laws of Allah are followed, fathers are obeyed, and wives are submissive. A proper life. He never thought he was doing anything wrong. He felt happy for the first time in years. Zoraida's brother Omar did not share the same opinion. He did not like the way women were treated: at the back of the mansion, no recognition, an empty look in their large eyes. He didn't want a life like that for Zoraida. She had worked since she was fifteen years old, helped her parents with money, and paid for half his education. She would never submit to a Muslim life. He exposed his concerns to his father, suffering a rebuttal from his father. Nonsense. Did he not conform to a completely different life and customs when he came to the United States? He was surprised when his good news was not received with the enthusiasm he expected. Even his wife walked away to show her disagreement. Papa Hosein was confused. "Did I not bring the best news to you? What do you do? You are treating me as though I committed a crime!"

Zoraida was sitting on a chair looking submissive as always. This time however, she found the strength to confront her husband in a matter that she regarded as being important. No, this time, she will not stay. She needed all the strength to oppose for the first time the will of her husband.

No, she will not agree to have her own daughter suffer all the tribulations that her own mother was exposed to. She was beaten up by her husband under the cold stare of his other wives. Her son was taken away from her.

"I was allowed to stay with my mother because I was considered an impediment, a hindrance, an obstruction. We were thrown out on the streets, our inheritance taken away from us. It was my fault. As a girl, I ran and opened the heavy door that separate the heavy and tall walls of the harem from the streets. My mother ran after me while the heavy door locked us out of the harem. My mother did not have her veil on.

"She felt practically naked without it, as it is forbidden for a married woman to go about without a veil. We knocked on the door again and again, but his other wives did not open the door. We were forced to go to the main entrance. The male servants were trying not to look at my mother's uncovered head. She was beaten up and thrown out on the streets. We walked fifteen miles to Marrakech to Uncle Jabal's house. Luckily for us, there were plenty of pistachio nuts to satisfy our hunger.

"We were taken in and treated as maids. My mother never protested. It did not matter what they asked her to do. She only asked for me to go to school. That wish was granted. I attended the local school, under the watchful eyes of Uncle Jabal. Would I want the same fate for my daughter? I tell you, Hosein, it is a big no. This is the first time that I do not obey you, but even if you threaten to throw me out on the streets, I will still tell you no."

Ah, my dear, a picture of an obedient wife," said Zoraida's Father. "I will tell you what will become of your daughter if she marries in the US. He will cheat on her with dirty prostitutes and exposed her to terrible diseases. She will be cast away by his family and rejected by our society. When he gets tired of her, he will divorce her. She will be forced to go to work and leave her children to tend for themselves. Her children will become vulnerable to gangs and to drugs. That is, if she is lucky, the unfortunate ones are found dead, scattered in the swamps and roads of Long Island, Brooklyn, or the Bronx."

Silence engulfed the crowded and small living room. One could grasp the thick laments of their souls, the bold and grave situation of Zoraida's future. "Above all," Papa Hosein continued, "my honor is on the line here. My family will not be discredited on the streets of Marrakech! I could just picture your fat uncle Jabal and family going about discrediting our family. My family! Do you understand? You ingrate wife, because of you, I left my family back home to migrate to the US. You didn't want to reside in Morocco, the very land that your eyes saw for the first time, Marrakech with its peaceful valleys, high mountains. Fruits and nut trees adorn the valleys with colors. You could see from the top of the mountains the Atlantic Ocean with its deep blue color and the gentle cool breeze bathing our very land. It is your land, madam!" His eyes were on fire, his fist slammed hard on the table while saying, "Have I not been a devout spouse? Thrashing someone else's land and working until the cold weather numbed my fingers or the summer heat abated my strength? Are you about to debauch your soul, to satiate your devious rancor?"

He looked down, trying to hide the tears that filled the cavity of his eyes, but stayed among his lashes, as if afraid to cascade down his face. A dreadful silence hung around the room, a deadly mist that one could almost touch, the truth emerging to the surface, that deadly silence that is harbored inside oneself and would burst out sometime into a fury or rage.

There was nothing to be said. Papa Hosein felt betrayed, his wounded Arab pride and honor discarded by his own wife and children. Would he be able to walk the streets of Marrakech with his head set high? His children and wife had passed sentence on him, making him an outcast confined to the curse of his own people.

Chapter 8

The problem was extensive: Reaching out to two opposite sides of the world. Different countries, different religions, different beliefs. Papa Hosein felt dishonored, his respectability stepped on, the honor of his family tinted, his public mark of respect in doubt, even the chastity of his daughter placed in an ambiguous position. Dignity was the word that characterized his American children. It was their egotistic being. It was personal. It was advancement, grandeur, believed to be of reaching out to the greatest of achievements without the consent of others. (Papa Hosein was Apollo presiding over religious laws, the averter of evil.) It is the haughty American. Like Zeus, the sender of thunder and lightning, Papa Hosein felt his honor stepped on, betrayed, discarded. His own son Omar felt offended by Mahmud's proposition. He felt that Mahmud was trying to buy his sister. He probably thought, "Who did he think he is?"

It was a big problem to resolve, and I couldn't handle it. I needed help. I remembered my attorney, the fellow that helped me set business with Joe. I forgot his name! I looked through my drawers, purses, shelves, until I found his card. I didn't know if he was still alive or if his office was still open or if the phone number printed on his card was still the correct phone number. I called. An answering machine talked to me, telling me that his telephone number has been changed. At the end of the message, I even said thank you to an answering machine! Mr. Landward is not in at the moment. Can I take a message? Sure.

Two days later, Mr. Landward called. "Mary, I am sorry, I thought that you were dead! I tried to call you a couple of times, they told me that you did not live at that address any longer. I didn't know what to do. What can I help you with?"

I tried to explain, but he cut me off and said, "I thought you were talking to me about your financial situation. You probably know about the market. You lost some of the holdings you had in the market. Luckily for you, the business with Mr. Joe Scorcia is doing well, and he is an honest partner."

"Well, Mr. Landward," I asked, "is it possible for me to withdraw $300,000 dollars?" There was a big silence in which I prayed that I wasn't completely defrauded, that I was not left without a penny, practically on the streets. In William's dreary grip, don't tell me that I am without an opportunity of running away if I needed to—trapped, groping in penumbra for a hidden exit.

Mr. Landward thought that I was exaggerating and laughed. "No, no, missus, you were not left on the streets. You could withdraw that much money. But you will have to invest it in some sort of business. Or the government will hit you hard with taxes."

"I'll think about it, Mr. Landward, and call you when I have an answer." The truth was that I didn't have an answer, and I couldn't be bothered. I told Omar what the lawyer said. He told me that we could open a construction business in both of our names. Papa Hosein would be very proud of his son being in business, and maybe he will forgive him.

"Do you know anything about construction?" I asked Omar.

"Oh," he said, "you don't have to know about construction to open a business. You will hire a superintendent. He will hire some construction workers, and we will be in big business. I will be responsible for getting contracts."

"Very well, we are in business!" I called the lawyer, and we both signed the necessary papers.

Citizens were losing their homes because of loss of work and high interest in their mortgage. We bought their dilapidated houses then fixed and sold them for higher prices. Omar proved to be a devout and wily businessman. I could sense that Papa Hosein felt more at home now and proud. It was the year 2005, and the market was down to practically zero. Most of the investors woke up to the news that they were left without their pensions.

Discarded like waste debris, abandoned when the bones were brittle and the rhythm of the heart slow, an inconsistent Mr. Landward called me and said, "You were lucky to withdraw most of your money. However, of the $200,000 left on your account, $80,000 remains." He was calling from my iPhone. Zoraida opened an account for me in her name and in her home address. I felt free for the first time in many years. I was careful to turn the phone off when any of the staff members were around. It made me feel secure. I could air out my feelings, get in touch with the outside world without risking its wildness, without feeling scared. I was in touch with other people. Other souls that like me felt the emptiness in their lives, reaching out to other souls, clamoring the computer technology, sending their sad messages into space to other people, to other worlds where no one cared, but pretend to. An unrealistic being, you will call a friend a world of deceiving, pornography and plunder.

But it was better than to feel lonely, confined to a stillness, surrounded by silence. It captivated me. For the first time in many years, I felt alive. All this information! I was awake most of the night. The next morning, I had a dragon look reflected on my weary face. I read about the Manorville Pine Barrens of 2000 and 2003 murder; the angel wing was a tattoo on her hip. More murders, this time, they found five cadavers in Gilgo Beach, the work of a serial killer who hates prostitutes. Sharon Gilbert's disappearance led to the discovery of five other victims believed to be prostitutes. There was a picture of the press interrogating the police Commissioner. All the way to his right side stood William. One could hardly see him. Hidden away by shadows, a stern look was on his face, hands locked by his stomach, a dark suit displaying the dignity of the occasion. I knew that the police commissioner and William were aware of my knowledge. I was grateful that I could sneak in and spend hours reading when he was absent. I was careful to place everything that I touched back the same way. I did not take the books that I was reading with me to my room. I didn't want him to know what sort of books I was reading. I didn't want William to acquire an opinion on the person that I was becoming and rob me what little dignity left on me.

The iPhone liberated me. I understood the young hordes of youth that cheat, lie, rob, prostitute themselves, and kill in the open while the old generation did the same thing in the shadows, using the tactics of surprise while plundering, deceiving, lying, robbing, and killing its victims. I like the young generation better. Are you stupid enough to let those girls charge you twelve to fifteen dollars per minute to show you their intimate parts? Or do you prefer to kill a client that is looking for an innocent wage. It is up to you. You have a choice. It is a lot better than being followed, kidnapped, and killed by a serial killer or by the nice old man that is always looking after you without giving you an opportunity to decide, to set your life or your well-being.

I looked at the meadow; somehow it didn't seem so frightening to me. On the contrary, a display of peaceful tranquility reigned in their light green virgin foliage. It made me feel calm and free, as if I could run through its vast tall grass and encircle its tall trees within seconds. I knew then that I had lost my fears. It evaporated away like the mist that hovered by the tall grass where the blue sea lays. I got dressed in a heavy jacket with a hood lined with fur, jeans, and sneakers. I didn't ask Zoraida to come with me. She didn't know. I ran. I circled through the narrow road and to the tall trees, some of them with decayed fruit still clinging to the dried branches or scattered on the earth where different birds were disputing its decayed remains. I ran, my legs getting stronger by the mile, my heart beating wild. I kept on pushing myself. I had to keep on until I reached the tall grass.

Why? I asked myself. *Does the tall grass remind me of William? Our love nest?* I wondered. There was the lake far to the left. I pushed and finally arrived at the tall grass. I laid there exhausted, filling my lungs with air, a beautiful feeling encasing my soul. A peaceful and free person, a second being of myself. The Mary that I used to be was a true human carved out of misery, shelling my outer being to show the strong heart that dwelled inside of me. I was going to be okay. I laughed with each breath, expelling the fears, the agonies of the past. I knew I was ready to meet William, a different feeling encasing my being, a calm feeling based on reasoning, not the crazy love that blinded the young, but a matured way of measuring and calculating one's actions. I decided that it had to be a casual encounter.

I focused my attention on Tinkle, my dog. Zoraida used to walk him every day after lunch, but lately I was walking Tinkle. He ran through the dried scattered leaves that covered the lawn, his tiny body momentarily lost inside the piles of late autumn debris. Before I knew it, he was pulling at William's pants. I bent down to pick Tinkle up, and as I stood up, our eyes met for the first time in so many months. The same elegant, impeccably dressed man I knew so well. Some gray hairs covering part of his temple, which made him look more attractive.

Yes, I said to myself. I still loved him! My heart accelerating its rhythm. I felt a flush rushing to my face. There I was. So many times I had rehearsed in my mind the moment of our first encounter and yet I couldn't talk. I felt as if a giant hand was shocking me and bringing about the scarlet on my face.

"Mary!" I heard him say. It sounded as if we were inside a tunnel and each word was bouncing around in my mind. "A pleasure to see you!" he shouted. "You are looking great!" No apologies, no emotion. Behaving like a gentleman. Just as I remembered him. Cold, astute, calculating. I did most of the talking, my fears, the terrible disease that I had suffered. He listened to me, as if he didn't know about it, his intense blue eyes trying to read from my eyes the veracity of each word.

Why did I feel intimidated? Didn't I learn about the calloused, insensible man that William was? Was I not acquitted of impudent men displaying and inflicting their bold conceited characters in women? It didn't matter. I rejoiced the time; I wasn't going to spoil this lapse of time in my life. The moments I wanted so much that I had dreamed for so long. The sun was giving life to our frozen souls. The rancid smell of dried leaves, the bright blue sky, and the pink clouds brought to our minds memories of our past. In the bright sunlight, his eyes looked more intense. We were lost in each other's arms. I didn't remember which way we entered the mansion.

I woke up from ecstasy in a different room, on a strange bed, our sweating bodies united, sharing only one soul. I talked for the first time about my past life to William: My grandmother. How happy I was when she and my grandfather were alive. My illusions, my hidden afflictions, my meager life, my desire to be liberated of my dreary existence. Tears flowed freely from my eyes. I was careful not to tell him about John Traves, the owner of Jig's Variety Shop. I knew William wouldn't be able to comprehend it. He did not live the miseries I had been subjected to. To live in a cockroach-infested house, being a disoriented child living in a chaotic, frightening world. He wouldn't be able to understand. He would see it as my fault. I felt apprehensive. I could sense a certain fear of rejection, of repulse. I was hoping that he would open up his fears and confide in me. Not William—he was not the type.

Our lives kept the same rhythm as before. Serene, peaceful. I had forgotten his devious ways, his other self. That abominable other side of him—the dark, dreary, impudent other self. I met Elizabeth! Very casual, strolling along the garden by the cursed statues of Zeus. I could have taken Zeus's thunderbolt and aimed it at him, stepped over his olive wreath, and killed his eagle! There she was hand in hand with William! I could have killed them both as well, but I forced myself to smile, just showing my teeth. She looked shy, disoriented, her long black hair covering her petite shoulders, an innocent look on her face.

I heard him say, "Allow me to introduce you. Mary, this is Elizabeth." She extended her hand, a very soft and small hand, so different from my large hands and long fingers. Tinkle started to bark. She bent down and caressed him. You could see that Tinkle liked her.

You treacherous little thing! I thought. I excused myself and left, sobs choking me. I could hardly breathe. I had to sit down on a garden bench to calm down. I looked back and saw their shadows mingling through the dark tall trees. It was the end of the week. I didn't want to think about William and Elizabeth right across the mansion! Did he take me to that part of the mansion purposely? Was it the same bed I woke up in? I started to hyperventilate. My nerves couldn't grasp the pain. Back came all of my resentments. I could kick myself! How could I have fallen for his lack of sensibility again? I had to be careful; Mrs. Blake kept an eye on me. I had the feeling that she liked Elizabeth. She could be a powerful rival.

Not even Zoraida could penetrate the hidden bramble of lies that bounced around the mansion's walls. I took some Demarol and calmed myself. I knew I couldn't walk away. I tried so many times to flee, only to gather again the clothes that were scattered about the room and place them back in the closets. It was Monday. I felt better. Helen was not in the opposite side of the mansion with William. She was a weekend sweetheart. She was a year older now than when she met William at sixteen. A virgin, an innocent girl, practically sold by her family. Nothing to say, there were lots of monies to spend, and William was very generous. I heard a tap on my door.

William came bursting in, grabbing me, pulling me. Trying to force me to my bed. Was he trying to rape me? I thought.

"Wait a minute," I heard myself saying, "harems are forbidden in this country! Do not treat me like one of those Muslim women that are forced to share their husbands, except, of course, that their husbands married every one of them!"

"Let me explain, Mary. I feel sorry for Elizabeth. She looked so fragile, alone, no money and with parents eager to sell her to the highest bidder. I desired you. Let me come back into your life again."

I felt a flabbiness running up my legs and into my back that made me tremble. A beastly ecstasy invaded my being. I was lost on his arms, his body. I thought that I even reached into his soul. I was lost forever. I tried to hide away my lack of courage by pretending that William loved me. But somehow inside of me, I knew I was helpless, a morbid sensation taking hold of me. I was glad to be his slave, to be controlled, despised, humiliated. I admired his virile stand, his conceited self. I was suffering from that crazy love that afflicts women, like Juana La Loca, queen of Spain. Some critics believed that she poisoned her husband Phillip. She suffered all of his abuses except when he tried to get the crown of Spain away from her. No drunken foreigner was going to reign over the kingdom of Spain. She made a stand. I often wondered, *What will be my stand when it concerns William?* I couldn't think of anything that would make me kill William. He was the man I love. I felt contented. I shouldn't have any more doubts. He was my man, and I a willing slave.

Autumn came with its windy air and mellow skies. I heard the howling wind by my window at night, scratching with its piercing sounds, its force racking the trees and sending its bared branches across the loan. A pale moon hid behind dark clouds. It was a tornado. The next day, giant trees could be seen lying on the streets or on top of houses, showing their tangled and decayed roots. No electricity. The garden looked as if a heavy machine had flattened every plant, a dreary picture to look at. Only the statues of Apollo, Zeus, Hera, and Dione (or Diana) stood majestic, their proud and contorted faces concentrated, rigid, decisive as if they themselves had struck Long Island with their thunderbolt missile and Zeus with his eagle set on his extended left arm had struck us with the ultrasonic planes. Finally, he claimed his victory by wearing his olive wreath, a symbol of victory. I could have bombed them.

Zoraida texted me, "Miss Mary, I am not able to work today. Some roads are closed, and a heavy wind and rain is still coming down."

"Don't worry, Zo, I am okay." I don't know why I had a strong presentiment that something had happened to my mother. I had that feeling inside of me that mortified me. I couldn't get in touch with her. The telephone that my parents had was disconnected years ago. I was completely isolated from everyone that I knew back then. I remembered Joe, my business partner. I was surprised when he told me that Betty had called and that she wanted to get in touch with me.

"Did she give you a telephone number?"

"No, she said she would call back."

"Please," I begged, "give her my phone number as soon as she calls." My heart accelerated by the seconds. Oh, thank God, I prayed I would be able to see her. I could help her if she needed help. *Please, Betty, call me.* Days passed by, and I didn't receive any news or a phone call from Betty. Anxiety gripped my soul and clouded my senses. What if something happened to her and I again was not able to help her? I kept on calling Joe, but the answer was the same, no news. Weeks passed by, until one day I received a call from Betty.

I heard my name, followed by the most terrifying sobs I had ever listened to. I knew it was Betty. I called her name, and I started to cry uncontrollably. I was practically screaming. A mixed feeling of joy and pain invaded my senses. After we had calmed down, we were able to talk to each other. What could we have said? There were so many mutterings that we were unable to hold a conversation. Finally, I asked Betty for her telephone number. A long silence followed. I realized then that something was wrong in Betty's life. I had the feeling that she was being manipulated by an impudent and cruel man. I felt like before, in a corner, when sadness used to invade my senses, leaving me housebound to a conceited man. Did we share the same destiny? Has she been stripped, subdued, deprived of all sense of honor, discarded? It was worse than I could have possibly imagined.

"Mary," she said in between sobs, "I cannot give you my phone number. I will explain when we get together. I will call you."

"Please do not hang up, Betty, I can help you!" But the telephone was dead before I could finish my sentence. I stood paralyzed, wallowed in penumbra. My knees gave away, my heart wilted. A dreary feeling invaded my soul. Betty was in danger, and I could not do anything to save her.

Winter hugged Long Island with its usual howling and cold winds. Fog seeped through, high above the trees. I felt sad and helpless, like groping to find something in the dark, but not knowing exactly what. Why hasn't Betty called? What must I do? I couldn't ask William to help me. I had the feeling that Betty was in a lot of trouble, and I knew how William despised young girls that sold their bodies. I was alone. I didn't even know from which state she called from. The telephone number on the iPhone was hidden. I felt despondent. I didn't want to find myself again in one of my crazy moods. I had to be very careful. Mrs. Blake was constantly on my back, checking the time, spreading false rumors, sending other members of the staff to check my room, interrogating Zoraida. I hated her brazen attitude.

I wanted to see a therapist. I called Hector, the chauffeur. First I had to call Mrs. Blake and tell her where I was going, the time, and why. I decided that this time I was going to write down my itinerary and hand it to her; I did. To my surprise, she called me when I was down the corridor and yelled, "Ms. Mary, you forgot the time you are supposed to be back."

"There are a number of reasons why a person could be delayed while traveling. I hope you could figure them out."

While I was sitting in the car, I noticed that Hector kept looking at me through the rear back mirror. I knew that I looked terrible. I had been crying. Mrs. Blake was the last knot that struck my delicate soul. I asked myself, *Why is William ridiculing me in front of the staff? Especially in front of the despicable Mrs. Blake?* Hector kept on looking at me, a sad look showing n his dark and piercing eye. I felt guilty.

"Oh, Ms. Mary. What do you know about misery? Have they confiscated your house? And your family living with sweating, alcohol-smelling castoffs? Running away with a shopping cart piled up with the few belongings that you had managed to save, like your naturalization papers. The good Lord protect you if you lose that document! They will send you to prison in shackles. Away from your family, no visitors. (The authorities check immigration papers, and if your wife is undocumented, they will arrest her and send her to prison, the children to foster care. You will never see your children again!) Deported to a forsaken country you never knew existed.

"I know, Ms. Mary. I had talked with these men that crossed the frontier again to find their family. There are no jobs in those countries. The only option they have is to join the revolutionary army and become a *guerrillero* (a warrior). You have to pass the word that you are *indocumentado* or someone will mug you to steal your papers and identity. I thank Mr. Bruckner for giving me the protection I needed. I felt lucky—I could work, I can drive without the cops stopping me and giving me a fine. There you are feeling sorry for yourself, when you should be thanking the dear Lord for all of your blessings. Be happy, Ms. Mary. I know that you are a good person. I never believed all the gossiping!"

I sympathized with him. It took me back to the days of hunger and poverty. I discharged all of my past miseries to a complete stranger. We had both sprouted from the same seed. One stem. Our fruits would nourish the others to continue, to strive, to share. It is the American dream. He parked the car on a dilapidated street on Seventy-Eighth Street and Amsterdam Avenue.

A small variety store was right across the street. Hector excused himself and asked me if it was okay for him to buy a soda. I did not see any problem. I knew that I had taken a long time today and that he must have been thirsty and hungry. He came back with a can of soda and a chocolate bar. I also felt thirsty, and I wanted to buy a soda. Hector wanted to come with me, but I felt sorry for him, waiting so long to quench his thirst and me depriving him. I walked along. The owner of the shop handed me a bag of hashish, or Thai. He probably confused me with someone because the drug was packed up and ready for distribution. Zoraida told me that in some parts of the Middle East, this drug is not prohibited. I needed something to relax. I paid him and left. His eyes were like the weather. It changed colors with each expression. I had never seen eyes like those. Romantic, inquisitive, powerful, deceiving, and loving. He was handsome, tall, and dark. A man born to command and to rule.

I arrived home very tired. Eager to be in my room to get into my nightgown, I would not have supper tonight. I entered the large receiving room, and to my surprise, she stood there looking like a grizzly bear, eyes focused on me as if she wanted to devour me.

"Ms. Mary," Mrs. Blake said, "you are two hours late." I didn't even look at her. I ignored her and said to Mr. Leeward, "Please inform Mr. Bruckner that I am indisposed and that I will not be able to sit with him for dinner, thank you."

I jumped into my nightgown and rolled a hashish. It felt good. The cold air coming from an open window aired out my brains and made me relaxed. I woke up from my relaxed sleep frightened. The highlights up in the ceiling of my bedroom were bright like the sun shining. The window panel hit the windowsill with ferocity. A chilly air in the room. I felt cold, and disoriented. Above me was a tall figure that I did not recognize. My toes were hardly touching the floor! His eyes looked menacing, decisive. He let me go with a blow to my face that sat me back on the chair and then to the floor. I hit the back of my head violently and momentarily passed out.

He said while walking out of the room, "Do not play with me, madam." He didn't look back. He didn't stop to see if I was badly hurt or dead. He didn't care! My head was spinning. The cursed ceiling lights hurt my eyes. I was bleeding through my nose, through my mouth. My face was completely swollen on one side, the left side. I should have called the police. Call an ambulance. Instead, I called my doctor. He wouldn't get involved. I had to call the police. Instead, I went to emergency and lied.

"I fell down a balcony," I said.

The doctors just looked at each other. "Are you sure, miss, you don't want to report this accident?"

"No, no, it was my fault, thank you." They kept me in the hospital just that night for observation. They said, "No head injury, no fractures. You were lucky the blow was with an open hand." Two days in bed, and cold compress on my face. If I felt dizzy, to go to the hospital immediately.

"Okay, thanks." I just wanted to go home. To a prison, to a man that was a cold permanent foe of my being! A devourer of souls, a devious being. A devourer of souls. I never thought of going away, of running for my life. That was my home, a place where I felt protected. Heathenism passed me and made me vulnerable, attached to a vicious, rapacious man. I was alone and felt frightened. I said to myself that I hated him and that I will never believe him again.

Zoraida came in early in the morning. "Ms. Mary, what happened? Some of the staff members said that you were dead, others are saying you were disfigured. That you were with another man. I didn't know what to think, Ms. Mary. I was afraid to walk into this room and find you dead!"

She opened the curtains and was disturbed. "Oh, Ms. Mary! That animal! I hate him, I hate him!" she shouted while tears were running down her face. We both cried. I needed a delicate being to hug, someone that cared, a friend, anybody.

Dear Lord, I prayed, *help me to carry this burden.* Zoraida didn't go home and slept next to me, on the floor, wrapped up in a rug that had crazy designs and beautiful colors. She was constantly taking my temperature and fussing over me. God bless her soul! Without her, I would have been lost. On the third day, I was able to stand with Zoraida's help and sit on the table for my daily meals. I was having coffee and yogurt. I was unable to chew anything solid.

William had the habit of coming into my quarters with a sudden impulse as if to surprise me in some sort of mischief. At the beginning, I felt embarrassed. I used to run and cover myself, and at other times, I used to feel abashed and blushing. I felt the adrenaline run up my body and cover my face a deep red. After a while, I got used to it, and it didn't upset me at all.

However, on that day, when William came rushing in, I was afraid. Was he here to accomplish the murder he didn't finish? I tried to get up, but my legs were trembling, my eyes focusing on his eyes. I could not detect fury in his eyes. What would be William's next move?

Zoraida was by my side, ready to defend me. I asked myself so many questions during those first seconds that my head felt as though it was spinning in a Machiavellian dark tunnel.

To my surprise, William was on his knees, begging me for forgiveness! "I spoke to Hector. He told me what happened. You sat on the park, relaxing before he drove you home."

"Well," I heard myself saying, "I don't hate you, but I will not continue to live subjected to the calloused insults and covert actions against my devotion toward you. It's Mrs. Blake or me! You choose."

Chapter 9

I could see the surprise in his eyes when he stood up straight, eyes looking at me. I couldn't tell by his expression what was in his mind. I was afraid that he would say something, like "Are you telling me how to run my house, madam?" I would have been cast out. A malevolent look on Mrs. Blake's fat lips, but he just stood there looking at me for what seemed to me a long time. Seconds passed by me as if they were hours. Anxiety flashed through my body and made it stone cold, like the stones that lay on the cemeteries. He took both of my hands and kissed me. He did not say one word to me; he just turned around and walked away, his tall figure almost touching the doorframe.

He left me devastated, as if a cyclone had passed throughout the room and left me wallowed, unable to get out from the chair. I asked myself again and again what he meant. It looked to me like a staged play, with Henry the VIII saying good-bye to Anne Boleyn before he ordered his execution. I lay there, unable to move, until Zoraida came in and helped me to my bed and covered my body. Hot water bottle and hot broth revived me.

William sent for Mrs. Blake. He probably was sitting in the office next to his bedroom. He used that particular office for his personal business. This time, however, his purpose was for me to listen to everything he said. "Mrs. Blake," he shouted, "you are a calloused and beastly woman! Because of your cruel and unjust gossiping, I hurt the woman I love and who had been faithful to me all these years. I am sending you away to England, and let me warn you, madam, if you in any way spread in England your evil gossiping, I will take care of you! Do I make myself clear? My accountant will set your wages, Mrs. Blake. No, I have not dismissed you yet! You will go to Ms. Mary and ask for forgiveness. Now!"

I had jumped out of my bed before as soon as William asked Mrs. Blake to step in. I knew she would come in, so I composed myself. Zoraida combed my hair. I put on my dark glasses and a robe that William loved. An Oriental robe with all sorts of gold and red designs printed on it.

I heard two taps on my door. I knew it was not William. He would have burst in without knocking! I was standing up with my back to the door when I said, "Come in." I heard Mrs. Blake saying, "Madam . . ." As I turned around, I saw the tall, impressive William standing behind Mrs. Blake. I almost felt sorry for Mrs. Blake! She went down on her knees and asked forgiveness, and she mentioned every one of her devious plots she had managed to concoct against me.

"Mrs. Blake," I said, "I forgive you, but I feel sorry for you because instead of growing wise with the passing of years, you have turned into an indictable old lady. Get off of your knees and live the years you have left in peace."

She left, looking so different from the haughty woman that used to induce the staff against me with slanders. William came to me, and we kissed passionately, me completely in love. I knew now that William loved me. I was completely pinned down to his will, a slave to my love. I felt free to go downstairs for the first time since what I used to call my incident with William. I was looking a lot better than two weeks ago when I was practically disfigured by William's wrath. With my dark glasses, rouge on my lips and face, and my hair combed toward one side of my face (the side that was swollen), I ventured to descend the stairs that led to the large corridor. I could tell the different treatment of the staff toward me. No more running away or vile whispering when I happened to be in their presence. They acknowledged me and were ready to serve. Then I saw Mrs. Blake. She looked one hundred years old, a silly hat covering her white matted hair, dragging the old suitcases.

Hector came to help her. I heard him saying to Mrs. Blake, "Only to the train station, Mrs. Blake. Those are my orders." There was no other human being that could inflict a moral knout like my William. He was a hawk, Mrs. Blake the prize, the spoils, or booty, snatched away before she had the opportunity to devour her prey. She would lie spiritually encased in the carcass of her soul, wasted. A hate toward William, the man that devoured her conceited ambitions forever.

William and I were like two young teenagers, running about, trying to find warmed clothing for a ride in William's red convertible. I found my

Russian fur hat and wrap. We were speeding in the Ocean Parkway, the stars above shining over a dark gray sky, the smell of dried leaves filling the air. We were happy, laughing, letting our minds run free.

We felt majestic, without being imposed on or influenced by the rules of society. We stopped for drinks, off the Ocean Parkway and into the Long Island Expressway. We found a discreet tucked-away bar. The liquor was taking effect. We could hardly keep our hands and our mouths from each other. We ran to the car and to our love nest. We felt like two animals making love in the middle of a jungle. No restrictions, to men's laws, wild, savage.

I understood William's changes of moods. He had a wife and a daughter that he adored, his life was almost perfect socially and economically, they had no worries, and then abruptly, his perfect world turned upside down. His arrogant wife had found a lover, a divorce followed. He lost the love of his life, little Catherine. The restrictions and the court settlements gave Elizabeth complete custody over the child. He felt cast out. No one to turn to. Growing up with cold parents, interested only in making money. A spartan upbringing. Left alone to fight! To struggle. No affections, love, understanding. The fear that another woman could inflict the same punishment made him wild, mad with rage.

Uncontrollable, I understood. Why? Did I understand his wild moods, his barbaric fury? *How could I understand the fact that he left me barren, unable to hold in my arms a precious piece of me?* Why could I have not seen the real William, the despotic wild man that he really was? It is a mystery to me, and I asked myself, was I really mad? Phantoms of the past clogged his brain and made him the callous man that he was. In my pitiful childhood, I did not heed at the wailing of my soul. Lurched alone, left to defend myself, caught in the web of my innocence. Devastated by neglect. I needed William, the father figure that I never had. A man that would defend me. Someone that I could trust. His fits of jealousy were false, make-believe that he cared. He was protecting me. No one could touch me there. I had William to defend me! I created a false mirage based on my past childhood and neglect. We were the perfect couple. We lived from the misery encaged deep in our souls. I was his slave and he my false protector. I always knew when he felt cast off from Catherine. Did she go to Europe and he didn't know? Was his grandson sick? And no one told him. Did the child have his birthday party and he found out about it in the newspapers? I fear him on those days. He would walk around, antagonizing me, talking out loud, displaying his hate toward Elizabeth, drinking more than he usually did.

Disappearing for days, I knew it will all pass and all I had to do was to keep calm! Those were black days, terrifying days. I couldn't tell if under a bolt and furious fit of anger, he will grab one of his guns from the collection displayed on his office wall and shoot me. I prayed for him to go away, to disappear like he always did, after one of his hysterical attacks. He came back one week later. Relaxed, new shirt and suit. His shoes shining. Where was he all this time? Jealousy filled my senses. I couldn't talk to him. He locked himself in his bedroom until the next day. A calm satiating his soul, the other William that I adored, his twin soul, would emerge. We acted as if nothing had happened. I was grateful that I was not the pivot of his wraths. William was next to me, even if he was someone else's, he always came back to me.

Then I remembered Elizabeth and wondered what happened to her. William never mentioned her. She did not exist. He did the same thing to me. I did not exist for almost three years. Never came to visit, to see me. Mrs. Blake probably kept him informed. I don't know. I wanted to believe that William loved me. That I was the love of his life. Didn't I hear him say how much he loved me to Mrs. Blake? He knew what he was doing when he mentioned to Mrs. Blake that he loved me. He knew that I was listening, and therefore I repelled from my mind any doubts about his love. He opened up another channel into my ascetic devotion toward him. I would remember those words every time I was in doubt, every time his haughty self provoked me and shattered my dignity.

Zoraida came to me with a message. Elizabeth wanted to talk to me. It was okay with me to meet her at the end of the brick walk, on the right side of the woods, at 6:00 p.m. In winter, that is the time when shadows start to cover the day and the horizon is bursting with colors. The woods seem darker than usual. I noticed a black shadow emerge from behind a tree. I didn't recognize Elizabeth. She wore a long black dress, a shawl covered her head, I could hardly see her face. She looked so sad I felt uncomfortable. Tears filled her large and mystic eyes.

I waited until she calmed down and then said, "Elizabeth, is anything wrong in your relationship with William that you feel you have to confide in me?"

"Yes, Ms. Mary. I'm so unhappy, and Mr. Bruckner is so difficult, I don't know what to do. I tried to be perfect but it's never enough for him."

"I don't understand, Elizabeth," I said. "What is it that you wish me to do?" Of course, I knew what she wanted to tell me; I could sense her grievances. She looked devastated. "What has William done to you, child?"

She let her shawl slip down her shoulders, and I saw with horror the hidden black marks that she was trying to cover up. Just like me, I thought, when I wore sunglasses and let my hair fall on one side of my face to cover up my injuries. As though shamed of my misery. As if I were at fault and wanted to erase all quiet from my calloused debaucher.

"Elizabeth," I said, "you have a family, friends you could confide in. Talk to them. Do not be ashamed of your injuries. You were not at fault!" I was giving advice and surprised myself! How come I never followed the advice I was giving? I had years of martyrdom, of suffering, and yet I kept on giving excuses to myself about my relationship with William! I guess it was because I kept on remembering the words that William said to Mrs. Blake about me: "The woman I love." Never did the word "love" been said with such a perverse Machiavellian meaning. It kept me isolated, trapped forever, encaged in a world of dreary existence. Its claws left marks in my soul to imprison me forever!

"Oh, Ms. Mary," Elizabeth continued, "my family doesn't believe me! They think it is all my fault. They said I am not a good housekeeper, that I am always attired in jeans, long blouses, that I am no good when it concerns my sexual obligations. I had no family, Mr. Bruckner bought them!" I could hardly hear what she was saying; her sobs were convulsing her fragile body.

"Stop, my child," I said. "You are too young."

"Yes, Ms. Mary. He is an old man. What young girl wishes to be dressed in long party dresses and lots of makeup? I don't love him!"

"Why then did you agree to be with him?" I asked.

"It was all so fast. Before I knew what was happening, I was caught up in a web of presents, restaurants, apartments, and a huge house he bought my parents. There are lots of relatives living off the amount of money Mr. Bruckner allowed my parents. He is never at fault. He looks so distinguished, so proper, they cannot ever imagine the injuries he had bestowed within my heart. I do not love him! I hate him!" There was a dark cloud shining in her dark eyes! "Oh, Ms. Mary, because of him, I left my boyfriend, the man that I loved."

"Listen," I said, sitting down on the humid grass. "Mr. Bruckner, as you call him, is a powerful, dangerous man. You have two choices. To stay with him and learn how to cope with his moods and violence, or run away, far away. I know you must have money. Take it and run as fast as you can. There are no other ways!"

She listened in silence, trying to compose herself, looking at the shadows around us, then looking at me, determination set in her shining red eyes. "I will think about it," she said. We embraced, a hug we knew was going to be the last.

"Be well." I stood there, the chill of the night encasing my body. She was now nothing but a shadow. A phantom vanishing throughout the night, a heavy burden set upon those fragile and young shoulders.

I went to my rooms, heavy with thought, a small light shining inside my decayed brain. I saw William for the first time; he was like a stranger in my mind, the most complex part of the play, the epitasis. The arduous, difficult, complicated side of my life. Scattered at my feet, it was there, visible, ready for me to gather and start anew. I watched William on those following weeks, his moods, his actions. He seemed impenetrable, as usual. I learned how to be on my guard from all of his persuasive actions. I watched him very closely. Did Elizabeth leave him? Or is she trapped in the web of luxury that her parents wove around her? There was no way for me to find out. Except of course, my iPhone. I looked for real estate; there it was, her parents' house up for sale. Elizabeth's apartment was not listed. William probably had the apartment in his name. I felt happy; there was a woman that stood up for her rights!

Somehow she didn't look so small and fragile anymore. She did it! Finally, someone showed William that he was not the gallant suitor he seemed to be. Would he appreciate me more? I couldn't help but be glad for Elizabeth. I could just see William's anxiety reflected on his face when he found out that Elizabeth had left him for another man younger than him. He must have felt abandoned, ridiculed. But William was a jackal! A knight from the medieval era. When a man challenged another to take away all of his possessions, including his wife and children, he will go after her, I had no doubt.

Everything in my household seemed to be okay. We spent the weekends reading, strolling in the park. He spent half of the day in his downstairs office while I ran to my rooms to speak with friends in my iPhone. I enjoyed those precious times, alone with the iPhone, texting other souls that like me were alone, where I could ease all of my pain and afflictions to strangers. William seemed to be very calm during the weeks and months following Elizabeth's elopement. His souls rest never lasted long. He accused me of spending too much time walking in the woods. It was true, but what else could I have done but visit the doctor's office? And walking. Lately, he had not taken me out. I walked to release the feeling that I was experiencing. I walked to satiate the feeling of loneliness.

I needed grass, that magic tea, the hallucinogenic drug (Mimosa) an analgesic tree from which trunk the pulp is extracted to make a tea. I saw it in the Internet, and I was wondering if that tall fellow that handed me the bag of hashish in Amsterdam Avenue knew about Mimosa, that anergesic drug that I wanted to try. I couldn't ask Hector. He would probably give me another sermon about the mysteries, the murders that were outside there, in that world that his fears had created. I asked Zoraida. She was afraid when I told her about the hallucinatory tea. She didn't know about it. This tree grows in the South and some parts of Central America. She sensed that it was something prohibited and refused. At my insistence, she agreed.

When she came back, she said no, that he was angry, that it was a dangerous hallucinatory drug. Hashish was the only drug that he would sell. Be careful, he had warned her. I wasn't disappointed; I liked to smoke hashish. I went out into the woods, my back resting on an old oak tree. I sat alone where the world collided and where the sun rest toward the east right above the clouds, feeling its white mists touching my body. Relaxed, almost happy. It was almost seven o'clock. I had to be ready for supper at eight o'clock sharp. I had to hurry; I had about twenty minutes of hard running and then a shower and dress. My heart beat fast with each effort.

Oh, dear Lord, I pleaded, *let me be on time*. William had complained about my disappearing through the woods. *God forbid that he thinks I am meeting someone! After Elizabeth, he will be on his guard over me.* I thought that I was in danger if he suspected that I was seeing a lover. I came to my rooms suffocated, sweat running down my face, my shirt stained with residues of sweat, undergrowth, and the distinct smell of hashish. I didn't see him when I entered the room, calling for Zoraida, giving her orders. He was sitting on my swivel chair, his back toward me; then he turned around, his eyes on fire, his face tinted red. I had seen that expression before. It was the time when he practically killed me! I couldn't avoid the first blow. I was not going to stay standing in front of him to receive a second.

I ran to the bathroom and said, "Listen, William, once before you accused me of being unfaithful to you, and you were wrong." He started to kick the door. "You are making the same mistake now. Does anyone that is in love going to meet her lover looking the way I am now?"

He stopped kicking and said, "Forgive me, Mary. I keep on forgetting that you are special. Do you truly love me?"

"Oh, William," I said, "if it wasn't because I smell so terrible, I will open the door and kiss you." I took all of my clothing and put them inside the laundry basket. I looked at myself in the mirror.

This time, he used his fists. Oh Lord, I said, thank you for moving my head to one side. The blow merely touched my ear. I trembled. What if he had hit me in my face? I showered as if the hot shower was going to erase the fears that dwelled inside of me!

I was really worried. I asked myself what really happened to Elizabeth. I pictured her delicate figure, her innocent face, in front of an irate bully of a man. *Oh God*, I thought, *let her be safe*. I descended the spiral stairs for supper at exactly eight. I did not cover the red, nor did I put makeup on my face; only my lips had a pink shade on them. My hair was tied with a black ribbon. We were silent. Only the tinkling of the silverware could be heard, like the thundering of a storm to come.

We went to my rooms, his fingers digging my arm while we ascended the stairs! He went straight to the bathroom and opened the laundry basket. "Why did you ask to remove the laundry?" he said.

"William," I lied, "I smelled so terrible that I was afraid the smell will reach my bedroom!" He demanded to see my laundry! It was so embarrassing! He looked at my laundry and smelled them! I turned around; this was the first time I felt embarrassed in front of William!

"Well? Are you satisfied?" I said. "You must feel like a hick in front of Zoraida!" He didn't say anything to Zoraida but said to me, "Your walks through the woods will be supervised by Zoraida. Be here at 6:00 p.m. Not later! Do I make myself clear?"

I knew this was going to happen! He walked out. Why did I let my guard down every time we seemed to be in good terms? I didn't know why I acted that way. For the first time, I was glad that I did not have a baby. Imagine a child subjected to such abuse! He probably would have hit the child! A chill ran down my body. I knew better—William will never let me go!

It might sound unbelievable to you, but I was glad that the punishment was not severe. He could have locked me in my rooms or sent me to a mental institution, or worse yet, he could have killed me! Dear Lord, save me. I had to stop smoking hashish. I would take only pills; after all, they are prescribed drugs.

William seemed to be relaxed. We went to see a Broadway play, *The Phantom of the Opera*. Impressive, unbelievable. I could identify myself with it. It was all about fear, just like the apprehensions inside of me; the efforts needed to overcome your fears, your doubts; the dread to face your demons, capitulating your destiny or to fight to reach your own ambitions. I needed a phantom. Someone who cared, who will make me find my hidden antagonizing apathy, make my noble self shine, to believe in myself. I looked at William right across the restaurant table. He looked so distinguished, I was probably the most envied woman in that restaurant. It was all a hidden illusion, just like me, displaying my beauty, and yet no one can see the gnarled trampled soul dwelling inside of me.

An example of violence against women is Guatemala, a small country with an area of 4,278.341 from the Caribbean Sea to the Pacific Ocean in Central America. Guatemala is known to be a violent country, especially to women. Statistics show that two thousand women were murdered in a period of four years (five hundred women murdered in one year, fifty-five a month, eleven in one week, one woman a day and sometimes two). Soldiers in that small country are trained to hate women and to kill them, claiming that they are responsible for begetting rebels. No one has been found guilty of murder. Their animalistic acts go unpunished.

I was glad that Zoraida finally was experiencing that wonderful feeling of love, but I wanted her to step back and try to study the man she loved. "Is he demanding, abusive, inconsiderate, conceited, haughty? Do you feel boundsmaid to him, inferior? Has he grabbed you or pushed you when engaged in an argument? Run, run away from him! He is an insolent being, a conceited man that will chain you and rob you of your honor and dignity."

Zoraida confided in me. She knew I wanted the best for her. The man she loved was Bob Nakib, the man with a variety store in Amsterdam Avenue. I met Bob, and I was impressed by his stern look and virile attitude, prevalent in a Muslim man.

"Zoraida," I asked her, "how does your Muslim father treat your mother?"

"She just makes him think that he is the boss. I had never witnessed any ill treatment toward my mother. Both my father and brother respect her."

"That's good, Zoraida," I said. "You have a model to follow. Does Bob display the same characteristics as your father? If he does, he is a good man, and I wish you the best."

My life never changed much; it was the same. I felt more trapped than ever. I think that this happens to all of us. It is when the first wrinkles show around our eyes and mouths that we realize how time slips away from us. How fragile and short our lives in this planet last. Why worry about anything? I learned to live with violence, submitted myself to abduction by force and deceit. To be submissive for the sake of peace. But peace was a mirage in my life. When I was ready to grasp it, it disappeared from my very eyes and left me discarded, ejected. A feeling of emptiness engraved in my soul.

William was acting again. He pushed me so hard that the chair that was close to me tipped over backward when he threw me. I hit the back of my head. He walked out and left me there with not a look back nor a care. I was discarded, rejected, thrown into oblivion, affecting my abated self with one push, a push aimed at my soul. I saw him throw one of the large stairway's windows, his brand-new Mercedes-Benz 450 speeding away, leaving behind a different world, trying to get away from pain and misery. I was relieved! No one knew when William was mad. Not even me! That day when he pushed me at breakfast time, he was the same passive, elegant, distinguished, polite man he portrayed to the world. His manly manicured hands did not tremble, his speech polite, a gentleman, with delicate mannerisms.

What happened to him as soon as we entered my rooms? He acted differently as if another self that love has recovered sprouted again, with a fiery thirst and lack of comprehension. As soon as he left I felt free. I felt free. I jumped into my jeans and ran away alone through the woods, way out to the lake, and sat down on a rock. It was so peaceful! The lake was blue like the sky. Its ripples and waves shone like diamonds with the sun rays. I had to think about William.

Is he crazy? Where does he disappear to? Why come back with a new attire every time? How come he never thinks that I noticed? If he did, why then was he not afraid that I will investigate, to meddle in his affairs? What happened to Elizabeth? He didn't know about my iPhone. I must investigate. I always carry the phone every time I went into the woods. Lady Elizabeth agreed to release him of charges if he gave up custody of Catherine. He agreed. The love of his life, little Catherine. He never stopped from providing everything her little heart wanted. He could talk to Catherine once a week. After three long years of good behavior, he could see Catherine at supervised surroundings. Later on, when Catherine was seven years old, he could see her unsupervised once a month. It took a sharp, intelligent, calloused English lady to set William straight. I admired her!

I found out that William had another residence listed. Whose house was it? I would love to find out. I wasn't allowed to leave the house, only for medical and mental assistance, and this was supervised by phone calls. (William was really afraid of me talking to someone! A person that will feel sorry for me and help me.) I called my lawyer.

"Mary," he said, "this is the second time that I told you that I am not a spy or an investigator, I am a lawyer." I felt embarrassed. He probably thought that I was losing my mind. I started to go in circles around my room for days, thinking, Who can I confide to check on that house, to investigate all about it? Whose name appeared on that house? Was it a house or an apartment? Was it the apartment he used to take Elizabeth? Is she there, tied down, abused, discarded? I couldn't think of anyone that could have taken such a risk. I forgot about it for a while. I asked Zoraida with tears in my eyes.

"Zoraida, you are going to go away! I am going to be left alone in this house. No friends, no one that cares for me. I don't know if I can stand it!"

"Ms. Mary, I discussed my working here after we were married. Bob was against it. No wife of him was going to work as a maid, definitely no. Well, I tried to explain to him how much you needed me."

She continued, "Of course, he doesn't know the situation you are in. Well, I put my foot down, just like my mother did! And said, 'I don't need the money now! My brother provides for me. Besides, I have my own bank account. I do not need your money.' Well, I could not believe that the tall impressive man bowed his head and agreed for me to keep working with you. Of course, Ms. Mary, I need a favor from you. He doesn't like the title of maid, would you change it for a lady companion?"

"Of course, my darling." I was so delighted!

"It is all figured out, Ms. Mary. We will buy a house close by, and I will get a small car for me to come to stay with you. Everything will be okay, Ms. Mary. You will see." And she smiled that beautiful smile that I adored. It made me feel happy. Our little secrets, gossiping, laughing, she was all to me. Without her, I would probably have killed myself.

Zoraida had left on top of a table in my room a catalog displaying a number of various trips that she and Bob wanted to take on their honeymoon. I paid no attention to the catalog, but William saw it. I was surprised when he asked me. "How would you like to take a trip to Paris?" I thought he was trying to tease me. "How many years has it been since we traveled together?" I didn't remember; I didn't want to. He hugged me and said, "We could be leaving for Paris next week."

I thought that it was one of his witty moods, so I didn't sound too enthusiastic. I just said, "Oh, it will be nice!"

"We are leaving next week so start to get ready," he said. I was not in a rush. What if he was making it up and then leave me there all propped up, ready to part, and nowhere to go? I waited until the day before the trip to get my suitcases ready. I didn't have to go shopping; I had everything I could take to the trip. It was just one week, one of the most beautiful times that I spent with William. Who was going to imagine that it will be my last trip with him? And our last beautiful experience together. I was excited; I had not seen Paris in such a long time, I almost forgot how it looked like. Everything came back to me as soon as we visited the crowded restaurants and sat on the small outside cafes, the good wines, the excellent foods. William made reservations in that old famous Hotel De Ville situated on the right bank opposite the Île de la Cité. We paraded through the public gardens of the Tuileries, designed for Louis XIV. The Cathedral of Notre Dame, the Theatre de l'Opera. The tree-lined avenue des Champs-Élysées, where the Arc de Triomphe displays its majestic past, where victories, troops, and enemy armies had left marks in its history. I was delighted. William was a gentleman and a lover.

The romantic atmosphere of Paris was contagious. We kissed and made love anytime we were alone. Was that the same William that had me sequestered and brutalized for so many years? I didn't think of anything then. I didn't want to. This was the man I loved. He was there with me, showing me off, displaying the part of William that I adored. I was lost, willing to be at the center of a web he had carefully tied around me. He told me that Catherine was there with little Philip and her husband Edward Hammeth. I was a little disappointed and thought that we were in Paris because of Catherine and little Philip! However, I understood well that it was nice to plan a trip so he could also see his daughter and grandchild. Of course, I was not invited to the reunion. I was not important enough. I did not belong to the aristocracy. I was part of his working society. That was why William was so happy, so generous, such a gentleman. I didn't see it that way then. We were vacationing for the first time in many years and probably Catherine as well. I thought it normal, proper, convenient, a magnificent opportunity for William to get acquainted with his daughter and grandchild. I was having a good time. After William's moods and ill treatment, I deserved a distraction, a residue of peace thrown in my path. Anything to forget my gnarled existence.

I was glad to be home! My familiar surroundings. My comfortable and controlled existence for some crazy reason was a refuge. A place where I could identify with the comfortable cage, where William kept me in, just like a canary that sings while his little eyes focus beyond his surroundings, far away into the blue sky, reaching with his melodies, that spacious infinite world that was strange to him. If set free, he will not live. His cage is his refuge, his home. A place where he was chained, deprived of his liberty, and yet he was happy. Happy to carry the slavery chains that kept his little body trapped while his soul wandered about to vast and greener woods and blue skies. That was me!

William was hilariously happy, attentive, the generous gentleman that he portrayed to be. A dried outer cast of himself. A refrained soul, ready to liberate his other self, that monster that used to dwell inside of him. I learned to live with William—his moods, his accusations, ill treatments, his physical brutalities. I was a slave to his wishes, a victim of his past misfortunes. I also learned to enjoy the good times. At the present, it was a good time. We walked hand in hand, visited museums, the opera, concerts. I was feeling so happy that I forgot my ill vicissitudes and confined treatment.

It was the day that Zoraida and Bob Nakib were going to marry. To my surprise, William assisted the ceremony. I cried when I saw her just as if she was my daughter. She looked so beautiful, so fragile. I prayed to God that they will be a happy couple. It was a Moroccan wedding, full of traditions, fine foods and expensive wines, and magnificent tents and hanging chandeliers. It was in the garden of Papa Hosein's house. It was three days of exciting celebration. William went to the first one. I had two days of being merry. I could not take the third day. I can imagine how tired the bride and groom must have been. They took a tour to Italy, Turkey, and Morocco. All these countries shared the same history. I missed Zoraida, but luckily for me, William was still in a good mood. I couldn't comprehend his happiness. He was never tired. We jumped from one activity to the next as if he wanted to waste all the positive energy left within him by being merry and showing his happiness. Definitely, Catherine was the pivot of all his happiness and his ex-wife his torments.

The devil and good in William—they were his soul's captors, his judges, the essence in which he existed, to be happy or to dwell in agony.

13 Consequence Street

It was time for William to travel to England again. He was going to meet Catherine and little Philip. Of course, Catherine could meet her father anytime. She was nineteen years old, and besides, she was married and a mother. William felt free. For the first time, he felt like a father. He could meet his daughter anytime they agreed. They were free. He had a daughter and a grandchild. No wonder he felt so happy. I was glad for him. Maybe our lives will be different, I thought. No more accusations, ill treatment. Will he ever confide in women? Will I be able to go out, to have friends, to feel free? You know, I didn't want to. If William will not antagonize me, I was ready to stay where I was with William as my partner. I didn't care if he did not marry me. Would a document change our lives? I had been his slave for about twenty years; lines on my forehead and around my eyes were visible. Who will give me a job or want me as a wife? My breasts didn't have the firm look that they used to, and my long and thin body looked as though some force had sucked out every muscle of my body and had left me like a dried-out skeleton. I looked well when I was dressed, my thin body able to accentuate the designer's style.

William didn't seem to care. When it came to lovemaking, he made me feel like a princess. That's all I cared. With William gone to England, I felt free to rest, to concentrate on the investigation about the house address. Who could help me? Joe! His name came out of my mouth all of a sudden. I shouted it out! I was afraid that someone was listening. I would not talk to Joe in my apartment, and it was too late to go out for a walk. I will talk to him tomorrow after breakfast when I go out for my walk. I couldn't sleep. Yes, I thought Joe is the perfect friend to help me. He knows about life. He was a tough, rough individual. He was not afraid. He was perfect.

Finally, I took three sleeping pills. I had to be rested in the morning. I had to go far into the woods to talk to Joe. I could not afford to have someone listening to my conversation. My life depended on it. A cloud was numbing my senses. The pills were starting to work. I was in a different world all of a sudden. A perfect world, no worries, no miseries. I felt carried away to distant lands, a perfect place.

The next day, I ran as far away as my body could carry me. Exhausted, I sat down on the humid grass soaked with the early morning dew. I dialed Joe's number. Too early. I forgot that it was a bar—Joe wouldn't be in until early afternoon! I had to wait until after lunch. I came back to the mansion full of frustrated expectations. To wait more! I have been waiting for this opportunity for almost a year; I felt that a strange force was working against me. Not much to wait now. That's what I tried to think then. I had to look relaxed. I didn't have Zoraida with me, I had to act as if everything was normal. As if I didn't carry with me a dangerous secret.

Finally, after lunch, I took my daily walk, but it wasn't a walk—it was a run for my life. I kept on asking myself, "Am I in danger?" I had to find out what happened to Elizabeth. If William hurt her, he'd probably do the same thing to me. I felt afraid, as I usually did of William. I had my doubts. He would get mad and sometimes he would be violent, but he would never kill anyone. He was too smart as he had too much to lose.

Finally, I was far away, deep into the woods. I dialed Joe's number. Someone answered the phone. "No, he is not in yet. He will be back in half an hour." Another wait. Dear Lord, when will I know the truth? Was I making all this up? Was I losing my mind and seeing shadows where there is no concern? I had to clear my mind of any doubts. I must find out. Thirty minutes of waiting felt to me like hours.

Finally, Joe answered the phone. "Mary! For Pete's sake, where do you hide yourself?"

"Joe," I said, "this must sound strange to you, it is very confidential and dangerous. Don't say anything."

Joe said, "Call me on my cell." That was like Joe, decisive, firm. He knew what to do in any occasion. I told Joe everything. I didn't know about all the rage I harbored within my soul. I told him of my tramped and wilted soul, his beastly treatments, as if I were an ascetic religious person giving confession. Was it because I couldn't see him? Read his eyes, perceive his looks? Sense his reactions? "What do you have to feel sorry for, Mary? I had seen in this very bar young kids, sexy attired, looking for men to prostitute themselves to. They are beaten, scared, even murdered, with no place to go. Lost in their meager existence, silenced and used. You have money, beauty. You can find a man who will respect you! Why have you not left that impudent man you claim him to be?" I detected mockery in his firm answer.

Oh please no, Joe! I thought in desperation. Was I really crazy? Everything he said made sense. I was the last person in this world that needed help, I felt lost. My lawyer and Joe. They couldn't be wrong! Definitely, I was crazy, William was right. I am that dreary person, the melancholic, gloomy wretch he accused me to be. I am lost, lost forever. I felt like the dreary Bloomington town, scorched by winter. Its filthy mud splattered all over my body, its naked, bare branches and gray sky surrounding me. I was on top of that hill alone. I couldn't find Betty. Betty, Betty I howled! I sat there, the iPhone still clutched in my hand. Lost, lost forever! The sun was hiding beyond pink clouds when I woke up. I took many pills. I couldn't get them away from me lately. I had a long way to go. It will get dark when I reach the mansion. I wondered what they will think. I needed Zoraida.

I came in late. Dirty, sweat covering my hair and body. They probably were thinking that I had a lover and that I was making love in the woods. On top of dried, dead grass. I couldn't blame them. I went upstairs to wash up and change. I jumped into clean jeans and an oversize blouse, brushed my hair, carefully throwing away any remainer of dead grass, just in case William walked in unexpected. I couldn't eat. Only soup could my sore throat swallow. I didn't recall, but it looked as though I was screaming, but didn't remember. Outside on the corridor, on top of a small table was the newspaper that William had subscribed from London. I took it and went upstairs. On the social page was the reception that Lady Portberg gave his daughter Catherine. Pictures of them were taken with baby Philip. William Bruckner Sr. was detained at the door when his ex-wife, Lady Portberg, dismissed the invitation and held William at the door. My legs started to shake. I knew how William must have felt. She was the devil on him. I dreaded to see William when he came back. What do I care? I thought, Let him kill me. It will be all over. No more suffering, no more tears and doubts. I know now that I am crazy.

I was tumbling down into a dark pit, trying to grasp, to seize, an impossibility. I was very calm when William bursted into my room. I looked at him with resignation clinging in my blue eyes. He was like a lion in a cage! Going about the room, roaring bellowing. I didn't care. I would not defend myself. Let him kill me! That seemed to aggravate him further. I didn't defend myself! I wanted to die. Finally in frustration, he walked away. Like a tornado, furious. I heard his car speeding away. He was gone! I did not cover my injuries. They were there for all to see. The marks on my neck, the swelling on my face, my black eyes, the black and blue on my arms, the pain in my stomach. No, I don't want to go to the doctor. No police, nothing. I was a wreck, a somber being afflicted, demented. What do I care if no one knows about me, no one cares! I did not have the devious ways of Lady Portberg; the strong character of Queen Victoria, Elizabeth, and Isabel of Spain; also of Queen Joanna of Naples.

I wish I had called the police since the beginning, before William had the time to plunder, deceive, and confine me to a life of meager existence. It's too late now. I am a shadow of myself, a carcass left to rot. Someone who was blinded by love, who believed, willing to give without asking anything in return, loving William to the end. I wondered what Joe will think if William killed me! Would he say that it was my fault? Would he think that I probably deserved it, because of my accusations, my craziness, or would he feel guilty? Who knows, who cares? I was like in a trance living off my pills, rarely eating. Out of this world, as if a fog had covered reality and everything was confused, obscured. Zoraida came again to save me. She was a darling attending to my injuries with love, the only soul in this world that loved me, that cared for me, that believed in me. I smiled at her.

"Thank you, Zoraida," I said. I went downstairs to eat after the first two weeks. I did not cover my injuries. I wanted everybody to take a look at me. I could only have soup, my hands trembling, spilling the liquid all over me. Zoraida was there helping me. I did not feel afraid nor ashamed. William did not expect me. It was the first time that he looked at me with horror, amazement, perturbation. It was a split second. As a gentleman, he moved the chair and helped me sit. He ate as usual, not a tremble in his manicured fingers, not like mine with broken fingers and nails. Hands that looked like a witch's—twisted and long, with unmanicured and broken nails. I knew that underneath that cold cloak he wore lay a feeble being, a weak, detestable, heinous, and confused William. I never went back to the dining room. But I did not stay in my rooms. I paraded around for everyone to see me. My counselor and doctor wanted to report him. I told them that I wanted to die. The doctors became alarmed.

"Who did this to you?" I didn't answer. They called William. I don't know what William said to them, but I was taken away and locked up in a mental institution right on Sunrise Highway on the border line between Suffolk and Nassau. I could see right across a beautiful complex, a gated community, and wondered. Mothers and fathers going about without rest, working long hard days with less pay and more working hours than our friends in Europe. I was placed on a recovery ward, together with patients parading about with blank faces. They looked defamed, despaired, anger reflected on their mad and distorted selves. Melancholy invaded my senses. Did I look like those affected abominable patients? It was all my fault. I challenged William. I knew what would happen. I had taken too many pills. Those little stars that shine through the jars and make you relaxed and contented, they aim at your soul and leave you groping for light! Encased in the dark part of you. I was not sorry I loved William. William was to me the ether, the perfume that emanates from flowers, a blooming aroma within me. Without his kisses, I was lost. It was the force that kept me slaved to his wishes, the crazy passion that kept my senses numbed. My king, my master. The elated love that few of us experience. Loving Helen, the Spartan princess that the Greeks sequestered many centuries ago who prompted a series of battles to recapture her back to the Spartan king.

The Spartan Achilles distinguished himself during that period. The love that ancient warrior felt for his horses, he and his horse shared the same dangers, fought to protect each other, saw their friends fall to their death on the battle fields. They became one, both fighting for their lives or a dream—Bucéfalo, Alexander's great horse; Bellacris, or Meteoro Tigranes's horse; hero of Issus against Alexander; Villain, or Lightning, Attila the Hun's horse. The injudicious love that every damsel dreams of I have experienced. Crazy love. Men and women had been writing about it, in ballads, verses, poems; many books have been written about it. I made a decision—I was going to stay with William until the end. I knew that our love was going to last forever. I mulled around the rehabilitation center for three months. Composed, serene, I wanted to go home. I missed William. I longed for his kisses. I was captured, enamored. I made a plan to go home. I started to eat. My matted, deteriorated hair was dyed and set. My hands and feet were manicured and pedicured. Doctors had to make changes on my treatment. They asked me what made such a drastic change. As if they didn't know! Did I blame William, didn't they see me when I first went to the hospital? Did I say anything, did I not look away, refusing to make charges against William? They knew that I wanted to go home. Why didn't they stop me? Why did they ask me? Were they blind? I told them that they were unlucky because they had never experienced true love, and still they did not capture my feeling, the danger they were releasing me to.

Chapter 11

My psychologist, Robert Tarantelli, had been treating me for years. Sometimes I used to get mad at him and stroll out of his office and stop visiting for some weeks. But eventually, I would come back and resume my weekly treatment. He couldn't understand why I didn't walk away from William. He used to tell me, "Why? You had money, are still young and pretty. Why take the abuse of a psychopath who could kill you someday?"

"Ms. Fletcher," he used to say, "you are in danger!" That's when I ran from his office and called him a fake, a midget. I thought at that time that he was making a wrong opinion of William.

"Sir William Bruckner is an honorable man, he will never kill anyone!" I said. "He has his bad temper." I used to refer to William's wraths of terror as "William's bad temper." What was wrong with it anyway? And then I started to enumerate all of William's good traits. Besides, I used to tell him I loved him. "Tell me, Mr. Tarantelli, have you ever been in love? Madly in love? Have you ever been lost in the fragrance of a kiss, looked into someone else's eyes, and felt lost in the magic? Have you not experienced that love, that crazy love that stops your heart? Have you ever idolized, adored someone?" He didn't understand. Obviously, he had never been in love!

When I saw Mr. Tarantelli for the first time, I realized how thin he was. He sat across from me, his black hair showing silver threads scattered around his small thin mustache covering the upper lip. His mouth was so thin that it used to look like a line when his lips were closed. Long eyelashes gave shadow to his black piercing eyes. He spoke very softly and was a very patient man. Only Robert (as I called him) could have taken the aggravations I had subjected him to. However, lately I was listening.

Everything he said was making sense. I started to listen, a black cloud hugging me, terrible dreary doubts obstructing my mind, leaving in me a sense of dejection. Did William love me? Was he a devourer of souls? A beastly human being capable of killing me? I tried to get into my clogged mind the meanings of Mr. Tarantelli's words. I was not ready yet to admit William's deception. Robert didn't know William. If he knew him, he would not have such a terrible opinion of him. So once more, I was trying to cover up, disregard a professional opinion in favor of William.

I came home experiencing a sense of loss. Lost in the safe quarters of my rooms. What Robert implied was true—I was not safe anywhere. I felt like I was against a wall, bound, blindfolded, ready to be shot. William came home, and with him, all the doubts disappeared. He came home happy, a malicious tinkle in his blue eyes, a long passionate kiss hugging my lips. I melted away. What does Robert know about love? Has he ever loved someone like I love William? I was a feeble sparrow under the talons of a bird of prey, lonely, spreading my wings in the surrounding woods, willing to fly and afraid to do so. Shedding with every mile my inner fears.

Zoraida came looking sad. Her eyes did not have the shining look of love that they had a year ago.

"What's wrong, Zoraida?" I asked. She tried to conceal her sorrows from me, but I knew her too well. I sensed that beneath that masquerade, dense clouds were gathering. I set my book on the side table and got up to hug her. She started to cry. In between sobs, she told me that her father was very ill. "You have to see him!"

"He has lost so much weight that it is frightening," she said in between hysterical spasms. "I can't think about it, I can't live without my father's love."

We entered the corridors of North Shore Hospital; even at six o'clock, the entrance hall was packed with people. The elevators were crowded. There was a mass of people getting in and out of the elevators. Their blank faces were without emotions; no pain nor disturbance reflected on their yellow faces. They looked to me like they were patients, the unfortunate creatures that lay in the various wards throughout the hospital. Floor number 5. It was a push and rush before we had the opportunity to get out. A small landing with signs (5-12). We rushed and stopped at the desk.

"Yes, Mr. Hosein." The nurse hardly took a look at us. What for? I asked myself. The computer will tell her everything she wanted to know.

We were ghosts, puppets, marionettes. The computer pulling the strings, we were at its mercy. Room 508.

We followed a long corridor and stopped. Zoraida needed some seconds to face her dying father. She opened door to number 508; the room was semidark. The only light came through a large window facing a faraway busy street. He didn't move; he couldn't. He was hooked up to various machines, his dark complexion looking almost green. He looked at Zoraida and then looked at me. Those eyes told me everything he wanted to say.

They reflected gratitude. Compassionate Zoraida was on her knees; a clamoring cry bursting from deep inside her. He talked to her in a low and deep voice, as if trying to alleviate, mitigate the pain that she was suffering.

"I am sorry about Mahmud. Forgive me, my daughter, I just wanted to do the best for you. I wanted you to be proud of your race. We descended from the Berber tribe, high in the mountains of Southern Morocco. We fought against the Hammadid and Zirid tribes and allied ourselves with the Christians. Our land is at peace. We are not terrorists, only hardworking people. I want you to believe that. About your mother. Do not abandon her, protect her. She is going to need lots of care. She had only me for protection. Take her to your house, she is a good woman."

"Oh, dear father, I will do as you say, but please do not leave me, Papa. I can't live without you!"

"Oh, my dear," he said, "you are young, pretty. Soon you will have your own children and you will rejoice when you see their little funny faces and small beautiful feet and hands."

We left the hospital in tears. We sat in the car. Zoraida's car was parked on a spiral parking lot that led to the top. The ravaging wind blowing with savage force, our souls felt the same as the wind—sad and cold. We hardly spoke as we drove through the Long Island Expressway. What was to be said? I was surprised.

The next day, it was a festivity in Papa Hosein's honor. Food lined up the numerous tables. Relatives and friends were everywhere, coming, going. People that didn't see each other for years met at Papa Hosein's funeral. I remembered my parents' funeral. The cold and desolate cemetery, the lack of friends, the lugubrious atmosphere. I cried. I cried for my parents, I cried for the affliction that I was subjected to, for my life, my rotten luck.

It was all for nothing. I wouldn't leave William, I knew it! As soon as I arrived home, I would see him and melt in his arms. I even missed him then. Surrounded by people, I was trying to, pretending to socialize. I miss him! I didn't see Zoraida for one month. I ran more than ever, trying to forget the tragedies that hit us so suddenly. During all the misfortunes and trepidations that ravaged my soul, for the last three months, I had forgotten all about Bruce, my neighbor, the wrangler, the athletic, smooth, and mellow neighbor that wrenched away my hopes from me, the conceited stranger that was trying to darken William's honor. He passed me, as always, with a smooth athletic rhythm and without any effort disappeared into the woods. Who was this stranger? I promised myself that next time, I was going to talk to him. Curiosity sparked my brain. I was going to dig into William's activities; I was going to search, look into his past. To find out for the first time who was this man, what secrets enclosed his past that I was unable to know, even after living with him for over twenty years. Was I so eager to please him, too afraid to investigate, too desolated for anyone to realize the danger I was in? Did William deceive me all these years? Was he a murderer? A silent, hidden, and somber assassin? An insensible monster that had me captive for so many years? No, it can't be possible. How can anyone be so stupid? I didn't consider myself stupid and yet there I was! Believing William, being his slave. How could so many people be wrong? What was wrong with me anyway?

Sweat dripping down my shirt, I didn't care. I kept on running as if I was running for my life. Running away from my shadow, from the dark clouds that encircled my mind. It didn't matter how fast I tried to run, the shadows were there. Following me, making my life miserable.

I arrived at my quarters, feeble, tired. A premonition hung in the air that left me cold. I needed something really fast. I took a shower; there were only Temazepam pills left in my bathroom's cabinet, fifteen milligrams each. That was not enough. One pill will make me pirouette around the fountain for about a minute, so I took six Temazepams; that was all there was left in the jar. I looked around for grass. In my closet, on top of the shelves, coat pockets, everywhere—nothing. I was frantic, like a lunatic going around in circles. I needed the black opium from the Paths and Mountains of Africa or the narcotic produced from the amapola flower in Peru, but none of these were available. It was my Temazepam and me. Nothing more. The pills made me relaxed. I pulled my comfortable chair by the balcony's window, looking at the traveling clouds, a rainbow of colors illuminating the sky. I didn't want to think. Oh, William, William, dear Lord, let it not be him. I drifted away into space. I felt wonderful. Life was nice again.

The maid woke me up the next day in late afternoon. "Ms. Mary, Ms. Mary, wake up. Sir Bruckner wants to see you for supper!" Oh, dear Lord, my head felt heavy, too heavy to move around. "Help me, Lisa." Oh, I needed Zoraida. She was still in mourning. Lisa helped me to disrobe to get into a hot tub, help me out of the tub. My head felt vain, empty, and useless. I needed something so. "Lisa, please bring me a strong cup of coffee, no milk, plenty of sugar."

I wore flat sandals, I didn't want to trip on the stairs. Light lipstick and rouge. Lisa brushed my hair. Oh dear God, I prayed. Let William be in a good mood! It must be serious.

The meeting was in his downstairs office. Mr. Leeward opened the door. A silent darkness engulfed the office. I could hardly see William! "William, my love," I said. "Is anything wrong?"

For the first time, there was William being honest with me. He said, "Well, I wanted to tell you before one of the staff members told you. Probably the police are going to be here asking you questions."

"The police!" I said. Fear encased my fragile state of mind.

"Do not panic!" His eyes shone in the dark like the eyes of a lion when it is ready to attack, hiding behind the bushes, targeting its victim. "Be calm. They said that Elizabeth was found dead in Gilgo Beach. They said that she ran away with her lover, the police are looking for him! The police probably want to know if you could give them some information." Those last two words were said between his teeth as he grasped at my arm, digging his fingers.

"I can't tell the police anything, I hardly saw her," I said with fear inside of me. Did he know about our meeting? I thought then. I prayed that he didn't know.

I walked out of his office feeling sad and sorry for Elizabeth. The poor innocent girl! Tears filled my eyes. She didn't deserve such a tragic ending, I said, without realizing the serious situation William was in. I ran out of the office with a feeling of culpability. I told her to run away, to save herself. The young couple didn't know that William was a jackal, a beastly hunter of young souls. I came to believe, to understand William's capacity for murder. There it was, her picture all over the newspapers. Her black hair and beautiful expressive dark eyes. Her parents were there too. Her mother crying, blaming the boyfriend. How much money did William give them?

The police came to the house to speak to me. "Did you know that Ms. Elizabeth Pattini was Sir William Bruckner's guest at his mansion?

How long have you been a guest at Sir William Bruckner's mansion? Were you jealous of Ms. Pattini staying at the mansion? Were you in a mental institution? How long? Do you experiment with drugs? Did you ever talk or spied on Ms. Pattini?"

I asked myself, Did William know about our meeting? I didn't think so. The next few weeks were a nightmare. Police searching the grounds, asking questions to the servants, following them. Unmarked cars stationed at a distance, watching. I was afraid to go to my daily walks with the media flashing news about a serial killer presumed to live in New York and come all the way through bridges and long highways to dump his victims in the outskirts of Long Island. Years back, there was another serial killer around the town of Manorville, not far from Gilgo Beach. Was the Manorville killer the same man? Someone that triggered by personal emotions ripped, cutting down his victims as if they were the dark tools of his imagination? Like William? Newspapers were displaying photos of the victims that were found murdered around Gilgo Beach. The victims' photos showing youth, their clear eyes showing determination. I saw their faces; only Elizabeth looked sad, her beautiful dark eyes showing distress. There were controversies in such a huge case. Like the case of a victim that was walking along a gas station after leaving the Hauppauge Holiday Inn Express. She went to meet someone she contacted through Craig's List although her remains were found at Gilgo Beach, investigators made the conclusion that she was drowned in the marshes. Her investigators believed that she was accidentally drowned when she was trying to run away while reaching for the lights of the Robert Moses Causeway, a mile or so away. She was found practically naked. Did she also take her underwear off while she was running? Running from whom?

There was lot of publicity that died away as time passed by. Then silence, not a word. I kept on looking for news about Elizabeth, and nothing. As if she never existed. Did William kill her and place her body in Gilgo Beach to make it look like it was the work of a serial killer? Or worse yet, was William the serial killer?

I hardly saw William. He came and went as though he were a ghost coming and going in shadows. I visited Robert, my psychologist. I couldn't wait for him to tell me about what he thought about Elizabeth's murder. He looked at me with compassion and answered me, "What do you think?"

I was surprised. I told him, "Look, we are paying you a lot of money to let me see the reality of life and yet when I ask you anything, you answer me with another question. Did you think that William killed Elizabeth?"

His answer was, "What do you think?"

"I don't know," I answered. "How could I know about something that is encased in someone else's heart? How could I be sure? Yes, William is a violent man, but there are thousands upon thousands of men that are violent and yet they have not committed murder."

"That is true," Mr. Tarantelli answered. "But there is a feeling deep inside that tells us when we are in danger, when we fear the person that confronts us, the expression in their eyes, the rage that one perceives through his actions. If one ever perceived this feeling of terror, this feeling while confronting a beastly person, that person is in danger. Run away, my child, run as fast as you can." I wished then that it were that easy.

"I know you become paralyzed with fear. The abuser practically has you in his power. You become stagnant, doubtful, perplexed. Terror grasps you in such way that you cannot move. There is no use. You are lucky if only bruises cover your body; it is the bruises left in your heart that one cannot erase.

"Did it happen to you, Ms. Fletcher?"

I looked at him and for the first time in so many years, I saw William as he really was. Cold, deceiving, a somber murderer. Yes! I believed at that moment that he was a murderer. An arrogant assassin of young souls, a debaucher of young girls.

I felt those words coming out from inside of me, as if they were hot pincers coming from my soul.

I had stood up, facing a large window, and I didn't notice all those feelings that for years were encased in the deepest fibers of my soul come rushing out. Words that I knew profoundly were burning my soul. I couldn't let them out. I felt free now, free of soul only because I was still a prisoner of love. I resumed my daily walks feeling liberated, as if I could have flown through the woods instead of running. I felt light, free. The rhythm of every step coordinated, my muscles relaxed, my legs flexible. Like a bird of paradise, flying, arms and legs coordinated, following the speed, accelerating as I ran along.

There he was! My rival, Bruce McKluskey, next to me, both of us flying through the woods with the same speed, with the same rhythm. Like two flamingoes, their thin and large legs accelerating to fly beyond the clouds. We stopped by the lake; I noticed that we came that far. Relaxed, energy reflected on our bodies, we laughed.

"How?" he asked me. "How come you run so professionally?"

"A long story," I said. "It comes from within."

We sat on that old log that heavy ice had dismembered it from its trunk long ago. For the first time, I felt at ease with this stranger. "I want to ask you something if I may." He looked at me with suspicion, his gray-blue eyes looking into mine as if he wanted to extract every one of my secrets. "Are you ready to tell me about Sir William Bruckner?"

"I don't know," I replied. "Not yet."

"Well, Ms. Mary," he said, "you let me know. You have my card." And he disappeared through the woods like a flash. I could not do this to William! An informer, a spy, never! One thing was to talk to my psychologist and another to become a deceiving lover to someone that had provided for me in his home, tenderly loving me throughout the years, never!

Life with William was very difficult after Elizabeth's murder. I felt that I was living with a stranger. Someone who could hurt me, who could kill me. I don't know how he perceived my feelings. It is another secret between lovers. One could sense the other partner's feelings. As if they were dual souls. Like twins that grow together sharing the same placenta, breathing close together to come to a world completely detached but sharing the same feelings. That was William and me! I could sense his moods, his happy feelings, his glories, his laments, his grumbles, his injuries, his somber moods and also his beastly, dark temper. For weeks, he was around, hunting up and down to pick a quarrel. I stood calm through his evil accusations and tribulations.

I knew I had to take him away from the mansion. To let him see, for some days, the other side of life, the happy side, and I said to him, "William dear, why don't we go away for a week? To the mountains, upstate. To that beautiful hotel encrusted up in the meadow where the rich pasture grows. Remember, darling?"

He stopped to meditate, to reconsider, looking beyond the garden, lost in the bend of his thoughts, fighting to choose happiness, to relinquish, to subdue the evil inclinations. He turned around and then I saw that it was my William, the one I adored, the easygoing and generous lover. I sensed his good side. His dense blue eyes told me he had pruned away the useless stems from his evil other self. He was happy!

We started to make reservations. A large room, I heard him saying, with a nice view of the mountains. For the first time in weeks, I felt his happiness. We looked like two crazy teenagers ready to elope, lost in the excitement of the moment, free of the consequences. We left in a red convertible, the spring breeze fluttering my hair, passing the George Washington Bridge, Route 80, bordering the skirts of the Hudson River and Upstate New York. Green meadows, beautiful mountains, small and large rivers. We laughed and sang. Never, never had I heard William singing! We were so happy! We couldn't wait to be in each other's arms, what can I tell you! I loved him.

We dined on the terrace, a beautiful garden below. From a distance were green meadows and orange, red, purple, and yellow mountains. Early spring in New York! A rainbow of colors bursting everywhere, a safe harbor, a refuge to alleviate one's soul. We danced close together, our bodies feeling each other's heart, caressing our senses. It was love. We loved each other. No one could deny, hinder, oppose, disregard that fact. It was really love!

I couldn't remember the last time we were as happy. Why? I asked myself. Couldn't we be as happy always? I guess love is like a mirage from far away you perceive your lover. He is a knight, brave and strong, pleading you to come to him, love showing in his shining eyes. Inviting you, seducing you, asking you to share his love. You run fast to grasp this beautiful being, this man that you love. It is an illusion and it is telling you that he loves you, but when you try to grasp it, it disappears before your eyes, leaving you doubtful, uncertain, perplexed. It didn't exist; it was all a mirage. That's how I felt with William. I knew that those beautiful and loving moments would disappear, to turn around to despair, anger, fury, and displeasure. I wonder if it was the same with other couples. I see older couples sharing good moments walking hand in hand, taking care of each other, and I wonder, Are William and I bound by passion only? Was it really love that we were experiencing, or were we defrauded by love? Two persons bound only by a meager existence of violence, one partner toward an unresisting, passive lover. A self-destructive and sick woman, blinded by the desire to be loved.

It was all over the news. Catherine's daughter (William's granddaughter) died of heart failure due to pneumonia. Little Lisa was five years old, the daughter of Lady Catherine and Sir Edward Hammeth. Funeral would be held. I turned my iPhone off. I couldn't read it any longer. William was not mentioned at all. His own granddaughter. I wondered if they told him that little Lisa was sick. I knew right then and there how this was going to affect William. God Almighty and powerful being, have mercy on me, I prayed. I dread the moment that William will burst through my door and attack me! Maybe I was wrong. He was missing for three days. I imagined that he knew, that he was with little Lisa on her last moments. I felt bad for Catherine. At her young age, she has gone through lots of tribulations. The loss of her father, her dominant mother and grandmother, and now, the loss of her precious child. I couldn't think about it any longer.

Thank goodness that Zoraida was back. I took her along so as not to upset William if he came in before me and found me gone. I took all sorts of precautions. I became cautious, sagacious. My closet was in order; my shoes set heel to heel. All sweaters together, coats, underwear. My bed and pillows set at a certain angle. The bathroom spotlessly clean, perfumed my room, opened the window just a little bit. Everything was ready. Zoraida looked everywhere and said that everything was right. We ran out of the mansion as if a ghost was chasing us. I had to stop for Zoraida a couple of times; she was out of shape. Too many good times, I told her and we both laughed. Finally, I was with someone I could talk to, someone who had perceived throughout the years all of my suffering, who believed me. Who understood the havoc, the penumbra I lived in, where light and shadows meet, just like my life.

Zoraida told me, "Run, run away. I couldn't stand another beating, Ms. Mary. I couldn't see you suffering any longer! I will not come back to this mansion ever again. Do you know what Bob told me?" She was screaming now. "He told me that I could be charged and even sent to prison for covering up an abuser. Imagine, Ms. Mary! Please run away, as soon as you see him in one of his dark moods. Run, run!"

I thought that's what I told Elizabeth and now she was dead. Maybe her lover was also dead. The police would never find him! I waited too long. I had my chance. On those long three years, I was alone and I didn't run away. Why didn't I? Now I was asking myself that question. Too late!

We came home and took showers. Zoraida changed into her suit and high heels and I into a serious gray gown and flat sandals. No makeup, I wanted to let him know that I was also in mourning. My long hair was knotted high with black pearls. I sat on my comfortable chair reading a book—*Assegai* by Wilbur Smith. One of the best historical novelists of our times. It made me forget all of my tribulations. I learned that there were people more miserable than I was and they managed to survive, to keep on going with their lives as I should. My thoughts, running away to dark Africa. Zoraida had left. It was six thirty to be exact. I kept on looking at the clock; that's how I knew the time.

Before I realized it, he was in my quarters, crying like a baby. Sat across from me, his head bent down. Tears running from his eyes and into his hands. I handed him a tissue. I made a mistake; I should have known better. I came close to him to caress him, to console him, and that's when he turned around. His face had that evil look I had seen other times. A somber and beastly look that I knew so well. He stood up, fists clenched, eyes wild, a deadly grin showing on his wry face.

"It is all your fault!" he said while coming toward me. I remembered the words of Robert, my psychologist: "The victim knows when confronted by a killer, they know it! But they become paralyzed by fear. If this happens to you, run, run as fast as you can."

It was of no good; the blow hit me straight on my nose. I heard the terrible sound of my nose bone splintering, blood running down my chin, my chest. I panicked, the blood did not stop coming out of the hole that the blow left on me. I ran toward the stairs. I couldn't yell nor ask for mercy; blood was choking me, staining my dress. I came to the top of the stairs, my head spinning. I stopped for a moment, thinking how I was going to go down all those stairs without William getting at me first. That's when I felt, or I thought I did, William pushing me down the stairs. It was strange. While I was falling down all those stairs, I kept on thinking. My brain kept on working, thinking, *William pushed me!* I kept on rolling but didn't feel any pain, as if the body makes its own sedative, a tranquilizer to ease the pain.

I woke up at the hospital five days later. I couldn't move or talk, strapped to a bed. Both of my legs were broken and one of my arms dislocated at the shoulder. They were calling me, "Ms. Mary, Ms. Fletcher, you are okay now. You had a terrible accident. Your partner is here." The nurse turned around and asked William his name. I heard William saying, "Sir William Bruckner." I wished at that moment that I could talk! But I was immobilized, motionless, only tears were running down from one of my eyes as the other side of my head was bandaged. I wanted to yell. I wanted to tell them that he was a monster. Oh God, I thought. Will he disconnect the tubes that were giving me life? Fear running down my spine, I couldn't talk, I couldn't tell anyone the fear I was feeling then. I tried to move my lips; no sounds came out.

Terror gripped me! *Please someone*—my brain kept on talking to me—*help me, get this man out of here! He is a murderer.* It was of no use. I had to listen to William explain to me how lucky I had been. How worried he had been when he saw me tripping down the stairs. "Why didn't you wait for me to escort you down the stairs?" Real tears were coming down from his eyes. I wished I could have told him if I was able to, to yell at him, "Assassin, monster, get him out of my side, away from me!" But I couldn't move. I closed my eyes; I didn't want to see him or listen to what he was saying.

I spent three months in the hospital. Reconstructive surgery was performed on me twice. My nose was broken, and my front teeth were missing. Part of my head was shaved. My legs were in traction, my head was bandaged, a deadly grimace on my thin and yellow face. I looked like a brave armored Zulu warrior from southern Africa, ready to confront his enemy. I cried, but tears kept on running into my mouth, dangerously close to the tube that kept on giving me life. I couldn't cry. I had to subdue the desire to scream, to tell the world how unfairly I had been treated by a cruel assassin. I considered myself murdered. I was dead to the world, dead to my dreams, but above all, I was dead to love.

I woke up early one morning as the nurse was trying to hurry me throughout my daily bath and change. "You are lucky, girl, you are going home! Sir Bruckner said you don't need to stay at the hospital. He will provide all the facilities needed for your stay at home. You will be in your own rooms, surrounded by the people that love you." I couldn't talk! Coming out of my mouth were moans that didn't make sense.

"I know" the nurse said, "you are excited after three months in this hospital, I don't blame you." They rolled me down the elevator, the corridors, and into a sunny June morning. The sunrays hurt my one eye. I tried to struggle to make sounds from deep inside my throat. It was of no use. Everybody was concentrating on doing their jobs. One, two, three . . . and they enclosed me in the ambulance and toward my jailer. Sentenced to life, to spend the rest of my life in a prison. I knew then that William brought me home so I wouldn't talk. He was afraid I would say anything that might incriminate him. He didn't care about me; he was protecting himself. I knew that I couldn't say anything, even to Zoraida! What was the use? Zoraida would get mad at him. She will not stay with me. I couldn't stay in that mansion without someone that I could trust. I was gagged for life. William was the rooster ready to strike his adversary to death. I needed three months to recover, not completely, but at least I was walking with the help of a rolling crutch. I still couldn't look at myself in the mirror. I had all the mirrors covered, but it felt nice to go out in the garden to feel the sunrays on my face. Every staff member was crying when they saw me coming down the electric shaft that William had installed for me to go down the stairs. At least, I thought at the time, I had made some friends. I had the impression that they didn't believe the tale of me tripping down the stairs. I still had to go for reconstructive surgery on my mouth, as all my front teeth were missing, but I could sit down in the garden bench and feel the sun's rays on my face, feeling a little alive after five months of torture. I resigned myself, I submitted myself to his will. I had given up to William. I had a scheduled appointment with an orthodontist; finally, my front teeth were going to be implanted. What for? I thought. Teeth were meant to eat, and I didn't care about eating or thought I will ever smile again. I was curious of how William would keep me from talking to the orthodontist surgeon and the nurse who was taking care of me when the doctor performed the transplants of teeth. He must have been fearsome, a dread, apprehension encasing his soul. Good! I thought. Now he knew how I must have felt. It was not that way at all. He had all his bases covered, like the baseball game, waiting for a little infraction to win the game. He won. I couldn't talk to the doctor; the nurse was with me every moment. Even if I wanted to, which I didn't care.

It took one month to finally finish my teeth. I looked at myself in the mirror; someone completely strange was looking back at me. The teeth looked too white to look normal; the expression on my face was completely different. My cheeks were pumped to resemble someone's face that wasn't me at all, and I cried. Who was that stranger that was looking at me?

"Don't worry, Ms. Mary, the next step is cosmetic surgery," the nurse told me. Another operation. It took me one year of pain and various surgeries to make me look like myself again. The surgeon shaved off my hair. To erase the wrinkles on my forehead, he pulled my skin toward an incision in the front of my head and then pulled my skin toward the back of my ears and both sides of my temples to erase the wrinkles around my eyes. After one month of recuperation, I looked like a movie star. Except, of course, for the fact that I was still walking with a cane.

Zoraida told me, "You must not be grateful. Remember, it was his fault."

"No, no, Zoraida," I said with fear. "I tripped, I tripped, Zoraida, don't forget that." I was afraid that if William suspected that I had mentioned the fact that he pushed me, Zoraida and I would be in danger. She lowered her eyes; she understood. I walked with a cane for about six months more; then little by little, my legs got stronger, my muscles started to relax. My bones felt stronger; it was a miracle, Zoraida said, but the orthopedic doctor had a different opinion.

He said, "Your physical condition helped you recuperate." But he warned me, "Do not break another bone again!" I left his office feeling free for the first time in many months. I felt young again; I wanted to run, to tell everyone how I did feel. But of course, there was only one person that I could talk to; that person was there with me, Zoraida.

"Hector," I said, "take us to a beautiful restaurant. No, better yet, take us to that small restaurant close to Central Park, where I sat with my friend Carmela many times, plotting, dreaming of ways to make our lives better."

It is dreadful, I thought then, the humans' resistance to acknowledge truth when it is placed too close to their eyes. I didn't see it then, but Carmela did. That was why she was always positive, full of energy. Sure of herself. She made it; she knew how to choose a partner and take charge of her life. So unlike me that had someone else to control me. Did I have an inferiority complex? Did I fall in love with William, or was his dominant and superior station in life that attracted? Did he feel the need to feel superior and bestow upon me the same treatment that his parents and ex-wife had shamed him, made him feel discarded, frustrated, annulled? I didn't want to think about it then. I felt almost happy. I was enjoying a beautiful view, and I was sitting next to someone I loved as my own daughter, with whom I shared intimate feelings. We laughed and talked like two teenagers out for a good time. No worries, no pain. We walked toward Fifth Avenue, chirping away like two sparrows, getting in and out of stores, buying things that we didn't need. Having an ice cream, laughing, living. We went home feeling tired, weary, exhausted, but very happy.

"Listen to me, Zoraida. From now on, it is only happiness for me," I said. I went to bed with the assurance and conviction of fulfilling my dreams. Becoming liberated, free. I started to run again, very slow at the beginning, but as the months kept on passing by, I was accelerating my rhythm, feeling the energy in my legs.

Bruce came close to me and welcomed me back. "Let's sit down for a while. I know that you have lots of explanations that I want to know," he said. Just like that! He was not asking me; he was demanding from me a confession!

"Why should I confide in you?" I said.

"Because, Ms. Fletcher, you are in danger."

"Oh," I said, "and what makes you think that!" I had to be careful; I didn't know if he was William's friend. How come this stranger came up out of the blue sky after and before each one of William's bad temper? Was he William's friend, a confidant, someone that knew of our relationship, a spy? I started to dislike him. That was none of his business, I thought.

"Ms. Fletcher," he said, "you have been in hospitals and in mental institutions three times. This last time, we will say that you were very lucky. Either you are completely insane to cover up someone that intends to kill you again and again, or you are held up by fear. Talk, I could help you!" He reached for his wallet and showed me his FBI identification card.

"Oh, dear me!" I said. "Do you think that you can help me? Where were you when I tripped down the stairs?" I almost said "pushed down the stairs." I had to be careful, I thought then. I didn't know this stranger. How many women have been killed thinking that the police would protect them? They cannot be with you twenty-four hours a day. "No, thank you," I said. "Bring me some proof that incriminates William and then I will talk." I agreed to the fact that I had tripped down the stairs. A lawyer—Allan Parker, whom I previously thought was a doctor at the hospital—came to the hospital with the Police Commissioner Richard Kormer. I was still in traction. Vulnerable, afraid.

"Ms. Fletcher, did you trip down the stairs on the . . . month, year . . . Is the mansion located at . . . ? Etc., etc. Sign here please." I had my only arm, the only part of my body that was not in traction. I wished then that I had broken my right arm also. "Sign here please." I signed that document without even knowing what was really written on it. I couldn't see, as my left eye was completely covered.

"Yes, I remembered how well protected I was by the police then," I said and I turned around toward the mansion. William and I were just friends then. He visited me about once a week; except of course, when he used to despair. I liked it that way. No rides, restaurants, shows, presents, but also no fears or bad tempers, nor abuse. He had to stay away from me!

He knew that another beating will certainly send him flying to the "big house." I was safe for the moment. But no one could predict William's swings of mood, his devious plans, his calculated and devoted vengeance, his hypocritical stance. I was a threat, someone that could have turned around the perimeter of his life forever. He felt vulnerable. I could still read his emotions, feel, touch, even grope in the dark of his mind his devious self. I was not safe.

Chapter 12

I was emotionally ready to move away, to rent an apartment right on Fifth Avenue. I would have no problem to rent, like before. I could just see the real estate person asking me my previous address. "Yes, 88 Court Street in the town of Dayville in Suffolk." They would probably move like a gang of monkeys, jumping and making noise, celebrating. Better yet, I will go to the real estate of Mrs. Rockwell, the odious person that made Carmela's life miserable after she tried to sell the apartment in Mrs. Rockwell's domain in Fifth Avenue. I wondered if she was still alive; she was in her forties then.

All these pains for nothing. I was dreaming, of course, because I knew that I was safer living in the mansion than living on my own, in an apartment in New York City. If something happened to me at the mansion, William would be responsible for any injuries or murder inflicted upon my person. However, outside the mansion, especially in New York City, a person can get lost in the dark hallways. William could contract anyone to get rid of me while he was at a meeting, or better yet, in England visiting Catherine. No, I thought then, it is not the time to be on my own, to recuperate in the freedom that I had lost so many years ago. I reasoned my move cautiously. I did not want to raise a doubt in William's mind. I had to be careful. I had to erase from my mind every negative thought against William in his company.

I knew that he could sense my innermost feelings, just like I used to. I pretended to be a good friend, someone that he could confide in, a protector, a defender, a guardian of his intimate feelings. We laughed and told each other stories of our past lives over a cup of tea or a glass of wine. He started to enjoy the weekly visits to my quarters. I wanted to keep it that way, the two of us good friends. Sometimes Zoraida joined in and made us laugh with the stories of Papa Hosein and his family in Morocco. However, all the time I kept an eye on William. Especially about his long absences. What did he do? I had to be careful never to ask him that question. It will come about; all I had to do was be careful, to pretend that I was not interested in it, to wait. I knew I was dealing with a sharp wrangler; a dangerous, quarrelsome, violent individual; a dark human being; a hawk, a jackal that was able to read my innermost feelings.

William came to visit me one early afternoon; the day was dreary, the last two days was snowing and raining. Dark clouds were covering the sky, a somber look spreading over the meadows. I didn't feel like doing anything.

I rested on my divan, nightgown on, feeling protected from the dreadful, ferocious, and rude weather outside. I was surprised to see William. Usually on rainy or snowing days, he dedicated himself to paperwork and stayed in his office for hours. He didn't look well; he had lost some weight. His handsome manly face showed stress, traces of time painted on his dreaded-looking self.

"Is anything wrong, love?" We still called each other "love." It was a habit that most couples have. A pet name. Ours was the proper word for our condition. It was love and nothing else but love that we devoted to one another throughout the years. Sublime love afflicted by no mercy, abuse, two mentally ill people bound forever.

It was an early lunch brought into my quarters. We had some wine and we felt relaxed, like two friends. It was a period dedicated to peace. Like two armies of opposing relatives that shared the same blood and yet decided to make peace and then war. Like the battles between Joanna I, queen of Naples and Charles of Durazzo and Marguerite, both raised by Joanna. Just like William and I and yet, finding ourselves on an adverse battlefield. William, who felt threatened by a woman below his station in society. And the stamp of his ill temper. Not knowing when havoc would strike, a harborer of madness or a mentally sick individual could be waiting in the shadows to harm me.

I made a calendar that depicted William's absences since early 1990. One week in November, Catherine's birthday. Two weeks in May, no record; doctor's visits, dentists, visits to the mental institution, the hospitals. Everything was checked; however, there were days when I couldn't tell what he was doing during those absences. There were many. What was he doing during those days? Curiosity knotted my brain with doubts. I had to find out.

Next day, I had to match his absences with the Gilgo and Manorville murders. I prayed that it was not so, that William had some girl that he visited to, or some kind of hobby or business that kept him occupied throughout his absences. I was mad at myself; how could I think of William as a murderer, a beastly individual, a monster that assassinated all those girls?

William was a refined person, a lord, a well-educated individual that happened to have a bad temper. Definitely not a murderer that disposed of his victims by cutting them up and then throwing their remains in the wilderness of Long Island. It was absurd. Not William, my refined and honorable lord; I thought that I was crazy! Imagine William full of blood, cutting up all those bodies? A limpid, neat, and elegant man. Manicured hands and feet, a great example of law and order?

But what about Elizabeth? She was found in Gilgo Beach! No, I thought; it must have been her boyfriend, the man that she loved, that she trusted. Only now, we have started to become aware of the abuses men have inflicted upon their wives and girlfriends. To awaken their victims from their fearful and sensitive gentleness, as I was. I saw William as a different person, only remembering the good times, his status, his refined manners, his looks, his manly self. I was living in the dark. If someone had shown me the light then, I would have reacted in a negative way. How can anyone get used to the sunlight after living in darkness? It would hurt your eyes! You have no idea of what is outside there. You feel protected inside your dark cave. Out there is danger. A freedom you never experienced before. Therefore, it is frightening. Sometimes we see a movie on television about tribes of people that manage to survive without the utensils of modern life and yet they do. If you removed them from their environment, they would become afraid, resentful. Some of them would die. They get used to be surrounded by wild animals, to hunt when hungry. No doctors, no facilities, but that's the way they like to live. Which one of the two groups is freer? That someone would have to hunt for his food; be exposed to wild animals, diseases, poverty; or someone that lives in a modern society that has to be strapped to a desk eight hours a day? Twelve years of schooling. During their lifetime. Working twelve hours a day (with the care of children) the payments of bills. People conform to their way of living and everybody thinks that their society is the best.

My own quarters were a refuge to me. I felt protected, just like the jungle people surrounded by dangerous animals and yet feeling protected. Perhaps I could find an answer in the Pedro Calderón de la Barca philosophical play

"La Vida Es Un Sueño" "Life Is A Dream," based on the struggle between reason and instinct. Yes, I know about dreams. How many times have I dreamed of William, our first meeting, our love, that first crazy attraction that drove us together?

I could still close my eyes and feel that I am in that beautiful garden. The moon through the tall pine and oak trees. The smell of the flowers reaching me with its perfumes, William looking so handsome, so refined. His manly parts reaching me, making me crazy. Running, running to find a place, a love nest to fulfill our desires, I feel as though I am there, loving William, feeling him.

Life is nothing but a dream or "La Vida Es Un Sueño". as Pedro Calderón de la Barca stipulated in his philosophical play. That's the way I was feeling then, dreaming to reach the pinnacle of my existence, feeling free, in love, protected by dreaming from the languor that sometimes was enclosed within my mind.

They found more bodies in Gilgo Beach; the police was searching the area with trained police dogs. The bodies were spread around the tall marsh that surrounded the beach. The police commissioner still thought that it was the work of a serial killer. The murderer would seek prostitutes in New York and discard them in Gilgo Beach. The police from Suffolk County were asking the police from New York City to help with the investigation. What about Elizabeth?. She was not a prostitute and yet the poor girl counted as one of the group.

Some of the bodies found in Gilgo Beach were so old that the forensic experts were not able to identify the victims; animals and birds had torn at their remains to shreds. Very little was left of their once fragile and young bodies.

Betty, Betty, were your remains scattered around the tall grass of Gilgo Beach? If so, what monster clawed, lacerated, and stroked at your innocent body? Fear ran through my body. Did she come to New York? Did she try to contact me but couldn't? She hasn't contacted her family, why? I couldn't sleep at night; I had to take lots of sleeping pills at night. Sometimes it would be late afternoon before I woke up.

"Not good," Mr. Tarantelli said. "I am going to cut down on the sleeping pills."

"It is my friend Betty," I said. "She is one of the victims in Gilgo Beach. She was, I mean is or was a prostitute and I think she was living in New York City. The last time I talked to her, she told me that she was moving to New York City."

"All of these are speculations, why worry yourself with something you don't know for sure? Maybe she didn't come to New York. Maybe she found someone and she is happy living some place in another state? Who knows? You are probably harassing yourself without any proof." I felt a lot better after talking with my therapist; besides, the last time I saw her, she practically told me not to interfere with her life.

So I kept on dreaming. Dreaming on the Christmas William bought me a beautiful cluster of red flowers and a Christmas card. "Just for you sweetheart with all my love." We kissed and danced to the tune of that beautiful song "Let me call you sweetheart, I'm in love with you . . ." I kept that card hidden in my heart, imprinted in every fiber of my brain, longing to have him close by and yet knowing that now it was impossible. Oh, William my love, why had we come to this end? Loving each other and yet unable to stay together. What was this fury that enclosed your soul that kept you unfit, useless, captive in a demon's den? Why did he look upon you to tear and claw at your soul? I miss William; I could have had him in my arms right then. Not caring, even willing to confront the demon that kept us apart. What did I care?

It was Christmas and days passed by slowly, leaving dense clouds on my mind. I was practically alone in that mansion. It was not like before; lights shining all over and a giant Christmas tree at the entrance. After little Lisa's death, William did not want to have lights on at the mansion or a Christmas tree. I didn't blame him. I felt lonely; most of the staff had gone home for the holidays. Only Mr. Leeward, the butler, kept an eye on the mansion.

I did not trust Mr. Leeward; I admired him for his devotion toward the English tradition of a butler, of a butler toward his master. William's rules were carried out in the household by Mr. Leeward with haste. No room for faults, for subtle excuses, there were no escapes nor excuses from any difficulties.

On that winter night, the night of Christmas, a current of cold air encircled the hallways and staircases of the mansion. A chill that penetrated through your body and made you run for cover. I wanted to see if William's downstairs office was open and I sneaked into the office. But there he was! Sitting down in that cold anteroom, waiting for the hour to lock the doors, in William's office, the lights, etc., a rigid attitude reflected on his serious face. He stood up and said, "Madam!"

Oh no, Mr. Leeward does not demonstrate all those fancy courtesies with me. Everyone knows what I am. Nothing but a discarded, impudent woman. "Do not pretend, Mr. Leeward, there is no one here now." Mr. Leeward's face did not change. He stood tall and indifferent as if I was talking to a statue—cold, serene, calm, unruffled. I wasted my time; I knew it was useless, inutile to get into William's downstairs office. Mr. Leeward was guarding the entrance as if he were a rear guard Roman soldier.

It was of no use; Mr. Leeward watched the entire mansion with a hawk's eye, his ominous dark clothes and somber figure appearing unexpectedly in front of me, in every staircase and hallway as though he were a phantom. Did he suspect then that I was looking for something? How? I didn't know myself what was it that I was looking for. Mr. Leeward did not allow anyone to stay alone in William's quarters. He stood impassable before the servant until all the rooms were clean; he was in charge of William's closets, his attire, his shoes, those chores he did with prompt accuracy. William's shoes were like mirrors; his shirts, his suits, everything was organized in a military fashion. I wanted to get into William's upstairs office, but I couldn't find the opportunity; the door was always closed. I wanted to find out about anything that would keep my soul at rest; Mr. Leeward kept the keys inside of his vest pockets. I had almost given up until I had an idea. William's bedroom was next to mine but separated by a heavy door. The door used to lock as soon as anyone passed through it. You could hear the heavy thump behind you when the door closed. No one looked back to check if the room was closed. Its heavy hinges closing, the door told you with a loud thump that the door was closed. The person never looked back; one could tell by the noise that it was closed. I gave up; I knew that I couldn't fight William. His control over people used to be rigorous, harsh, severe. I couldn't blame Mr. Leeward; he was following orders.

The sky kept on crying. A fine rain swooping down my heart, wounding it, making it remember Tinkle, my dear little pet, my companion, who shared my pains. He knew my suffering. He was there also in my good times, I adored him. I buried him in the garden, right by the first bench, a place that I chose, where I could see him from my balcony and remember him. It was so suddenly; I didn't notice how sad he looked then until it was too late. The veterinarian told me it was cancer.

"Ms. Taylor," he said, "he lived for fifteen years, a record if you ask me. I had never seen a small dog lasting this long!" I ran out of his office; he didn't understand! I felt as though I had lost a child and he was telling me that I was lucky. I cried for days, not wanting to eat, feeling his small fur warming up my rigid shuddering body. It was fifteen years ago, and it felt as though it was yesterday.

I saw him then. The small monument I made for him. The pedestal was white and his fragile small brown body standing up on top, alert, his little tail up, his big eyes looking toward my balcony, searching for me. *Oh, my little Tinkle, I loved you! Maybe*, I thought then, *I could get another dog to keep me company, to be with me.* I was feeling sad. I guess it was the weather; the endless, turbid, obscure, and gloomy days; the empty house; or maybe I missed William, our lunches together, the friendship that we experienced lately. Why was I feeling depressed? I knew then that I still loved William.

It was New Year's; I could hear the racket, the music coming from other homes. I even wished that I were in a house party, the parties that William used to have. Facing those terrible society ladies like the Richardsons, the millionaire couple from New York. Anything was better than the silence I was experiencing then. I slept most of the time; I smoked weed and didn't care about Mr. Leeward watching me, his blank face not caring. Displaying the same cold attitude.

Lisa, my maid, came to work two days after New Year's Day. She was also in charge of cleaning William's quarters under the strict supervision of Mr. Leeward. I had a crazy idea; I wanted to get into William's rooms. I wanted to browse around, to find anything that will prove to me that William was innocent. I kept on remembering my friend's words, the phantom, as Zoraida and I called Bruce. I remembered that I had his personal card, but where? With all the pills I was taking lately, my mind was confused, perturbed, and dull. I pulled out every drawer, shelf, and nothing. I was frantic. Where did I place the card? I wished that Zoraida was there with me, but she asked for an extended vacation and I gave it to her. I felt weary, tired; there was no use. I lost it. I laid down on the reclining chair and closed my eyes.

This was the perfect time to meet Bruce. William was not at home; the staff was on vacation and, most important, Mr. Leeward was busy supervising Lisa. Then I remembered. I was wearing the jeans matching jacket. The jacket I had on the "incident" day as I used to call it; I never wore it since. It was there hidden in the inside pocket; I was out of the chair like a flash!

"Bruce, it is me, Mary. I want to talk to you! Please, I'll be running—or walking," I corrected myself since I was not able to run as fast as I used to. "I am leaving now, I need your help."

I put on my jeans and a heavy coat as the weather was still very cold. The ground was slippery, muddy, and slushy, covering my heavy boots with a sloppy-sticky mud. The sky was gray and drowsy, a morning dew sprinkling my face, sending chills over my body. There he was, as always, when I least expected him—relaxed, coordinated. He slowed his pace to mine and just said, "Happy New Year." We ran for a while and then stopped on a clear ground away from the drops of dew that were frozen on the tree branches and dropping down hitting us. It was a slight bump that melted down and it hit us.

I said, "Bruce, I am ready to cooperate, but I want you to understand that I am doing this to erase any doubts about William's culpability in this case. I know that right now you don't believe me, you just have to trust me. I will do whatever you tell me to do as long as I feel that you are not trying to incriminate him on purpose."

He agreed. He asked me a question. "How do you want me to help you?"

I told Bruce about William's secretive quarters, how no one was allowed to enter. Mr. Leeward's supervision, the heavy door. "It is very simple, Ms. Mary. Is that heavy door connected to your quarters?"

"Well, yes, it is a very heavy door and it locks behind the person as soon as you pass through it."

"It is very easy, Ms. Mary. Have a card in your hand, and as the person enters, before the door closes, stick the card close to the hinge. The door will look closed, but the card will prevent it from closing completely." Just like that, he disappeared from the meadow, his tall figure gaining speed, flying, spreading his wings like a bird. I stood there stupefied, petrified, all this time thinking on how to get to William's quarters and just like that, Bruce told me what to do in seconds. It showed me a trained mind, a mind able to capture every small detail, to think fast, quick, swift. I turned back, eager to get home to see if I would be able to get into William's quarters. Curiosity knotted my brains with expectations and fears. What if I found something that incriminated William? What would I do? Would I tell Bruce? I couldn't answer those questions then. In a way, I felt afraid. I didn't want to see William being hurt. Why? I asked myself. Did I want to do this?

I came into the house through the garden entrance just one hour away from lunchtime. The house looked empty, desolate, dark. I removed my dirty boots and soaked jacket. On my way up the staircase, I met Lisa. "Ms. Mary, I will bring your lunch if you want me to."

"Thanks, Lisa, I will be taking a bath later." I relaxed in the Jacuzzi, with perfumed candles and salts. I had to think what was it I wanted to accomplish. Was it vengeance that wrapped my heart with a malicious, wicked corruption? Or did I want to protect William? To erase from my mind once and for all, all negative suspicions that I had against him? I knew in my heart that I still loved him. If I could go back in my life, I would not hesitate to be with William again. His kisses, I still felt them burning my flesh. The wonderful times we spent together. His manly perfume, his serene, quiet, unruffled self and fair eyes, like the blue color of the deep sea or blue sky. I loved all of his manly being. Did I also love him when he was abusive? I guess I did. Was I one of those rare creatures that liked pain? Who gets high when her man turns around and demonstrates his vigorous masculinity against a defenseless female? I knew that I couldn't turn around and betray him. Even if I found evidence, I couldn't turn William to the authorities. I couldn't see him being dragged about, living in misery and distress. No, I'd rather see him dead.

"No!" I heard myself screaming, not realizing where the noise came from. It was me screaming. We were meant to die together. It was our fate, our destiny. A macabre appointment. Everything my love, I didn't care what awaited me, as long as we were together. Then I knew what I wanted. Even if I found evidence against him, I would never betray him! I felt calmed and relaxed for the first time in many months. I knew the truth; I admitted it to myself, my feeble, weak, and fragile self; and the truth set me free. I felt almost happy, longing to see William again. Feeling the emptiness of the house flattening me, crushing, smashing me, he called me. It was long distance.

"Hi, love! I miss you. I am staying a little longer, two more weeks, not more. I told Mr. Leeward to call back half of the staff so you wouldn't be so lonely."

"Oh, William, I miss you too, hurry back, love." I could tell that he was happy. He didn't know then and I didn't tell him that I would be lonely with a house full of people if he was not there with me. I asked Lisa over lunch if she had finished cleaning William's quarters.

"No, Ms. Mary," she said. "Just cleaned the bathrooms and shampooed the rugs. Mr. Leeward said that we would finish it tomorrow. I understand," she continued, "that Sir William Bruckner is coming back in two weeks."

"Oh yes," I replied. I knew what it meant: windows clean, rugs shampooed, lamps and chandeliers polished. An army of maids and men cleaning, painting, decorating, the chef arranging a menu. William, on these occasions, had company. Usually male company, the chief of police was never absent on those occasions. People were everywhere, even in my quarters. I had to leave my bedroom; rooms were full of debris and workers. Walls were painted, new furniture rearranged, curtains, bedspreads, pillows, and rugs were changed, my closet set in perfect order. Shoes heel to heel, skirts, pants, and intimate clothing rearranged.

I called Mr. Leeward and asked him why I was not asked about those changes. "My orders, madam," that was all he said. There was William again, taking control, letting me know who was the master. Crushing, pulling apart my only trace of privacy and dignity. My door was changed, a new lock set in. I knew that William had an extra set of keys, my new keys left on top of my new nightstand. My quarters and William's were separated by a corridor, along which, all of William's private quarters were. It was a long and narrow hall. A large round window high up gave some light to the opaque and gloomy hall.

I would wait until Lisa was scheduled to finish William's quarters and then I would try to get in. Everything by then would be set, walls painted and his quarters in military order. I had to be careful. I must put back everything exactly the same way. Mr. Leeward had hawk's eyes; he could detect the slightest change in William's quarters. I asked Mr. Leeward if it was okay for Lisa to come and help me after she finished cleaning up William's quarters. "She will be there, madam." I wanted Lisa to come back to my quarters through the small hall that separated my quarters from William's quarters, not for her to exit through William's quarters outside corridor to the main staircase and toward the rest of the mansion. I wanted Lisa to come out through the back door, the door that led to the small corridor and into my quarters. I stood in the corridor waiting for Lisa to come out so I could place the card close to the hinge and see what happens. Lisa was carrying so many cleaning utensils that she was hardly able to get out of the heavy door. I had no difficulty in placing the card by the hinge. I heard a heavy thump after the door closed after Lisa went through it; I thought that the door was really closed and that I couldn't get into William's quarters. But as soon as Lisa went through my door, I tried the heavy door.

At the beginning, it was difficult for me, as the door did not have a handle to pull it. But somehow, after trying to ease my fingers through a small opening, I managed to get the door open, being careful to remove the card before the door closed after me. And there I was, for the first time, standing in his secret room! My heart was pumping wildly. There was the smell of William everywhere. I felt as though I had walked into a secret place. Afraid to move, uncertain, doubt filling my mind with fear, I approached a large mahogany wall unit. How many hours would it take me to browse through all those drawers and doors? No way. I knew that anything of importance, of value would be placed in the high doors and drawers that were locked; it was of no use. I turned around and left. I didn't even try to look into the connecting rooms. What for? It was like a fort. I asked myself, When will I be able to browse into William's quarters again? I didn't know what was it that I wanted to find.

Was it a predicament? I didn't know. Somehow, someday, I would find out, I was sure of that. I did miss William, but I felt that being back with him again, I would lose the little freedom that I was enjoying then. In my new quarters, I could not smoke weed nor could I go into any excesses like sleeping for long periods of time, etc. I would feel that William could burst into my quarters once again and for any reason at all attack me. I had that fear! I longed to be with him, but for the first time, I was afraid of William. Well, at least there was still a lock on the door. It gave me a few seconds to react in case of trouble.

I called Zoraida and told her everything. She was not happy about the new changes. "Don't you see," she said, "it is all a big show to mesmerize you, to interfere, to influence, to impose upon you his will." I knew she was telling me the truth, but I couldn't help myself. All those months I longed for his kisses, his lovemaking. I knew I was enslaved to his will, a masochist. A weak person that likes to be flogged about by a dominant male, to enrage and abuse. A feeble woman that thought she was in love. I had to think, I had to go out. I put on my boots, sweat pants and a heavy jacket. I was out walking, running.

The snow that a week ago was crystal clear with specks of ice shining through the sun's rays was mushy, dirty, and slippery on that day. I couldn't run; I couldn't take the risk of falling down. I didn't want to spoil William's arrival. The cold air felt nice on my face. I met Bruce. He asked me what had happened. Did I uncover anything? I explained to him my experience.

He reflected a moment and said, "It is a job for a professional." He looked into my eyes and knew. He read a hesitation, a consecrated devotion in my eyes, and didn't say anything. He understood; we never spoke about it again. I lost the only friend that could have helped me; I didn't know it then—I had made the biggest mistake of my life.

William was coming early in the morning, arriving at Kennedy Airport at 6:00 a.m., will be at home about 7:00 a.m. No traffic at that hour, the expressway would be free. I couldn't sleep that night; I couldn't take a sleeping pill. I was afraid that I wouldn't be ready on time. I wore a rose-pink-colored long-sleeved gown and gold sandals. My long shoulder-length hair was loose and I wore a light-pink makeup. Everybody was in place, the staff checking out every little mistake. Mr. Leeward was giving out orders right and left.

The entrance was packed with flowers and exotic plants. New rugs, artwork, and paintings were rearranged. The smell of flowers filled the senses. The king is coming, I thought. There he was! William, the elegant, the proprietor, the authority, and respected owner. A big smile, shaking hands with Mr. Leeward, telling him the wonderful job he had done, and then he came to me. Those shining and beautiful eyes smiling at me, telling me that he loved me. We kissed for a long time, not caring about the staff nor of ill memories.

I felt his hands opening my blouse, caressing me. He picked me up and carried me up the stairway and into my bedroom. We did not come out of the bedroom until next morning, eating very little out of the tray that Mr. Leeward sent to us. The next morning at eight, we went down for breakfast. Our eyes were half open, traces of a sleepless night reflected on our faces. I could hardly eat. Why, I thought, couldn't we stay in bed for a week?

After our second cup of coffee, we looked better. Mr. Leeward approached William, handed him something, and proceeded to ring a bell. All the staff came over and surrounded the table. William stood up and handed me a small blue box. I knew that it was probably jewelry, but I was afraid to open it. What if it was one of William's practical jokes?

I said, "Oh, William, you shouldn't have." I opened the box with trembling fingers; it was a big solitary diamond.

I heard William saying, like in a dream, "You are my fiancée, the only person I wish to share the rest of my life with." I started to cry, big tears falling down my cheeks. Lisa was crying too. Oh God, I wished that Zoraida were there with me! I kept repeating to myself, "The woman I love," those sneaky words I heard William say to Mrs. Blake many years ago. For the first time, I felt truly loved and that I belonged in the house. Not just an old house guest that was kicked about at William's whims but someone to reconcile with, to be respected. I was called Ms. Fletcher from then on; I liked that better. I sensed the respect that members of the staff displayed toward me. Not like before with mocking eyes and a sneer reflected in their faces. I was so happy; I knew it all the time—our love was to last forever.

I felt as though I had met William for the first time. He was a different man, patient. His eyes didn't have the sparkle, glitter, splendorous look as of before. Eyes that looked as if they were dreaming; a faraway look that lets one know the languor, the decay of his soul. I was happy; I wanted to think that he was happy too. We sat in my sitting room for hours, reading, talking.

Walking hand in hand, we looked as if we were the perfect couple; but underneath reigned doubts, uncertainties, and hesitation. I kept up my guard, trying to read on his face any trace of violence, feeling afraid every time I heard the key opening the door. I was alluring, trying too hard to please. He sensed this attitude on my part, and it probably made him feel doubtful, perplexed, and empty. I knew that my fears made him nervous, but I couldn't help it. There were too many "incidents" in the past, I didn't feel completely secure. Dread filled my clouded mind with fears. It was going to be that way, I couldn't help it.

In a way, the living arrangements I had with William before turned better for me. I had no fears of William bursting into my quarters. I knew a new lock was placed on my door. A lock was no impediment for William to come in, but at least, I had some time to react, to respond to any of William's "incidents." I used to feel free, a relative freedom, of course. I knew then that I was still confined to William's dreadful and rude, bestial attacks; but for some reason, I cannot explain today, I felt safer. However, being his fiancée at that time gave him some legal discussion in court.

If anything happened, a lawyer would argue my credibility: why did she accept to be engaged to someone that treated her so badly? Was this engagement ring a mendacious object, I asked myself, that kept me bound to his imprudent attacks? Everyone, staff members, saw the love on his face, the diamond's splendor, and I accepting his offering with love and tears in my eyes. A perfect alibi in any court! I kept on adoring William even with all those fears pounding my mind. I tried to brush away any rapacious thoughts, I wanted to enjoy those beautiful moments with William. The William that I was enjoying then. The elegant, courteous, transparent, loving William. Not that other self, the sardonic, dreaded, and rude man. That was not my William.

Time kept passing by, measuring every split second, crawling slowly, sneaking into your body silently, softly, a hushed breeze touching your body. One cannot feel its gentle weapon strike in silence, its thunderbolt aiming at the world. No exceptions, no pity, no mercy. That's the way I felt when I looked at myself in the mirror. Was it yesterday, or was it twenty years ago that I was pretty, desirable? Not like the image reflected on that mirror, with wrinkles around my mouth and eyes, my neck filled with lines. A bulge under my chin and my blue eyes losing the sparkle that made them beautiful a long time ago. But time passes, desiccating you slowly, touching, creeping. Even my dear William looked worn out with age, stricken by years.

The thunderbolt of time struck William's mother. The fragile, stern old lady collapsed, her lineage of aristocracy forgotten, her station in society under six feet of dirt. They called William, telling him that he must go immediately. When he left, Zoraida and I started to jump around, celebrating the fact that we were going to be alone without William's constant observation and disregard for our privacy. We walked through the meadow, singing, laughing, chanting like two excited parrots out of a cage. We couldn't wait for William to go; of course, I had to pretend that I was sorry. Thank goodness I had never met the lady. I had never visited England; it was a forbidden land to me. The land of William's ancestors, the land of his loves and misfortunes. I just wanted to be with a friend, to talk to Zoraida, to share our laughs and our pains, to walk and jump, walk through the woods, rest on the meadow. Pick wildflowers and come back home with rosy cheeks, matted hair, and bright, shiny eyes. We talked for hours under an old oak tree or sat down on the garden bench looking at Tinkle's statue, remembering him, the time when he started to run away from me, his small frame hardly visible through the grass, barking, tearing at Elizabeth's gown. How did he know then that she was my rival? He also knew when William was in one of his dark moods. He used to warn me! My little beautiful dog!

Zoraida and I had a wonderful time; we sneaked a bottle of wine and paper cups into the woods, far away from the watchful and vigilant eyes of Mr. Leeward. Zoraida was a new woman, not that very young girl who came to me when I needed her the most. She had become a refined lady; her two boys were twelve and ten years old. She didn't work for me anymore; she was a friend, someone that visited me three times a week to keep me company, to guard me from the uncertainty I was suffering then.

She knew I couldn't help myself, and she used to worry. We walked or ran when she came in, laughed and giggled like two teenagers, confiding our innermost feelings to one another.

We were sitting on a stone, right in the middle of the meadow. A soft sun was warming up the chill of a young day, laughing. I was looking at my diamond ring, turning it around again and again. Zoraida knew something was bothering me. "Tell me, Mary, or I wouldn't be able to sleep." I told her about my fears, the engagement, and the display of gratitude to reward me, the ostentatious and boasting vanity in front of the staff. Even the fact that Mr. Leeward was the one who kept the diamond, not William; it was not like William. Never before had he brought the staff into his private life. It was unusual for a lord to intermingle with any staff member. Just a century ago, no member of the staff talked directly to their masters. William would not break this tradition unless something was in his mind, but what?

A display of new rugs, furniture, lamps. The exotic plants and flowers of different colors throughout the house. My new furniture, the diamond ring. Giving the staff a long Christmas vacation and huge Christmas bonds. The fact that Mr. Leeward kept the diamond ring instead of William. The prompt arriving of the staff, as if they were expecting the call. William standing up and handing me the diamond, instead of kneeling down as it is supposed to be. Telling the staff members that I was the love of his life, the woman he wished to spend his life with. Lisa's tears, my tears. The respect that the staff granted me from then on sounded very suspicious to me and especially to Zoraida.

She said to me, "Mary, you have to be on guard against any of the old tricks he used against you to set the staff, doctor, lawyers, the police, and everyone that you were in contact with against you. If he starts a fight, get out of the house or open the doors, windows so everyone will be aware of his ill temper. Be careful with the stairs, go through the back entrance. Promise me, Mary." Zoraida was practically in tears.

"I promise you, Zoraida," I said.

Chapter 13

Zoraida came to visit me about two days after I told her of my fears. While we were sitting, resting, and drinking the last drops of wine in the meadow, I told her of my fears of William maybe trying to trick me once again, making everyone to think that I was demented. Zoraida visited me on one of those lazy days full of sun and the smell of flowers, feeling the air. She looked very excited and refused to speak to me inside the mansion; we went running. It was not unusual for us to go out running when the weather permitted it. I was anxious to stop and find out what was it she had to tell me. We sat on the same rock that was in the middle of the meadow, perspiring, our throats dry with the excess of heat. We drank greedily from our water bottles and proceeded to look everywhere to see if Bruce was following us.

No sign of Bruce. After a small pause that seemed to me forever, Zoraida started to talk. She said, "Mary, listen carefully to what I have to say. I was worried about you when I left you the last time that I spoke to Bob about William. I just told him that you wanted to find out about William's background in England. That we had tried to look on the computer but couldn't find anything." Bob knew a fellow who was a computer brain. He had the ability to get into files that very few people could get into. You can imagine, I was jumping up and down when I heard the good news.

His name was Robert. He worked in the basement of a dilapidated house in the Bronx. Bob did not want me to go in. I sat in the car while Bob talked to Robert. I was anxious to find out about William's history, a past that seemed to be wrapped around his somber presence. But I was nervous; I was not sure if I really wanted to know about William's past. I heard Zoraida speak as though we were in a tunnel, the sound of her voice tumbling around my turbulent brain. I took with trembling hands the report that Zoraida gave me. I had to sit down to gather all my strength. Inside that envelope laid the truth about William, and I was afraid to find out what affliction had he done to others that he hadn't tormented me with.

I couldn't open the report; it lay on the desk for two days before I had the courage and the strength to open it. I read with trembling hands that report, asking myself why I wanted to mortify myself. I knew very well the results. Would I leave William? I think not. I read that his mother, Lady Helen Portberg, had disinherited William after all the scandals, commotions, shameful and disgraceful rumors, and violent passions. William was notorious for the seduction of young girls and the habit of excessive drinking. The mother, in an act of desperation, managed to marry him to a nice society lady. Finally, William was arrested; his wife accused him of domestic violence. He was disinherited. The legal papers stipulated that Lady Portberg and Sir Ronald Portberg will provide William with a fair allotment if he was willing to leave England.

That was more than twenty years ago! About the time that William and I met. I kept on reading: violent passion, drinking, seduction, defilement of young girls. *How could you have degraded yourself, deluded your family and lied to me!* He probably inherited a large amount of money when his mother died, which doubled in value in the United States as the English pound was more valuable than the U.S. dollar. The ingrate! The detestable, despotic, alluring, and rude man. The sick, mendacious liar! I took off my diamond ring and threw it away as far as I could. I didn't see Bruce, but he approached me and simply said, "I believe this ring belongs to you." And just like that, he disappeared as fast as he had appeared. Zoraida and I looked at each other and laughed. No wonder we used to call him a phantom!

Why was William giving me the honor of being his fiancée if he could now have any society lady? He dreamed of belonging to the "cream of the cream" to one of the most powerful, ancient, and distinguished society, a society of famous kings, princes, of descendants of earls, dukes, lords that distinguished themselves in the battlefields, and he chose me? Practically a hick, no education, titles or honors. I was a regular woman who achieved some fame while young. Even my beauty has been taken away. The thunderbolt of time aimed at me, touching me throughout the years with its hushed gentle breeze, leaving in my body the havoc of its force. There was no doubt in my mind then that William was trying to get rid of me, but how? He was still handsome, tall, rich, and belonging to a powerful society. A magnificent marriage for any English society beauty. I felt jealous; suspicion filled up my soul with dreadful vengeance. He cannot do this to me! I thought as if William had scruples or any tenderness of conscience. He was the same rude, manipulative, and despised human being I knew. I had to play my role; I couldn't let William know that I was aware of his background, nor of his recent achievements and possibly devious plans. He thought I was an idiot, a complete deranged and ignorant person; maybe I was! It was going to be very difficult for me to play the role of a feeble female again, a devoted human being that believed in him. How could I look at his face and his eyes and not see my dear William, my hero, the man I loved?

I came home from my daily walks desolated, as if I were sinking in a stagnant marsh, trying to grasp at anything that could help me out; instead, I sank deeper into its sluggish and dirty mud. It seemed to me then, that I had squandered away my life. I felt unwanted, discarded. I went into my quarters and cried. Rage shocked my body with furious spasms. "You," I cried, "malicious, treacherous, avaricious, and wicked example of a human being, I'll show you!" I was warbling each word with a rage that left a rancid, stale, and bad taste in my mouth.

I met William for the first time since his absence. I thought, The king was coming! The staff was running around, making everything to look perfect. There he was! A perfect example of a male figure, his tall frame almost touching the doorway! The perfect human being, affable, kind, agreeable, the female members of the staff practically drowsing on their feet. He came to me, his manly perfume exhaling, reaching me. He looked different! Younger, not wrinkled around his mouth, around his eyes. He looked twenty years younger! I knew then, "plastic surgery." Another sign of his obvious plans. He was going to be looking for a young society lady. Very young, preferably a virgin. He used to hate everything that was previously used. I stood in his way. Imagine William introducing me to a high-class society. "This is Mary, from Bloomington, Monroe County, in Southern Indiana." They would probably think that I was an Indian. They would probably gather around me to hear the sounds from savage Indiana.

Instead of a long kiss, he gave me a short disgusting, repugnant kiss, with the excuse of being very busy. Lord Kentville was coming to dine; the staff was moving as if a tornado was about to hit the mansion. Running, gathering, setting the table. The cook, the menu, everything had to be perfect. Mr. Leeward knew how to direct, control, and demand the best from the staff, no problem. William went up the stairs without giving me a glance. I felt humiliated, discarded. A look of pity was reflected on Lisa's beautiful dark eyes. I had better get used to it until I discovered his plans. How he was going to get rid of me? Will he let me go free, knowing all of his secrets? Will he take a chance of letting me go, the risk of scandal that would wreck his most desirable dreams? He was too smart to provoke a wounded lover. Someone like me, mad enough to bring to justice the ruffian that devastated my life. There are three ways of getting rid of a foe. One is the most common—a knife, a gun, anything that could cause injury to the foe. The second one is the sneaky, devious ways used mostly by women—a venom, a poisoned ingredient that has saved the lives of many women, like the life of Joanna, the "crazy queen of Spain".

The third way of killing is the most dreadful, callous, and barbaric way of discarding an enemy. Lots of care while in front of others and then when alone, destroy the person's vital qualities by mortifying, afflicting disgust, making the victim think that he or she is wrong. Alluring, making the person think that he or she is at fault, working on the fibers of the brain. Usually, the victim is taken to a mental institution or he or she dies with an overdose of drugs. He or she doesn't have to do anything to kill that person with their hands. The victim does it. A perfect alibi. Everyone feels sorry for the perpetrator. They would whisper, "The suffering, the patience that he or she went through taking care of the deceased. What a pity!" The next day, he or she will go to see their lover or sit next to a lawyer to receive the inheritance, the perfect crime. The perpetrator wraps its evil abuse in the fiber of the brain like a small worm named convolvulus that wraps itself in the vines and destroys the plant. Obviously, knowing William, he will use the number three option. It will be perfect for him. A perfect lover taking care of me even though I was in a mental institution, giving me presents, making me his fiancée. The perfect setup for a perfect crime. He was the heir of an estate; misconceptions were forgiven, his faults, deceits, and mistakes thrown in the scale of power. It could be a cheap fiction play. William was out most of the time, traveling to England, setting up his business, keeping an eye for any young virgin that holds a title. It was best for me; I did not have to listen to his cold words or feel the despise, contempt, and disregard displayed toward me when he was home. I had to endure it if I wanted to win. It was a battle of two Titans. Which one of us would succumb, yield, or sink under pressure, I didn't know.

I had time to think, to analyze, to set in order the events of my life. I thought of Bruce (the phantom); of course, he knew as an FBI agent. He probably investigated his past. He knew what William was capable of doing. He couldn't tell me. He didn't trust me; he knew I was too much in love, I wouldn't understand.

William arrived yesterday. I didn't see him until early that morning. "Come down for breakfast," he urged me. "I miss you. Sports clothing, we'll go for a walk after breakfast."

I was excited. Maybe everything that I suspected was a figment of my imagination. Trying to control my inner feelings, I tugged my sports jacket and went down for breakfast. I could always sense William's feelings at breakfast. Under the carcass of his inner self laid a pool of somber, anguished feelings he used to hide from me. We were too much alike. I asked myself while I was observing him, Why the pain, mistrust, and the suspicion reflected on his eyes? The heir to a vast estate, recognized in high-society circles, he had everything he used to tell me that they took away from him. Something else was bothering him. It couldn't be me! He had left me before for a poor young girl. He could have done the same thing again. He knew I was too much in love and mentally unstable to make any sort of trouble. It was something else, I will find out, I was sure of it!

We left through the garden door, into the terrace, and toward the Zeus family. Zeus's thunderbolt aimed at the sky, ready to strike, crowned with an olive wreath personifying victory. The eagle on his left arm signifying that he was the king. Apollo the averter of evil presiding over religious laws and expiation, his manly parts covered; not like Zeus, completely naked. The statue of Hera, his wife, was there and his daughter Dione, or Diana. The whole family that I hated so much was there, staring at me. Diana pointing her arrow at me, a crazy look reflected in her eyes, the entire family chasing me away. William stood there! In reverence as if they were gods. I couldn't take it anymore; I pulled away from William and started to walk away. William hit me on my shoulders with a discarded piece of wood. I looked with horror as he was coming toward me, grasping the piece of wood, a crazy look reflected in his eyes.

"William," I called, "wake up, do not let that demon take hold of you! It is me, Mary."

He stopped as though he was in a trance. He looked down and let the piece of wood go. Crying, we embraced, both of us crying, kissing, crawling, creeping, dragging ourselves on the ground right in front of the odious Zeus family, William's heathenism gone for the moment. We were too much alike, as if our souls were chained, captured, seized forever.

We came back home with a look of lust reflected on our faces, happy, exhilarated. Eager to soak our remorseful selves in a tub of hot water. I cannot explain to this day what happened in the garden in front of all those statues. Was Diana aiming her arrow at me? She was known for the lust and sharp aim, I will never go to that part of the garden again. For the first time, I felt ashamed of our lovemaking. It was not like before, full of love and enchanted magic. It was lust that drove our bodies together that morning, as if we hated each other and wanted to scratch from our bodies the remains, the last vestige from a past love. William was away from the mansion most of the time. I guessed he had already found another girl, an English lady, not an uneducated woman like me that took his abuse without complaining, protecting him, giving excuses for his erratic behavior.

Zoraida came this morning; she brought me the most adorable little dog! It looked just like Tinkle—brown and black except for a white mark on the tip of his tail, a red ribbon around his adorable neck. I cried. I thought that the good Lord had sent Tinkle back to me! I named him Tinkle. He was my lost Tinkle.

"Zoraida," I said, "you found him." I was not alone; I had Zoraida and Tinkle, but something was missing. Deep inside of me, I knew what it was. Who else but William? I tried to disregard it but didn't say anything; Zoraida could see it in my eyes. Tinkle and I took long walks in the garden. I let him loose to roam around. He used to stop at Tinkle Number 1's statue and piss on it. I didn't mind; he was marking his territory. He used to run after a ball, his little body lost in the tall grass. His barking pierced my ears, but I didn't mind; I loved those moments together.

The news was all over the Internet, the newspapers, TV. Sir William Bruckner married Lady Jean Sokolvsky. The ceremony took place in Dublin, Ireland, in Saint Patrick's Cathedral. Reception was held at the Blarney Castle. I remembered my grandmother telling me about Blarney Castle. The various white towers that shine under the sun, its beautiful terrace along the banks of the River Liffey. The land of my ancestors, Dublin, my grandmother's place of birth, my inheritance.

How could you, William, marry another woman in Ireland? I wanted to see Ireland so much but never pressed you to take me. I could almost see the towers of the Christ Church Cathedral. The limestone cliffs and caves along the northern coast at Portrush County. Now I will never visit Ireland again, my child dreams gone forever. He had taken everything from me. He left me naked of soul.

Chapter 13

Was she beautiful? I didn't want to see her pictures then, but later on, I ventured to look at a picture of them. A honeymoon around Europe, including Russia, where her relatives came from. Oh, William, did you remember me in Rome, when we tossed a coin in the Trevi Fountain? Or across the Tiber climb, the Fontana del Gianicolo, the Eiffel Tower, and Notre Dame in Paris? She was probably tired of touring all of those places. But to me, it was a wonderful experience because I was with you in all of those places that we only visited together. They were magic to me only because I was with you. I knew that you remembered me. You probably avoided those intimate places where we were together. She looked beautiful. Almost like I was when William and I met. Tall, blond, and blue eyes. Languid, sensual, and lustful looking like I was, tossing my hair, moving my hips every time I passed a group of hicks in my hometown. She was engaged twice. I wondered if at seventeen years old she was still a virgin and if William had the surprise of his life on his wedding night. Good young girls of today could care less what men think about virginity. I wished then that she was one of those modern girls, but maybe she probably had a Russian upbringing where tradition is hard to discard.

I passed most of my time reading. Mr. Leeward stood by me while I chose the books that I wanted to read, and then he locked the library after me. I didn't think any evil thoughts about him; after all, I was not William's fiancée any longer. Just a visitor. I read all day. Tinkle by my side tucked on my lap looking out at the blue sky adorned with a mix of bright colors, a tribute to the sun before it withered away, toward the west. Zoraida came to visit me; she was astonished by the way I looked. I didn't go running for a while; I didn't take Tinkle for his daily walks. I just showered and jumped into a clean pair of pajamas and read, ate very little. I guess that I must have looked terrible. William dismissed half of the staff before he left and took Hector with him. Good, I didn't want Hector driving me around telling me how lucky I was. My driver's license was due for renewal a long time ago. I couldn't rent a car or purchase a new one. I was lost. Zoraida said she would drive me. She wanted to take me to a Broadway show and afterward to a restaurant. How could I be without William? No, I'll wait for him! I knew that he was going to come back. Zoraida did not want to hear about it! She had the Broadway tickets. Went to the closet, took out one of my gowns, and told me to hurry up. We had a long way to travel.

I pretended to be happy. To ignore the fact that I was happy only when I was with William. I couldn't forget the wonderful moments we spent together. The years of faithful resignation. Years of cavil trying to escape from all our difficulties. The devoted and pious feelings that I demonstrated toward him. Even murder, my dear William, I tried to conceal to save you. I had lived with the fears of dreadful attacks. I laid my chaste and wounded dignity at your feet. Asking very little. Dark thoughts came into my mind. Sitting down in that restaurant with Zoraida until I heard Zoraida say, "I wonder if he said anything to that innocent girl that he married that he couldn't procreate." I laughed out loud without realizing it, slapped the table with my hand, at the same time I said, "Aha! There goes the malicious liar again!" Will she find out about it? I wondered. Maybe a malicious person was waiting for the proper time to tell her and I laughed. A laugh that was like a thunder; it cleared the clouds away from my tormented mind. I couldn't deny then that I was jealous of a young girl that was miles away with my lover. A lover that had confined and defiled my honor, my dignity, and had left me alone, desolated.

I came home feeling different. Going out with Zoraida, I experienced a fling of liberty, something that I had not experienced for a long time. I felt somewhat different in a way of thinking, of course.

I made a decision after spending days thinking what was it that I wished to do. First, to feel free. I would have to renew my driver's license. The mansion was too far into the woods, and there was no transportation for miles away. I lay on the divan thinking and reading, giving myself all kinds of excuses why I shouldn't go and get myself a car. Why should I wait for William? Didn't he leave me before? Didn't he come back after Elizabeth? Even his marriage. I gave an excuse for why he couldn't marry me. He would have lost all of his privileges, the money that the mother used to send him. His social status. I knew that he shouldn't ever marry me. Why complain now. I had lived under that shadow all my life with William, and I didn't care. Why now? All of these excuses I was giving myself until I received a telephone call from Joe. My partner in the Joe and Mary Bar.

"Mary," he said. "I am tired. I am old now. Some of these tough young punks are very violent now and I had to hire bodyguards. It is not like before when we used our fists. Now they come with assault rifles. They don't care who they kill. It is getting dangerous."

"Joe, please give me a week," I said. "I will be there next Monday. I know you are closed on Mondays." The punks are too sick to go to work or too sick to drink.

I had to do something to get away from the prison I was living in. I had no choice. I dressed and went to renew the driver's license. I called a taxi, simply telling Mr. Leeward that I will not be in for lunch. I left in a taxi. I told the taxi driver to take me to the Department of Motor Vehicles. "What for?" I was surprised when he asked me that question. "Well, Miss, they have different departments, in different buildings, in the same area, of course."

"Oh well," I said. "I want to renew my license." He didn't say anything else and drove for about one hour and said, "This is it, Miss!" I was afraid of what to do. Which door! I felt as though I had just come from Bloomington, like a hick. If I felt this frightened just to renew my license, how would I manage alone? It made me think of how protected I had been. How would I be able to survive, to strive in a world that I didn't know? I felt as though I was in a vessel between wind and tide. Not knowing which way to wield, to arrange the threats of my life, to knot together the difficulties of my life. I felt afraid. I was ready to run back into the protection of my quarters and never get out! Oh Lord! I prayed. I was ready to turn back, to suspend that madness, to give up.

I closed my eyes and looked for the taxi. He was not there! I was used to being driven. For the first time, I missed Hector and heard his words pounding in my head, "You are very lucky." I asked myself, "Am I really lucky?" At that moment, I thought that I was. I didn't even have the taxi driver's phone number. I leaned on a wall, and I started to cry. Tears of pain, tears of rage, of fury. As if William had cut one of my arms and left me abandoned in a dangerous world, in a different world, full of mysteries.

I didn't know how long I was standing against that wall when a security guard approached me and asked me if he could help me. I told him I needed to renew my license. "Follow me," he said. Following was what I always knew best to do. I followed him as though I were a little dog. Like my Tinkle, following me throughout the garden.

Oh, I wished I was in my garden. I didn't know if I wanted to do this. There I was! In a long line, waiting and waiting. I felt cold, hot. I wanted to go to the bathroom; will I lose my turn? Of course. I looked at the customers' faces and decided not to move. There were lots of arguments. People yelling. Customers arguing. Why would you take my license away? How would I be able to feed my family if I can't get to work? There are no buses or trains close by me. You cannot take my license away! Another customer saying, "I only had a martini, why don't you close up the bars? Oh, oh well." The guards came and tried to detain him. There were others that were complaining and saying, "How could I pay $200 for a fine? I only make $150 a week, and I have three children." Others were crying, cursing, babbling. The horror, the pain. I flew out of that place as though the devil was chasing me.

Outside, the cool air felt nice on my face. Then I remembered my cellular. Operator 411 answered, "What state? The number is . . ." I realized that I didn't have a pencil! I heard with trepidation the operator say the number for the last time and then a long trifling noise that told me that the line was closed. I had to call Mr. Leeward. The only number that I remembered. I swallowed my pride and called. I tried to act cool, composed, but it was of no use; my voice was trembling.

"Will you please send me a taxi, Mr. Leeward?"

"Where, madam? Of course, madam." Just the sound of his voice made me feel comfortable. I sat in the cold bench that surrounded the building. A beautiful garden full of sun, and the smell of flowers. A peaceful atmosphere. So different from the uncertainty, the labyrinth and obscured atmosphere I experienced inside. I came back trembling, thanking the good Lord for blessing me. I remembered Hector; maybe he was right. I should be grateful. I came back home feeling grateful. I took a look at the mansion for the first time and saw its beauty. The gray structure with its large windows and its deep-set arches and manicured garden. The gray stone and marbled fence. The iron gates that opened by pressing a button. The beautiful background of peaceful gardens and tall elegant cypresses. Farther up, a forest of hazelnut, cashew nuts, hickory nuts, pecan nuts, where I loved to run and pick up nuts with Zoraida, just like I used to do with Betty. A paradise for me! I didn't need to be in bars or in those buildings, nor did I have need to run fancy restaurants and magnificent shows to be contented. I was a farm girl. A girl that looked upon nature and saw its beauty. I was also a woman in love, and a frightened sparrow.

After the incident at the driver's license building, I was scared of facing that world outside again; there was only misery. As if facing death in the world I used to live in was not misery enough! I guess that is the way humans are. One gets used to misery, poverty, ill treatment. I read somewhere that hostages get used to their environment, and with time, they even get to idolize their captors. We are like children. Some of them grow up with very little to eat, in a very poor environment, and yet they don't realize that they are poor until someone tells them. Or ugly until someone makes fun of them. Just like me. I didn't know I was mentally imprisoned. Held by a despotic tyrant until it was too late, no one told me. I continued with what I thought was my pleasant life, full of luxuries.

William and his bride took a long honeymoon for six months. I had plenty of time to think, no worries. I decided that I was going to enjoy those months the way I used to like it best. Running, running to exhaust myself, to fatigue my body, to weary, to erase from my mind the confinement I was subjected to. It was better not to think, to live in a make-believe world. A world full of fantasies and enchanted dreams, a fancy world, a fake world that did not exist.

What role did I play in this drama? William's bride probably knew about me. Would she ignore me and play the role of a wife, that untouched creature that the law protects, providing them with half of the husband's estates and the custody of their children? It's like having a loaded gun aimed at the husband's head. I was sure that Lady Petrowsky knew about me. The question was, how would she get rid of me? Will she wait in the castle like a snake, waiting for the right moment to strike, to spread her poison on me? Or worse yet, will she wait, serene and poised, while spreading rumors, talking to the press through a friend, making me know when William was with her, treating William with love and understanding. Waiting like a snake in her dark cave until scandals are so vicious that William will have to dispose of me? She will win! I will be photographed with lovers that she will contract to discredit me. Or will she be like Queen Catherine who ignored her rival Anne Boleyn and kept on adoring King Henry VIII through Lady Boleyn's manipulations, even making his shirts with pearl buttons and lace. She died on her bed while the fake queen Anne Boleyn was executed.

In my heart, I knew how it was going to be. I will be docile, obedient. No fuss, hardly known by anyone. William knew what he was doing. The slick panther waiting in the tall grass, watching, plotting, to finally ambush his victim. I couldn't talk. Who would listen to me? The crazy lover. The ingrate woman that had caused William so many problems. She is unfriendly, doesn't like to go out. Locks herself in that mansion as though she were a wolf. I couldn't win. I knew it was just a matter of time.

Zoraida said to me, "Mary, what are you waiting for? She will probably complain about the cost of the mansion. They will probably sell it without you even knowing about it. What is keeping you?"

I finally admitted to myself I was afraid, afraid to face the world. Every time I thought about the experience at the driver's license building, I trembled. What had happened to me? I faced a lot more troubles when I first came to New York looking for a job, getting practically thrown out of that building. My career, my traveling alone. Me, facing the world all by myself and never feeling scared. Somehow, I had to face that world out there again. I had to find the courage I had before.

It took a lot of courage to do as Zoraida told me. She wanted me to buy a car. "Mary," she said, "you are rich, wake up! You can buy the car you wanted. I will take you to a dealer. He will tell you what to do. Don't worry!"

There I was! Sitting down in an office, facing a stranger, a fancy office on Sunrise Highway! I was nervous, he probably noticed. He invited me to look at the cars. They were parked all over the office. Red, white convertibles, two doors, trucks. I didn't know which one of those cars was good for me. The dealer introduced himself as Bill, made me feel comfortable.

"What do you need the car for?" he asked. I didn't know what to say. "Well, let me help you. Do you have children? A business? Do you need the car to travel long distances, to different states? No? Well, can I make a suggestion?" he said. Sure. "This Mercedes Benz 550, two doors, sporty looking, is the best car for you. We have it in different colors."

I sat in that car for the first time in many years; it made me feel somehow different. As though I could have conquered the world on those four wheels. Yes, I love it. I was very choosy about the color. It was a brown, almost a gold color that they had to paint especially for me, at a cost, of course. "How would you like to pay? A loan or lease?" A lease, loan, I was confused. He explained and asked, "Do you have a business?"

"Well, yes. I owned half of a bar downtown, I have a partner," I said. I called Joe. Joe gave him my bank account. He made some telephone calls, and bingo! I leased a brand-new Mercedes Benz.

"You can come and pick it up in two days."

I was so happy! Zoraida and I stopped at a coffee shop and had breakfast at two thirty in the afternoon. They took care of my license, everything. I didn't have to face those large lines or feel afraid. I felt happy.

However, I had one big problem: I had driven very little, and that was thirty years ago. I remembered when I was still living in New York and visiting William on weekends. I needed transportation; I had to rent a car. That was when I first had my license. I didn't drive a car for a long time; therefore, I felt very scared to go into highways. I drove at thirty miles per hour. Cars were beeping, cursing me: "Lady, get into a retired home! What's the trouble with you, need glasses?"

To my misfortune, that was a very modern car and I was not used to all of those electronic devices. It was raining, but I was not sure which button to press to activate the windshield wipers. There I was, in the middle of a highway, and I didn't know which button to press. I stopped on the side road and started to cry. Pressing buttons, feeling old, almost incapacitated. I didn't know how to set the mirrors. Police cars came. The first question was, "May I see your driver's license?"

Well, I was carrying a large bag. To save my life, I couldn't find the accursed license. I could see that the officer was starting to get frustrated. I looked at him with tears in my eyes and told him, "I had left it on top of my night table."

"Give me your telephone number and I will call. Is anyone home?" he asked.

"Yes, Mr. Leeward, the butler." He looked at me with suspicion reflected on his dark and penetrating eyes.

He positioned himself away from the car to talk. He came back and said to me that someone was bringing the license to me. I confessed to the officer that I had just leased the car. I didn't know how to manage the electronic devices. The officer showed me how. The car that half an hour ago looked to me like a space rocket, I realized, was very easy to manage. Press button to answer the phone, to set the mirrors, open the skylight, lock the door, etc. The license was brought to me by a fellow I hardly saw around the mansion. He used to tend the horses, but after William sold the horses, he was a helper, doing whatever Mr. Leeward told him to do. His name was Jeff. It was the second time that I had to call Mr. Leeward for help. A good record. Two out of two. What's wrong with me? I thought. I had to calm down, be able to think. I was so used to other people taking care of me that I was losing the ability to make important decisions. I had to stop being afraid, to resume the courage I had once. I felt ready.

The speedometer at forty miles per hour and then fifty. The police car followed me for about five minutes. No problem of how to get to Joe and Mary's Bar. It was programmed into the GPS. To come back, I will have to press Home, and the car will take me back home. I was surprised to see Joe. He looked old and tired. Weary face and sunken eyes, his face almost white. The lines about his mouth told me of all the hard work and frustrations. He flashed a big smile when he first saw me. I could tell that he was happy to see me. The smile as I remembered—white teeth and large wide lips. His eyes lit up when he saw me! As if someone had turned on a switch inside of him. We sat down with a cup of coffee to talk. We had to resume, to renew our old friendship, to get acquainted all over again.

He was not feeling well. He had a hernia operation from lifting all those cases of liquor. His wife had divorced him. His children were doing well. Joseph Junior was graduating college in three months, and his older child, Arlene, was married and working as a registered nurse at the Presbyterian Hospital in uptown New York. I noticed that he was very proud of his children. I was listening with a sad passive look that I knew was reflected on my face. I felt sad. A languid feeling encased my soul. I had to talk. I couldn't sit there with Joe and pretend that I was happy, that my life had been the sublime dream of every woman. I confessed to Joe as if I was in a confessional booth and a priest was sitting down on the opposite side of me. Tears came down in a rapid stream. We were alone in the bar. The dimmed lights from the wall lamps cast a shadow on our faces. He was surprised, and then he was mad.

"The bastard!" he said. "Just tell me when, Mary, and I'll have that despotic assassin banished from your life!" We talked for hours about our misfortunes and about our happy times and business. "Mary," he said with a serious face. "Because of your absence from the business, when we sell, three-fourths of the profit will be mine. Your contribution toward the business thirty years ago was $100,000. Today, you have in your bank account the amount of $400,000, a lot more than a bank would have given you in interest.

"They have offered me close to one million dollars. Mary, we don't have to sell," he told me. "We could work together."

"No, Joe, I can't. If William walks into this room right now, I will run to him and melt in his arms. The psychologist said it is a disease. You see, I have been infected with this plague called crazy love."

William came back to me a year later. I thought for sure that he was never going to come back, but he walked right into my arms, happy, displaying the flickering flame of his desire in his eyes. Telling me that he adored me. I was so different from Lady Jean Petrowsky. She was cold, conceited, and arrogant. I was perfect. Docile, innocent. He said, "You waited for me, you knew that I would come back, that I loved you." Those were beautiful days that ran into weeks and then into months. Four months we spent together. Four that were for us like heaven. I didn't care if we were enclosed in a cave. I was with William. Oh love, I thought then, why couldn't you be a regular fellow? Not a lord. I would have loved you the same way. For richer or poorer, in sickness and in health, I am married to you. Even if no man ever pronounced those words to us. They were written in the sky. Our love was eternal, endless, everlasting.

It was time for William to leave. "When will I see you again, love?"

"I'll be in touch. I have a different cellular. Hector keeps it with him. Remember, he will answer the phone and take the messages."

I hate to talk to Hector, his attendant, his plotting friend. How many secrets did you keep? Do you know what triggered William's madness? Why did you keep quiet and didn't warn me? Didn't advise me to run away, to save my life?

I kept quiet. I didn't want to spoil the beauty of those four months. He left specific instructions to Mr. Leeward. "Yes, my lord." William was called lord after his title and his inheritance were restored. I could tell that he was proud. Life after William's marriage was not pleasant in the mansion. I liked it better before; no one had their evil eyes on me then. The press was following me, asking me questions. "Are you Lord William's fiancée?" "No, I have never been his fiancée." "What are you, then?" "I am his guest. I'd appreciate it if you do not disturb my privacy." I kept on running, sweat covering my face. No makeup. My hair in a knot. My long and skinny legs looking like those of herons, and *flash!* My picture was in every magazine and TV news. Oh my dear Jean! I knew then what will be your strategy. You will sit calm and tranquil inside your lair, protected inside your cave while others stained my reputation. You had turned out to be a snake, sitting, waiting for your victim to be devoured. Displaying an innocent look while suffocating her. Playing the role of an innocent victim. Never complaining. Listening to William's complaints with devotion, tears of understanding bathing your eyes.

Do not worry, I thought then, that she was telling William. She probably was like a lioness, waiting in the tall grass, silent, reserved, waiting for the male lion to go forward, to begin the chase. She helped bring down the prey. Ferociously ripping the carcass away. Enjoying the feast. Everyone will get their turn in the feast, the vultures, jackals, and birds. She would morally destroy me, I thought. Pictures were circulating in magazines. Showing every wrinkle on my face. My skinny and long legs like two old long sticks. She was on the next page. The innocent young victim with lots of makeup, wearing a long gorgeous light-green gown. I thought then that I wouldn't ever win. There were many obstacles in my path. I was on William's mercy. I was afraid that eventually he would despise me. A desperate woman in love. I would have done anything to keep William; I had the trump card. I could have won that game. I would have let the secret of William's sterile condition float in the air. Its evil thunder will strike her and leave her tormented, anguished, dried. Like I was when I found out about William's condition.

But I couldn't destroy her. She could have been my daughter. The daughter that I fancied being in my arms a long time ago. She will find out about it in time. She could have been an heir to the vast Bruckner's inheritance. A vast inheritance obtained by William's great-grandfather before the first WWI. Importing to England merchandise from India and China. A rupture in William's marriage will be the loss of some of his inheritance. A blotch on his newly obtained social status. I kept quiet. I knew that if William found out that I was the pivot that could remove the mask of his hidden secrets, he would hunt me down, wherever I hide, and kill me. I thought that killing me would be more compassionate. I asked myself, What will my life be without William? Jean won; I knew that she would. There is always a lover in practically every man's life. The wife always wins over the lover. The wife has the house, the kids, her furniture, his life. The wife is bound to win every time.

I didn't care about any of his belongings; the trouble was that he did. How could he leave all the efforts his great-grandfather must have expected to push his grandson into an ancient noble and stratified society? Even I understood. I would have never imagined wrenching away a title or a position to get inside high society, as one or two ladies of lower social status had managed to do to acquire a title. I just loved William, as simple as that.

The communication system took away my most precious gift—my privacy. Even running in the woods that I used to love so much. The press had cast a cloud on my daily walks. I had to run through trees and bushes, getting stung by bees, and ants, and needles. Coming home to see a car stationed at a distance, watching, watching every one of my moves.

I was afraid to go and visit Joe or Zoraida, the only two places that I ventured to escape when William was not around. I did what I had always done when confronted with a problem that I felt I couldn't cope with. I tried to escape through drugs. I slept most of the time. I liked hashish. It was a slower high. It wrenched away my troubles in a slow sublime manner until it left me hanging in a cloud, my pains drifting away. They were left way below where there was only dark. I sat under a tree, the smell of spring filling my senses. The moistness of the winter passed, reaching me, wrapping me, reaping my troubles away, not for long, of course. Pain was embedded in me. It clung to me. Clawed at my lacerated heart without pity. I felt as though I was suffocating. I had to get away. To see someone or just talk.

I took my car and, without thinking about it, headed to Joe and Mary's Bar. I was programmed just like the car! A ringing bell told me when to turn. Take the right lane, the left. I felt as though I was possessed. I couldn't turn back. I sat at the booth with Joe. I couldn't talk. Joe saw the condition I was in and reached my trembling hands to console me. *Flash!* The light from a camera blinded me momentarily. Joe chased them, cursing them. There were pictures all over. Is he her lover? TV cameras showed Joe's bulky and tall figure chasing them away. It looked bad; we were holding hands. Like two people in love, my eyes cast down, a loving innocent look on my face. The paparazzi were experts in deceiving. Debauched individuals whose positions were and are to inflict pain or to take anyone to the highest pinnacle. I didn't blame them. There were also honorable broadcasters and newsmen who exposed their lives and had died to broadcast the news. In my case, it was as though a judge had passed sentence on me. The verdict was death.

I never told William about my car, my license, my business with Joe, and my partnership with Zoraida's brother, Omar. Why? I always used to complain about William's secrecy and there I was doing the same thing. I took it for granted that Mr. Leeward would inform William of all my moves. I mistook Mr. Leeward's integrity. He would only answer William's questions. He was not an informant. He was a respectable figure. It was Hector, of course, that used to keep William informed. Did William know about my business ventures and was watching me, testing my loyalty, my integrity?

Well, I thought then that as soon as I saw him, I would tell him, hoping then that the pictures of me and Joe did not affect him as it would before. I was nervous I could hardly sleep. I lived on pills and on hashish. Pills I drank on late afternoon, and hashish during the day. Of course, I always found an excuse for slipping three or four pills during the day.

Instead of William coming to New York to punish me or call me from London demanding an explanation, I heard with doubt the news. "After three years of marriage, Lady Jean Petrowsky and Lord William are expecting a baby, an heir to the vast Bruckner estate." The news depicted William with a broad fake smile and Jean showing the small and cute figure of a pregnant woman. I knew that it was not William's baby, but did William know about it? Oh my Lord! I thought to myself. William would kill her! Could I warn her? I thought about Elizabeth and erased from my mind any desire to help. I had warned Elizabeth and had always felt guilty about my advice to her. No, I thought. William wouldn't dare kill such a high-society lady. Her relatives would be chasing him like a pack of wolves after prey,

William called two weeks after the pictures were published. I didn't know what to say. Too many things had happened, and I was confused. To my surprise, he didn't mention the fact that I was in Joe's bar and that pictures of us were taken holding hands. Why was he acting so cool and composed? This was not like William. That was not my William. The macho man, the rooster that keeps his female hens secured in their nests. Tending his offspring while he secures his territories from other roosters. Climbing onto a fence or trunk to sing, a yell that challenged any male, a shout to defy, to dare any other rival to death. That was more like my William.

I received a telephone call from William months later. "Love, I'll be seeing you soon, arriving this coming Monday. I'll give instructions to Mr. Leeward."

"Great, can't wait to see you," I said. The king was coming! Mr. Leeward hired some help. William had dismissed half of the staff and he needed some outside help. Everything was ready early Monday morning. The smell of the flowers reached my senses, almost choking me! Too early in the morning for me. Everything was ready, even breakfast was set in polished silver trays to keep it warm for William. I stood at the foot of the steps, dressed in a flowing floating gown and open-toe sandals, my hair loose upon my shoulders. I thought that I heard the trumpets blasting away. The noise of a car arriving. Someone rushing to open its door. The king had arrived. Mr. Leeward said to him, "My lord, welcome home!"

He stood there handsome as always, flashing a wide smile at me! My knees doubled up, I felt as though I was falling. I had to hold on to the balustrade before I flashed a big smile at him. We kissed.

"Love, wait for me here," he said. "I am going to freshen up. Mr. Leeward, please, breakfast will be in fifteen minutes."

"Yes, my lord." That was all. I waited impatiently, restless, fidgeting, with the small purse hanging about my shoulders, the smell of food filling my senses. I felt hungry for the first time in months. I did not have the opportunity to wish him well. To congratulate him for the baby. I was going to act as if I didn't know about William's sterile condition. I never told him that I knew. I swallowed my pride back then. I was not letting him know that I was such a naïve person. I blamed myself for not being able to conceive. I was glad on that day that I didn't tell him and that I knew of his devious manipulations.

There he was! Standing tall and handsome. Kissing me. The smell of his skin, the feeling of his manly organ reaching out for me. We had to abruptly separate and sit down to eat. I reached for his hands and said, "I congratulate you, William, with all my heart. You know how much I love Catherine and the children. I will love this baby as well."

We went for a walk through the garden. His face showed the impressions, the tracks, the prints of a wounded soul. We were twin souls. It was something that even I couldn't understand. We sensed each other's feelings. Our souls infused in one thought, sharing our thoughts to one another without talking. I knew that he was disturbed, distressed, but kept silent. I didn't want to bring about his evil self and spoil our first encounter since five months ago. Why was William so sad? Shouldn't he be happy? Did Jean have a lover? Did William know about it? There were so many questions that I asked myself, but I couldn't find an answer. I thought then that it was better to ignore the problem and concentrate on our time together. After all, I thought, I felt lucky that William had not mentioned the incident with Joe and me. He probably knew about the paparazzi, I thought.

"Love," I said to him, "why are you so sad? I want you to feel free and happy when you are here with me. There are no problems or obstructions waiting for you here! I am all yours, there are no prints, no existing past memories that your love cannot erase. I never loved anyone. There is only you."

He stopped, kissed me, and said, "I love the new you, the refined lady that you have become. Yes, let us forget about any problem. Here, there is only you." We kissed, a long loving, sublime, and marvelous kiss. I felt my knees trembling, the strength of my body plundered away. We were like two turtledoves, encased in a cage, not caring what happened outside its cold bars. Snuggled together, happy, and free. Good and bad things always come to an end. A Spanish proverb says, "There is no illness that lasts a hundred years".

We said goodbye. I was bathed in tears. William came back again and again to kiss me. I couldn't go to the airport to say goodbye. The cameras were there like a pack of hyenas ready to devour its victims. After his departure, I didn't see William again for the next eight months.

There I was, counting the days, the hours, the minutes. Eagerly reading every scrap of news to know what was happening in William's life. There were no telephone calls. Nothing. Even Mr. Leeward was concerned. I tried to call several times, but the cellular that Hector kept had the same message: "The box is full." I couldn't complain. That's how lovers are supposed to behave. We entertain husbands. Listen to their complaints like their wives were loving and sexy looking, but after two or three children, they become fat and tired. They were only interested in the children. When I worked in the bar, some of the girls that worked with me had married side lovers. They even had to give them money. They couldn't afford a side lover. Just for a while, they would say to me, until he gets a divorce. Our place is in the red zone. We had the time to listen, to enchant their fantasies. To have sex every time they wish to. In this environment, he is free of bills, kids, electrical or plumbing problems, the roof not leaking. Men feel well in a place where they are able to relax, to feel free. We don't ask about their whereabouts. We don't care. There is always a roll of bills left discreetly on top of the night table. Practically every man that has the position to have a side lover set on a house or mansion will have a woman that is willing to live under these conditions.

Sometimes these women will have one or two children practically hidden away in private schools. However, there are the majority of men that cannot afford to have a woman set in a house. There is always a sexy office girl that is willing to listen and let them come into their apartment. Those are the worst. They are liars, cheaters. They are psychological murderers of both. They are liars, cynic, detestable, brazened, and vile women. They set one woman against the other, covering their meager self with feathers of chastity so they could float in the putrid waters of their existence. I was a lover, yes. But a dignified one. I did not go around talking evil about William's wife. I was first in William's life. I did not need his money; I could have lived on my own comfortably. I was his sweetheart only because I loved him.

William was always talking about Catherine. He knew the inheritance would always go to a male descendant, his heir, and now Catherine had two lovely boys and a girl. William was so happy when the first male child was born that I didn't see him for one year. He called me practically every day to tell me about little Edward. Finally, he used to say, I have an heir! I suspected that it was why William had his vasectomy done. He did not want Jean to have a baby as his heir. He only wanted Catherine's descendants. He did not expect to have a young and smart girl for a wife who probably suspected his plans and tried to resolve his sterile condition by having a lover. It was obvious that she didn't know about William's sterile condition. When William knew about the lady's planned pregnancy, he played the role of a devoted spouse up to the last minute. Being with her all the time. Tending to all her desires, bringing presents to her. He was a fox. In a fox chase, trying to outmaneuver the foxhounds by digging numerous foxholes, leaving their scent in different places to confuse the hounds. Running in different directions to give their lives in exchange for their brood's safety. That was William; he would give anything for Catherine and her children.

He came back to me after a year of plotting, of deceiving like a sorcerer, roving about in the nighttime, casting spells, bewitching a young girl with presents and love to implement his devious plans. It was a boy, beautiful and healthy. A little angel that was born. William insisted on having a DNA test before he would recognize him as his heir. Checkmate. She was outmaneuvered by a devious, wry, and impudent individual. William had a herd of lawyers planning, conspiring in his favor. The DNA test decided by 1.0 percent that William was not the biological father. Legal documents depicted William's condition to conceive. Therefore, the inheritance was passed to his descendants—Catherine's children. Well planned. He was telling me about all of his plans. Except of course, the part about not being able to conceive. He omitted that very important part to me. He did the same thing to me, or worse, at least she had the courage to get a lover, someone to love and to give her a baby.

I was taken as a naïve fool, my dreams cast away, leaving me dried and resentful. He was denying, refusing to admit the evil he cast upon my soul. I kept quiet, my heart beating wildly, a bitter taste in my mouth, the smell of infamy in the air. William and Jean separated, but were still married. Somehow, I did not feel happy about the fact that William was all mine then. We didn't have to pretend. We were free of the press. Nothing changed between us. He was still traveling three, four times a year. Business was growing. He was part of the 1 percent in the world—the billionaires that hold the world's pillars. William worked hard on the years that he was cast away, forgotten. He traveled, investing his money, making friends, building his own future to present it at the proper time. He didn't go into his inheritance with empty hands. He sat on the board of directors with something to offer, his head high above the respectable middle-aged gentlemen that sat on the board, full of dreadful speculation and unaware of William's hawk tendencies. He had them in the palms of his hands, and they didn't know it.

"Gentlemen," he said, "I came to this board not to waste my time, but as president of this organization that is rightfully mine." At that same time, six lawyers walked in, reading a drawn statement, the retiring of his father from the board and business because of old age and mental conditions, the mismanagement of funds. Every one of those charges were backed up by numerous paperwork, which were distributed among the board members. A roar as loud as a herd of wild elephants filled the large room, a shout of protest from the delicate, sweet, and dainty old gentlemen, their faces red with anger.

William was prepared for such outburst of protests. Two nurses walked in to keep his father out of the head seat of the board, and sat him on his left. William sat at the head of the board. And from this seat of power, he said, "Gentlemen, do not mess around with me! As the Americans say, I could take you one by one and send you to the pits of hell. I beg you, do not try."

They all looked at William's father; they saw the resignation and submission and abnegation reflected on the old man's face. "Like father like son," someone got up and said: "Gentlemen, we have to vote on this matter. Please say aye and then stand up if you approve of William Bruckner for president of this organization." There was a huge roar as chairs were pulled back, falling on the floor, a shout of aye filling the room. Only the father did not get up. Tears of remorse filled his tired eyes. William went to him and stood next to his father and helped him out of his chair. Another applause filled the room. Congratulations were handed left and right. The same gentlemen that one hour ago were full of futile, trifling, worthless, and intense conclusions stood under the huge skylight that embellished the ceiling, surrendering their pride, their haughtiness to William. He won! He was the king. The male lion that fights to death to win another lion's pride. A roar like thunder bounced about the deep extensive jungle. Claiming his rights, subjugating the members of the flock, he is king. He kills and eats the little cubs. Only his seeds will prevail from that moment on. William followed the jungle rules step by step and won. I was fascinated when William told me about all of his adventures. Somehow, it was as if I was living it myself. I admired him so! I couldn't wait to see him again; it was better this way. I didn't have to live afraid. I thought that he had changed.

William was fond of children. He adopted Jean's boy who had no rights to his vast inheritance. Funds were provided for little Peter. Jean was born in Ireland after Ireland's independence from England, running away from an oppressive Russian system at that time. Jean insisted, and she was adamant about having little Peter baptized as Catholic, which was her religion. William didn't care about religion. You could see that he loved the boy. He was often photographed with the four children around him, a big smile on his happy face. Sometimes when he was with me, he would tell me that he missed those children. It was not like before when Catherine's child died and he knew about it in the newspapers. He was in control. He could see Catherine and her children every time he wished. They often had lunch together, or he was invited into their home. He could see little Peter every time he wished. He made sure it was stipulated on the legal adoption papers signed at that time. The adoptive father Lord William Bruckner could call one hour before he visited or take little Peter Bruckner Lord William's adopted son for walks and fun times during the hours of 9:00 a.m. through 7:00 p.m. William had everything covered; he was the boss. You could see that he was satisfied with himself. I guess he felt free. I wished I could also feel free. What was that mental cloud that was afflicting me? I didn't know. I lived only for William. I didn't exist.

I knew then why William did not contact us for such a long time. After almost eight months, he called me and told me that he was coming. The house was alive again with the arrival of William. People running all over the place. The mansion looking its best since many months. He looked confident, haughty, proud. There was something different about William that I perceived right after I read his eyes. He walked straight and swollen up with pride. Rapid, long, firm steps that covered in seconds the distance from the car toward the entrance walk, and to the front steps of the house. Displaying an intellectual power, letting us know of his higher, greater, and superior power. He had changed, I thought then. There was something about him that I could not recognize, a different William, like someone carved out of a discarded dried piece of wood and turned into a masterpiece of art. I knew then that he considered me as his slave. A docile creature that he manipulated at his will. I asked myself then, What can I expect of this sudden change? I was soon to find out! For the first time, William was telling me about all of his legal and business deals. Talked about his family, the children, Catherine. That's how I knew about all of his activities of the past eight months. The DNA tests, the adoption of little Peter. His position as head of the board. Everything said with an arrogant attitude. As if he was standing on, top of a rostrum, and I was one of the audience subjects. I waited until he finished with all the slurs aimed at practically anyone that had come in contact with him. His business association, members of the board, his wife Jean, just about anyone that happened to stand in his way. I listened patiently until he finished. We were in his bedroom and I was standing up, looking at the garden.

From his balcony, I could see the odious Apollo and Zeus statues. I turned around and asked William, "How did you know that little Peter was not your child?" I saw his terrifying eyes, and I knew his answer, how did I dare such questions, was I questioning his manhood? Had I been unfaithful to him with that repulsive Joe? I just looked at him, terror clasping me as he came closer to me, his old despotic self casting a somber shadow over his tall frame. He pushed me hard, throwing me against the light curtains that covered the wide doors that led to the balcony. I thought for sure that I was going to fall down the balcony. Luckily, I was stranded in the mist of silk curtains that came down over me, as if I were in the middle of a web and a big spider was about to get me. I just lay there while I was trying to untangle and get free from the silk wrapped around my body. I didn't know how scared I was of William. Certainly, I remembered the last time when he pushed me down the stairs. Since then, I had become more submissive, fragile, and more afraid of his outbursts of anger. I knew what William was capable of doing. I had felt his anger and looked into his eyes on fire. I knew then that he could kill, that William was a killer, a murderer. Suspicion distressed my mind. The ruffian! He was mad because he didn't want to admit that he was barren. He was not the male lion that could engender cubs and spread his seed. He was the man that left me dried, alone, with no children to hold.

I laid there, wrapped up in a tangle of silk, looking through the curtain's transparency the face of William. Nowhere to run, trapped. The cool air that came through the open balcony doors lifted the silk from my face at intervals, exposing through a blur of silk the menacing face of a killer. He stopped, fists clenched, ready to give me a blow that will send me to the hospital or to the cemetery but stopped suddenly. The expression of his face changed. A heave lifted from his wide shoulders. Somehow, with the change, he didn't seem as tall as before. The evil twin of his subconscious mind had lifted, blown away. The evil that possessed him, torturing his soul, had left.

During the next weeks, he took control of the mansion, giving orders, changing things. Meals taken downstairs. No more business with Joe. His address erased from the GPS. Copies of the car keys given to Mr. Leeward. Copies of statements of my business given to him annually. I was only allowed to visit Zoraida and Zoraida to visit me when he was traveling. Proper dress attire when seated at dinnertime. He let us know who was the boss. He had control. He was leaving in three weeks. For the first time in many months, I couldn't wait for William to leave. He mortified me in different ways. He had a banquet given in honor of Lord Kentville. I was never allowed in the past to sit in his business gatherings or dinners. There were never ladies on those reunions. This time, however, there was a woman sitting in the middle of all those gentlemen—me. Because it was a formal affair, the table was set with all the protocol that the occasion demanded.

There was silverware displayed at each side of each serving. I did not occupy the seat of honor, either to his right or to his left, but I was tucked in the middle of two very stiff and distinguished-looking gentlemen. I was so confused as to what silverware I should have taken I was tempted to get up and run away from the table. Mr. Leeward was supervising the staff. His duty was to see that everything worked to perfection. I was perplexed, confused as to what to do. There were so many goblets and wineglasses. I didn't know what to take first. Mr. Leeward noticed my confusion and immediately sent with discretion, a member of the staff to help me. I was completely ignored by William. There were presentations and toasts to practically everyone while I sat there taking all the humiliations. I felt like a discarded old piece of rotten wood. I learned my lesson—never again to question William, to dare, to challenge the boss, the king. He certainly let me know how insignificant I was. I faced my poor and proud Irish background, against the haughty lords and superrich businessmen with dignity. No pretense on my part. I told my background to the gentleman next to me. My career as a model, etc. He was fascinated with my life as though I had landed on earth from the moon and all those life misfortunes existed in a faraway unknown land. I made one friend. William kept an eye on me all the time. That was my time to ignore him, but I wouldn't dare excuse myself and leave. I didn't know if I should stand next to William and thank the guests as I used to do in the past.

Mr. Leeward saved me. He announced, "Gentlemen, drinks and cigars are being provided in the next room." He practically pushed me to stand close to the door. Standing there, I said thank you to every member of the party that were going into the room, a room that was forbidden to women. I practically ran upstairs. I turned around and looked into Mr. Leeward's sad eyes and said to him, "Thank you." A complete stranger felt compassion for me, prevented William from making a laughing show out of me! How cruel, hardhearted, merciless human being he was! I couldn't wait to get into bed and take my pills. I thought of taking all of the pills at once. No, I said to myself. I had to know what happened to Elizabeth and to Betty. I had to know!

Long Island is beautiful during the summer, its extensive landscapes shining through the thick forests next to the pale sea, thrashing above the rocks with force and then fainting delicately upon the sands. Its suave rhythm enchanting, charming, fascinating you. The smell of flowers reaching your soul. I walked through the night; I didn't care about feeling afraid. Tinkle was by my side, smelling, running as though he was also feeling the night's beauty. It was a long walk. My feet tramping on the humid undermold that covered the ground where the tall grass grew. I had to carry Tinkle.

His little teeth showing, somehow he jumped off my arms, his little body disappearing through the thicket and tall plant's blades, me following his bark with a flashlight. There he was barking and moaning, his beautiful fur straight up like a fan. I cried out. The odor of death reached me. I could see bright-colored garments, mixed with bones and dirt. I ran out.

Somehow, the night's enchantment was gone, the putrefying odor of death surrounding me. I couldn't think; I just wanted to get out of that place. Dark shadows followed me. "Can somebody help me?" I was screaming, running, running. The grass blades scratched my tired legs. Far away to my left, I could hear the rumble, the clamor of the passing cars traveling on Ocean Parkway. I didn't know I had traveled so far; it looked to me as though I was traveling in circles, lost somehow in a jungle and wild animals following me, my mind, like my body, going in circles too. Is the killer following me? Am I stepping on the discarded bodies of some other victims?

My heart accelerated its rhythm until it felt as though it was going to come out of my mouth. Finally, I perceived at a distance the cement bench, the solitary square with its dense yellow light. The empty parking lot closed. It was not a safe place to be, but at that time, I had to sit down and think. I should call the police, but I was concerned about the paparazzi and all the fuss and trouble that they could bring into my life. I didn't have to give my name. What if the remains were those of Betty or Elizabeth? And William knew that I had found them?

I couldn't call the police just then. Police cars would be around Oak Beach in no time at all. They would stop me for questions. No, I thought then. I will wait until I reached the mansion and then call. It was half an hour later when I finally reached the mansion's garden. I sat down on the garden bench and called. "No," I said to the police. "I don't want to give my name. The killer could come after me."

The police searched the area. Trained dogs ran, sniffed, their teeth showing. A great show for newsmen parked in the Oak Beach parking lot, waiting for relatives, shoving their microphones on their noses. They were hounds too, with teeth just as sharp as any shark waiting for its victim. The relatives of those young innocent girls. The police were investigating. Waiting for the DNA tests. "It's a long list, we are doing the best we can," so they said. Zoraida came. I wouldn't talk to her over the phone. She knew it was something important. We clung to each other, waiting, praying that the body that I had discovered was not the remains of Betty or Elizabeth.

13 Consequence Street

It was all over the news! The remains found in Gilgo Beach were those of Elizabeth Pattini. Her picture was all over the news. She was seventeen years old.

I cried for days, remorse invading my devastated soul, dreading William, knowing that the man I loved was a killer. Her parents were the worst. Praying to the Lord that they will find the killer, knowing very well that it was William. They said that it must have been Elizabeth's boyfriend, Paul Taranto, who killed her. The Police Commissioner said that Elizabeth's case was not connected with the serial killer case and the numerous ladies found in Gilgo Beach. As if running away with your lover was a transgression against the law and that deserved the penalty of death. A phone call to Mr. Leeward. "I heard the news, be there as soon as I can, alert Ms. Mary," William said. Was I ready for the big show? Could I look into his eyes and still love him? Forget his murderer's instincts, his shady and gloomy self? A killer that discarded the carcasses of young girls and then seemed oblivious to his murderer's instincts, to all the pain inflicted on those girls and their parents? Well, I didn't know if William was the serial killer. The police said Elizabeth's case was not connected with the serial killer case. I knew deep in my heart that he killed Elizabeth only.

I didn't see him come in. He arrived at Kennedy Airport at 2:00 a.m., a big show of sorrow, grief, affliction, and mourning displayed in the funeral parlor. Elizabeth's parents and the Police Commissioner were at the mass. William showed a shady and gloomy face to the press. Another victory for the champion of deceiving. To delude, to impose upon its victims a shroud that will cover their souls forever. I was not allowed to be present in the events. Too many victims gathered in one place. I was glad; I couldn't stand next to William and pretend to agree with William's sardonic behavior. Instead, I decided on hashish, looking out the sky, stars shining far away, the cool breeze of May surrounding my body. It was all a bad dream, a nightmare. The pain that lacerated my heart was gone. Ripped off my life until morning. I didn't see William at all. He came in the middle of the night and left the same way. He tried to avoid the press. They asked him, "Lord, was Elizabeth Pattini your girlfriend? Did you know her?" No comment. The mothers and relatives of the Gilgo Beach victims were there.

Elizabeth's parents answered all the questions. "No, my daughter was not Lord Bruckner's girlfriend. He just wanted to help my husband and me. Why don't you ask the same question to Robert Tarantelli?" The old fool probably thought that Elizabeth's boyfriend killed her. But why was she covering the fact that William was her lover? I will not be influenced by their hypocrisies, their expressions of sorrow, their lack of dignity. Her parents were hyenas, feeding on the carcass left by the lion. William came in the night and left the same way. He probably didn't want to see me. Didn't want to read in my eyes his wickedness, the abominable corruption that dwelled within his soul. Just as well, I didn't want to see him either. I didn't know that he was gone.

Were the rules that he previously imposed still being followed? Breakfast, lunch, and dinner at the table. I didn't know that he was gone. I went down the steps, looking out, feeling my way through the corridors like a soldier in enemy territory. Feeling the terrain, ready for an ambush. Expecting the enemy around every corner. I yelled out in fear when Mr. Leeward turned around the corner and into the corridor where I stood. My knees trembling, he had to hold me, help me to a chair. I was embarrassed; Mr. Leeward knew. I didn't have to pretend.

"Lord Bruckner left early this morning," Mr. Leeward told me.

A sense of fear flushed out of my body. "Thank you," I said and ran out of the dining room, up the stairs, along the corridor and into my room, my heart accelerating, relief bathing my body. I felt free! I changed into jeans and went out into the woods. It was safer out there!

I ran away from the pestilence of Gilgo Beach. They were searching for more cadavers, their hounds creeping, crawling, dragging along their masters, sniffing the air. Their cries rebounded against the loneliness of that early morning and reached my ears. I didn't want to hear; I wanted to forget. I went far away into the woods. I saw my old friend, a hollowed-out old trunk that lay in the midst of a tall grass. I sat on its humid and crusty bark. How long has it been since I saw you fall heavy with ice on that early cold winter morning? I had heard the screeching howling as though a shout of pain and then the hard thump against the icy floor. How long have you been lying there? I asked myself. It was just like me, carrying along the harshness of time, experiencing the rigors of nature and its beauty. You are probably still lying in the middle of the forest. Rotten away, eaten up by ants, like the vermicides that are eating at my soul today, tormenting my mind with remorse, uneasiness, missing William with all my heart. Two winters had passed by, approaching the third spring. Little birds nesting, the sun's warm rays touching the earth with an explosion of nature's best.

Flowers emerged from its stems. The moss rose of Portulaca crawling in the garden with its yellow, pink, and orange blooms. The California poppies filled in the rocks and harsh terrains, the buttercup, the hepatica filling the woodlands, crawling on top of decayed leaves. Pink rhododendrons filled every corner, tucked away, resting against fences, changing colors. Pink and blue flowers everywhere. Roses that crawled up to my balcony, leaving a delicate perfume into my quarters.

Lady Jean knew from the beginning that I was not a threat. She had to deal with William, and that was not an easy task to deal with. She could not get a divorce without losing custody of little Peter, but little Peter was ten years old then and in private schools since he was aged seven. She owned the mansion she was living in. It looked as though she had accumulated enough wealth to ask for a divorce. Outside of a monthly support, which amount was not stipulated, she did not receive, as previously agreed, any part of William's inheritance. In case of Lord William Bruckner's death, custody of little Peter would go to Catherine. It was a harsh decision for any mother to be subjected to, but Lady Jean was in love, and as I well knew then and even now, she would have given her life to keep her lover. William drifted away from me like the leaves of autumn give way, carried by the wind, to far meadows, to lie still, tumbled on by the harshness of winter.

He came to the mansion after about five months, or was it six months? I had stopped counting. He looked old, beaten, fragile tears reflected in his tired and still beautiful eyes. "What's wrong, love?" I asked. He said to me that Lady Jean's lawyers had found a break on William's harsh custody settlement. Jean insisted back then on having the baby in Ireland. William gave way to her demands. Ireland's court demanded that since the minor Peter Bruckner was born in Ireland's soil, therefore, the child was an Ireland subject and documentation to be included in both parties' legal papers. This was Ireland, the land that suffered under the strict orders of a new religion, established by King Henry VIII and followed by Queen Elizabeth I. The sacking of every church in Ireland and England, to enrich the coffers of the throne of England. How dare them, the lord and lawyers shouted, the child is an English subject. Lawyers waved documentation, sweat dripping out under their white wigs.

William won, only financially. Jean could not keep up with the expenditure of the lawyers. Jean's rebellious attitude left a sour mark on William's tired soul. He came home devastated. He called me and said, "Love, I'll be home soon." He called the mansion home. That was the first time he admitted that the mansion was his real home. My heart was full of expectations. That was the longest period that William spent with me since he first married Lady Jean. Catherine's son Edward was the heir of his vast fortune, and he was being trained by an advisor and by William. Edward used to travel to New York City. I had seen his pictures. A handsome, tall young man. He looked to me so much like William when he was young that tears welled up in my eyes. I remembered beautiful times. Times of love, beautiful, and also of lonely memories. The fight for the custody of little Peter left William with a feeling of vulnerability. He was challenged. The old tired lion was afraid of competition. He remembered what he did to his father, and now he felt he was in the same situation. His plan was to release some of his power to his grandson, Edward. But what if his grandson was a devious and rapacious as he was? The old lion afraid to be challenged by a more young and vigorous male. He was back to his old tricks again. A despotic, gloomy self. I knew what he was thinking. I held a secret against him; my secret's name was Elizabeth. Did he see her in my eyes? Was his conscience tormenting him? Was he so fearful of defeat that he had to prove his manhood over defenseless women?

Back to his old tricks again. He disappeared just as before for one or three weeks. Coming home with brand-new clothes all proper. A new haircut and manicured hands. He seemed oblivious to what was happening around him, relaxed, eased, less tense. He would stay away from me and then burst into my quarters impromptu without regard to my privacy at all. I had to pretend that I was glad to see him, that I didn't know that he was home. I couldn't tell him that I ran to the other side of the mansion throughout the corridors to spy on him. To see with my own eyes how fatuous and incensed he had become. "Love," I said, "you look as though you have been chased by a phantom. You need something to relax." I handed him a drink. I noticed that encouraging words, easy, slow movements, and a soft calm voice quieted his soul and made him feel relaxed. We sat by the balcony, the smell of the roses filling with perfume our nostrils. He looked relaxed than the real William sat next to me.

Forgetting everything, enjoying the warm rays, casting away his gnarled self. Furbishing his soul with calmed, and relaxed thoughts. That was my William that sat next to me then, not that odious, evil being of before. The mansion was his home. He tried to stay away from England as much as he could. Only Catherine and his grandchildren he wanted to see. He told me of all the progresses his family was going through. The kind and easy character of Edward and James and of little Catherine. A proud smile was reflected on his face when he spoke of Peter.

"You know," he said, "that Peter is all Bruckner. He earned the respect of Edward and James, not by being nice, but by the strength of his character. He set straight the boys at the school that tried to make fun of him because of his Irish background and religion.

"The school administrator used to call me and complain about Peter using his fists, but I did not pay attention to their calls. Why didn't they talk to the other children? I was so mad that one day I took the headmaster by his neck and threatened to kill him and told him if I withdrew the funds donated to that school, he would have lost his position. That finished all the complaints. Checkmate. I could see that Peter was more qualified to carry the burden of the vast enterprise than Edward was." He seemed to be a devoted, rude, and walloped young boy, a frank attitude reflected on his self. He was just like William, as if he had engendered him! His pose, his manners, his looks. My life kept on running away like a frightful rabbit, afraid of predators hidden in its den, looking out to the bright sun, enjoying nature's beauty, crawling inside in cold winter days. The mansion was William's home now. His business was conducted in his private office downstairs. We never shared the same quarters. I thanked God for it. Nevertheless, every time he wished, he would come in. I made sure that he would find a peaceful atmosphere. He looked lonely. He knew that I was the only person he could trust. That's how I knew about his business deals and about his family cares and problems. I couldn't wait for William to leave the country, to go and visit his family, but he looked tired. Ready to capitulate. The old rooster falling down, its crest down, a look of defeat reflected in his yellow eyes. But, he stood his ground to death. William was sixty-three years old, but looked as an old refined man that he was. The few times that we went out, women of all ages looked at him. A jealous look toward me reflected in their eyes.

I didn't mind. I was used to women and gentlemen looking at us, but it made me uncomfortable. Finally, William told me that he was going to England. He missed Catherine and the children. "Love," I lied, "make sure you come back to me soon." This was the time that I was waiting for. Mr. Leeward was sixty-four years old then, and he was not the shrewd man that he used to be. I wanted to get into William's quarters, and that was the time I was waiting for. I would browse to my heart's content and see if I could find any clue, any dark secret on William's life. I knew. I knew for sure that he had killed Elizabeth. What other secrets was he hiding from me? I was curious enough to find out about William's other self, his dark side. The side that I had often enough experienced, his evil side, but at the same time, I was afraid. What if William was the serial killer? What then? I couldn't see William shackled, taken to prison, morally destroyed, dreaded, deteriorated. Curiosity won. I waited for Lisa outside the corridor by William's back door and inserted the credit card in its iron hinges (as Bruce McKluskey, the FBI friend showed me to do). I waited for a while until Mr. Leeward closed the front door leading toward the front stairway on William's quarters, and I got in. everything looked the same to me. Nothing had changed. The same symmetrical order throughout the rooms. The shiny slippers next to the chair where he changed his shoes. The large room where he kept his clothes that were all set in pairs and in colors. Another smaller room for his shoes.

Another room for all of his coats, hats, and ties. How could I move anything without it being noticed? And then I saw an old leather jacket that I had not seen William wearing for years. I browsed into its outside pockets, and in the inside pocket of the jacket, and I felt something. It felt too thin for me to take out, and the inside pocket was too large for me to reach the bottom. I tried one time more, scratching my nails against the pocket's wall. It felt like a thin chain. I tried again, and there it was! A white gold chain with a half-moon full of diamonds. Betty's chain! I cried out. I didn't care who heard me. I ran out of that room as if the devil was chasing me, my heart pounding against my chest. "Murderer, murderer!" I screamed, clutching at the chain I had given Betty on her birthday. I couldn't breathe.

Lisa came rushing in, opened the balcony's door, and took me out in the open while I was panting. The cool breeze hit me, filling my lungs with fresh air. After a while, Lisa sat me down and brought me two aspirins. I was holding that chain as though it was Betty that were there sitting with me and I was holding her. I was drained out, no strength left in my body. Lonely, betrayed by a deceiving murderer. "William," I said, "you just killed me. I was just as dead as all those innocent girls whose remains are still lying under the tall grass in Gilgo Beach."

I don't remember how many days, maybe months, I spent sitting down, not moving at all. Looking beyond, out into the empty space. I hardly had the strength to bathe and change. Zoraida was next to me, giving me hope, telling me to leave William, that I was in danger. Fear was reflected on her dark and beautiful eyes. I didn't know for whom I should grieve. Fear clawed at my heart, lacerating, tearing it apart. I knew then that I couldn't have never seen William dragged away by the police, indicted as a serial killer, forsaken, friendless, alone. Betty, my dear friend, my bosom friend, how could I let the assassin that defiled your innocence be free? And I sitting in the middle of this tragedy like a lone cypress tree casting a shadow over your grave. There were lots of grumbles and grudged gossip among members of the staff. They were openly exposing their opinions without any regard for the consequences. Zoraida and Cindy told me. But what do I care? I must confront William. The Lord will give me the strength to face him. I was confused and asked myself, Would I have the courage to face him? What if I would be weak, mesmerized by his strong personality? Persuaded by his elegant, majestic figure and beautiful blue eyes?

I must remember Betty and Elizabeth at all times. He cannot get away with murder. It must be an explanation. He must be able to speak his mind with freedom to me before I lay open the road to false charges and slander. I had time to think. William was taking his time in England, enjoying his family. Will this trip to England be for him the last wish before a prisoner is taken to the execution chamber? I had chills all over my body. Maybe I should just call Bruce McKluskey and let him deal with it. I knew it was not going to be easy. I'll have to testify against William. I would have to sit facing him in court and explain to the jury all of William's tortures, battering, and afflictions that I had endured throughout the years. My heart scattered in bits, fragmented. I wouldn't want to keep on living after such an audacity. I knew that I couldn't betray William. There was no other way but to let him go free or confront him. I could never forgive him for the killings, nor could I live with such a burden upon my shoulders. It will be a slow death. I'll be haunted by Elizabeth's somber figure in the meadow. The white attire she wore on that day resembling a shroud that covered her petite figure. The happy and innocent look in Betty's blue eyes when she saw the pendant, the same pendant that Zoraida advised me to wear under my clothes today, the pendant that brought into light the somber evil beast that killed both of you.

I ran through the woods shouting aloud and crying, "Murderer, murderer, how could you have killed those innocent girls! You somber, beastly man." An anxiety attack wrapped up my body. It felt like someone had swathed my body, making my breathing difficult, painful. I calmed down, practicing the breathing exercises that the doctor advised me to do. Sitting there, on top of my old friend, the old log that lays alone in the middle of the meadow, its outer darkened skin giving away, showing a white and yellow skin underneath. I sat down on top of my old friend, relaxing, thinking, cursing the day that I met William. The hashish was taking hold of me, letting me forget, feeling as though I were suspended in the air. My soul set free, my mind lost in a dark labyrinth in the obscure matter of my brain.

The household staff was divided. They didn't know the real story. All they knew was that I found something belonging to another woman; they didn't have the faintest idea of the truth, that their master was a killer. Only Zoraida and I knew the truth, that terrible secret that kept us united and tormented. Mr. Leeward called William. "My lord, you have to come home. It's Ms. Mary. She looks indisposed." I heard that word before, "indisposed." It had a familiar ring to it. In the sophisticated English language, it means "crazy" Oh no! I thought. William will not cart me away to an asylum. I had to get him away from the mansion. Allure him into a corner far away, but to allure him into a corner. To accuse him openly. To be able to open up my blouse and reveal the chain that I had given Betty. To make him mad, to provoke him to murder. To kill me!

I knew that he would not reveal his evil instincts for everyone to hear. He would treat me like a demented person, agreeing with me, making me shrivel to past injuries. Everyone would believe him! I had to get out of the house. Confront him alone. To a place where he will feel free to confess, no witnesses, no evidence. His abominable self exposed to me alone. His dreaded being out in the open.

It was the time I dreaded the most. William was home! Everyone was running around. No time for flowers or the shining of silverware. This was an emergency. He was cunning, fixing in his mind his way out. "She probably lost her mind again," I heard him say. "What's wrong with her?" members of the staff were saying. "Didn't she have enough?" But I knew him more than anyone. He will come up and burst into my quarters. But I had locked it. I wanted to open up the door and let him see my eyes. I wanted him to feel the hate in my face. To incite him into chasing me.

I said to him, "Murderer!" and ran through the back entrance and into the backyard running fast. William straggled along behind me. My powerful legs like a projectile bolt, taking space, steering him away toward a neutral territory. Aloof, to a place where he could confess, I wanted to hear him, look into my eyes, and ask him about Betty and Elizabeth. Satiate my thirst for vengeance. To raze him, destroy his image. His impatient and haughty, evil self.

I turned right and into an inside fenced space where the horses used to wander about for some exercise. To the house where Jeff used to take care of the horses, where all the horses supplies and fixing tools were hanging on the walls or inside covered rolling carts, a two-room house where Jeff used to work. I tried to run inside the covered yard and closed gate, but I couldn't lock it. Its swinging large doors were wide open. There stood William! Blocking the only exit in that tall fence, but its iron rings were too small for my large feet to climb up. Fear took hold of my senses. I ran to the house, praying that the door was not locked, and I got in. There was no lock inside the door. This is it, I thought. The moment I've been waiting for, getting myself closed in without realizing it and toward two gambrels that were hanging from the wall behind me, where a saddle and its trappings were suspended, its sharp points protruding out from the wall on top of me.

This was my time! I saw him coming from the opened door, his macabre figure obstructing the sunlight. I could hardly see his face. I knew that I was going to die, but before I died, I wanted to hear him confess. I heard myself talking. "You miserable being. You killed Betty and Elizabeth," I said while at the same time tearing at my blouse, exposing Betty's chain. "Here lies the truth of all of your infamies. You haughty murderer." A rage taking hold of my senses, I was telling him what I wanted to shout to him months ago, but I didn't dare.

He did not speak; the whole time he was getting getting closer to me, fixing a knout in his right hand. A terrible instrument made out of rough leather, an instrument of torture used in Russia many years ago. William was a dark knight, ready to carry me to the pits of hell, his eyes were on fire. A somber look was reflected on his distorted, twisted face. I was backed into a corner, fear invading my senses. He stood there, impassible, insensible while fixing up his knouted glove. I didn't know how I found the strength, the courage to accuse him, to scream the words that were clogged up inside of me since I found Elizabeth's remains.

"You miserable murderer, confess be a man! There are no witnesses here. Tell me to my face that you are the serial killer, that you killed Elizabeth and Betty," I said while I was tearing at my blouse to reveal the white gold chain with its diamond half-moon, Betty's birthday present so many years ago. William stopped momentarily, a surprised look on his eyes. Then, I heard what I refused to admit all along—William was the serial killer! I didn't care to live any longer when I heard William confess.

"They were prostitutes," he said. "Contaminating the world, they deserved to die." He was Zeus, his body muscular. In his extended left arm stood an eagle, the knout set in his right arm ready to strike, holding a scepter, crowned with the olive wreath of Lordship, opening the door of his conscience without guilt. The eagle, ancient symbol of Rome, was set upon the wall, its dried eyes looking at me.

"They deserved to die, just like you and Joe. You are just as guilty," he said. "You deceived me, plundered away my dignity while I trusted you!"

"But you chose me instead of Joe, a man", a man," I said, "a man that could kill you."

He looked surprised. "He will have his turn," he said. He was almost on top of me; I could smell his sour breath. He reached for my throat with blinding speed at the same time that I avoided his knouted hand by moving quickly to the left.

The force of his hate thrusting hard on my throat, darkening the light of reason within me shutting down the windows of light, his hate blinding him from seeing the gambrel's hooks set on the wall, piercing his left eye. He was left hanging there inside that two-room house, as if he were a butcher's piece of meat suspended from the gambrel, blood flowing from his body, twisting in agony, mumbling, grumbling, growling, grunting like a wounded hog until his body laid rigid, inflexible, dead. Blood running down my face, covering my vision.

I screamed, saying, "William, please do not leave me! William, William, my love." How could I keep on living after such a tragic end! A lively description stamped, imprinted on my memory forever. I was lost; I might as well be dead. Jeff came in but stopped when he saw the horror. I was yelling, "I killed him!" The gambrel's hooks pierced my brain just like it did William's. I died on that day and I was left dry, useless.

Chapter 14

Why do men kill one another? We had even categorized the killing according to its victims: patricide, a man that kills his father; infanticide, the man that kills his children; cannibal, a man that eats human flesh, etc.

Is the justice system around the world ignoring the mass killings of women by men? Men have been killing each other ever since our past ancestors learned how to hunt. We have finished all predators. We have conquered them all. Has the circle of life vindicated us? To become antagonistic, bold, dreadful criminals? We became our won predators. We had to kill each other in order to keep up the global mass of men stabilized. We had gone against the laws of life and killed all our predators to become the killers of men.

I didn't know why William had to become a serial killer. He had everything. My psychologist said that every time he killed a woman, it was revenge against his parents and grandmother, but I didn't believe it. Women are the pivot of hate created by psychologists. Ever since children have become bold and hateful, they blamed their mothers for every one of their actions. Very seldom do they blame their father; there are no faults in their actions, they are always somebody else's fault. I said that I was guilty, why didn't they believe me? I knew the truth, I set him up. I was just as guilty as the two gambrels that were hanging on that wall.

I was subjected to the laws of man. A defendant is innocent, he has to admit that he is guilty in order to get a reduced sentence. But on the contrary, if he or she is guilty and does not want to admit that he is guilty, they get the maximum penalty of the law. I did not change my plea of guilt; I wanted the maximum sentence. They gave me five years in a mental institution. Lady Catherine and Sir Edward Hammeth and the children were sitting in different benches, close to William's lawyers. All the witnesses came or were called to testify.

When Mr. Leeward was asked if he ever listened to any misconduct or abuse toward the defendant, he answered, "Yes, sir." "When?" He did not recall the days nor the time.

They called Mrs. Rockwell, the real estate woman that made Carmela's life miserable. "Yes," she said, "they were two vicious opportunists. They tried to take over my business." She looked old and beaten and had to be helped into the witness chamber. She was still the despotic and somber person that I remembered.

The Richardsons, the billionaire friends of William who owned a penthouse in Park Avenue, were asked, "Did you see any wrong disposition with the victim?"

"No, sir, Sir William Bruckner was a perfect gentleman." Mr. Richardson looked at me and said, "She did not get along with any of Sir William Bruckner's guests." One of the lawyers stood up and said, "Would you call the victim by his proper given name, Lord William Bruckner, sir?"

My lawyer stood up and begged the court pardon. I was surprised to see Mrs. Blake, the old head of household staff. She looked as though they got her off the hospital to testify. "She is evil," she said. "She didn't want me at the mansion. She knew that I was going to warn Sir. . . excuse me, Lord William Bruckner of her evil." She took out a large handkerchief and started to cry and continued. "I had to kneel down in front of her and ask for forgiveness. I was dismissed and forbidden to talk to anyone while I was in England." Sobs like fire were coming out of her tongue.

Bruce McKluskey's testimony was very effective. He saw my bruises many times while we ran through the woods; he even remembered the dates. He was glad I was alive. He thought I was going to be the victim. Yes, he showed the defendant how to get into Lord William Bruckner's quarters. The prosecution tried to imply that Bruce and I had a "close relationship" but changed the line of questioning when they saw Bruce's face.

I didn't pay much attention to all the testimonies. I didn't care. I was like in a trance, rapture, sinking deep into oblivion. What were they arguing about? I was guilty; I wouldn't change my mind. My attorneys tried to warn me, but I wanted to be locked up, never to see the sunlight again. How could I ever see the waves to impact upon the rocks and then disappear over the sands without William being next to me? Never to visit

Barcelona again without him. Walking hand in hand through its winding alleys of the Barri or to climb the heights of Montmartre. I couldn't keep on living without William; I wanted to be locked up in a dark dungeon, never to see the sunlight again.

Instead, I sat in a courtroom surrounded by lawyers, lords, the press, and by everyone that met William and were mesmerized by his charmed personality. The prosecution lawyer displayed an image of William in the court. It was there for everyone to see. The handsome, tall Lord William Bruckner displaying all of his ranks and privileges. I fainted when I saw that picture. I had never seen a picture of him nor of the oil painting that was at Lady Catherine's house. Why did they keep on tormenting me?

Finally, the jury had a verdict. I couldn't believe it; I was innocent on charges of murder, guilty on psychological conduct. The judge's sentence was of five years in a mental institution. They always thought that I killed William. Could I have picked up and smashed his face against the gambrel that was on the wall above me? I knew I was guilty. I led him on, I made him mad. At the end, William was looked upon as a hero and I as a crazy, terrible honey pet, a cherished kept woman that was ungrateful of the loving care of Lord William Bruckner.

Chapter 15

The first two years were hell in the mental institution. I didn't want to eat. I laid in a windowless room with no furniture, nothing in it. They put a straitjacket on me whenever I made trouble. I sat on my own dirt and didn't care. I scratched the walls until my nails were a bloody mess. I calmed down and eventually I was able to sit somewhere in a corner of a large sunlit room, but I didn't want to see the sunlight! It took a lot of effort from the staff to convince me. Lots of therapy to be able to sit on a garden bench and be allowed to enjoy nature.

I had received many offers of reputable writers and newsmen to write my life's experiences. But I was never interested. They did not let us read the newspapers. At the rehabilitation center where I was moved to after my recovery, the Staff that we had enough drama in our lives without adding more. But they could see me reading every book that I could get my hands on. One member of the staff thought it interesting that I was able to read an article in the Long Island Press by Arlene McKrugger. She had written various articles about Gilgo Beach victims and seemed to be a champion on defending Comen's Rights movement. I tried to get in touch with her, but there were lots of obstacles, impediments, and obstructions thrown on my path. I couldn't get in touch with Ms. McKrugger.

I had one more year to get out of the rehabilitation center if I behaved, took my medications, get away from troublemakers, and sat quiet somewhere in a remote distant corner. They would probably let me go in a year. I would have to go to court again and stand in front of a judge so that he could pass sentence hoping that the assigned judge had forgotten all the past evil rumors against me and give me a fair sentence. William's family thought of me as a crazy old lady that no one would ever listen to, a discarded old being that should be kept in a mental institution forever. I had an evil thought. I would like to tell my life story, and I thought that Arlene McKrugger was the proper writer that I would like to contact. It was too dangerous to start making a fuss while I was still in a mental institution. William's relatives would be after me. Especially Peter, who by then would be a young distinguished gentleman, helping Edward in the various businesses. I had to be quiet, peaceful, rested, tranquil, waiting for the proper time to contact Ms. McKrugger. I wanted her to write my story; I wanted to tell all. I had to wait one more year. I had to be far away from the mental institution. I kept the article by Ms. McKrugger titled "The Long Island Serial Killer." I also kept the articles from other writers in *Newsday*. The picture of Elizabeth was printed for everyone to see, her killer a fugitive of the law.

I had nightmares at night. I heard William growling, crying, and calling my name, sticky blood running down my face, making me blind. "Someone please help me!" I pleaded. "He cannot chase me; he has to leave me alone!" The nurses would give me injections and then my body and my mind would feel relaxed. The dark clouds drifted away, my body felt light. In my dreams, I could hear someone calling, "Mary, Mary where are you?" "Betty, Betty, I am here." We ran through the woods, happy, laughing with our mud-caked rubber boots, dirty dresses, and matted hair. Chasing butterflies, picking up nuts. Dreaming, dreaming, an empty feeling in my soul. I didn't want to eat or to look out at the sunlight. My spirit was overwhelmed with dreaded memories. The mental institution had a reunion to check on my condition. Psychologists, doctors, lawyers were there, looking at all the records, asking me all sorts of questions. They arrived at the conclusion that I couldn't leave the institution until I was cured of the nightmares. It was dangerous for me to be out there on my own. As if the institution could harbor me from pain. I realized that I had to make an effort to be cured, feel free. But how could I get rid of my nightmares?

To live over and over again such horrors. I wanted to feel well; I wanted to leave the institution, to go back to my old town. To my dilapidated old house with its turned-out 31 number to read number 13, the same house where I lived with its small windows and broken-down front steps. The house that I wanted to run away from so many years ago.

The institution felt like my home then; people get used to their environment. I was used to my small room with just one bed, a night table, and small lamp. The window was high up; I could only see the treetops and the birds flying. I wanted it to be that way; the sunlight and the ecstasy of the meadow brought in me feelings of remorse, a guilt that I thought was encased in my soul forever. I was shackled to William as if I was hanging with him on the gambrels set on that wall. It takes time, the psychologists told me. How long would my suffering last? It will never end, they told me. With time, you will be able to accept it. How much time, dear God, I had been in this institution for eight years and I still loved William and remembered every detail of our lives together.

Hector came to visit me. "I am so sorry, Ms. Mary," he said to me. "I didn't know, the house staff and I had an idea as to what was happening, but people are reluctant to interfere. I just saw the good side of Lord Bruckner, he was very nice to me."

"Tell me, Hector," I said. "Did you ever see him go to prostitution houses?"

"No, Ms. Mary, he was too much of a gentleman to let anyone know. Sometimes he would ask me to stop the car. I used to leave him downtown."

"Where?" I asked him.

"It was never in the same place. He just said he would call me when he was ready."

"Thank you, Hector, do you need anything?"

No, madam, I just need a job right now, sorry."

That was the place where William used to find his victims! He hunted them down like a lion after a deer, camouflaged within the light tall grass that resembled their tan coats. Waiting patiently to pick up his victim and then charge without pity, aiming at their throats, no mercy. The victim's beautiful eyes looking at the monster while he quenched and extinguished the last breath left in their innocent bodies. That was William; I started to dislike him! Maybe, I thought, I was on my way to recovery. And yet Hector saw in him a gentleman, a refined, subtle person; I knew better. I could count, even to this day, the grievances, injuries, and scars left imprinted in my body and soul forever. I did not want to blame William for everything he inflicted upon my physique. I was to blame too; I could have walked away, continue with my life, explore other horizons, be free. As soon as he first stroked me, lacerated my dignity, I could have left. He held the whip in his hands, but I didn't have to humble myself to a haughty lover by staying at his mercy. Love has a boundary. There is no love in violence. Love is free, unmingled, modest, and chaste.

Therapy was having its effects on me; I was able to reason, to allege, to take a memorandum of my experiences and bring them up to the present. To be able to clarify my past life with William. It was working; I no longer saw William as the hero, refined gentleman that I thought he was. What refined gentleman kills and mistreats women? He was a mirage, and I was living in an arid deserted place. I thought that I could have reached out to him, and yet every time I tried, he vanished into oblivion. He never loved me! That was the hardest truth that I had to face. I refused to believe it for many years. I remembered our beautiful experiences and asked myself why a human being would lie and tell you that he loves you.

Perhaps the perfect example of men's brutal competition for the love of a woman was that of King John of England. He stole Isabella of Angoulême away from one of his own vassals, Hugh of Lusignan, Count of La Marche, to whom she was legally betrothed. She was twelve years old and King John was thirty-four when he stole her. The count, as revenge, allied himself with the king of France, and King John lost his biggest possession in France.

My psychologist explained to me the secret of love. Men love women in a different way. A man desires a woman, and he wants to possess her, make her his own. She is like a trophy acquired in a competition, like a knight in ancient times when they exposed themselves to die in dangerous games, the manly way to be. Then the ribbons of victory made them celebrities. They could marry the most beautiful maiden; she was a trophy, and he was there to claim his prize. Nothing had changed, I said to the psychologist. Today, all they had to do is be popular, tall, handsome, and lucky. The large screen will make them heroes, there is no limit today in the hero they wish to portray. Why do women get mesmerized by a rustic, manly man? Why be submissive? I think it has to do with childbearing. But what about me? I could have been free and yet I chose to be his slave.

It looked like though that therapy was working on me! Those long conversations with the psychologists helped me. I saw through their experiences the meaning of life. I was also able to express my feelings, to communicate with someone, to be free to express myself. I was on my way to recuperation; I was feeling a lot better. I could stroll through the garden, see the beauty of nature. Listen to the chirps of birds, their broods chirping away, urgent, pressing their parents. It sounded like music to me.

I felt free, like a heavy bundle was lifted away from my shoulders. I was almost feeling happy, but William was like a dark shadow in my life. Just like when he was there living with me, sharing beautiful moments, making love, traveling, walking. Then everything turned around and he took me to the pits of hell. He was there then hiding in the shadows looking at me. A shining light in that obscured room. As if he had reconstructed himself and sprouted again with fury, thirst, and lack of comprehension. Urging me, telling me to come to him. He was not finished with me yet! I was backed against that wall. His knouted hand grasping my throat, the gambrel's hooks over my head. I couldn't breathe. "Help," I cried, "he is there, can you see him?" I was back to my old self again. I had to have bright lights at night and then I couldn't sleep. Afraid to take pills. He could carry me away when I was sedated. Will I ever be cured? Will I ever get out of this institution? The psychologists think I could have. What do they know? It doesn't matter what I had told them throughout the years, they still though that William was innocent.

I couldn't answer him. I really felt happy in my dream with William, remembering the beautiful times. He wanted me with him.

Zoraida came to see me, and she knew the instant she saw me that something had happened. "Oh, Zoraida," I said, "it's William again. He wants to take me with him. I cannot escape him. He is hunting me down like all of his victims. I felt desolate, wasted, sad." Zoraida looked sad. She had brought Tinkle with her. A red bow on his silky and fluffy fur, he was nine years old then. I could see his tired eyes and the sadness in him. "Tinkle, my darling," I said with tears in my eyes. "Do not leave me." But we both knew that it was the last time that we were going to see each other. He started to howl as though he wanted to talk to me, telling me why I abandoned him. He was reproaching, blaming me for rejecting him. "No, my sweet little toy, I have always loved you." We somehow knew that it was the last time that we would see each other. After that day, Zoraida never said anything and I never asked but didn't see Tinkle again. I had therapy every day, especially after every one of my visions and crazy dreams. The psychologists acted as though I was to blame, I was making up everything. They never believed that William was to blame.

In desperation, one day, I tore my blouse open so they could see the gold chain with its half-moon full of diamonds, Betty's birthday present from me. "This chain," I cried, "I found in in one of his leather jackets." I couldn't believe it but they said, "Well, there are lots of half-moon chains around." After each one of my accusations and outrage of contempt, interrogation followed. Did you feel afraid when you traveled with him? Did you sleep well at night even though he could burst into your quarters? How long were you smoking hashish? Were you ever deprived of food, money, attention?

I used to leave those sessions crying, thinking that it was all my fault, that it was all a figment of my imagination. Oh, how desolate I felt! I was back into the mansion again, afraid. I couldn't think. Past thoughts numbed my brain and planted doubts. Did I see William at night? Calling me, or was I suffering from nyctalopy? He looked so real, only his eyes had that evil look that I had seen twice when he tried to kill me. In my next session, a young psychologist came to observe me and said something that made sense to me back then. He said that I was still afraid of William, that I had to face him the next time he came to me! He said, "Tell him that you are not afraid of him anymore, that he cannot hurt you again." There were no other ways. I had to confront William. I remembered how afraid I was to confront William before, and I had to do the same thing all over again. I asked myself, "Will I ever be free of William?" I was not as afraid as I was the last time he came. Still, at night, he came into my dreams, enticing me, calling me to him, telling me that he loved me.

"William," I used to cry, "do not leave me, and come back to me, my darling." Sweat covered me. His face engraved in my memory. There was a strong aromatic fragrance surrounding me, a familiar essence in the air. "William, William," I woke up calling him. "Wait for me, William. Do not leave me alone." I had to do something. I had to feel free. Would I say goodbye to William, or would I go with him? To be at his will. Two tormented souls damned forever.

I had to find the strength to confront William. I still had scars left in my soul from our last encounter. I remembered how afraid I was. Would I ever be free of William? One day, just like I feared, he came to my bedroom. He stood surrounded by a red evil light, coming toward me, trying to reach me. Fixing his knouted glove, ready to kill me. I remembered then how a calm and reassured voice used to calm him and mitigate his rage, the rage and furious pain that used to agitate his troubled soul. "Love," I said, "you are free. You cannot hurt anymore. Go in peace, my darling, follow the light. You are free from evil. No one can hurt you!" He stopped from coming forward. I heard myself saying, "You cannot hurt anyone anymore, my darling. You are free, follow the light, and be with God."

Chapter 16

He disappeared little by little, that red light going away, liberating, unshackling him from the sins he had committed, a rested look on his face, a peaceful repose invading his being. "Go in peace, my darling." I felt sad, but at the same time, I experienced a calmness that I had not felt since I met William. Finally, I was liberated; I felt liberated, no more dreams, nightmares. I felt sad when I left the mansion. I looked around the place that I adored. The balcony where William and I spent beautiful, peaceful times together, and yet at other places, a remembrance of tearing each other apart clouded my mind. I walked the garden and the forest one more time. The Apollo family looked sad to me. There was a yellow stain on their firm, sad faces. Where are the flowers that covered every nook and lurking place? Grass covered the statue of Tinkle I, I cried tears went from my eyes and into my heart. Even the meadow looked sad. I found the old log dismembered, separated, and divided, its dark outer skin infested with piles of weeds covered with soil in which ants were breeding. My old friend on which I sat many hours, wondering, dreaming. I couldn't take it anymore, and I headed toward the mansion, leaving behind me the agonizing sun with its yellow rays of colors.

I wanted to go home. Home to Bloomington, to Ohio. The staff were there, wishing me well. Most of them had gone away, and I was crying. Zoraida and Cindy came with me to the Newark Airport in New Jersey. We passed uptown Manhattan and up to 181st Street and into Riverside Drive. I remembered Doña Ana and the gray tall building overhead, high on top of a cliff overlooking the Riverside Road and river, the rippled waves of the river purling, flowing gently.

Zoraida wanted me to stay in New York. "No, my friend," I said. "I am a hick, I don't belong in this fancy town. I belong in Bloomington, where I was born. I belong in that old dilapidated house on 13 Consequence Street." I said goodbye to my friends, sobs coming from within. I said, "Zoraida, thank you for being my friend, for giving me strength, the courage when there was none left in me. You encouraged me, you embedded in me hope when my soul was lacerated, when I was left alone with only you as a friend."

At that time, Cindy asked me if she could help me, if she could come to Bloomington and stay with me. She did not have a job. "I'll be happy to have you, Cindy," I said. "Wait until I settle down and find a place to stay." Zoraida felt confident with Cindy's proposition. She knew that Cindy could be trusted. I said goodbye to New York City. Its tall buildings embellishing you, as if a premeditated enchanting was grasping you, fascinating you. A place of Broadway shows, expensive restaurants, billionaires trotting along the crowded streets, rubbing shoulders with the populace and no one caring. It is also a city with its infested blind alleys. A place of treachery, fraud, deceit, and murders.

Hector offered to drive me to the airport. We passed uptown, Manhattan to get into the Washington Bridge, and up to the one hundred and eighty street. I remembered Doña Ana, and the gray tall building overhead, high on top of a cliff, overlooking the Riverside Road and river. I looked up toward that small room that I rented many years ago. The rippled waves of the river, purling, flowing gently. It was time for me to part toward my old town.

We landed at Ohio Airport in the early morning, the sea-like Ohio Lake wrapping around the horseshoe Ohio State, the sun and the moon present. The dark shadows of the moon was on my back, the glimmering small sparkles of light facing me, lifting me up to heaven. My beautiful Ohio State. I cried tears of happiness that were dwelling inside of me. I knew that I was going to be okay as I experienced eagerness, an ardent desire to start my life again. I would be making my own resolutions. I would be the pivot, the axle that would tread upon my future life. Free, dear God, at last, I am free forever!

I went to my old neighborhood on Consequence Street. The old family house with its number turned around to read 13, the front steps demolished. I wanted to lie by this old house and wait for the passing of time to kill us both off. I couldn't give up now, vexed by a dreaded feeling of fear. I would fix the house, everything would be different. I noticed that the neighbors were in a different financial situation; they had built about half a dozen beautiful houses around my property. New roads and sidewalks, electricity posts were installed. Flowers and landscaped lawns added an elegant touch. I sold the house I had given to my parents. Stale smell reached my nose. I had to open the windows. Junk and dirty clothes were accumulated all over the house. The kitchen and the bathroom had to be demolished. Bottles of whiskey were spread out all over the place. It looked as though the house was broken into; some windows were broken, no televisions, no cash anywhere. I sold the house that was sitting on two acres of land and decided to fix the house on Consequence Street. Two bedrooms and two baths and an extralarge room that was living, dining room, and kitchen. Hot water and gas, a big fireplace on the large room that covered one-third of the room. It had a large block patio with a built in barbecue. Life was good again. I spent hours in the garden or talking with Cindy, contemplating the flowerpots that adorned the patio. I liked to visit Betty's family. It was such a large happy family that I delighted myself with all the children running about, asking questions. But most of all, I remembered.

I was not crazy about the house. I was used to living with lots of comfort but I earned my freedom. The house had a high brick patio, with sliding large doors off the kitchen. It was nice to look out in the winter season and see the squirrels jumping, staring at me asking for bread.

When Betty was a girl there were nine boys in her family. That was why the boys used to look after her constantly, protecting her. Betty didn't like the idea of helping her mother with all the house chores. Just cooking for all of those boys must have been a very hard job for such a fragile girl like Betty. All the boys worked hard in the field since they were young. They all looked healthy, tall, handsome boys. Today they were men and still working hard for their family. I missed Betty most of all. I walked the cold winter field that separated our houses, remembering my dear friend. When I used to see her, she was so fragile, no gloves, and no hat, walking through the snow-covered fields to visit me. I used to wait for her with a cup of tea and a chocolate bar and then sit her by the fire, her face flushed with the scorch of winter's ravaging winds.

Paul Handerson is my new psychologist. I told him that I still think about William. I tried to get busy, but I couldn't get him out of my mind. "Write about your life with William."

"It would take me forever!" I said. "Besides, what do I know about writing?"

"A short poem, anything that brings out the evil that you were subjected to."

I tried a short poem, and I wrote,

I remembered you every Fall
When the trees bloomed with colors
Our walks, and our talks
Our dreams and our sorrows

Paul was furious when he read the poem. He said, "You don't really feel that way about Lord Bruckner. You are covering up your feelings."

"I don't know," I said. "Besides, why dwell on the negative aspect of my life? It was both sublime, and evil. We had beautiful times together. Wonderful moments that very few people have experienced. I know how it is to fly beyond the stars, to be on top of the highest mountain sitting on the clouds, and looking down to green valleys, the aroma of flowers invading my senses."

"You forgot to say some important words. 'Mass murderer,'" Paul emphasized. In this town, William's family could not influence Mr. Handerson. William's family coaxed New York psychologists. Paul treated me as a victim, not as a demented being. He said, "He played with your mind by being polite and sweet to confuse you. The jackal had the field open to inflict beastly punishments."

I realized the injuries and beastly sufferings that I was subjected to. That I was a victim, he was a vile mass murderer. I read the poem I had written and tore it to pieces. As the wind blew the pieces of paper, they separated, scattered into the wind, to then fall on top of the mud, shrugging into the black dirt. The pieces of torn papers resembling William's soul. I almost felt cured. That was my past life. Biggest horrors had stroked, shaken, and beaten up humanity, and yet we continued to dwindle at the edge of time without remorse, forgetting past horrors, ready to excuse ourselves in order to commit new ones. I was trying to understand, but somehow, it was hard for me to do so. One cannot live a lifetime of submission, shackled up to a man you loved or thought you did, and then forget him like magic. The tragic end that I was a witness too. The experience that I provoked, that had me almost killed by the man that I loved. Someone that I trusted. Someone that I wanted to spend my life with.

My life at Bloomington was pleasant enough to forget all the horrors and also beautiful moments that I had experienced with William. Lately, though, I only dreamed about the beautiful times that I had shared with William. I dreamed that we were in Naples, looking down from the sea cliffs of the Amalfi coast. Walking up the narrow streets hand in hand, buying little trinkets at the plaza, listening to the troubadours sing romantic songs. William and I in love all over again! I woke up with a feeling of remorse, a sting in my soul that made me feel uneasy. As if I didn't want to wake up and let it go and live with William forever. Paul Handerson, my new psychologist, was worried. He was afraid that I would commit suicide for the wrong reasons.

"It is like a vengeance against anyone that they feel had harmed them. Of course, that is the wrong reason to commit suicide. Their torturing beings stay free, having fun, dancing, raising a family, while the boy or girl that commits suicide are gone forever. Never to see their children, never to experience life. The best punishment for those bullies is for their victim to do well in their lives. To ignore their bullying (as they call it). To become a better person than their tortured beings could ever be, work for a better life. Those dreams you had are a mirage; it is a cunning fine way to incite you, to be with William, but it is false. Would you really want to be with him again?"

"I don't know," I said. "The dreams are so beautiful. It gives me the peace that I would like to experience in life."

"You are just remembering the good times, the two of you spent together."

"I want you to say 'mass murderer' every time you experience this great love that you said you experienced for Lord Bruckner. Agree?" I agreed. I thought then that I could erase from my mind every dash, every humiliating stroke inflicted upon me by a devoted and somber being. Unfortunately, life sometimes leads you into oblivion. As if you were suspended on a giblet, ready to let go, to finish it all. Somehow, I managed to hold myself up. I was not alone. Not like in New York where neighbors don't talk to each other. This is the South, where neighbors talk to you, where people make you feel that you belong. A state where they show compassion, where you feel welcome. I was lucky, so I kept on living.

It was springtime again. Children everywhere in the McKlusky family, Betty's family. Grandchildren came from near towns to experience life in the farm, picking up pumpkins, learning how to milk a cow, picking up the corn. The farm bursting up with colors and the smell of peaches, pears, wildflowers, and of children running everywhere. Among them was a fragile, small girl with chestnut hair and enchanting deep blue eyes. "Betty!" I cried out, my heart accelerating by seconds.

"Yes," her mother told me. "As soon as my husband saw her, he said that she looked exactly like his sister Betty, so we named her Betty." Little Betty was to me like a little angel in my life. She was the child that I dreamed to have a long time ago.

She looked at me with those innocent eyes that reminded me so much of Betty. I wanted to keep her with me all the time; she liked to run in the fields, picking up flowers, feeling free. Just like my friend Betty her aunt, little Betty escaped with me, high up into the mountains. Running, feeling the icy wind burning red our faces. I loved that child so much my heart dreamed of other times, past moments, as though I wanted to live my life all over again and be of little Betty's age. Go back in time. Feel the same sensations I once felt. To be a child again and run and play with little Betty, as if I was her age. Free of all my experiences. She liked to run with her cousins and did not like to do any of the farm chores. She would come to me when the family was looking for her to perform a farm or house chore. She would play with Tinkle until my delicate little pet would feel tired and he would hide anywhere where Betty couldn't find him. I took her with me on my daily walks. I didn't go into the mountains where my friend Betty and I used to go many years ago. I couldn't face being on those mountains without Betty.

There were plenty of woods around my house to let us run free. The woods in this part of the country are not flat, like the feasible terrain in New York. The Ohio State has a rocky, craggy type of woods, with rolling hills and hard terrain, thick with nuts, hickory trees, and fruit trees. There was magic in the air. One never knows what to expect after one reaches the nearest hill and looks into the wilderness down below. Sometimes, there is the smell of the magnolia trees, with its pink large bulbs set upon the tree, as if by some enchanting magic. Their tree's flowers are set at perfect intervals. There are also fruit trees that bloom in the spring with pink-and-white flowers. The smell of life fills up your soul with new and beautiful illusions. The exercises in the woods were hard for my tired body.

I was not used to hard, broken, and uneven terrain. During late fall, these woods would turn stormy, gusty, tempestuous. I couldn't run during the fall season like in the New York woods. I often wondered what happened to my old friend, the discarded log that I saw that had given way, to disjoin, to separate from the mother tree, and then lie plundered, cast off like me. I also thought of the tall grass. The smell of saltpeter in the air and the smell of putrid, rotten flesh in the tall grass. I wondered about the mansion, about the garden, the peaceful setting, the flowers. Whatever happened to the Zeus family? To our love, to the years we spent together? Everything was gone as though they never existed. Was it real? I asked myself many times, and yet I craved for my past existence. As if the suffering years that I had experienced at the mansion were erased from my mind and only the enchantment, the charm (like a spell) were there to coax, to deceive me. I thought of William when he was charming. His elegance, gallantry, and refined manners fascinated me. I admired him!

Perhaps it was the common and ordinary parents that I had. It hurt me tremendously when I saw my parents being so dishonorable, lewd, and dishonest. I wanted to run away as far as the bus could take me then. They accepted merchandise from a nine-year-old daughter and never asked where I got it from. Happy to open up the bottles and to run away to their bedroom and gorge themselves with liquor. They never fought, only strange noises (that I didn't understand then) came from their bedroom. They hardly ate. Whatever potatoes and eggs I could collect was my everyday dinner. Milk and chocolate bars were given to me by John Traves, owner of the Jig's Variety Shop. He was a devil too, giving me liquor so my parents remained drunk and wouldn't care to question me! I found a discarded old wheeling cart so I could carry the groceries home. I walked five kilometers to our house; nevertheless, it felt good to come home and know that I had something to cook. I browsed about the groceries to see what surprise Mr. John Traves had included into the bags. Sometimes there were socks, ribbons, dresses, and even shoes included. In my innocence, I didn't understand the evil that John Traves was inflicting upon my physique. I thought that he was a good man. The first time I went to the shop, I was standing next to a shelf packed with chocolate bars. I stole some chocolate bars; I couldn't wait to eat them in his shop. After stealing some chocolate bars, instead of calling the police, he gave them to me. I remembered how starving I was! It was the next time I walked into the store that he suggested to see me in the room at the back of the store. There were sacks of grains and all sorts of merchandise stacked high up in the shelves, also a large desk with a large black chair next to it. It was there that John Traves touched me.

The first time, he only sat me on his lap, asking me questions, touching my hair, kissing my face. I looked at him like the father that I never had! Was that the way fathers acted with their children? I thought then. I didn't know. He told me that it was a secret between daughters and fathers. So I kept on going to Mr. Traves's shop. I could still feel the rancid smell of his body, his fat lips sucking up my delicate pink skin, remember the bad sensation that I was doing something wrong, but unable to know what and why. I used to feel ashamed. Flush used to tint my face with a red-hot color that I felt was covering my entire body. Why, I asked myself, was that woman looking at me with those intense and devilish eyes?

I felt dirty, discarded, but I couldn't understand why. It was Betty three years later that let me know what was happening. We used to disrobe in front of one another with the innocence that children at that age have. That's when Betty discovered the black and red marks in my body. She was alarmed and asked me who was making those marks all over my body. I told her who it was, and Betty said she was going to tell her parents and have John Traves killed. Betty came from a large family where all her brothers used to go through the adolescent stages of life; living in a farm with animals teaches children the facts of life. I didn't know of those factors that make a child aware of sex. Betty had seen those marks that I had on my body more than one time on the skins of her brothers. Besides the fact that being the only girl, her mother or brothers had warned her about men and what she should do. When she explained it to me what that old shady, gloomy, and abusive dirty old man did to me, I cried. But Betty was there to console me, to tell me what to do. The next time, I went with Betty, and we both walked into the back room. The old fool thought that Betty was there to submit herself to the same abuse. Instead, Betty told him that if he ever tried to do anything to me again, she would tell her brothers and they would kill him like a dog.

After that incident, I went to the store and right to his face took whatever I needed for our survival. He couldn't say anything. Betty came with me the first couple of months. After that, I became wise and even teased him, bending down so he could see my back side or picking up some merchandise close to where he was sitting to expose just a little of my small breasts with the two little pink buds that he used to love so much. He sat there! His face turning purple, a bulge in his pants growing by the second. I used to laugh then and leave. I had to see John Traves now after all these years to face him. Paul Handerson, my psychologist, told me that I had to confront him. That my submissiveness toward men had started with the abuse I experienced as a child by John Traves and my parents. I wanted to believe Paul, but then I thought of Betty. She was never molested when she was a child, and yet Betty was wise enough to understand what was happening to me then. She knew what to do at only seven years of age. I was eleven years old then. Betty was not wise enough to perceive later in her life what a detestable, despicable man she was in love with.

I visited Jigs Variety Shop. The shop looked different. It was a new building with large windows, bright lights, and separate rooms for different merchandises. There was not a back room anymore. Instead, offices were located on the third floor of the building, a long white corridor with oak wood doors. A desk was set in the middle, and a receptionist was there welcoming us. "May I help you?"

"I would like to see Mr. John Traves please."

"John Traves Senior or John Traves Jr.?"

"Senior, please."

"Your name?"

"Mary."

"The last door to your right, number 2 door," the receptionist said.

I walked in, and I was repulsed by the condition that John Traves was in. He sat on a wheelchair; bottles of medicines were stocked up on top of a small table. His eyes looked so old as if a cyclone had hit him, left him blind, and discarded in the middle of nowhere. Like an old branch left to rot away, to decay. A nurse was wheeling him, and she said to me, "He insisted on coming in today. As vice president of the corporation, he had to have an office. May I ask who you are and what do you want to see Mr. Traves for?"

"It is an old story that I had encased in my soul for a very long time," I said, "but you see, that innocent old man took my innocence away from me when I was only eight years old. He devastated and defiled my innocence. He is a dirty old man." Tears covered my face; sobs closed my throat and disabled me to continue.

The nurse turned the wheelchair around so I could see him. Tears of remorse were covering his face. He didn't have to say, "I am sorry." It was written all over his red-purple face. At last, my feeble and stumbled innocence was in the open. It lay free for everyone to see. I felt guilt leaving me that this evil and sick man had encased in my innocent being many years ago. I ran out of that office as though the devil was chasing me.

Outside, the cool air hit my face. I breathed, a deep liberating feeling surrounding me. I told Paul about my experience with John Traves, and he was very happy. He said it was an occasion to celebrate, and he invited me for lunch at the local restaurant. I hesitated. Since I met William, I had never had a date with any man. "Paul," I said, "I don't think I am going to feel comfortable going out with another man."

"Don't you see," he said, "Lord Bruckner is still pulling the strings in your life, dominating you beyond his grave." Reluctantly, I consented. We ordered wine instead of coffee. I felt relaxed talking to Paul; after all, he was my psychologist, my confidant. Paul knew everything about my life as if I were standing naked and bare in front of a mirror, in front of him, disrobed, just like a child when it comes into the world. Afraid, innocent, displaying my innermost intimate emotions to him. A complete stranger. It made me feel relaxed, like having a good friend. I felt free and confident with Paul.

However, I didn't want to get involved in any type of relationship. I didn't trust men. I asked myself why I wouldn't trust Paul. But of course, I knew better. I remembered William and how nice he was at the beginning of our relationship and how much he changed after the first year. I didn't trust men. I told Paul about how I felt. He said it was understandable that I shouldn't rush into any relationship until I felt completely secure. After my experience with William, I was not able to love again; my heart together with my soul were dried out, lacerated. William had clawed and torn it to pieces, leaving in me a dreadful feeling of fear. I was a victim of William's hegemonic and gnarled self; there was no cure for me. I was doomed.

Time passes by with incredible speed. Every second in one's life has its boundary. Your heart palpitates at the same speed of time. It follows a rhythm. I asked myself, why worry or harbor in my mind, past mistakes, or gloomy, ill-fated experiences? Everything will be forgotten, dismissed by the passing of time. I tried to follow this philosophy, and it helped me a great deal. But like the weather, with its sunny and bright days, tornado days, it was the same in my life. I still remembered William. Always the beautiful times, why not? Why mortify myself with past dreadful experiences. I wanted to continue my life without past and devious memories.

It had been two years since I left New York. I had accomplished more in those two years than the twenty-six years I was in New York. I remodeled my house, sold my parents' house. I found Paul, who has hard with me, trying to emancipate me, to extract from me the shackles that William had imposed on me for a long time.

I was practically a part of the McKlusky family, Betty's clan. However, sometimes I felt that I had to look around as though someone was following me. I then became apprehensive, afraid, my heart hastening, accelerating by the second. Paul said that I had to renounce, to set aside my fears, to keep on running through the woods and tall and to be careful of bears hiding, where a bear could hide, eating the berries they liked. I ran in the hard terrain, with its dusty paths or musky wet holes. I was getting used to the change. I also took with me Tinkle. Sometimes after a long run, he used to sit down and refused to continue. I had to pick him up so I could continue running.

I found little Betty. I helped her every day with her homework and bought her all kinds of dresses, shoes, etc. The McKluskys said that I was spoiling her. I was going to make a lady out of her. I felt as though I owed her aunt Betty the attention I should have given her. Betty was to me like Zoraida was when I first met her, shy and gentle, a good human being, my dearest friend, a child that I miss so much.

I felt the gentle passing of life. The generosity, the liberated state of mind that one feels when surrounded in a peaceful environment. I felt emancipated, free. My heart did not skip a beat when someone opened a door or when I heard a car stopping in my driveway. I just felt curious, eager to see who was at my doorstep. I felt that it was a nice change for me. It was not like that in the first year. I used to feel scared when someone, a stranger, came close to me or when I was in the woods and heard strange noises coming from nowhere. I stopped in fear; I still do sometimes. I also missed the beautiful and lonely feeling of the past. The mansion's surroundings. The peaceful garden. The times we spent talking and sometimes crying with my dear friend, Zoraida. The balcony from my quarters looking down on the flowers and the statue of my first Tinkle. The aroma of the roses reaching me at the balcony. The magnificent luxuries, my gowns, all the jewelry that I had left. I didn't want to take anything with me. I never looked back, nor did I claim any of the luxuries that were left behind. Only Tinkle number 2 did I ask Zoraida to keep with her and to bring him to visit me. I remembered like a dream all the accusations I was subjected to at the trial. I was called a dreadful, old adventurer, a devoted, extravagant, wily, and abominable murderer. A display of party gowns and jewelry, they said, I wore every day like a queen. I was a haughty person. I treated the mansion staff with contempt.

William was a hero. The honorable lord that was caught up by a dominant and rapacious woman, a murderer. I didn't care then, but when I used to read the magazines that circulated then with the trial's faked rumors, I cringed with the injustice I was submitted to. At the time of the trial, I was in limbo land, unaware of what was going on around me, vexed by my enemies, weakened by the sardonic speculations, feeling remorse for a crime I didn't commit. My soul satiated, afflicted by a garrulous and eloquent district attorney. He held the facts, opening the doors into my guilty conscience. For every severe, harsh, and frothy injury that came out of the attorney's mouth, I thought then that I deserved it. What did I care then? I was guilty. I loved William, and because of me, he was dead. What did I care if I lived or died? I couldn't possibly live without William.

Didn't I tell them that I was guilty? What's all the fuss, I thought then. I felt like a somber dirty murderess. Didn't I take an oath with William? I said that I was going to be loyal to him for the rest of our lives together. I remembered it was in the garden. Springtime, when flowers are in full bloom and the aroma of lilies was in the air. It was a cool day, but the sun's rays were warm and soft. He embraced me as if to cover me from the morning's chills. Our bodies together, facing each other. He lifted up my chin and looked at me with those blue eyes, as tranquil as the ripples of a lake. I swore to him then that I was going to be faithful, loyal, and true to him forever. It didn't work out that way. I killed him, I knew I did.

At the trial, on the front seat, sat Lady Catherine in a high-necked black dress and hat, a veil covering her forehead and eyes. I couldn't see the color of her eyes. I wondered if they were as intense as William's blue eyes. Sir Edward Hammeth and their two boys, Edward and Peter were there, silent, composed. I did not listen to the lawyers nor the DA. I was not interested in what they had to say. I was guilty. I didn't care. I just didn't want to live. Lock me up forever. Shackle me to a wall; hang me from the highest gibbet. Cover me with a somber shroud. What did I care? I just wanted to be left alone. Be able to mourn. The lights, the lawyers, the witnesses, the DA. "Can you please leave me alone!" I cried. I was hysterical. A big crowd was trying to see me. The press, the judge. "Please help me! I killed him, I killed him!" I kept on crying while they were taking me out. "Leave me alone!" But it was not that simple; doctors argued among themselves. Lawyers, even the witnesses, argued against the lawyers. Everything was a big show! To me, the lawyers were all pettifoggers, presumptuous, insolent beings that wanted to wrench away from each other the little fame they could acquire. They very well knew that I was not guilty. How could I have hung William from a gambrel? William was about six inches taller than me, at the same level as the gambrel hung on the wall. They very well knew that it was a sentence of acquittal. No phenophene positive test was found. I thought the jury was going to give me a sentence of guilty. Didn't I tell them I killed William? Instead, I was declared insane. I remember that I was shouting that I killed him while I was dragged away from the courtroom and into an insane institution.

Everything was gone now. As spring runs into winter, so our souls run also through different stages of life. One gets entangled in the intricate passing of one's life without realizing its beauty; an outcry, a clamor of past ill memories reaching us, destroying the beauty within us. I would not let that happen to me; I wanted to remember William, not as a volatile verified killer, but as a sick person. Someone who was not aware of his somber side and who thought that what he was doing was for the good of humanity. Like a doctor who first experiments in his lab with rats and then when he feels confident of his hard work will experiment on his patients, or like a sick person, who, vexed by the rigors of life, kills his family and then himself. Are they to blame? Can we call them murderers? I knew the other side of William—the gentle, compassionate, and loving side of William. How he rescued Hector when he was in need of help. How nice he was with the staff; they loved him! And then also how nice he was with me and with his adopted son Peter. He gave him his name. One could perceive his love for life by visiting the mansion. The beautiful decorations, most of them imported from the hills of Morocco and from Italy, Germany, Greece, Spain, and even the jungles of Colombia, where some of the selected pieces of furniture were designed with wood from the Muzo tree. Its black and red veins were displayed in the beautiful pieces of furniture displayed throughout the mansion.

How could I not remember him also as a loving human being? I lived in his mansion. He never once asked me for money. Beautiful and expensive jewelry was given to me. I will always see him as a loving, generous, but sick human being. Paul said that I was stubborn as a mule. He was right.

I guess that my weak character prevented me from leaving William years ago. Did I want to change him? To see the William that I dreamed of? Not the William that he was, the antagonistic and despotic human being that his tormented soul made him to be. I had no idea if I loved William immensely or not. All I knew was that I would never love anyone like I loved him. And now that I had lost him forever, I would keep on loving him like I never loved him before. This was my choice.

Paul couldn't understand my position in reference to William. "How could you keep on loving someone who treated you with the inclemency, severity, and harshness the way Lord Bruckner treated you?" Paul always referred to William as Lord Bruckner. I didn't know if it was to incite in me the somber situation I was in or if he felt envious of William's superior status. This was the first time that we looked at each other with wretched suspicion. I didn't like the feeling, and I guess he didn't like it either. We said sorry. He knew I would not change my position in reference to William. Maybe I needed a lot more psychological help.

Every day, I felt that I was gaining confidence in myself. Now I used to leave my Ford parked on my driveway and walk through town. I remembered the time when I was young and full of life and I used to pass by a group of other young males and females. How distressed I must have been to act the way I did, swinging my hips and flipping my hair, but this was a new generation. Some of the boys had tattoos all over their bodies. They looked at me with indifference. However, others would greet or extend their hands to help me cross the street. I walked through the shops, and the experience was somehow strange for me. I heard people talking.

"Is she the high famous model and ex-partner of some lord from England?"

Some others would say, "She murdered him, didn't she?"

"Yes, I, remember her."

They used to say to one another, "She used to live in that old house."

"Oh yes," they answered. "The house on 13 Consequence Street." Others felt admiration for me and secretly told me that they believed in me and of what happened to me. They proceeded to tell me of a friend that was experiencing the abuse I was subjected to when I lived in New York. People sometimes feel apprehensive, ashamed of abuse committed by members of their family. They will say, "It's a friend they know"; everyone wants to feel proud of their family. Especially of their children. I suppose that every parent that has wasted their energies, youth, time, and money would want to experience the thrill to see their children being successful and grateful for all the efforts that both parents did to accomplish their children's goals. Even when parents are ridiculed and abused by his or her family, they will deny the accusations. They feel rejected, desolation and despair encasing their souls. They feel like failures. The real failures lay on those who swing the whip of hate. The abusive, despotic, ungrateful, brazen, devoted foe. Those who had devoured their parents' time and left them old, alone, and fragile just like me!

Can a parent stop loving their children? I don't know; I couldn't say. I didn't have any children. I asked Paul why most psychologists blame mothers while consenting the girl's father's mistakes. On TV shows (with some exceptions), young girls of today look as though they are in love with their fathers and are jealous of their mothers; mothers are the rivals, the antagonists, the enemies, and the foes. Fathers are rarely mentioned, and yet most of the time they fall in love with someone else while they are still married to their wives. Children would complain most of the time (especially girls) about their mothers. If the mother has to earn a living, they will hate her for leaving them alone. Is this an extremely distorted era? Is this society more corrupted now than it was in my time?

I am a fair example of what society looked then. I was still fearful of accusing William. It felt as though I would have been unfaithful and despotic toward William's old and proud inheritance line of Lords. I thought then that he did not deserve to be the first in his family to slur the well-deserved line of English gentlemen. William will haunt me forever! I was still afraid of him. Nothing had changed. Children today are more aware, better informed than their predecessors. Their intellectual capabilities tuned in with their electronic devices. However, there are today vast open fields for predators, computer sex for minors, drugs, rape, and murder. We cannot discard the fact that one of the Gilgo Beach victims had contacted her killer through Craigslist to later lay humiliated on the vast cemetery grounds of Gilgo Beach. Are the victims' names still displayed for everyone to see, on the outskirts of Ocean Parkway? Was William the serial killer, or was he bragging when he said before he tried to kill me "they deserved it"? I couldn't picture William dragging those innocent girls on the thick tall grass on Gilgo Beach. He was too much of a scrupulous man, a fastidious being. His manicured, distinguished hands, his impeccable appearance. And then I thought, Did William have a partner? Someone that would do the dirty job for him? I thought of Hector. But I remembered what Hector told me that he had left him in different places. Besides, Hector thought too highly of William to help him commit such horrendous crimes.

"Stop thinking so much," Paul had warned me! "And live your own life. Why torment yourself with past ill memories? You are free; look at you! You established yourself back into your old town without looking back. Meeting new friends, ignoring the volatile, antagonistic people of this town."

"Well," I said, "with all the therapy I had received, something was meant to rub on me." We both laughed. A clear, sincere laugh. Paul had a beautiful smile. Large and perfect teeth. He was not as tall as William was, but he was tall enough to carry my height, with heels, by about one inch. What I liked the most about Paul was his open sincerity, his sense of humor. When we walked into a restaurant, people did not stare at us because of our lineage (as it was true with William), but as a well-loved, and respected member of the town. People loved his sincerity and easy charm. Sitting down in his office, I talked to Paul about trying to analyze everything in my present life. I asked him, "How come I didn't analyze the events in my life back then when I was with William? Perhaps if I had analyzed the events in my life then, I would not have had to suffer captivity for so many years. All my time was dedicated to please him. He drove me out of my mind. He would hide my rings in different places. He would tell me to get ready to take me out and then deny that he told me. My medications were hidden in different places every time. One earring, one shoe was missing. I couldn't figure out that it was William that was doing all those horrible acts of mischief to me. Even Zoraida sometimes believed that I was taking too many pills.

"Why," I cried, "would a person do something so humiliating if he loves someone?"

"Let's make one thing clear—Lord Bruckner did not love you!" Paul said.

There he goes again, I thought then, with the "lord" title, and he continued. "He kept you busy so you wouldn't have time to think of your situation. You were busy with all of his malicious inclemency and severities against your physique that he gave you no time to think. Serial killers are smart individuals. They challenge detectives, threaten the police, and laugh at them over phone calls. They keep detectives busy with false leads. Most of the time they are never found. They move to different towns, fade away, impassable, impenetrable. They have no friends; they are unconquerable, invincible, obscure beings."

I did what I always do when confronted with the truth. I ran out of Paul's office and into the cold fall weather of Bloomington. I breathed deeply, the scent of decayed leaves in the air. Even the fumes from the transit felt better than the encased office where I was in before. I had trouble thinking. Paul's words kept on ringing, a familiar ring to it: *Serial killers move from town to town. They are smart. They make fun of police. Kept you busy so you wouldn't think, you would be so worried about problems he lays on your path, so he would give you no time to reflect.* William would disappear for weeks and come back. Every piece of clothing was new. His manicured hands, a recently done haircut. He would greet everyone, give me a light kiss. Did he travel on those weeks? Why the new clothes, manicure, and haircut?

He would give orders to Mr. Leeward. He will not be in for dinner. He wanted breakfast at 8:00 a.m. as always. Next day, he was refreshed and attentive to me. There were beautiful quiet times for a while. We walked in the garden (William did not like to walk in the woods). But the garden was long enough for a nice walk. He would stop at the "Zeus family" with reverence, which used to bother me. I tried my best to be respectful. Inside of me, however, I felt repulsed, smudged by vicissitudes, afraid, disgusted. And then I thought of William's instincts of killing. He tried to kill me; I knew this to be true. How about Betty, Elizabeth, and her boyfriend Paul Taranto? William fit all the pieces as though it was a macabre, gruesome, and gloomy sky map that only I could see. It was hard for me to fully admit that William was a vicious, a mass murderer. A beastly human being that lured innocent girls to devour them. Just like a tiger or a jackal feeds from their booty, William used to feed himself from the victims' souls. I vomited right on the street, people looking at me with pity.

"Do you need help?" they asked.

"No, no, thank you." I wondered then if I could have exposed William to the public. Tell everyone what he did to me. Paul told me that I could not use his name nor title; I could be sued. William won again.

It was time to gather, to harvest. The ripened wheat in the fields released their kennels, working and bounding the stalks together. The fields displayed a light yellow color that shone with the sun's rays. The smell of hay was in the air. I could see as far as the horizon meets the eye, the harvest fields from the tall mount I was standing on. Smoke from the tractors lifted up the suave scent of the harvest.

I could see, like little specks from where I stood on the ground, the McKlusky family and farther up, like a distant winding road, the Ohio River, peaceful, serene. I was never in this part of the woods before. I walked for about five miles, trampling on the tracks of hundred other generations. I was tired from the long walk. Going through holes, mounds, tumbling underneath bushes, and walking, running, rushing away from my shadow. That somber shadow that was always trying to encase me. I was tired. I sat down with Tinkle at my side. We fell asleep. When I woke up, dark clouds were covering the silent woods. I was scared, my sense of direction gone, running to one side and then the other. I was trapped, entangled. I yelled a hollow cry that filled the woods with my fear. Tinkle saved us! He knew where to go. At times, I couldn't see him, lost in the woods' dark foliage; but I could follow him, the moon's rays, letting me see at intervals his raised little ears and tail. We finally arrived home.

Cindy was scared, her dark eyes showing concern. "Ms. Mary," she said, "I was so scared I almost called the police."

Tinkle and I were hungry and thirsty. I ate like I never ate before, hungry, thirsty, and happy.

It was the first day of autumn; it marked the beginning of the harvest. The smells of oranges, pumpkins, apples, pears, and grapes were in the air. Big sunflowers and yellow wildflowers filled the fields. People rushing about buying, storing merchandise for the sloshy fall and severe winter to come. It was the old routine. Soon it will be winter. Snow will cover our vast fields. Trees will hibernate as if they were bears, their long dried branches gray and silent. Their firm trunks rocked at the wind's rhythm, giving a sound like a shout filling the night. It was winter here in Bloomington.

It was a time of rest after a busy summer for farmers and their families. Children had collected the sap from the maple trees; a rod hammered into the bark and a bucket attached to it to gather the sap. It takes time, so most of the time, the bucket was left to be filled for hours. Stocking up wood for fire. Collecting fruits that are left to make marmalade. Buying boots for the slush to come. Stocking up on canned foods. It was a busy time, and then a quiet rest throughout the winter months, when the snow covers the fields and it is dark and gloomy. As if a curtain is set upon the sky and lingers on until the spring months.

It was during the winter months that I felt lonely. It never happened to me in New York. It was always sunny. Even as the snow was covering the grounds, the sun was always not far away. It is different in Ohio. People in Ohio get what they call cabin fever. After much resting, we feel the weight of idle hours, looking at the swirling of the snow, at the sky without sun, without birds. The quiet of the night, the thunder of time slowly passing by us, and there is nothing we can do but despair.

I felt the urge to fly away on those winter months. I was taking more sleeping pills; the pills made me tranquil, sleepy, relaxed. It discarded the shroud from the sky to let the sunshine in. I dreamed of William. I flew with him to remote places, to unknown caves, the warmth of his body encasing me, making me feel secure, unafraid. Why should I feel this way? I asked myself. The urge to be with William lingered within me, the desire to be with him! "What's happening to me?" I asked Paul, but he always told me something that I didn't want to hear: that it was all in my mind.

"You have to be able to release William out of your mind! I am afraid for you, Mary!" Tears filled his greenish eyes, which used to change like the weather. This time, however, they were firm, intense, trying to send a message to me that I didn't want to hear. I thought that I knew better. I clogged my brain with false illusions. I asked myself what harm can dreaming do to me. Doesn't a man that is fastened in shackles dream of being free? Or the captive wife, the ransomed child? Can they not break the chains that hold up their spirits by dreaming? A man dreamed of flying, of riches, of conquering the world. How many lovers looked up to the sky and wondered about the moon? Did they dream of scavenging its grounds? Of conquering other horizons? Do we look up at the stars and wonder about the universe? Are we dreaming now of leveling, flattening, of tumbling down this beautiful blue planet?

"No, my dear," Paul said, "You are not the pivot that makes this world turn around, nor is the beggar, the alcoholic, the drug addict, the abused child. The captive wife, neither is the murderer."

I saw the sadness on Paul's face and felt sorry. "I dreamed," I said, "of becoming a model, of being rich, and above all, I dreamed of William. I had all of my wishes, now I cannot complain. I just wanted to keep on dreaming, to be with William every night."

"Mary," Paul said, "you are in danger."

"Do not worry, my friend." I got up from the sofa where I was sitting down and approached Paul. I went close to him, feeling his breath, looking at his eyes, and said, "Paul, if I were capable of loving anyone else, it would have been you." We embraced, crying.

Cindy taught me how to crochet. It took lots of effort on my part as my fingers were too long and didn't have the elasticity that they used to. It made me feel good to be entertained in the winters without looking out at the gray sky. It was me and my dreams. *Don't tell anyone, Mary, they just don't understand.* I put on my boots and went out for a walk in town.

"Ms. Mary," Cindy warned me, "it is dangerous, you could fall down." Did I ever listen to anyone? Except of course, William.

Chapter 17

When did the front steps break down? I had not noticed. I fell down and landed on my back, my right leg broken. Doctors were astonished by my medical condition.

"Ms. Fletcher," the doctor said, "you are suffering from osteoporosis, a debilitating weakness in your bones. Unfortunately, your bones are too fragile. You have to be operated on. The operation was successful, but the rod we placed in your leg could not be attached effectively to the femur. I am afraid you will limp forever."

Just like that. He told me that I was going to become a freak. A discarded, old deprecated being. I lost control. I started to shout, "Help me, get me out of here!" But when I tried to get up, the pain was so terrifying that a shout died on my lips and my eyes became rigid. The pupils disappeared and hid under my eyelids. Nurses came running out of nowhere and gave me some kind of narcotic. I slept until the next day. Still, months later I couldn't drive. The narcotics were so strong that the police gave me a warning. I limped into town carrying my cane. Futile and worthless. Stares following me. "Is she the one?" I heard them talking. "My son said that she is a drug addict. "Imagine?"

I headed toward the rough part of town where the tall, tattooed, rough young boys and girls gathered. At the beginning, they made faces at each other every time I passed by. I wanted to get some drugs. The pain in my leg used to shoot up right to my hip. I needed help, but the doctors said that they could not provide me with more drugs, that it was dangerous. Cindy didn't want to drive me; what if a policeman stopped us? She was waiting for her citizenship and she didn't want to get a ticket, or else she would lose the right to become an American citizen.

I didn't know how to approach them; in New York, it was an easier job getting drugs. One day, I asked this lonely fellow that I wished to buy some marijuana. I was surprised when they all disappeared from the streets, the alleys, the corners, and out of sight a suspicious look in their eyes. It was as if a curse had fallen down and wiped out the young people. I looked around me, not knowing what to do and then I saw this bar called Kimo, where I imagined prostitutes, killers, etc., dwelled. I sat at a table that was available.

After a while, a woman approached me and said, "Look, lady, we don't cater here to old invalid persons. This is a rough bar. If I were you, I would get out of here fast."

"Listen, please, I suffer from this pain on my leg, and I need narcotics to calm it down a little. I have the money," I said, shaking the contents in my purse.

"I'll be right back," she said and proceeded to speak to two rough young fellows that kept on looking at me "Okay," she said, "what do you need?"

"How about some crack?"

"We have some envelopes of five dollars, but I think you need a more expensive drug."

I hurried home, eager to block out the pain that was shooting up my spine. My bad leg tried to stay behind every time I walked forward. Eager to get home and dream. I couldn't see a taxi. Where did they all disappear to? I was waving my cane up so they could see me. "Thirteen Consequence Street, please." Oh finally, I will be able to go home and dream. Wait for me, William.

I stopped seeing Paul. I always had an excuse to why I couldn't go to the appointments. My leg, I can hardly walk, that I needed help to just get off my chair. However, every time, Paul will threaten me with locking me up in a mental institution. "Why can't you leave me alone?"

One day, I woke up anguished, anxieties oppressing my mind. Betty, I have not seen Betty, was it two weeks ago, or just two days? I used to lose count of days and even weeks. Betty, my darling, where are you? Has she been here? I didn't remember. Was I dreaming then when I thought I was awake? Or before, when I laid still and Betty was with me, running in the woods? The smell of decayed leaves in the air. A bright blue sky following us, laughing, happy. I was afraid.

I went to see Paul, too many days sleeping. He tried to hide from me the effects that my deteriorated body caused on him after I had the operation. I knew how much I had changed. I had seen a reflection of myself on a glass door, and I couldn't believe it was me. I looked back thinking that it was someone else, not me. It was me. Tears ran down my face. Tears of remorse, uneasiness, bit and clawed at my soul, leaving me spent, solitary, and sad. Life kept on crawling, pestering me. Dwelling in one instant memories that had taken a lifetime to harbor. I had flashbacks of my previous life, the life that I had on this earth. I considered myself dead then, as dead as a stiff corpse, yellow and blue, my skinny arms and legs with blue marks from the punctures of needles. I was bound, gagged to my habits, unable to save myself.

I visited Paul; we embraced. He looked into my eyes. Sadness covered his face and said, "Psychologists in New York made an addict out of you, they kept on giving you narcotics to keep you in a languor state of mind, vulnerable. So you wouldn't be a threat to Lord Bruckner." I could tell that Paul hated William. Did William rob him of his love? Or did he feel sorry for me and blamed William for my condition? I thought that every human being makes his or her own decisions. No one could have dissuaded me from taking that bus out of Bloomington back then. I could have skipped the bus, gone to college, work, and maybe I could have had the luck of meeting Paul; but I didn't. Paul kept on blaming the psychologists in New York, my parents, John Traves, and every blasted person that had the misfortune of meeting me. Everyone except me!

I said, "Paul, I could have walked away from William after the first slap he gave me. He didn't have me strapped to a chair. I was free to leave."

"No," Paul said. "He had you strapped to your mind. You were sitting on that chair, gagged, in heavy chains and ropes of silk and silver threads connected to your brain! He coaxed you, mesmerized you. Like a spider or a silkworm weaving in his evil intentions. Convincing you he was a female spider, persuading, inducing the male to mate and then killing him. She will devour, swallow him up. His remains will be food for her brood. You were the food that nourished his evil soul. You could not have gotten out of that chair. Do not blame yourself, my dear. You were an innocent doe that happened to laid on the path of a hunter." We embraced, crying. The tears turned his eyes the color of the weather in a clear day; two crystal pearls, diaphanous, lucid and clear. This time I didn't run away from Paul. We were friends. In a way, I loved him. A friendly love.

I went cold turkey for a while, my entire body in a state of mental deprivation, immobile, shaken, but I wanted so much to see Betty that all the aggravations in this world to me were worth it back then. Helen, Betty's mother, had stopped Betty's daily visits to me. I first saw Betty when she was four or five years old. I was mesmerized by her innocent large blue eyes, her chestnut hair, but most of all, how much she resembled Betty (her aunt), my dear friend. The friend that William had killed. She was always wearing the half-moon pendant I had given Betty. I remembered that I had told Zoraida to look for the pendant and keep it. I didn't want the police to know about it, but the police somehow discovered it and my lawyer presented it as proof of Lord Bruckner's intentions; they never said the word "murderer" but "his intentions." I was glad that he was not presented into the world as a murderer. I felt then that I was guilty. I didn't do enough to save Betty; I could have looked for her in New York. I didn't know she was prostituting herself right under my nose. The prosecution's lawyers argued that there were hundreds of pendants that look exactly like the pendant I had given Betty. I couldn't believe it when the prosecution's lawyers exhibited other pendants just like the one I had given Betty. They were given to the members of the jury to examine. Betty's pendant was placed in a plastic sealed bag, the fake pendants for every member of the jury to touch and see.

I called Helen, sweat covering my face as though it was summer, as if the sun was shining directly on me. I tried to speak, but words lingered on my lips, slow, sluggish, and tardy. Betty answered the phone. "Aunt Mary!"

I heard her. "Darling," I said, "why don't you visit me?"

"But, Aunt Mary, I was in your house yesterday, don't you remember?" Betty answered me.

I was lost and I knew it. Looking across the fields at the McKlusky family, I felt lonely. A dark loneliness that wrapped up my spirit with shadows, thinking of what would have been of Betty and our lives if I had never left Bloomington. Perhaps Betty and I would have been married to ordinary men. A house full of children. Our children playing together. Betty would have been alive today. But would I have been happy then thinking about leaving? Would I have felt trapped, disconnected, disgusted? Would I have felt afflicted with my life if I didn't have achieved my dreams? And hated my life?

Above all, I wouldn't have met William. I couldn't think of a life without William. I felt lucky that I experienced a love without a heap of earth from where to hide my emotions. A disregard for the consequences. I didn't care what Paul told me, I knew that William loved me! He was sick. Do you abandon your loved ones when they are sick? I loved my life with William; thinking back, I wouldn't have had it any other way. Even when

I felt dejected, spiritless when I was living with William. I still waited for him with love in my heart. I knew then that I would be always "the other woman." He could have never married me! I was not of the same social status, the same privileged society that William belonged to; I didn't care. I knew that he would always come back to me. That I would see those deep blue eyes, his elegant posture, his refined self, and his manly personality. Every time I went out celebrating with him, I felt like a little kitten set in a vast dangerous jungle and William was the male lion that protected me. I knew it to be so. He had been challenged more than one time by the rough, strange, and big men; sometimes we used to walk in out-of-the-way bars. William's eyes at about five inches taller than the rough fellow challenging him. They could sense that William was a killer. I felt protected, sheltered, defended.

Not like how I feel now, a decrepit, ragged old lady. No one to care for me, dragging my gnarled leg throughout the streets of crime and iniquity to get some drugs to release my pain. Necrosis—that was what the doctors told me I was afflicted with. No cure; it was a death sentence. His words were as clear to me as an offender standing in a culprit listening to the judge say, "May the Lord have mercy on your soul." What else was there for me to do? Take treatment, the doctors told me. What treatment will do for me? It will prolong your life. How long? I asked. Six months, maximum. I couldn't help it, but I laughed. A laugh that came out from my soul; I thought a criminal had a better chance of coming out alive than me. He could appeal to a higher court, say that he was guilty, appeal to the governor, and come out with a life sentence, To whom shall I appeal? To God, the priest had said to me. Oh dear Lord, I implore you, take me to the other world in haste. Break the chains that are fastened upon my soul, and let me go free. Free to meet my only love. Free to meet William.

I felt comfortable living in my dark cave, afraid of the sun's rays outside, hesitant to face the dawn of my existence, hidden inside the cold walls of 13 Consequence Street. I was ready for the inevitable. The following months were calm. Peace shot through me like a tempest hitting a barren rock. One could be frightened by the actions of a storm, overwhelmed by the intensity of its force, trying to protect yourself from the gusty, tempestuous, and violent rays. The dark that encircled the atmosphere, the shadows that follow, and then calm encircled the earth again with its beautiful and bright tranquility, and everything comes to pass. The immense fields were still there, the trees, the mountains; nothing had changed.

Like everything in my life, my feeble condition started to diminish. Cindy had been working with me all along. She would cry if I refused to take my medication, refused the drinks or broths that she was constantly bringing me. Miraculously, her efforts started to show on me. I couldn't believe when I saw a reflection of myself in a mirror. Did I see some rose color in those sunken cheeks, or was all a fragment of my imagination? No, it was real! I started to feel better. Zoraida bought a variety of vitamins that she was constantly telling me of their miraculous healing power. Helen, Betty's mother, came to give Cindy a hand or simply to speak to me, but it was little Betty that made the difference inside of me. She was constantly telling me to hurry up and get better so we could take long walks in the woods. At the beginning, I just wanted to lay down and die. Didn't a doctor say that I had six months to live?

"Leave me alone," I used to yell at Cindy. Zoraida came to visit me, and I knew that I was in for some rules and regulations. She was not sympathetic with me at all. She brought the broth, and without asking me if I wanted it, she just started to feed me. "Now," she warned me, "you will take different types of broth, Cindy will help you. You will take a tea of this root," and she proceeded to pull out of her bag this twisted, terrible-looking root that I thought was some type of worm.

"It is ginger," she told me. "It is known to cure cancer. It was used all over England by the eleventh century." She also displayed a large jar with a brownish liquid. "This is honey, your teas are going to be sweetened with this honey." I had no choice; I had to do as she told me. She also told me how they collect that honey in Morocco.

"It is a little bird called honeyguide, they are brown and gray and they have a white tail. The bird chatters loudly to guide people toward the wild bees' nests. It waits patiently until the hives are open and then comes down to feed on the bits of honeycombs that are left. This is wild honey, very hard to find anywhere in the U.S. Cindy will call me when she is running low," she continued, "and I will send you more honey." She also hired a woman to do the cleaning, shopping, etc. Not the cooking; she told Cindy exactly how to prepare the different broths. "I have no time," she informed us, "to be traveling. You are going to do as you are told." And then she left.

I thought of Zoraida, that delicate, innocent-looking child that I adored, and how much she had changed. I knew better; it was a front, a shout to cover up her anxieties. Like a soldier saying goodbye to his family before going to war. "It is nothing," he would say," "We have the best equipment; I'll be back in no time at all," but inside of every soldier, his heart is bleeding, and he has to withdraw from them because he feels that tears are starting to flow to his eyes. He doesn't want to show weakness to his family. "Hey, little Anthony!" He would address his small son. "Want to give a military salute to a soldier that is going to war? You did very well, I'll see you soon!" He will sit in the back of a green military truck, two lines of soldiers facing each other. Silently, somber looking. Not talking, wondering. One could see which ones are the new recruits, the ones that have not tasted the experience of war. They sit quietly, looking down at the rough floor beneath them, afraid that other more experienced compatriots could read in their eyes their fears. That was how Zoraida felt about me. She gave me all the instructions for me to do my best to recuperate, but it was all to God and for me to do our best. I wish, I thought then, that I had the same faith, the conviction deep in my heart, of recuperating from this terrible disease.

Everyone said it was a miracle. I was able to stand up and walk a couple of steps. I still experienced some discomfort, but it was a giant step, considering my previous condition. I gained some weight. The yellow and green face, the harrowed look on my face was gone. I felt life coming to me again, as if a lightning bolt had given my feeble body the force to push forward. To give me life. I didn't feel like this for the longest time. How long? Cindy said three months. "I massaged your legs and turned you around so you wouldn't get sores on your back. A twenty-minute exercise twice a day." "Thank you, Cindy," I said. "It must have been hard for you, I thank you."

The sun came shining through the heavy curtain that used to cover the sky. I could hear the birds tweeting away, the trees displaying their tiny and light-colored leaves. The smell of life was in the air! I felt like I wanted to live again, to run, to go shopping, to visit Paul, my dear friend. He came to visit me. I heard his smooth, soft, and mellow voice asking about my welfare and then retired politely. His voice was to me like a suave echo that rebounded inside the fibers of my brain and made me feel relaxed. Sometimes, I thought it was William that had come to visit me and I would shout his name. "William, William, did you come to visit me? To take me away with you?"

That was months ago. I couldn't count them; time didn't matter. I didn't care, and then one day, the telephone rang. It was Paul. "Can I go and visit you?" he said. I didn't know what to say. He must have felt my doubt and promptly continued to say, "For therapy, Mary. You cannot come to my office so I could come to your house and give you the therapy, agree?" "Agree," I said. I couldn't ever say no to Paul.

Except when it was on the subject of me loving William.

It was the beginning of May; I remember it well. Zoraida had sent me a birthday present; presents brought in me different emotions. Emotions of happy times. Waiting for William, feeling beautiful, young. The mansion's surroundings, the ever-present smell of flowers in the air, but most of all, the garden, the woods, the lake. I couldn't help but look around my existing surroundings; they were so different! Here, I felt protected. No luxuries. Living with the everlasting ghosts of my childhood experiences. Wilting away for the inevitable living confinements of 13 Consequence Street.

Cindy worked so hard to have me ready to meet Paul. My white hair was covered with the original gold color of my hair, ringlets covering my head to conceal the bald spots. Manicure, pedicure, was I so deteriorated and detestable before that I was in need of so much care? I looked at myself in the mirror, and I was astonished at the reflection. A cheap reflection of my old self. It brought in me deliriums of megalomania. I saw myself in the mansion, surrounded by servants, dressed with the finest of gowns, wearing the best jewels. The courtesan that I used to be, the lover, the lord's toy, and then I felt ashamed. I ripped off my gown and kicked off my sandals.

There! I said to myself. *This is the new me!* If Paul doesn't agree, I wouldn't care. I dressed in my summer silk robe and fuzzy slippers that little Betty had given me to match the pale yellow of my robe. *There*, I said, *this is me.*

Paul didn't seem to notice anything. He was the same compassionate, relaxed, and sweet fellow I first met. Sometimes I stared at Liberty Road, as I used to call it, and wondered. What if I had never left? Looking at its dust-covered path, dreaming of freedom, experiencing the same sensations I once felt, I knew it was impossible. Liberty Road was to me then a murmur, a clamor encased in me that satiated my thirst for adventure, to make haste from my past, as if I was running away from my shadow. It was destiny.

Therapy had helped me throughout the years, especially with Paul throughout my stubbornness. I finally agreed that William was a murderer and that he didn't love me. William not loving me was hard to understand. To admit that I was in love with a hegemonic, gritty, and gnarled, evil person was hard for me to admit. Attracted forever to a garrulous and evil being. I cried, attacked Paul, accused him of being jealous of William, told him that I hated him, that I didn't want to see him again; but I knew deep inside of me that William was deceiving me. With time, peace entered upon my soul to sweep away any doubtful residues. I then felt calmed, composed. I told Paul that I agree on two terms. That he was a murderer and that he didn't love me! But that I was still in love with William and that I was incapable of loving again. It was to be like that forever.

How did I become poor again? About that time, Omar, Zoraida's brother, told me that the construction firm was in trouble, the economy went down, and thousands of people were left without jobs. Some lost their hard-earned retirements. We practically lost everything. My lawyer told me almost the same thing. Joe, my partner in the Mary and Joe's Bar, had retired. The funds that were left in the bank were practically gone. I was not sixty-five years old yet, no retirement payments.

And to add to my "good luck," they raised the retirement age to sixty-six. I sold my car. I cancelled the gas, so it was back to the fireplace again. The stove and the water heater were electric. The house started to deteriorate—no money to fix the steps. The windows were rotting away with the impact of the winter winds. I couldn't paint the house. It looked dreadful. To my dismay, the number 31 had turned around to read number 13 again. Was God punishing me?

I dressed the best I could for Cindy's pledge. She was to become an American citizen; I was her sponsor. It took her eight years to become a citizen; she looked so proud! She had a small gathering at her apartment. There was a tall young fellow holding hands with her; she was in love. Cindy had moved away after my recuperation; she came every day and took care of me. She drove every day, cleaned, and prepared the broths that by then I was used to and fond of. As the economic situation changed in my household, I couldn't be as generous as I was before with my financial position, and Cindy needed money to pay her bills. We cried when it was time for her to depart.

"I will come every day after work and bring you the broths and take you shopping on Saturdays. I am moving five miles away, don't worry! The McKluskys will not abandon you, neither will Paul." She mentioned Paul with a flashed dark look reflected in those dark beautiful eyes. It was an outcry, a clamor, to accept Paul into my life. I would be safe, no more financial situation, and then I asked myself, safe from whom? I thought I was safe with William, but who protected me from him? A woman should not look for protection when getting together with a man, nor for financial stability. It should be a union of love and trust.

A man should not feel as though he is carrying on his shoulders all the responsibilities. He would feel trapped. Children would add dreadful thoughts to his hidden fears while the mother would look at her child as her little angel. He would be taking notes of his tremendous responsibilities. Can you blame them? I refused Paul when I thought that I was a wealthy, independent woman. It would not be fair for him to accept him now that I was practically destitute. I was not looking for stability; neither was I looking for love. I felt alone for the first time in my life.

When I was living with my parents, I had Betty. In New York, I had Doña Anna, Carmela, Joe. At the mansion, I had Zoraida; and here, the place I chose to die, I had Cindy and Paul. But they both had responsibilities; even though I see them momentarily, I still feel very lonely.

The dark winter months were the worst. Sometimes I couldn't find wood for the fireplace. An old-fashioned rubber water bag filled with hot water saved my life. I would carry it around as though my life depended on it because it did. Paul came to visit me once a week. I saved the little wood I could spare for Paul's visits. He would bring cookies, cakes, cheese, cold cuts, milk, etc., on those visits, enough to last me the rest of the week. I looked upon those visits with great expectation. I would clean and polish the best I could. During the spring and summer months, flowers and fruits were placed in large bowls around the house and the upper patio. We shared great moments of peace and contentment, our souls bonded by friendship and trust. We could have been the perfect couple if it were not for my fascination with William.

Did I like rude, dreadful, and controlling men? Not a generous, easygoing man like Paul? I didn't know. All I knew then was that I loved Paul as a brother, a twin soul, united forever. I often thought of Paul and other women. Was he in love with someone else? Why not? He had the position, a divine gift of looks that could have attracted a beautiful young girl, and yet he was still not married. Why? I then imagined Paul with another woman and felt jealous. What if another woman had won his heart and was parading herself all over town with Paul? I'll be the other woman again, that creature that wives hate so much and spread all sorts of malicious gossip to impair and damage the relationship with the partner you are in love with. I said to myself that it will never happen to me again! I knew that people around town were talking about our strange relationship, but Paul and I paid no heed to gossiping. He was still loved around town; however, his acquaintances and friends flashed a half-bold smile at me, showing their teeth, as if they were a pack of hyenas ready to devour a discarded carcass.

Paul was so careful about my financial situation. He never offered me any sort of cash to alleviate my lack of money. However, on every holiday, he gave me expensive gifts of clothing, flowers, baskets of fruits, cheeses, and wines, as well as taking me out to restaurants and to a few town balls that I couldn't tolerate because of the slight suspicion I had that I was not welcomed. Life kept on vibrating, oscillating at the same rhythm as the world's turns.

Little Betty was going to graduate with a high school diploma and going to college. Her college funds that I had set aside for her were not touched. I was very proud of her. I was going to miss her tremendously—my companion, my friend, my daughter. Tears ran through my eyes as leaving on Liberty Road, in her new Chevrolet her parents had given her. Its dusty path encased her car in a cloud of mist. Liberty Road, where my past dreams, lay, on its road paths disappear in a cloud of dust, as if I was still watching and dreaming through the small and dirty window many years ago. The puff of smoke and dust of Liberty Road was just a cloud of dust, nothing more.

Right after Betty's departure, Paul was acting strange. I couldn't tell exactly what it was, but he was unusually quiet. His eyes, like the weather, seemed to have changed to a stormy and gusty color. He was eluding my questions. There was an increased awareness in my mind that something was wrong. I kept on telling myself that it was all in my imagination, but I was worried, like there was a tweaky sensation puckering at me, letting me know that something was terribly wrong. He had lost some weight; sometimes when we were sitting down eating he used to excuse himself and ran to the bathroom. I waited for the proper time to confront him. We used to park the car up on a cliff from where we admired nature at its best—the rocky slopes, the green foliage in front of us, the descending cliffs, the blue sky and the Ohio Lake, as big as a sea, shining with the sun's rays, the far horizon.

I came close to him. For the first time, I held up my hands to clasp his and kissed him. It was just a brief innocent kiss, but it made him tremble.

I looked into his eyes and asked, "Paul, please tell me what sorrows, hardness, and pain is tormenting your soul."

"You are tormenting me, Mary," he said with those pitiful eyes. "Please do not feel sorry for me! It makes me feel oppressive, discarded. I couldn't take it coming from you!"

"Paul, please," I said, "you had seen me in one of my worst stages of my life. I presented myself to you spiritually, came out to you from the shady and gloomy corners of my life naked."

"It was different," he said. "I was your psychologist."

"I prefer to think that you were and still are my friend," I cried. "Was I a residue, a rubble in your life? Don't let me wonder about it in vain, Paul, with the suspicion that you mistrust me."

He bowed, looked down, and said, "It is bad, Mary. Pancreatic cancer." We both cried holding to one another as if we wanted to stop the rhythm of time. I wanted to die right there; why continue living?

I looked at the dark cliff below and said to Paul, "It would take just a gentle push on the accelerator."

"No, Mary, you could continue your life, you have always managed. It will pass."

I was with Paul throughout all his sufferings and tribulations. I saw him decaying little by little. No deferment or delay in that terrible disease. Every time I was next to him, I was to be a witness to the catastrophic effects of this disease on his body. He lost his hair, his head displaying an unnatural shape. His skin was green, and his eyes bulged out of their sockets with a look of fear. I asked myself how such a horrendous treatment that causes so much damage on a body could cure anyone. But Paul was a doctor, and he believed in medical science. I could hardly see him on the bed. Such a handsome, tall, and charismatic man decaying away before the earth covered his body! I made an effort not to show my fears.

I knew he wanted to tell me something. I came close to him, placing my ear next to his lips. I heard him saying, "I loved you, Mary, I was always in love with you since I first met you."

I kissed him, crying and saying again and again, "I loved you also in a different way. I could have given my life to save yours. Paul, there are lots of different loves, ours was special. A given type of love poets write about." I wished I could stop the clock and perpetuate this moment forever. "I didn't love William with the trust and friendship that I have loved you.

Our love was beyond sexual attraction, it is pure, sublime, heroic, majestic. I love you, Paul, please don't leave me!" I cried in pain.

Nurses pulled me out, away from Paul, and gave me a sedative. When I came to my senses, Paul was gone. There was not one of his relatives at the funeral. He ran away from home when he was sixteen years old. He didn't want to become a farmer like the rest of his brothers. He was smart, and he knew it. He worked at the supermarket while he was going to high school and college. Everybody knew and respected him. He was the town hero. Mothers would point out to their children his good qualities and speak about him as if he were a hero. I understood then the look of hate they used to give me. A murderer, a detestable, presumptuous evil woman, who debauched the town's hero. I was accused of poisoning Paul. Rocks were thrown at my windows, making my life more unbearable. A conference was given by the doctors that took care of Paul. Was Dr. Paul poisoned? No, Dr. Paul was being treated for pancreatic cancer for over a year. No traces of poison were found in the autopsy.

There were still evil tongues that were saying that I killed Paul because of his inheritance. Paul had left me $90,000 dollars, but most of that amount went for hospital expenditures, which were $45,000 dollars, $20,000 for his funeral and place of rest. The $20,000 left I donated to the orphanage, for those children that ran away from home and had no place to go, just like Paul when he was young. I made sure all the legal papers were printed in the local newspaper for everyone to see. Rumors calmed down in town, of course. There were others that were asking the same question that I asked myself. How come Paul did not have a substantial amount of money for his retirement years? It was a small town. Most of the people were unable to pay him, and he was so generous that he didn't charge them. That was Paul! That is why I used to adore him.

It was another epoch in my life. The last one, I hope. Some of my neighbors that saw my destitution, the lack of money, I guess they understood. I ate because of the generosity of the McKlusky family. Counting the days, minutes, and seconds left for my retirement, will I be able to make it to sixty-seven? I had no income. I couldn't apply for welfare because I owned a home. Those ladies in the welfare departments were adamant about it! "You cannot have money in the bank or own a home and apply for welfare!" they yelled at me. And then I looked around the office, and I felt devastated. I couldn't afford a doctor; if I was sick, I had to go to the emergency room and wait forever. Luckily, some of the doctors knew

Paul; they asked me to go to their offices at no charge at all. I didn't want to receive psychological help. I felt that I couldn't find anyone like Paul. However, I was able to get medicine for my pain, for the discomfort I was experiencing lately. Did I have my old disease again? The maligned disease ontologists call necrosis?

Will the doctors tell me after they had examined me that I had to have treatment? I'd rather die than subject myself to the infamy of those treatments. I didn't want to die like Paul. I was experiencing some discomfort lately. Did I have the old disease again? The maligned condition Ontologists call necrosis? If I do, I'll be stubborn again and will refuse those treatments. I didn't want to die looking like Paul. To be stripped, plundered, plucked of every one of my female possessions. Cast off, dying by the seconds as though I was in a torture chamber and they were stripping me little by little of my internal organs. I saw Paul when pain racked his body. The force of the pain sat him up. Wild eyes staring at you, not focused, a shout of pain dying on his dry lips, no strength left in his body to shout aloud in pain.

Throughout his agony, he was left without pain medication. They couldn't give him any more painkillers. They argued that it was dangerous for him. He could have died of an overdose. Paul was suffering tremendously. I ran to the desk nurse and talked to her about Paul's condition. "He is in need of help, please give him something for the pain!"

The desk nurse would look into her computer and say, "His medication is due at twelve thirty, and it is twelve o'clock now. He will have to wait for a half an hour before his next dosage." That's when I decided to bring some pills into the hospital so I could alleviate his suffering. Call me a murderer, anything you would like to call me. I couldn't see someone I loved suffering as much as Paul was suffering and not help him. He would have done the same thing for me.

I was getting worse, little by little, dying from loneliness and the lack of love. Only the letters from little Betty brought calm into my decayed soul. Why was my life so dramatic? Was I being punished for abandoning my parents, for bringing them alcohol? I knew it was detrimental to them, and yet I handed them the poison that eventually killed them. Did I mortify Paul by not being with him like a man and a woman? Did I make him suffer?

It was fall again, the worst of my life. Pain racked my body every time I moved. I howled as though I were a wolf. Yes, I had to go and see the doctor, I finally admitted to myself. They will give me medication and strong painkillers. So I went to Paul's best friend, Dr. Samuel Kentbourg, oncologist, for a diagnosis. I knew what was ailing me! I wanted a diagnosis so I could get painkillers to alleviate my suffering. Dr. Kentbourg wanted to see me. He had seen me at the local hamburger stop before, a look of pity reflected in his dark eyes.

"Come see me, Mary, come close to me," he said. "You do not have to worry about payments." I sat in his office wondering. There were young people sitting across from me, already showing the ravages of cancer disease, a yellow complexion, lack of hair, etc. Some of them came with their children, and I thought, who took care of them when they felt so tired that they couldn't even sit? Who brought them a cup of tea or their medicine? What did those innocent children thought of what was happening? The change in their household, the worries about the medical bills. Will they lose their home? Some of them will lose their homes and fathers who run away, pursued by the harsh economic situation. My heart bled for them. The children sat in silence, calm, serene, a wondering look in their innocent eyes. I couldn't sit there and be a witness of so much misery.

I tried to get off the chair; a sharp pain racked through my body, making me sit again. I could almost see the wild look in my eyes. The same look that I had seen in Paul's eyes! *This is it!* I thought. I waited until the nurse came for me and helped me out of my chair, a screeching sound coming from the rolling wheels of the walker as I walked toward the doctor's office, just like a one-year-old child.

Wheeling about the house as though I was learning to walk. We reverse back to our infancy. Will I lose the gift of communication? Some of us do. Dr. Kentbourg saved my life, not my physical life, but my mental state of mind. He sat me at his office and said, "Mary, you know what you have. You are a smart woman."

"How long do I have?" I asked.

"Who knows?" he said. "I don't like to set a time when my patients should live or die, no one ever knows! But I assure you that your stay in this earth from now on will be comfortable." He started to set out lots of papers. "You need transportation, medicines, help in the house every day, a hospital bed. Are you Catholic?" he asked.

"Yes."

"Well, a priest will come to you every week and give you the holy sacraments." I started to cry. Tears that were hoarded, accumulated inside of me for a long time gushed, rushed out of my eyes to wash away the fears I was experiencing before. "Do you want to go to a home?"

"No, Doctor, I would like to stay in my house."

"Very well then, Mary, call my secretary for your next appointment." I was helped toward the sidewalk and into a taxi. I felt wealthy again. A wealth that I never cared for before. I let people rob me of my well-being. Too late now, I thought. The lawyers, the market, the taxes, the construction company that I funded was practically out of business. The little assets were collected by the Hosein family. I didn't blame them. They were doing all the work and I sat back and never even asked how the business was coming along. Did I think myself a member of the aristocracy? Was I avaricious, insidious, and treacherous? I sat back and let other people do the work for me. I cannot complain now.

Zoraida called me, complaining that Papa Hosein kept on blaming her because she didn't marry Mahmud, the millionaire Arab that Papa Hosein had her engaged to so many years ago. He kept on crying, as if in mourning. He called himself a destitute old man. We couldn't help it, we laughed. A laugh that came from within, depicting our hopeless and mournful state of mind. I didn't want to give Zoraida the "good news" about my welfare; it was not the proper time.

The Internal Revenue Service had been coming to my house. I did not have a phone, demanding payment. I owed three years to the IRS. It was worrying me tremendously; I had medicine, transportation, food, etc., but I did not have income, cash at all. I had just turned sixty-five last month, and I was hoping that by next year I would have my Social Security check. It was a whirlwind of mental outcry every time the officers stopped at my house. I kept on saying my house, but is it really my home? If I don't pay the taxes, it is taken away from me. It made me feel vulnerable, as if I were naked in the middle of the street. No place to hide, exposed to the rigors of destiny. Will I ever live long enough to receive my Social Security checks? I was lost, thinking of the taxes situation, when a knock at my door awakened me from my dreadful situation. I thought the officers from the IRS were coming to take me out of my house. I felt destitute, afraid. But instead, I had the surprise of my life!

A journalist came to visit me, Ms. Arlene McKrugger, a journalist from New York. Her presence impressed me. She was not like the rest of the journalists I had seen, properly attired and immaculately manicured, with a flat stomach and surgery. It was the end of fall, and mud was still covering some areas. And slush still on the ground. Ms. Arlene wore simple boots, pants, and a large sweater that covered her knees. She looked so familiar that I invited her immediately into my household, the heavy wind closing the front door with a loud thump after her. There was a look of surprise in her inquisitive dark eyes.

"Excuse me, madam," she said. "I think that I am in the wrong place. I am looking for Ms. Mary Fletcher. Could you please tell me where I can locate her? I am a journalist."

"You are in the right place, madam," I said while I invited her into my sitting room. She kept on eyeing me as though I was a strange creature from outer space, but I didn't mind. I knew that she was expecting a long-dressed heavily made-up, sophisticated woman living in a mansion as they depicted me in the newspapers and television back then. "Yes," I said, "this is me, Mary Fletcher. You see, the rhythms of life have changed. They could be fragile, vulnerable, sometimes stormy, tempestuous, and violent. This is me today, a destitute old lady. Riddled, affected by disease, paying for all my weaknesses, a lonely soul. Living off the government charities, counting the days until I will be sixty-six so I could collect my Social Security checks, pay the IRS, and be able to keep my home." She looked at me and couldn't believe that I was really Mary Fletcher, that she was in the wrong house and that she was talking with an insane, ill-riddled old lady.

"Would you like to have a cup of tea?"

"Yes, Ms. Mary," she said. But as I was trying to get up, I experienced one of my worst pains and I couldn't talk. She came toward me and helped me up. As we were walking toward my small kitchen, I felt better. I had comfortable chairs and a small table. We could look at the terrace; there was light in that part of the house. Ms. McKrugger walked into the kitchen and observed some of the pictures Zoraida had sent me. In the pictures, I was standing on my balcony, all dressed up, next to Zoraida. In another picture, I was at the entrance with William, welcoming the guests, Mr. Leeward close to the entrance. A fake smile was reflected on my face when I greeted the Richardsons, the billionaire friends of William. Zoraida and I laughed so much at these pictures that I decided they were great memories and I framed them. Ms. McKrugger believed then, when she saw the pictures that I was Mary Fletcher. Had I changed so much that there was not a trace of my old self reflected in me? Had I dwarfed away, to erase the mental plunder that I was subjected to?

"Yes, Ms. Mary," Ms. McKrugger told me. "You have changed but for the better. I can read in every wrinkle in your face the wisdom, the determination that is still reflected in those beautiful deep blue eyes."

"Can you please tell me what sort of business brings you to this remote part of the country?"

"Certainly," she said and proceeded. "I have followed your story throughout the years, and it seems very interesting to me. I know of all of your pains and tribulations. Your life's story fascinated me."

"Ms. McKrugger, what is it that you would like to accomplish?" I asked.

She hesitated for a moment, stood up facing the terrace, and said, "I would like to write your story." She turned around to face me and continued. "A book, Ms. Fletcher. A book that will shake the foundations of true, real, and sincere love, the story of your love, Ms. Fletcher."

"Oh, the story of William and me," I answered with sadness. "I promise that I would think about it."

"Will you, Ms. Fletcher?"

"I will stop by the day after tomorrow, is that okay with you?" She looked stimulated, excited. A flush covered her face while she went about collecting all of her papers. She rushed out of the house and disappeared in the early afternoon cloudiness.

I had read in a local Long Island newspaper an article written by Ms. Arlene McKrugger, where she stated that she had been chasing serial killers all the way throughout the gloomy and somber streets of Hart Island, where the poor and the unidentified dead rest. No necrology list for the poor unidentified females or males, only a rustic cardboard box headed toward their last resting place, Hart Island, a floating mass grave. Her article was very impressive. Her compassion for these victims clawed at my heart with pain.

Were Betty, Elizabeth, and her boyfriend's remains resting in Hart Island? Tossed away from the isolated Fordham Street in the Bronx? I remembered Elizabeth; petite, young, and beautiful body, so much in love with Paul Taranto. What heinous and despotic human being vanished your beauty forever? Was it William? My William? He was sick. I knew then what I was going to say to Ms. McKrugger.

My name, Mary Fletcher, was going to be printed in this book, but William's name could not be used at all. Let the public guess who it was and who I am, but nothing more. I decided that I would tell my life story step by step to Ms. McKrugger. It has to be printed the same way I say it. Thank the Lord I had no mental incapability, no trace of memory loss in me. I had to think very carefully of what I had to say about my life with William; I didn't want to make him the murderous assassin Paul believed he was. Maybe he was! But I would like for the readers to understand that when a person kills without any reason, when the perpetrator does not know the victim and still commits horrendous crimes against any of those persons, it is because they have a mental incapability.

Can mothers detect an erratic behavior in their children when they are very young? Torturing animals, hitting their siblings, etc.? Are the parents brutal, despotic, and detestable? Do their mothers protect them from a brutal father? Did they teach them what is right or wrong by example? Or do the parents look the other way when their children bring them money from any drug deal? You have to know who you are living with. The house belongs to their parents until both of them are dead. Children have to understand that fact. There is not one room in their parents' house that belongs to the children; they have the privilege to have their own room, yes. One should knock on their bedroom door before one comes in, but if the parents suspect that there are dangerous drugs or arms in their rooms, the parents have every right to search their bedroom.

I knew that William was sick. Why was he obsessed with prostitutes? Did he observe as a child or as an adolescent a sexual act that he considered horrendous? Why was he barred from his inheritance and thrown out of Boston; England? Did they talk to him, give him psychological help? I know that under his hard shell dwelled a great and compassionate heart. I had seen him acting with elderly people, the poor, the rejected. There was always someone that needed some sort of favor that William was ready to accomplish. I knew the good in him. He was a discarded plank from an old warship, riding the waves, going under to the dark bottom pit of the ocean and then coming up again to see the light. I wouldn't want to shackle him to a horrendous crime forever. His family rejected, wrenched from the wealth they fought so long to acquire. His memory would be a disgrace in a society that does not exempt anyone from committing an infraction. They are the pillars that hold down the world. Pure, unmingled, uncorrupted, diaphanous. As they used to say in old Rome, *"Un ruin ido, otro venido"*

("One evil is gone, another one comes"). There will be others that will ride on the waves of freedom from punishment, why not William? I decided that I had to talk to Ms. Arlene McKrugger about it. I do not want to have William's reputation tarnished. The sun was coming through the veil that covered the sky all throughout the winter and fall. It looked as though it was going to be a happy day. Perhaps I would be able to pay the IRS if they get to publish the book. Of course, Ms. McKrugger would be the author. She would be writing my life's story.

In the morning, as I peeked through my front door, I saw a big van, cameras, and about four to five fellows following Ms. McKrugger. I didn't open the door. "That's not what we agreed before!" I yelled. I didn't open my door! And I wouldn't answer the telephone; they were all alike, all they want is publicity.

Helen called me. "Mary," she said, "there is a reporter here that says that she would like to write about your life. She said she is sorry and that she will only bring with her a lawyer and that you should have a lawyer as well."

We sat in the terrace; it was March, but the sun was shining and the lilies were in full bloom. I needed a relaxing atmosphere in which we were able to resolve the differences. After a nice cup of hot chocolate, we were able to air out some of the problems. I didn't want to portray William as a murderer. There were no proof of his guilt; a jury had acquitted him. I didn't want to implicate him in such a horrendous crime. Most of all, I loved William; he was the love of my life.

"Ms. Fletcher," Ms. McKrugger said, "if I have to write about your life, it is imperceptible not to be able to mention Mr. William, he is practically the main character of this book."

"What if I changed names?" I said.

Arlene looked feeble-minded. "What? Change the name of the main character?"

"Yes, what if instead of William Bruckner we will call him Stephen Vanderbilt instead of a lord from England, belonging to the Boston society."

"You got it!" Ms. McKrugger said.

There were lawyers in the signing of papers. All I wanted was to have enough money to pay the IRS. I gave up on my Social Security checks; I knew I wouldn't be able to make it to sixty-six. Eight months is a long time for someone who is dying. I thanked the good Lord because I was not thrown out of my house while I was dying. These were my roots, and this was my house. I looked at the sign outside the house; the number 31 turned around to read 13 Consequence Street and I laughed. A laugh that came from within my soul. I didn't want anything, not without William; he was my master, my only love. I considered myself as being an old warrior, loyal to his king to death. As Tigranes was loyal to Dario, General Parmenio to Alexander, the legendary Roland to Charlemagne, the Roman soldiers to General Aetius in the battle of Chălons against Attila. I had fought lots of battles with William, always loyal to him, ready to give my life for his. Loving him unconditionally, ready to fight anyone who dared to speak evil against him. I reached the epitasis of this book—the complex, the most arduous, difficult, and complicated part.

Chapter 18

My name is Arlene McKrugger. I am writing the story of Mary. As a Journalist, I intend to dig up the truth about Mary's story. Journalists, have changed the course in the life of some war heroes, like the story of Genghis Kahn, his memoirs were written by his enemies; the people that he conquered. He was portrayed as a savage warrior, a Mongol out of the Gobi Desert; they never mentioned the fact that he respected all religions, that a trail of monks and preachers followed his army. They were exempt of paying taxes. I intend to write Mary's story without passion, with a clear mind, no conspiracy, no deceit in my mind.

I left Ohio with a heavy heart, I couldn't attend Mary's funeral. I refused to see that house and remember all of Mary's pains. I wanted to fly away, my mind trembling unable to focus. A veil of shadow wrapped up my mind while I was going through the Long Island Expressway, passing me as if a movie camera was filming me, and I sat in my car enjoying the ride. I remembered Mary and so many beautiful and sad days; raising her fingers when she was too weak to talk, to let me know how many days were left to collect her Social Security check. Sobs were choking me and then, someone was talking to me asking me questions, "Can I help you"?, a police officer was asking me. I realized that I was in a paying booth at the Tri-Borough Bridge heading towards the Bronx, far away and in the opposite direction from my apartment in Queens. The officer directed my car towards a small building that was surrounded by a fence. The officer could not find any felony to charge me with; they had monitored my speed at 95 miles per hour. They took me to Jamaica Hospital; the doctor said that I had acute symptoms of anxiety. "I would not recommend you to drive". Luckily, I had good people to help me; like my Landlady and her family.

My apartment is situated on Rosedale Road, Nassau County in New York. I live in a two-family house right at the end of the road, two blocks away from the line that separates the towns of Queens and Nassau. My landlady, Doña Caterina, has an ancient barbaric look about her, flashing dark eyes, a full mouth, and silky black hair that makes a shocking contrast with her very white oval face. She looks as though she is of a mixed descent from the horde of Yakka Mongols and from Alexander's marching phalanx of Argead, Hellen, and Greek descendants. She is the matron, the boss of her household. She came from Lucania, close to the Basento River, at the heel of the map of Italy, tucked in between Campania and the Apulia districts, just like Queens and Nassau counties. Doña Caterina couldn't understand why the children that live in Rosedale couldn't go to the nice schools in the Five Towns area.

I pointed toward the other side of a small bay toward the town of North Woodmere, with its manicured lawns, parks, and Bay View, and said, "Those are the middle-class people, the taxpayers that carry America on their shoulders. Their taxes are very high. Unfortunately, if the Rosedale children are allowed to assist the Fine Towns school districts, they will have to increase their taxes as the need for more teachers, schools, etc., will be necessary."

"Madonna mia," Doña Caterina said, like the Guelphs and Ghibellines in Italy. Doña Caterina was superstitious. Her house looks different to me; there are rare statues placed all over her house, and a large picture of the Madonna di Viggiano placed on the opposite side of the entrance wall. She has a pleasant, cheerful attitude, and she is always eager to please you.

She introduced me to her family. "My Antonini, (her husband), my Geovanni, my Garebaldi, and my Peter." Everything in her household was her possession while Doña Caterina was talking to me. I heard a loud bang, and then pieces of paper and small sparkles of snow came rushing in from the front door. A pack of swarthy children rushed in as though they were a herd of wild creatures. Doña Caterina was not surprised, but as agile as an eagle, she grabbed the last boy that passed her way and held him by the back of his pants, leaving little Geovanni hanging in midair.

There was a look of surprise in his beautiful large dark eyes while Doña Caterina was trying to explain something to me that was hard for me to understand at the moment. "Lookee at his face, pinkee he no sickee he, no male dell'arco he healthy. Mal dell'arco is jaundice, an illness that affected some children years ago in Italy." Doña Caterina took me in as part of her family; therefore I was expected to sit down and have lunch and dinner with the family, but I felt trapped by the schedule. I wanted to be able to think, to be alone to see if I could write this book that kept on hampering and hammering at me. I pretended to be sick as an excuse for not eating but couldn't avoid Doña Caterina's stern and rigorous character.

"L'Pancia," she said and disappeared, then, came back with her famous Punzoné, packed with calories. I decided to go to a doctor and obtain a diet prescription. I crossed the border toward the other side and into North Woodmere, and to Dr. Bugulaski's small office situated on Rosedale Road across from the Temple Hellel. Dr. Bugulaski is of Jewish descent from Argentina. He is extremely professional. A believer of the old medicine, Dr. Bugulaski and his wife cared for the poor at his second office situated in Broadway, in the town of Lawrenee by the railroad tracks, next to number four school. He is a pleasant, soft-spoken man with fierce intelligent eyes. After he examined me, he told me that I was only about fifteen pounds over height and gave me a diet plan to lose the weight. Dr. Bugulaski's diet plan saved me from Doña Caterina's rigorous schedule. Now I have time for myself; I walk to the Woodmere Park, wrapped around by a beautiful blue-water bay, extensive walks, trees, flowers, pools, and a variety of birds, followed by a trail of scents that brought to my senses forgotten memories. I felt the piece within me tumbling, precipitating the fears that encased my soul.

I had to go back to Ohio. I had to face the pain, be able to feel the love and tribulations that Mary had felt. I went back to Ohio and to 13 Consequence Street, to the old dilapidated house from which Mary's story began. I opened the rotten and old mailbox that Mary used to dread because the accumulations of bills she could not afford to pay. As I looked through the mail, I saw her SS check. I couldn't help it; tears of anger and rage filled my eyes. I could see her pleading eyes, raising her fingers when she couldn't talk, counting the days left to receive her SS check. I tore the check into thousands of pieces and threw it against the air, the frozen pieces of papers dancing, vibrating, and vacillating up and down in the air toward Liberty Road.

"You are free now, Mary!" I came into the house and sat by the old table, drinking a cup of tea, overlooking the large terrace and remembering the good times I spent with Mary looking at the bare trees far away, their dry branches racking, vibrating as if dancing to the rhythm of the sharp and rigorous wind. I looked around the house, trying to capture its essence, the mystery encased in the old house.

I went to the front window to see Liberty Road as Mary used to call it, to perceive, trying to capture its essence and the mystery encased in this old house. "Mary," I said, "I am ready to write your book. I hope I can bring about your feeling. To let the readers of your book walk through the whirlwinds of your mind, feeling the love you felt for William to the last. Your eccentric being the enigma that desiccated your soul and turn you into an eccentric old fool." I packed my old traveling bag, put on my long coat, hat, and gloves. I looked around the house for the last time, tears flooding my eyes, sobs coming up my throat, trying to choke me. I ran out the back terrace two steps at a time and toward the vast field that separates Mary's house to the McKluskys' field and house, feeling the same frozen wind that Betty Mary's friend must have felt when she walked these frozen fields through stormy, gusty, violent, and tempestuous winds to see Mary.

Helen answered the door. I practically ran inside, stamping my feet on the front mat, scattering pieces of iced dirt on the floor. My coat was frozen; my clothes and shoes were placed by the fire. We sat by the fire with a cup of hot chocolate. Helen was there sitting with me, a warm and peaceful atmosphere surrounding us.

"Helen," I said, "there is one thing hidden in Mary's well-being that disturbs me. It looks as though Mary was wrenched out of her inheritance. I visited Zoraida, and they lived as though they are wealthy while Mary lived in poverty."

Helen stood up and took a long breath as if she was encased in a dark cave and was trying to reach the light by touching, feeling her surroundings. Finally, she turned around and, with sadness reflected in her eyes, said, "I suffered so much when I realized the conditions she was living in, but she loved little Betty so much she wanted to make sure that little Betty graduated from college." Mary had a lawyer make a trust fund for little Betty and her. No funds were to be released to her or little Betty, not before she graduated from college. A sum of money was to be given to little Betty periodically, but not to Mary. There is no delay, no deferment, no obstacle, or obstruction in my path now to start Mary's book.

I headed home to my upstairs apartment in Queens, New York, my small desk looking at the blue bay. A few ducks were dancing in the waves, the sun departing toward the west and leaving on its path a rainbow of colors. A tape with Mary's voice bounced in the wind, her clear voice reaching me. I felt as though I was back in 13 Consequence Street, feeling the warmth of her kitchen, the smell of fruits and flowers in the air. Beyond the trees, the meadows cast light and shadows over her voice. It was Mary telling the world of her sufferings, uncovering the truth of her love life, the other side of William, and the sick attraction she felt for him. This is her vengeance.

THE END